Sisters i

Looking around Cheryl's driveway, studying the faces she had known for so many years, Jackie thought about life and its many mysteries. So much had changed, so many miles had been traveled and yet, once again with Cheryl and Doris, Jackie could have been standing anywhere in time. High school, college, the marriage years . . . they all blended together. It was nice to feel that familiarity and have the knowledge that there were two people in the world who, no matter what, would always be her family.

"I missed you girls," Jackie said. "I'm glad to be back."

Cheryl let out a breath, putting her hand to her head. "After I got hit, Stan asked me who to call and I realized . . . you're my only friends. My real friends, I mean."

"Well, we all certainly hit the jackpot," Jackie chirped, adjusting her bag. She was beaming inside. "Momma Jackie's in town," she said, glancing once again at the SUV. "I'm taking care of you now."

For a moment, the three friends stood silent. They might be a triangle of broken hearts, broken heads, and—Jackie glanced back at the rental car—broken dreams, but at least they were together.

"Je t'aime," she said. "I love you guys. Let's go."

The Whole Package

Cynthia Ellingsen

BERKLEY BOOKS, NEW YORK

THE BERKLEY PUBLISHING GROUP
Published by the Penguin Group
Penguin Group (USA) Inc.
375 Hudson Street, New York, New York 10014, USA
Penguin Group (Canada), 90 Eglinton Avenue East, Suite 700, Toronto, Ontario M4P 2Y3, Canada
(a division of Pearson Penguin Canada Inc.)
Penguin Books Ltd., 80 Strand, London WC2R 0RL, England
Penguin Group Ireland, 25 St. Stephen's Green, Dublin 2, Ireland (a division of Penguin Books Ltd.)
Penguin Group (Australia), 250 Camberwell Road, Camberwell, Victoria 3124, Australia
(a division of Pearson Australia Group Pty. Ltd.)
Penguin Books India Pvt. Ltd., 11 Community Centre, Panchsheel Park, New Delhi—110 017, India
Penguin Group (NZ), 67 Apollo Drive, Rosedale, Auckland 0632, New Zealand
(a division of Pearson New Zealand Ltd.)
Penguin Books (South Africa) (Pty.) Ltd., 24 Sturdee Avenue, Rosebank, Johannesburg 2196,
South Africa

Penguin Books Ltd., Registered Offices: 80 Strand, London WC2R 0RL, England

This book is an original publication of The Berkley Publishing Group.

Copyright © 2011 by Cynthia Ellingsen.
Cover art by Claudio Marinesco.
Cover design by Rita Frangie.
Interior text design by Tiffany Estreicher.

PRINTING HISTORY
Berkley trade paperback edition / August 2011

Library of Congress Cataloging-in-Publication Data

Ellingsen, Cynthia.
   The whole package / Cynthia Ellingsen. — 1st ed.
   p. cm.
   ISBN 978-0-425-24134-9 (pbk.)
  1. Female friendship—Fiction. 2. Businesswomen—Fiction. 3. Restaurateurs—Fiction.
I. Title.
   PS3605.L43785W48 2011
   813'.6—dc22

                                                                                    2010051952

PRINTED IN THE UNITED STATES OF AMERICA

10 9 8 7 6 5 4 3 2 1

For Ryan, with love

ACKNOWLEDGMENTS

I had a ball writing this novel—thank you so much to the amazing team that helped to make it happen. Wendy McCurdy, you are my hero. I am eternally grateful for your kindness, insight, and clever editing. Katherine Pelz, thank you for your amazing support. You show me how it's done. Stephen Barr, you know how much I love your e-mails. And Jon Cassir, just when I thought it couldn't get any better, you came along. You are absolutely brilliant in every way.

Finally, where would *The Whole Package* be without Dan Lazar at Writer's House? Dan, thank you from the bottom of my heart for your support, expertise, and incredible humor. I am so honored to work with you. With each and every note, you've dragged me kicking and screaming toward being a better writer. You're a rock star.

Huge thanks to my fabulous friends and to my wonderful Whole Package of a husband, Ryan. Mom, thank you for a lifetime of enthusiasm and can-do spirit. Carolyn, thank you for teaching me to read when I was way too young. And, Dad, everywhere I look, you're still there. I love you all madly.

Love demands infinitely less than friendship.

—George Jean Nathan

The Whole Package

Chapter One

FRENCH IS A SEXY LANGUAGE. EXCEPT, OF COURSE, IF YOU ARE standing in line at a French café and the French you hear is a nasal, drawn-out, "Fat American." Unnecessary, especially if you are simply trying to buy a chocolate croissant to dip into the first cappuccino of the day.

Jackie—and yes, she still preferred to be called Jackie and not Jacqueline, even though she was closing in on forty instead of the throat of the snickering girl behind her—whirled around.

"Did you just call me fat?"

A French girl stared back at her. The girl had the audacity to cock her head. A yes.

Jackie was stunned. Okay, fine—and a little hurt. Such a judgment was the last thing she expected in this cheerful neighborhood café with its brightly painted walls, kitschy produce art, and erratically placed wildflowers. Even the French sayings on the wall, written in such careful, scrolling script, were meant to inspire good cheer, not snappy little insults.

"Well, I am not fat!" Jackie said. And this was *not* in French, because after two years in the country she spoke French perfectly, and proving it was no longer important. "I am *sexy.*"

A mustached host had been writing out specials on a blackboard with squeaking chalk. At this, he paused and took a look. Jackie ran her palms over her curvy hips and considered giving a slight shimmy. The man gave a nod in agreement and went back to the specials.

The French girl sniffed. She was dressed in all black, a total cliché. She was holding a sniveling, trendy dog. Its shaky face was framed by a bejeweled collar and its droopy eyes stared, along with everyone else in the cinnamon-scented café.

"Perhaps *you* should order something to eat," Jackie said, pointedly eyeing the girl's bony frame. "You're probably just suffering from low blood sugar."

"*Casse-toi.*"

Jackie's jaw dropped. Drawing herself up to her full height of five three (five six with her three-inch pumps), Jackie said, "If you want to live off of cigarettes and red wine and ignore the delicacies your country has to offer, you go right ahead. But I would rather get chased out of Le Bon Marché by a firing squad than strut around in a body that looks like it was stolen from an eight-year-old boy."

The French girl gasped.

"I am going to *embrace* my sensuality," Jackie said. "I am going to improve upon it. And," she stood a bit taller, "it is gonna happen with a chocolate croissant."

There was silence in the café for a moment. Even the hiss of the cappuccino machine stilled. Then a gray-haired lady in the corner clapped. Just like in the movies. One by one, the little tables with their fashionably angular, well-dressed guests joined in until the majority of the café cheered with a passion not unlike the drunken crowds spilling out of the Stade de France after a futbol match.

Jackie rewarded them all with a sugary smile and a toss of her blond, Goldie Hawn–inspired hair. She flipped back around to the counter to pay for her treat.

"But, madame . . ." The cashier practically whispered. "We have no chocolate croissant today."

The skinny kid at the cash register was pale. Jackie had come to loathe pale men. France did not have enough sun. She leaned forward, showing cleavage soft as the dough of an unbaked roll. "Then how about a hot chocolate . . ."

". . . And a tartlette?"

The kid was trying. "Are you American?" she asked.

"British."

Jackie considered his pallor. Yes, he was. "Thanks, honey," she said, rewarding him with a smile. "That sounds nice."

The cashier handed over a rich cup of steaming hot chocolate. It warmed Jackie's hands through her black leather gloves, the ones with the pink hearts in the center.

"No charge," the pale kid assured her. His grin was thousand-watt.

Jackie hesitated, caught up.

Ever since her husband had died two years ago, there had been arm-prickling moments when she felt Robert was still present, popping up in the strangest places. Not as a phantasm or anything like that. After all, Robert had been much too vain to channel through, for example, the body of this kid. Much more his style was that Frenchman in the corner with the perfectly coordinated scarf and beret, or maybe that sultry redhead nibbling at her macaron. No, Jackie just saw his memory in other people. There was a certain sparkle Robert had that drew her in from the very start, that day at the Taste of Chicago festival, so many years ago. Granted, that sparkle might have been the diamond nestled in his Cartier watch . . . but Jackie wasn't one to dwell on trifles.

"You are so beautiful," the cashier said now, staring at her.

The French patrons began to stir. Characteristically abrupt in their enthusiasm, a cloud of impatience was settling over the line behind her. There was a definitive clicking of umbrella tips against the tile floor, keeping time like the second hand of a clock. Euros jangled, rubbed together in restless palms.

"I could be your mother," Jackie told him. With a wink, she laid a few extra euros on the counter. "Go buy your girlfriend something nice."

Smiling at the anorexic French girl on her way out, Jackie made a point of banging that door with the bells. They jingled as she left the café. The sound reminded her of the holidays more than those white lights always hanging from the trees along the block.

Jackie breathed in the crisp air and looked around in delight. The French bustled in and out of brightly colored doors, carrying paper-wrapped parcels, bottles of wine, and boulangerie-bought pastries. A small farmer's market flourished on the corner, practically spilling its wares out into the narrow streets. The fresh fruits and vegetables were plump and plentiful for the old ladies, who, with their sensible black shoes and string bags, came every day to paw through stacks of potatoes, onions, carrots, and parsley, speaking loudly to each other in heavily accented French.

"*Pédaler dans la choucroute,*" Jackie liked to mutter when she walked by, as though she were in on their conversation. The French phrase made her laugh. Literally, it meant "to pedal in the sauerkraut," but *pédaler dans la choucroute* really meant getting nowhere fast. It was the perfect description for these old ladies on the hunt. After all, they were going to do the same thing the next day and the next day and the next . . .

As Jackie walked by a sidewalk café, a group of women drinking garnet-colored wine lifted their glasses and cheered as a pretty French girl dashed over to them. With perfect grace, the girl kissed her friends and then placed herself in the center with a ceremonious flop. They all started speaking at once and Jackie put her hand to her chest. Scenes like these made her miss her best friends, Cheryl and Doris, so much that she almost wanted to cry.

"But you are in Par-eeh, darling," she tried saying out loud. "Who needs Schaumburg, Illinois?"

Jackie passed by a wine bar filled with French patrons, all shouting gaily to one another. A man by the window was smoking, drawing from his cigarette as if he were kissing a lover. Noticing her, the man gave a little nod and Jackie nodded back but kept walking. Smoking was something she no longer indulged in. Of course, this rule did seem slightly perverse in a country where smoking was practically the national pastime but Jackie was not willing to risk death for something so silly.

Back in the day, Jackie had started smoking only because Cheryl had made her. Cheryl had stolen pack after pack from her older brothers but refused to gasp and choke on them alone. So, Cheryl and Jackie would sneak out behind the high school, giggling and puffing and feeling very adult. By college, Jackie was the one who had ended up as an Official Smoker.

"It's the tortured artist in me," she'd kid Robert, whenever he eyed her Virginia Slims with distaste.

Robert finally got her to stop with that impromptu trip to Vegas, gently pushing her toward the roulette table. "Now *this* time," Robert had said at the very end of the game, when she was left holding only one chip, "pretend every spot on the board, except the number you pick, is lung cancer. Just try and win."

Clapping and cheering, Jackie dropped her last chip on number seven, the number of years she'd been smoking. The little ball bounced around the helm, carelessly deciding her fate. When the ball landed on fifteen and the table runner swept Jackie's last chip from the table, Robert said, "Hmm. Not great odds . . ." and Jackie had mashed out her cigarette for the last time.

"Thank you for that, my darling," Jackie said now. Her voice echoed down the cobblestone streets and she stomped her feet a little, just to hear her shoes clickety-clack on the walk.

Turning the corner, Jackie saw her building loom into sight and she smiled. It was so very French; too bare yet too ornate. The skeleton could have been a jail, all redbrick and intimidation, but it managed to find its beauty in the details. Those whimsical stained-glass windows, the way those copper pieces hung like tassels from the roof gutters, and, of course, those wrought-iron balconies lined with ivy at every twist and turn . . .

Letting herself into the lobby, Jackie enjoyed the high ceilings and bright murals as she clickety-clacked her way to her mailbox. After turning the tiny gold key in the lock, she pulled out bills and another piece of airmail from the lawyer who was handling Robert's estate. The sight of the weathered envelope made her stomach turn. Jackie had hoped that by ignoring these letters she could make them go away. Clearly, that wasn't going to be the case.

Once upstairs, Jackie made a point of jiggling her key loudly in the lock. Hopefully, it would be enough warning for Christian. It was. By the time she had made her way into the main room, the Chinese partition had been pulled across his work area.

Christian had purchased the screen at some rummage sale, and it depended on Jackie's mood whether the red serpent chased by golden scrolls was the most beautiful thing she'd ever seen or the most disturbing. Either way, the rip in the lower corner gave her a view into his workspace but Jackie didn't look. The rustling and soft moans told her everything she didn't want to know. To her friends, she excused the philandering of her young boyfriend with his very own argument: "But he's an *artiste*."

An artiste with brooding Italian eyes that kept her hooked. That and cherry red lips coupled with cheekbones higher than any woman's. And his body hair—you would think, gross, who wants to think about hair in any form, but Jackie wanted a rhinestone T-shirt to share it with the world: CHRISTIAN'S HAIR IS SPUN SILK! Not pubish, like American men's.

Finishing the last nibble of her pastry, Jackie tossed its waxy paper bag into the trash and eyed the envelope from the lawyer. She imagined chubby little George with his chubby little fingers painstakingly sealing it. Typically, a successful lawyer would leave such tasks to his assistant but George liked to joke that licking an envelope addressed to her helped him pretend he was brave enough to send her a love letter. Jackie had thrown back her head and laughed loud and long at that one. George was such a shameless flirt.

Taking a deep breath, Jackie slid a manicured nail under the lip of the envelope and tore it open. The letter was written on George's gold-embossed paper and read:

Dear Jacqueline,

Jackie couldn't help but smile. Even from across the globe, George insisted on calling her the name no one else did.

I have left you several messages that you have not returned. And are you checking your e-mail? Your cell? It is critical we speak. Your late husband's estate has been used in its entirety. I will need to meet with you regarding your situation. Your monthly allowance is no longer available due to insufficient funds.

Contact me at your earliest convenience.

Regards,
George Edwards

Jackie dropped the letter. As it fluttered to the floor, her full weight fell against the kitchen counter.

When Jackie first moved to Paris, her goal was to reconnect with her art and mourn the loss of her husband. Thanks to her striking looks, the money Robert had left her, and some helpful contacts, Jackie found herself caught up in the glamour of Parisian high society instead. Practically overnight, her life had been filled with fashion events, gallery openings, charity balls . . . so many delightful distractions. One of her favorites was hosting extravagant dinner parties for her new friends.

From where she stood, Jackie could see that ridiculous cheese wheel from one of the many dinner parties. It sat in the dining room on a medieval cart where its unsanitary, gooey concoctions had horrified and entertained countless French guests. They found the cheese wheel hilarious, just like any gimmick from the "fun American." Covering her eyes and looking out through splayed fingers, Jackie took in the confetti-colored paintings, large and small, that covered the rooms' walls. Every piece was gifted by the friends and artists who had come in and out of her home with the freedom of hotel guests. They had filled her life with art, wine, candies . . . any trinket that might make her clap her hands with glee.

Now, Jackie's hands simply shook. In the beginning, she had believed so much in her artistic abilities—the French would love her Americanized paintings and she'd be a celebrity overnight!—that Jackie had failed to plan ahead. In spite of George's consistent financial warnings, she had treated the best Bordeaux like tap water. By the time she finally noticed that his predictions were coming true, it was too late to do anything about it. Although some of her early paintings had sold, it was not enough to support a career, and certainly not enough to support her extravagant lifestyle. The money had run out. And there was nothing she could do about it.

"I have nothing," Jackie said. It was like confessing to a stranger that her husband was dead, as though hearing it out loud for the first time made it true. She said it again, louder: "I have nothing."

"*Chéri?* Are you speaking?" Christian called her from the next room. That voice she knew so well was off-key.

Jackie pressed her fingers under her eyes and raised her head. She swept out of the kitchen into *her* living room—the living room she had been paying for out of her dead husband's money, the living room where she and Christian had made love in every corner, the same corners where he felt up sculpture models while she was out—and pushed aside the partition. Christian was naked, as was the girl. They were on the sheet, entwined next to the clay. It lay wet and forgotten.

Seeing her, Christian gaped like a dead fish at the Sunday market. Apologies began tumbling forth in French.

"Christian, I have something to tell you," Jackie interrupted. "I am not thirty-one. I turn forty in one year and three months."

The model, bless her, appeared more shocked at Jackie's age than her sudden presence.

"And I have nothing."

His surprise and protests sounded like a horn out of tune.

"Do yourself a favor, Christian," Jackie laughed. "Learn English."

The French model gasped; the sound of so many French girls.

"Good-bye, my darling," Jackie said, reaching out to touch the soft hair on top of his head. No matter what Christian had done, she still appreciated him. Their casual romance had helped her to move on. "Good luck to you."

"Where do you go?" Christian panicked, struggling to stand.

Jackie let out a breath. "Home."

Chapter Two

"NICE SHOT, JACKASS!" CHERYL SHOUTED HAPPILY.

Stan grunted, and this time made contact with the racquetball. It thwacked sharply against the wall. Although the red rubber was like lightning, Cheryl was the jar. She was on it faster than her boss could have dreamed. It flew right at his head.

"Aargh!" he screamed, ducking.

They laughed. It was part of their game to try to kill each other because both knew the other could handle it.

"Pipsqueak," Stan taunted.

Cheryl swiped at the sweat on her forehead. Her wristband was already sopping wet, as was the rest of her body. Her legs ached but she relished the physicality of this sport. Where else could you be so violent and have nobody get hurt? She swung powerfully, aiming for a corner. The ball ricocheted as she'd hoped, bouncing just past Stan's left ear.

"Damn," he swore, then they both stopped for a moment, taking deep breaths. "Are you beating me?"

"What do you think?" she said, grinning.

Stan was resting his hands on his knees, looking up at her through a lock of dark hair. Moments like these, Cheryl could appreciate her boss was a good-looking guy. There were probably hundreds who looked just like him on the East Coast; thick body, strong jawline, Italian. Still, Cheryl would never let him into her bed. Stan was married. More important, he was obnoxious.

"So," Stan drawled, poising himself for a hit. "I saw your wet dream in the locker room."

Cheryl had lifted the ball to serve, but lowered it back down. The rubber was hard in her hands. Hot from the beating it was taking. "And who would that be?"

"You know," Stan said, flexing his elbow. "Andy. The new guy."

Setting her jaw, Cheryl said, "Great sentiment, Stan. But to be honest with you, I don't plan on getting arrested for statutory."

Stan laughed. Leaning back on his heels, he shook his head.

Andy was at least ten years younger than she was, smart, and incredibly likable. He'd only been with TurnKey for a month but had infiltrated the firm like a partner. He practically waltzed into meetings, throwing around high fives like free beer. Of course, the guys at the marketing firm immediately handed him the respect Cheryl had to spend years cultivating.

"You guys buddies now?" Cheryl asked.

"Nah," Stan said. "But I'd watch out for that one. Andy knows what he wants and it very well might be—"

"My job?" she scoffed, swatting at him.

Cheryl was second rung at the firm, right behind Stan. She liked to tease him that his hairy ass was the only thing blocking her way to the top.

"Just saying." Stan shrugged. "Glad we brought him in. Seems to know what he's doing."

Stan was famous for giving the young guys the benefit of the doubt. With the girls, he would say things like, *Think she can do more than flush a tampon down the toilet?* to the other execs while the new girl was just out of earshot. Cheryl had always wondered what would happen if one of these girls overheard and decided to fight back in court. But Stan was an expert at walking the line. The poor new girl might sense something was very wrong from the muffled laughter and inappropriate glances but good luck trying to prove it. Cheryl empathized in these situations but didn't dare intervene. She'd lived through the hazing. It was up to them to do the same.

"Per usual, you're giving the new guy too much credit," Cheryl said. "Andy just started. He has no *idea* what he's doing."

Stan positioned himself to hit. "He's here, isn't he?"

Cheryl bit her lip. Joining the Racquet Club *had* been a savvy move on Andy's part. It took most of the male executives years to cough up the membership fee and gain that all-important after-hours access to Cheryl and Stan. Maybe the kid was brighter than she thought. As if that thought wasn't irritating enough, there was another thing about him that had been pissing her off. Andy was good-looking. Distractingly so. And within the past week his floppy brown hair, omnipresent dimple, and piercing green eyes seemed to be everywhere. Cheryl grimaced and rubbed her right arm. As a matter of fact, everywhere had included the Racquet Club hallway, just before her game with Stan.

Cheryl had been walking out of the locker room, sending a text and unwrapping a PowerBar when she crashed into a hard block of male flesh. "Fuck! Watch where you're—" she'd said, before doing a double take. It was Andy. He was wearing silver soccer shorts and a close-fitting white T-shirt that showed off everything.

"What are *you* doing here?" Cheryl demanded, staring him down.

"Sorry." Andy reached out a hand to steady her, which she brushed off. He held up his racket as way of explanation. "Racquetball. I'm a sucker for it."

The motion of his arm shot a scent of something spicy and extremely male in her direction. Cheryl found herself tongue-tied, which was absolutely baffling. She was the type of girl who knew how to small talk a man. Forcing herself to hold his gaze, she took a big bite of her PowerBar.

"Just got a membership," Andy said, smiling like she might be happy to hear it. When Cheryl didn't say anything, he put his racquet behind his head and used it as a prop to stretch. "Heard it was where all the execs hang out. Figured if I wanted to join them, I'd have to pay up."

The stretching was really distracting. Every time Andy moved from side to side, the white T-shirt would creep up, exposing his taut stomach muscles. Cheryl kept her eyes directly on his.

"You're tan," was all she could think of to say.

"Single White Female." He winked, indicating her bronzed form. At her confusion, he added, "You're tan . . . I'm tan . . ."

Ugh. He was funny. No one was funny. It was so . . . bothersome.

Cheryl's eyes betrayed her and wandered down. She could see It outlined in his soccer shorts. And It was not small. Her stomach did a flip-flop. There was no reason to sit in the sauna post-workout.

"What time's your game?" Andy asked.

Cheryl jumped, peeked at the clock. She was late. "Right now."

"I'll walk you," he suggested.

Shrugging, Cheryl let him follow her down the hall. She could feel his eyes on her legs.

Cheryl was the type of woman other women loved to whisper about: "She's not pretty—she's just put together. She doesn't even have boobs. I don't get it. Why does *every* guy want her?" The answer was simple—older brothers.

Cheryl had been good-naturedly bullied by David, Tom, and John her whole life, ever since she was a little kid. She learned that the way to show affection was to punch, hit, insult, or ignore; that simpering and whining was the fastest way to lose respect; and that challenging a man was fine if you could make him believe you'd acquiesce in the bedroom. Most important? Never let him get you there.

Cheryl had been successful in that arena. The only guys she rewarded with sex were ones she didn't need. As a rule, she only slept with men who were hot and dumb. The famous tennis player, the surfer who lived in Maui, the Italian who owned the winery . . . not to mention all the model-perfect conquests from ski trips, tropical vacations, and college . . . her online albums were littered with pictures of them. If it wasn't for social networking, Cheryl wouldn't remember any of their names, but they all remembered hers. Her in-box was constantly inundated with little notes designed to win her heart but it never worked. Cheryl was done saying those three little words. Those words took your power; she learned that in her first and only marriage. Of course, that left her almost forty and single, salivating over some thirty-year-old in see-through shorts.

The locker room and the racquetball courts were on different floors and Cheryl usually took the stairs. When Andy stopped at the double doors of the elevator and pressed the Up button, she snorted and followed him inside. "Lazy," she said, sliding an elastic band off her wrist and pulling her hair into a sleek ponytail. "Don't you know you're at a gym?"

"Yeah," Andy said, grinning, "but I ride in elevators with girls whenever I can. Elevators remind me of that Aerosmith video."

Cheryl crossed her arms and leaned against the wall. "Okay. Let's live out that fantasy. Press that emergency button and we'll go for it right now."

As soon as the flirty words were out of her mouth, she looked forward to his response. Would Andy be the type to blush and stammer? Take her seriously and try to make a move? Or meet her eyes with an equal challenge, with a secret hope to take her up on it later?

Cheryl smiled angelically. "Well?"

Andy gave her a quick look up and down . . . and *shrugged*. His shoulders rose and fell in a slow, singular movement. It was like a gavel dismissing a bid at an auction block.

Cheryl's mouth dropped to the floor. Quickly, she reached up to smooth her hair and found herself also adjusting her Nike sports bra, her tennis skirt, even the gold tennis bracelets on her arm, all while sneaking horrified glances at Andy out of the corner of her eye.

"I wonder what that video would have been like if Tyler had been scared of elevators," Andy mused.

"Are *you* scared of elevators?" Cheryl stammered.

The doors slid open and Andy tossed her a dimpled grin. "I'm not scared of anything."

Somehow, Cheryl managed to be cordial on the walk from the elevator door to the racquetball court. She made some funny remark that had made Andy laugh out loud. Cheryl even gave him a lazy wave and a nonchalant, "Welcome to the gym," as he strutted away like some oversexed peacock. But the moment he was out of sight, she yanked a travel-sized mirror out of her gym bag and peered into it, hunting for signs of expiration.

In the reflection gaping back at her, Cheryl saw tan skin, taut and clear. A small and slightly upturned nose, with a smattering of freckles across the ridge. Hair that was perfectly cut and highlighted, falling just past her shoulders. Breathing a sigh of relief, Cheryl snapped the compact shut. She looked good. *Damn* good.

Andy had just made her shit list.

"Don't waste your time getting attached," Cheryl told Stan. "That kid will leave us for New York in six months. And if he doesn't, I'll send him there myself." She bounced the ball. "You ready?"

"Sure, sure."

Cheryl drew back her racket.

"It's just so funny that you don't like the kid," Stan mused.

Cheryl rolled her eyes, once again dropping the ball. "And why's that?"

Stan grinned. "He certainly seems to like *you*."

Cheryl didn't even bother to aim. She whacked the red ball as hard as she could. It flew against the wall and just as she felt the satisfaction of a firm hit, she realized something was wrong.

The red ball was not flying at Stan's head. It was coming straight at hers.

Chapter Three

DORIS PULLED INTO THE PARKING LOT OF WOODFIELD MALL, self-consciously easing her Lexus sport utility into a tight parking spot. The car was a bit too flashy for her taste, all silver and chrome, but Doug had chosen it for her based on its safety rating.

Doris thought she looked silly in it; a slightly overweight, middle-aged woman decked out in conservative clothing. Mandy was counting the seconds until her sixteenth birthday, expecting her mother to just hand over the keys. Doris and Doug had discussed whether to give Mandy the Lexus but in their generation, a car wouldn't have been a gift. It would have to be earned. After all, look at the first car she and Doug had bought together.

When he'd first found that old tank, Doug had called her from a pay phone. He was talking way too fast and too loud, something he did even back then when he got excited. Apparently, there was a navy blue Volvo parked at the side of the road, a bargain at four hundred dollars.

"It's perfect for our little family," Doug had crooned. "Grab the cash from my drawer and come down and see. We'll celebrate with ice cream."

They'd spent the evening kissing each other with cold mouths as the radio crackled from the speakers. When the stars came out, Doris found herself staring up at them as she and Doug made love on the scratchy seats.

Of course, as Doug got promoted and their bank account got bigger, all that early frugality gave way to luxury. Eventually, they donated the Volvo to charity. On days when she was feeling particularly nostalgic, Doris looked for it on the road, wondering if it was still puttering away. Maybe it was silly but Doris couldn't help but miss that time when things were simpler. She was grateful for the security Doug gave her but sometimes it bothered her that Mandy didn't know what it was like to save up cash in a drawer to get anything. They had raised her to be an only child who expected everything, and typically, she got it. What else was Doug working for? Certainly not them.

Even though Doug and Doris had talked numerous times about going on a second honeymoon, they had never agreed on a location. Doris wanted to go to Hawaii but Doug was worried that the plane ride would be too long. Doug was interested in playing golf in Naples but Doris didn't like the humidity in Florida. One of them had looked up Tahiti but in the end, trying to figure out where to go and what to do was overwhelming. Planning a vacation had turned out to be more stressful than their daily life.

With a shake of her head, Doris removed the keys from the ignition and opened the door. She gasped as the wind whipped across her face. A light slush seeped into her gray boots the moment she stepped into the cold. Yes, somewhere warm would be a nice getaway. Doris tried not to be irritated that she was bustling across the mall parking lot in this weather instead of at home reading a good book by the fire.

Then you should have been more careful, she thought, pulling her coat tighter around her.

That morning, Doris had accidentally shrunk a pair of her daughter's jeans. Instead of confessing the mistake, Doris decided to replace them. That would be easier than dealing with another one of Mandy's tantrums. Instead of handling the news like a normal person, Mandy would most likely start screaming and crying, just before slamming the door to her room until it shook on its hinges. More and more, Doris found herself the victim of these attacks. They could be loud and dramatic or much more subtle, but they all had the same theme in common—Doris was the worst mother in the world.

Every time she dared think the opposite, Mandy would prove her wrong. Like last Saturday, when Doris had been reorganizing her closet and humming something she'd heard at the symphony. She was right in the middle of placing her sweater sets into a color-coded sequence when Mandy had barged into her room.

"Mom, what is wrong with you?" Mandy demanded, sneering at Doris from the doorjamb.

Doris felt a familiar heavy feeling in her stomach. "What . . . what do you mean?"

"Are you seriously reorganizing your closet *again*?" Mandy said. The young girl was wearing too much eyeliner and a concert T-shirt that was way too tight in the chest. There was something blue and sparkly on the front that matched her daughter's dangly earrings.

Doris suddenly felt unbelievably old. "I like to know where everything is. What's wrong with that?"

"Nothing," Mandy said, examining a fingernail. "If you don't have anything else to do."

"I have lots to do," Doris said. A sensible sweater dangled from the hanger in her hand. Quickly, she smoothed its soft material and hung it in the closet.

"No you don't." Mandy sighed in a tone bordering on pity. She flung herself onto Doris's bed, wrinkling the white coverlet. Doris opened her mouth to tell Mandy to get off her bed or, at the very least, take off those dirty shoes, but nothing came out. Instead, she gritted her teeth and turned back to the closet.

"I have lots to do," Doris repeated, trying to keep the slight tremor out of her voice. "Go look at the calendar." The family appointments were concise and color-coded, hung neatly in the kitchen. On paper, there was never a dull day.

"Anyone who has time to color code a calendar *and* her closets clearly needs to get a life," Mandy said, lying on her back and raising her sneakers toward the ceiling. She was chomping gum and popping it after every other word. This was a sound Doris had grown to detest.

When Mandy was born, Doris's mother had been gleeful at the shock of red hair sticking out of the baby's head. "That red hair is a warning flag," her mother had said, laughing, practically smothering the baby with kisses. "When this one's a teenager, she's going to be a handful." Now, Doris wondered if her mother was laughing all the way from heaven. Or—and this was her biggest fear—shaking her head in disappointment.

Handling Mandy had been so easy when her mother was alive. In part, that was due to proximity. Doris's parents had moved in down the street a week after Mandy was born. Instead of finding this oppressive, Doris loved it. Her mother was her best friend. The two jogged every morning, went shopping together, joined every club in town and, of course, raised Mandy. There was no one in the world Doris admired more than her mother. The woman had been a genius at all of the little things that meant so much to a kid. Things like whipping up green eggs and ham on St. Patrick's Day, suffering through those giggly sleepovers without saying a word, oohing and ahhing over the first gag-worthy dinner her only child had cooked . . .

When her mother had died, Doris was at a loss. To get through that time, she focused her energy on helping others to cope. Time passed in a blur of putting her mother's things in order and disposing of them properly, helping her father sell the house and move closer to his brother in Florida, and even getting Mandy into grief counseling. Doris became something of an expert on the topic of death. She read book after book that clearly outlined the steps of grief and how to cope with losing a loved one. Doris was happy to share this information with anyone who needed it. Doris spent hours talking with her daughter about the loss of her grandmother. She was a friendly shoulder whenever her mother's friends needed it. She even talked Jackie through Robert's hospice.

During this process, Doug kept a close eye on her. He was worried that Doris couldn't handle losing a mother and a friend. He even tried to get her to talk about it a couple of times, but Doris would just quote from whatever book on grief she was reading at the time. After two years passed and Doris seemed fine, he decided she had handled the loss quite well. So had Doris . . . until she found herself gorging on sweets because she couldn't sleep, snapping at Mandy for no reason, or fighting back tears over the tiniest thing. The day her mother's favorite song, "Let It Be," came on the radio, something finally broke inside her.

Doris had been out running errands, crossing items off her checklist at a stoplight. The window was open and the sun was hot on her arm. "Let It Be" started, and out of habit, Doris began humming along. As the light changed and Doris pressed her foot on the gas, it dawned on her that her mother would have enjoyed running errands with her and that, if she hadn't died, she would be singing along in that out-of-tune way of hers. Suddenly, Doris got light-headed and darkness seemed to seep into the very marrow of her bones. Doris managed to drive herself home but once there, she got into bed, pulled the covers up to her chin, and fell fast asleep. Once awake, the reality of the loss finally hit her. She stared up at the ceiling with tears rolling down her cheeks.

"This isn't about your mother," Doug told her, the third day he found her in bed with the shades drawn. "It can't be. Too much time has passed. You need to tell me what's really bothering you."

Doris just shook her head, staring at the wall. That's when Doug had forced her to meet with a therapist and the medications began. Slowly, that terrifying blackness seeped out of her heart but it left a layer of gray that she couldn't quite shake. Some days, Doris wished she could feel like her old self again, but without her mother, it was impossible. She would just have to learn to live with who she had become.

Shaking her head as though to clear the memories, Doris smoothed her coat and stepped through the heavy double doors at Macy's. The warm air gushed onto her head, rifling her pageboy cut. As the scent of new clothes and perfume hit her, Doris decided it was a good idea to be at the mall. It was her and Doug's anniversary. Since she was here, Doris could pick up something special, like lingerie. It would be nice to make that extra effort Doug had stopped expecting from her.

Inside the store, Doris hesitated. The lights were bright and she had no idea where to start looking for anything so for the moment, she allowed the Godiva chocolates display to grab her attention. Fondling a gold box, she debated whether to snack on truffles or just get a mocha at the bookstore. Doris was in the midst of this mental debate when she heard whispering from the teddy bear display.

"Omigod," said a husky voice. "That's Doris MacLean. The one I was *just* talking about."

Doris stiffened, her heart suddenly pounding in her ears. That voice was familiar . . . and certainly not pleasant . . . but she couldn't quite place it. Who on earth would have been "just talking" about her?

"Yuck," said a younger voice. "She looks ninety. Was she a senior when you were a freshman?"

"No, she's *my* age," the first whisper continued. "She used to be super popular, can you believe it? I love it when they get fat and old." Doris almost dropped the box of candy. "Doug dated her right after me and that was the biggest mistake of his . . ."

It was Katherine Rigney! Doug's girlfriend from high school. What on earth was *she* doing back in town? Hadn't she married some trucker and moved to Tennessee?

"She got knocked up in high school," Katherine was saying. "They got married, then *lost* the baby . . ."

Whirling, Doris searched the clothing racks for her high school nemesis. There she was, leaning against a display of colorful sweat-shirts. She was sporting brassy highlights and gossiping with a girl who had to be Mandy's age. They both wore Macy's name tags and French manicures.

"Hello, Katherine," Doris said, voice cold. She took a few steps forward but then stopped. Why was she even talking to this woman? For a foolish moment, Doris had an image of herself racing out of the store, covering her head, and screaming, "I hate Katherine Rigney!" But then she'd still be stuck without a pair of jeans for Mandy and she would have given Katherine something to talk about for a week.

Katherine Rigney strutted forward through the juniors section, running her hands across the racks of clothing as though she were shopping for herself. Doris tried to remember—hadn't Katherine been busted for shoplifting in junior high? Something about jewelry and perfume from the display counters? It had been a big scandal at the time. The principal had come into their classroom flanked by two police officers and everyone had started whispering. Katherine had given a little sigh, packed up her Trapper Keeper and jean purse, and then followed the officers out of the room. Even though Doris would have liked to have seen her put away for life, Katherine had gotten off with a warning.

"Well, hey, stranger," Katherine said, cocking her hip and giving a lazy wave. She was smiling too big, showing off crooked front teeth that could have used a few years with a Whitestrip.

"Nice to see you," Doris lied. "You look well."

But Katherine did not look well. She looked like what those reality shows called a cougar—but a cougar who had spent too many hours in the sun. A cougar, Mandy had explained to Doris, was an older woman set to compete with a younger girl for a younger man.

"Like Cheryl," Mandy had compared, digging her hand deep into a bag of microwave popcorn.

Up close, Doris could see that Katherine was wearing black eye shadow and liner, pounds of mascara, and a slick, lacquered lipstick that had to be from the eighties. "Whatcha up to? How's Doug?" Katherine asked, leaning against a display and tossing that overprocessed hair.

Doris bristled. She tried hard not to let it show on her face.

Doug had dated Katherine during their freshman year. Katherine had dumped him right before the Christmas dance, so she could go with a boy old enough to drive. What did this . . . this . . . *tigress* want with her husband now?

"Why do you want to know?" Doris asked.

"Just curious," Katherine said, snapping her gum. The sound reminded Doris of Mandy snapping her gum. Irritating. "I moved back to town so I've been thinking about old friends. Oh, wait!" Katherine slapped her hand to her forehead in that old Chris Farley "stupid" move. Funny, Doug had recently started doing the same thing. "I forgot. I just saw Doug the other day."

Doris felt something tighten in her chest. Doug had *not* mentioned that.

"Where did you see my husband?" she asked, suddenly suspicious.

"Who knows?"

"*Where?*"

The younger sales associate was holding her breath, watching the exchange like a match point in a tennis game. Katherine, Doris. Doris, Katherine.

Katherine's eyes were wide, mocking. "Oh . . . the mall, I guess?"

Doris felt frumpy in her heavy winter coat. "He doesn't shop," Doris mumbled, stuffing her hands into her pockets.

"Downtown then," Katherine said. "I can't remember." Once again, the woman flipped her hair. Doris hoped the move would give her whiplash. "He's looking good," Katherine continued, cracking her gum. "You got lucky."

"You're too old to chew gum," Doris spat. "My teenage daughter chews gum." As soon as the words were out, Doris felt a little jolt of pleasure. She didn't know where the words had come from but they sounded strong. They sounded like the woman she used to be.

The two salesgirls regarded Doris with surprise. Then the younger one elbowed Katherine. "She's right. We're not supposed to chew it on the floor," she said. The girl glanced over her shoulder like a manager could pop up at any moment. Katherine rolled her eyes but she spit the gum into a tissue and stuffed it into her pocket.

Doris shifted her weight from one foot to the other, fists clenched in triumph. For a moment, she wondered what it would be like to have a job she would be scared to lose. Even a job like this, folding and refolding prefolded T-shirts. It certainly would give her something to do, but Doug had always been very against it.

"Your daughter is your full-time job," he'd said, more than once. "You should be focusing on her."

Katherine's catlike eyes appraised Doris's expensive handbag. "Doris, why don't you let me help you find something? Maybe we could upgrade your purse. Or even better, that jacket?"

Doris's jaw clenched. The gray-checked coat had belonged to her mother. Years ago, her mother had pressed it lovingly into her hands and said, "I've had this since the sixties. It's yours now." Although she had appreciated the gesture, Doris had never worn the coat—it just wasn't her style. Instead, she had stuffed it into the back of the closet. A few months ago, she had found the coat in the basement and sat with it, silent, for hours. She had worn it ever since.

"It makes you look lumpy or something," Katherine added.

"The *coat* doesn't make me look lumpy," Doris said. With all the dignity she could muster, she said, "I have put on a little bit of weight."

"I guess you have," Katherine said. "You know, some good lines could hide those rolls. Let's trade it out. We'll find you a new coat."

"No, thank you," Doris said. Her voice sounded steady but inside, she was screaming.

It was at moments like these that Doris wished she and Cheryl hadn't gotten into that fight. If Doris still had Cheryl to turn to, she would have stormed out of the store, picked up Cheryl, and brought her back to help put Katherine Rigney in her place. Doris might have said, "I wanted to talk to you about my mother's coat—" and Cheryl would have cut in with, "Your broken-down trashy ass shouldn't even be allowed to look at it, let alone talk about replacing it." Then they would have busted into giggles, stalking away with their arms around each other. Cheryl probably would have added something over her shoulder, like, "Congrats on minimum wage at *forty*." But without that type of support, Doris did not feel brave enough to take on this horrible woman.

"My coat is fine," Doris said. "I just want some blue jeans for my daughter." She dug around in her purse. Finally, her fingers found the piece of paper where she'd jotted down the size and brand of Mandy's jeans. Even though she was loath to get Katherine's help, Doris needed those jeans. She had no idea how to find them on her own and would feel even more foolish if she had to come back and ask for Katherine's help.

"Yup," Katherine said, reading the brand. "I've got just what you need. Follow me."

Doris walked beside her, feeling slightly foolish but unable to pinpoint why.

"Your daughter must trust you," Katherine said, suddenly elbowing Doris like they were friends. "Most girls would rather die than have their mother pick out a pair of jeans. You two must have a great relationship."

"I am very lucky," Doris lied. Immediately, she felt a little better. Sometimes it amazed her how easy it was to lie.

"So . . ." Katherine gave her a quick glance. "Are you still friends with Jackie Greene?"

High school never died.

"Of course," Doris gushed. "Jackie's in Paris. She's an artist."

"What about Cheryl?"

Doris's face darkened. "Cheryl's doing very well at her marketing firm. She'll probably make partner."

"You guys still BFFs?"

"Always." Doris smiled too brightly. "Ever since . . ."

"The crash," Katherine said, nodding.

The two women stood in silence for a minute, then Katherine picked up a pair of jeans, considering them. "What do you think of these?"

Doris took in the ripped fringes and flashy buttons. They looked exactly like the jeans she had shrunk. "Those are them."

"See anything else your daughter would like?" Katherine asked.

Scanning the crowded area, Doris shook her head.

"What about these?" Katherine pressed, holding up a pair of dark blue jeans that tapered at the bottom. Mandy had just been drooling over those in one of her fashion magazines. Doris felt a pang. How did Katherine Rigney know what her daughter would like more than she did?

"Those are nice," Doris admitted. "Why don't you pick out a couple more pairs in her size? I have to go find a couple other things. It's my anniversary. I'm going to find something special. You know. To surprise Doug."

Katherine's eyes narrowed. "Sure. Bring everything back to me. I'll ring it up."

The moment Katherine turned back to the jeans, Doris darted away. She ducked into the customer service area and ripped off her coat. Leaning against the wall, Doris took a couple of deep breaths before moving to the water fountain and taking a long drink. After splashing cold water on her face, Doris stood up straight and tossed her hair just like Katherine had. Determined, she set out for the lingerie section.

Maybe Doris wouldn't look good in black spandex or a leopard-print leotard but there must be something she could find that Doug would like. Something that wouldn't remind him of that cougar.

Chapter Four

CHERYL CRINGED AT THE BRIGHT WHITE LIGHT MOVING toward her.

"What the hell?" she said, trying to raise her hand to block it. "Did I die?"

The way she felt, it was certainly possible. Her arm was not cooperating and Cheryl could barely focus. Plus, that backlit figure kept darting in and out of her vision. Was it an angel? If so, Cheryl had to admit she was impressed. This particular one had floppy brown hair, green eyes, and a cherubic dimple attached to the hard body of a man. Giving her best Mary Magdalene grin, Cheryl managed to raise her hand. She stroked it against his soft curls.

"She's coming to . . ." a voice said. "Cheryl, can you hear me?"

Something passed in front of her face and a putrid smell raked through her nostrils.

"Aargh," Cheryl cried, trying to move her head away. Another jolt hit her, longer this time. Sharper. "Stop!"

"Yup. She's back with us," the voice half chuckled.

Cheryl's eyes flew open. The man in front of her was no angel; it was Andy. He was leaning in close and studying her with concern. Yanking her hand back, Cheryl turned away in distaste. She wondered how long she'd been touching his hair.

"Cheryl, I am so sorry," another voice boomed. A pair of muscular calves walked toward her. They were covered with matted, curly black hairs. In a flash, it came back to her. The elevator, racquetball, Stan . . .

"Nice work, Stan," Cheryl said, letting out a jagged breath. Bringing a hand to her head, she followed the pain to a puffed-out welt. It felt like a hard-boiled egg. "You've officially incapacitated me."

Stan crouched down, rocking on his heels. His bleached white socks were practically glowing. Cheryl couldn't help but suspect he bought a new pair every time he played. "Well, I certainly would have hit you if I could've," Stan laughed, "but you did this one to yourself."

"Don't doubt it." The swiftness of her retort, the husky sound of her voice calmed her.

Cheryl made a move to get up but her head throbbed with pain. "Ouch," she whispered, eyes smarting with tears. "What the hell happened?" Wildly, she looked around. Cheryl was willing to do anything to get away from the pounding in her head, the view of Stan's neon socks, those pulsing pendulum lights on the club ceiling.

"Cheryl," Andy said, jumping back into her line of vision. "You're all right. The ball just hit you in the head. I promise you'll be okay."

What was he even doing here? Hadn't he looked her up and down and *shrugged*?

Andy's green eyes sparkled. "Just so you know, I have medical training. The Heimlich, CPR, all of it. Tell me what you need."

What Cheryl needed was for Andy to go home; to get away from her and stop acting like some knight in shining armor just because their boss was standing there. This kid *was* trying to get her job. Cheryl jerked her head back toward him and really looked. He was younger than she was, cocky . . . clearly desperate to hang out with Stan or he wouldn't even be here. Cheryl wondered if she could get him banned from the club.

As if on cue, a club employee appeared. Hopping back and forth in a pair of lime green alligator shorts, he peered down at her. "Is she okay?" he asked. "I hope she understood that playing was at her own risk."

"She understood," Cheryl said.

"That's good." The health club worker hesitated. "Um, I've got some stuff I need you to sign and . . ." He was biting his nails and half-holding out a stack of papers toward Cheryl.

Cheryl gave a little laugh. "Give me a pen."

Visibly relieved, the health club worker passed her the papers. Cheryl knew she should be irritated that the club was more worried about the threat of a lawsuit than her well-being but she couldn't help but be impressed at their bravado. "You should have people do this when they join," Cheryl said, handing the papers to him. "Streamline it into the membership application."

The health club worker nodded, gushing, "I've been trying to get them to do that for years."

"Membership application?" Stan repeated. "That wasn't for the health club. You just signed your salary renegotiation." Stan laughed loud and long at his own joke. To Cheryl's surprise, Andy didn't laugh. Instead, he sneaked a look at Cheryl and rolled his eyes.

"Hilarious, Stan," she said, confused by Andy's response. The fastest way to get ahead was to laugh at Stan's stupid jokes. Everyone knew that. Maybe Andy was dumber than he looked.

"Your color came back," Andy said, reaching out a hand to her. "Do you want to sit up?"

"Um . . ." Cheryl adjusted her position on the floor. She just wanted to rest for one more minute. Every time she talked, it felt like a freight train was running through her head. "Maybe in a sec."

Stan cracked his knuckles and smeared on some cherry Chap-Stick, studying her like a sick stingray at an aquarium. Shifting her knees, Cheryl realized how cold the floor was beneath her. Her teeth started to chatter. Almost immediately, Andy noticed and draped some club towels over her. They smelled like chlorine and were slightly scratchy—maybe someone should talk to the Racquet Club about Egyptian cotton.

"Better?" Andy asked.

Cheryl let out a jagged breath and said, "I'm fine. Haven't you ever seen a woman on the floor before?"

Stan laughed. Cheryl took in another deep breath, trying to focus on a rhythm to separate herself from the blinding pain inside her head. Bummer she'd never had kids. Lamaze would have come in handy in this situation.

"Did you find anyone to call?" Andy asked. His voice was sharp and directed at Stan. Suddenly, Cheryl realized Stan was holding her BlackBerry.

"Give me that," Cheryl barked.

The last thing she needed was Stan's fat fingers navigating through her e-mail. As it was, the wrong file could pop up at any moment. Cheryl kept folders on everyone at TurnKey. She had documented failures, successes, and weaknesses because she never knew when she might need the information to get ahead. Nobody would be happy if he saw what she had written. In fact, most of it could get her fired.

"Stan, give it to me," Cheryl insisted. "Give me my BlackBerry."

Unfortunately, this was said along with a natural effort to sit upright and grab for the phone. The sudden movement jostled Cheryl's bruised brain with a headache so intense that a horrific wave of nausea hit. "I think I'm going to . . ."

The health club worker squealed. Stan and Andy groaned. Cheryl, thankfully, blacked out.

THE MACY'S BAG was bright red, waiting by the bedside table. Doris eyed it, excited to finally try on her purchase. She hadn't done it at the store because the lighting always made her look sickly and those three-way mirrors seemed to enjoy showcasing the dimples in the back of her thighs. In spite of this, Doris had taken pleasure in telling Katherine Rigney that the size 14 fit just fine.

The bag had sat by the bed for most of the day. Doris built the anticipation by finishing up little tasks like making phone calls, organizing her bridge game, and coordinating a holiday donations committee for her church. Then she vacuumed, dusted, and straightened the house, just like she did every afternoon. Now, the time had come to see how her slinky anniversary gown looked.

A bubble of anticipation built in her stomach. With trembling hands, Doris removed her glasses and necklace. Closing the bedroom door, she hesitated for a minute, and then locked it. If Mandy came home from school early, there was no doubt her daughter would burst into the room and offer some unwanted opinion. Once the room was secure, Doris got undressed, folded her pants, and hung her sweater set back in the closet.

In three quick strides, Doris was across the room and grabbing for the white box the gown was lying in. Opening the lid and peeling back the red paper, she lifted the light fabric. The slight beading against the creamy silk bodice sparkled. Doug would be very impressed. It would remind him of their wedding day.

Taking a deep breath, Doris lowered the gown over her head. The silk got stuck at her shoulders. After giving a slight tug, it fell into a gentle cascade, embracing her body like the arms of a lover. Doris smiled girlishly, put on her glasses and turned to the mirror.

Seeing her reflection, Doris nearly screamed. The nightgown did not look like a wedding gown and Doris certainly was not a blushing young bride. She was a woman approaching forty with a thick waist, conservative haircut, and glasses. Dressed up in a gown that was too tight around her stomach, hips, and thighs. A gown that made the fat on her arms look like overstuffed sausages.

"Doris," she could practically hear her mother say. "Don't be so hard on yourself. You look just fine."

Doris peeked into the mirror once again and shook her head. The silk on the evil outfit was sticking to folds of fat that weren't fit to be seen. She pinched the lower part of her belly and cringed.

The cover of the bed gave slightly as Doris sank into it. Taking off her glasses, Doris pressed her palms against her eyes. Even if she was her own worst critic, she wasn't an idiot. There had always been a marked difference between her full figure and someone with a naturally petite frame, but somehow she had gotten by. Until now.

Doris had noticed the weight gain as it happened but chose to ignore it, fully expecting her body would bounce back. Even with a full-bodied figure, Doris had always been fit. She'd played sports all her life and jogged with her mother every morning. After her mother died, someone . . . Jackie? . . . had suggested Doris join a yoga class instead but all of the stretching and breathing was a little too reflective, so Doris had dropped out after a week. Then, life just seemed to get complicated. Doris was helping her father sell the house, driving Mandy's carpools, working with various charitable organizations . . . Physical fitness became a low priority. Getting energy from sugar and caffeine was a much easier choice.

If Doug had noticed the change in her body, he hadn't said anything, but if he saw her in a gown like this, what on earth would he think? She looked ridiculous. She looked fat. At the thought, a sudden onslaught of hot sweat made her underarms swampy. Doris's head got light and in a moment, her heart was pounding.

Deep breaths. Take deep breaths, she reminded herself. That's what the doctor had told her.

After filling her lungs with oxygen in a slow, even rhythm, Doris should reach into the drawer of the bedside table and find the bottle of Xanax. The cap would stick a bit—it always did. Instead of throwing the bottle across the room in a fit of frustration, she should stay calm and keep trying until the lid popped off. Even the smallest piece would help induce a Pavlovian response, calming that dreadful, panicky feeling that made her feel so out of control.

Doris followed the steps. For once, the lid came off easily. The pill was bitter in her mouth, chalky. But unlike the acrid bile in the back of her throat, the taste was familiar. Safe. A few minutes passed before Doris felt her body go numb. The sensation reminded her of high school parties; getting drunk and performing comedic strip-teases as her friends cheered her on.

Always the wild child, Doris had been the one to lead Jackie and Cheryl to mischief. They toilet-papered houses on Halloween, flashed boys during spring break, bought Pink Floyd albums and that first bag of weed. Doris was always thinking of the next prank, except when they were on school grounds. There she was always careful not to get into trouble, thanks to her commitment to Florida State. Doris had been scouted as a freshman for her soccer skills. As a freshman! Even today, that thought made her flush with pride.

Doris had been so careful to protect her reputation at school, not wanting to risk her scholarship. If Cheryl or Jackie tried to get her to do anything crazy like smoke cigarettes with them out back, Doris would take only two puffs. Then, she'd douse them with Love's Baby Soft perfume and spritz her tongue with spearmint Binaca until it burned. At the memory, Doris gave a sad little laugh. If she would have known how her life was going to play out, she would have been a lot less diligent. In fact, she may have just gotten drunk every day at first period.

With a sigh, Doris watched as the room softened and came back into focus. The strands of the rug looked like soft, bleached wheat. Their purity soothed her. Taking a deep breath, Doris lifted her head and looked around the room.

The walls were a bright, clean white and matched all the touch points in the room. The wicker by the bay window, the porcelain vanity table in the corner, the ivory brush set on the dresser . . . Doug had once complained that their bedroom was too white, that it felt like something out of the "Imagine" video. Doris thought that was ridiculous. A piano would never fit and Yoko Ono certainly would not be invited.

Standing up slowly, Doris put her glasses back on and sneaked a glimpse of her reflection in the mirror over the dresser. The color had returned to her cheeks. Her glasses were no longer steamed and blurry. She was fine.

Tearing off the gown, Doris decided to return it. Knowing the act would affect Katherine Rigney's commission made her feel better. That conniving woman had picked out five hundred dollars worth of jeans for Mandy and then managed to sell Doris on a sparkling, perfumed body powder, just because Doris was afraid to say no.

Doris went into the bathroom, turned the shower to full blast, and stepped in. The new plan was this—have a cup of coffee, maybe a handful of cookies, and put on a sensible, Doris-style dress. After all, Doug had loved her just the way she was for more than twenty years. What could make him stop now?

"WE ARE PREPARING for our final descent into Chicago," the crackling voice came over the loud speaker. "Make sure your seat backs and tray tables are . . ."

Jackie shot up like a rocket, fluffy pink face mask askew. Her tongue was stuck to the roof of her mouth and her platinum blond curls smelled like something had curled up and died in them, probably somewhere mid-Atlantic. Fumbling underneath the seat, Jackie pulled out a pastel leather purse.

The cool satin lining brushed against her fingertips as she searched for her compact and trusty cylinder of Angel perfume. Even after the romance of the French scents, this sweet and spicy blend in the light blue glass bottle had always been her signature scent. After spraying it onto her hands, she ran them through her hair. Breathing in the familiar smell, she sighed. Aromatherapy.

As Jackie slid her purse back under the seat, her seat mate's eyes fluttered. The elderly woman seemed to smile at Jackie, before closing her eyes again. Her blanket had fallen around their ankles so Jackie picked it up and retucked her in, silently wishing her dreams of fairies, unicorns, and of course, a handsome prince.

Shifting around in her seat, Jackie decided to lift the thin plastic covering the window. *Schwwwwahhh!* went the film, such a great sound. She was surprised the little monster behind her hadn't discovered it and repeated it for six hours straight. She turned her head and peeked back. The kid was fast asleep or dead. Either one was fine by her.

When Jackie had first boarded the plane, loath to fly coach for the first time in ten years, the "*au contraire, au contraire . . .*" singing through her head was punctuated by a rhythmic vibration of her seat. She had whirled around and caught the eye of the perpetrator—an evil five-year-old with a freckled face. His poor mother had her eyes squeezed shut, determined to pretend the kid didn't exist even if he hijacked the plane.

Jackie gave a disapproving shake of her head. The kid smiled, waited until she started to turn, then gave her seat another good, swift kick. This time, Jackie had spun around with the slit-throat sign, indicating the kid, then his mother. The little snake went still with fear.

All kids were mass manipulators in little bodies. For Jackie, that knowledge made them much easier to handle. Doris's daughter had learned to respect Jackie at a young age because she wasn't given another option. After watching the two of them together, Doris and Cheryl had even dubbed Jackie "the kid whisperer." That said, perhaps her abrupt exit to Paris had been just as hard on Mandy as it had been on Jackie's friends, but if it had been she hid it well. There had been many phone calls where Mandy had chirped on and on about her life over the transatlantic line.

In spite of a general aversion to kids, Jackie had to admit it would be nice to see Mandy again. It would be nice to see everyone. Jackie's presence was going to be a big surprise—Doris and Cheryl had no idea she was on her way home—but Jackie lived for dramatic entrances.

Giving herself an excited hug, Jackie pressed her nose against the window. Snow was melting against the plastic glass. Wet streaks reflected in the lights on the wing; red and white shimmering against the dark sky. Squinting, she waited for Chicago to appear below, enjoying the sensation of the plane lifting and turning underneath her. Jackie loved flying. The risk, the adventure . . . the strange things it did to her body. She moved her feet around in her pumps. They felt like elephant paws.

Suddenly, the plane dipped through the clouds and Lake Michigan appeared as a dark pool below her, the lights of the skyscrapers blinking red and green—and oh!—there was the Drake! So many romantic weekends well spent. Peering hard, she spotted the miniature skyline of her hometown. Schaumburg's industrial centers and clock tower loomed in the distance.

"Ladies and gentlemen," the voice boomed once again over the loudspeaker, "please have your customs cards filled out and ready for landing."

Jackie jumped guiltily. She hadn't even started. Running her fingers through her hair, she once again looked at her empty customs form. The first question had tripped her up.

Destination? Unknown.

Chapter Five

"Where's my BlackBerry? I need my BlackBerry!" Cheryl said, opening her eyes.

Looking around, she realized she was in a portable hospital bed. The starched sheets were cool against her hot legs and medical bracelets were hanging from her wrist. A blue curtain had been pulled to make a semiprivate room. Andy sat in a chair in the tiny space, flipping through a magazine. Stan was nowhere in sight.

"Hey, you're back," Andy said, hopping up from a chair and strolling the two feet over to her. "How you doin'?"

Those green eyes studied her with concern, probably because her hair was matted to her forehead and she was still dressed in gym clothes. Cheryl turned away, tugging the sheets up to her chin. "Shut up. Where's Stan?"

A pretty nurse pulled the curtain, the sliding metal hooks announcing her entrance. Her hair was in a perfect blond bun, her eyes wide and gray. Andy already had her on a first-name basis.

"Hey, Molly," he said. "I think this one needs some more happy juice."

"Molly?" Cheryl mimicked. "Do you have to flirt with everything that moves?"

Molly regarded Cheryl with the same look of surprise she must have given her first cow-eye dissection in biology class. Cheryl blushed. Maybe the comment had been uncalled for but Andy's whole "I'm nice to everyone" thing was really starting to get on her nerves. Because he wasn't nice to everyone. He was Mr. Look Her Up and Down and *Shrug*.

"Cheryl, you do seem a little angry," the nurse mused. "Everything okay?"

Cheryl didn't bother to answer. It was pretty obvious that everything was not okay.

Molly pulled out a pen flashlight and started an assault on Cheryl's pupils. "Blink. Blink again."

"Where the fuck is Stan?" Cheryl said. "Andy, where is Stan?"

"Calling the local news, I think," Andy said, shoving his hands in his pockets. "It's a good story. Star marketing executive, downed by angry racquetball."

"When I get out of this bed . . ." Cheryl tried to sit up but Molly put out a gentle hand and pushed her back. The penlight moved forward again.

"I haven't been drinking, Officer," Cheryl mumbled, squeezing her eyes shut tight against the glare. The back of her lids appeared orange. Cheryl adjusted her position, groaning slightly at the sharp pain in her head. "Molly, I better get some good drugs out of all this," she said, trying for levity.

"Drug seeker," Andy sang. "Drug-seeking behavior!"

Cheryl's eyes flew open. Molly was biting her lip as though wondering if she was indeed a criminal.

"Andy," Cheryl said, "the mere *moment* it is confirmed I am not dying, you're fired."

"Please tell me she's dying," Andy pleaded.

Molly giggled, then slid on her stethoscope and started listening to Cheryl's heart.

Cheryl pursed her lips, forcing herself to hate the plain gold necklace with its single pearl that Molly was wearing, instead of the nurse herself. It was swaying back and forth as she moved, making Cheryl dizzy and drawing an unnecessary amount of attention to Molly's cleavage, a view Cheryl could have lived without. Unable to take the humiliation of being such a total victim, Cheryl grabbed the metal disk of the stethoscope out of Molly's hands and spoke into it like a microphone.

"Seriously. I'm fine," Cheryl said. "Let me go home."

Molly flushed, then made some furious notes on Cheryl's chart.

"I am so sorry about that," Andy said. "She's edgy. It must be the head wound."

"She's been through a lot," the nurse agreed, reaching out and patting Cheryl's hand. "I'm sorry this happened to you."

"That's really sweet," Andy said, touching Molly's elbow. "I wish *everyone* had a heart like you."

"This isn't a bar," Cheryl said. "If you want to pick her up, do it on your own time."

Molly blushed again, sneaking a quick look at Andy. He was wearing that dimple like an accessory.

Pocketing her stethoscope, Molly turned to Cheryl and said, "You do have a slight concussion. We don't have to keep you here for observation as long as you have someone to stay with you . . ."

"I'm taking her home," Andy said. When Cheryl opened her mouth to protest, he said, "Stan's not here. He had something planned with his wife."

Cheryl's heart sank. "Where's my BlackBerry? Does he have it?"

Andy glanced around the room. Cheryl's gym bag was on the chair. He walked over and sifted through it, shaking his head. Cheryl couldn't help but wonder if there was anything embarrassing inside. After a minute, he said, "Maybe it's at the gym. It's not here."

Staring at the lights on the ceiling, Cheryl felt her head spin. There were few options. If she had Andy call to demand her phone back this instant, Stan would probably pull over and start snooping through it right there on the side of the road. No, Cheryl would have to wait until morning and hope Stan had more faith in her than she had in him.

"Andy, are you . . . Are you staying with her?" the nurse asked, tapping the pen against her teeth. "She needs to have someone stay with her."

"No way," Cheryl said. "I'm gonna call a friend."

"Apparently, that's not me," Andy said with a grin. "Want to change before we go?"

Cheryl wanted to shake her head but it hurt. "Let's just go," she said, slowly bringing her legs over the side of the bed. After a minute, she stood up. The world wobbled around her but she brushed away Andy's arm when he offered it.

Andy grabbed her bag and they headed toward the entrance. The halls were filled with families and couples and, in spite of herself, Cheryl was grateful for Andy's company. Hospitals were horrible places to spend time alone.

"It might be cold out," Andy said. "Want my jacket?"

"I'm fine."

Outside, the air was icy against Cheryl's legs and she regretted her answer. She also wished she had taken the time to change. As she shivered, Andy ran around to the driver's side and started the car, immediately turning the heater to high. The vents blew out cold air.

"Sorry. It should be warm in a minute," Andy said, glancing in his rearview mirror and carefully pulling out. "Listen, if you feel sick or anything, tell me. I'm supposed to take you right back. Where do you live?"

Cheryl gave him her address and he punched it into his GPS system. A pert, female voice started giving directions. After a moment, Andy flipped on the seat warmers.

"You really should start kissing Stan's ass," Cheryl said, absently watching the scenery as it went by.

"Huh?"

"You didn't laugh at his jokes earlier," she explained. "Bad idea. If you want to get ahead."

Out of the corner of her eye, she saw Andy rub the back of his hand over the dark stubble on his cheek. With his strong jawline and perfectly white teeth, Andy was one of those guys that would be a perfect fit for any of their clients' commercials. Of course, Cheryl found it hard to categorize Andy as classically good-looking. There was something too relatable about him, an amiability that naturally made him one of the gang.

Cheryl thought back to Andy's first day at TurnKey. At lunch, he'd sat quietly at the end of the table at Hooters, observing how the team interacted. Stan had been harassing the Hooters waitress about Buffalo wings, deliberately emphasizing words like *hot* and *spicy* while leering at the young girl's breasts. Granted, the breasts were quite an eyeful (or mouthful, as Stan always said), pushed up to the ceiling in the tight orange bra, but Cheryl was annoyed by the teasing. Maybe it was—Cheryl had peered at the name tag— Susie's fault for choosing a career that seemed to beg for harassment but still, Susie should have dumped a pitcher of beer on Stan and gotten it over with.

"Just order already," Cheryl finally cut in, irritated with Stan's performance.

The waitress smiled at Cheryl in relief.

"I think we already know how much heat this guy can handle," Cheryl said, rolling her eyes. "Can anyone say Cabo?"

The men at the table groaned, instantly getting the reference to that company sales conference in Mexico. Stan had gotten hammered and passed out on the beach, turning redder than a Mai Tai. Cheryl liked to joke that Stan's massive amount of body hair was the only thing that saved him from death by sun poisoning.

Stan threw his hairy arms up in dismay. "It was the worm!"

"Too bad your date didn't know that was all she was getting," Cheryl quipped.

The men pounded the table with glee and a beer got knocked over into the breadsticks. Cheryl folded her napkin and gave a ladylike smile. Feeling Andy's eyes on her, Cheryl had taken a deliberate sip of her margarita, slowly licking the salt from the rim.

Every guy at the table had stopped what he was doing and stared.

Cheryl was smart enough to make the move look mindless. Out of the corner of her eye, she saw Andy shift in his seat. She looked back at him for a split moment and his eyes darkened—that tiny, universal sign. Unfortunately, a piece of salt had chosen that very moment to lodge in the back of her throat. Cheryl choked and had to grab for a nearby glass of water.

Jack Thompson looked over at her in surprise. "You okay, there?" he said, grinning.

Jack was such an asshole. Cheryl almost wanted to sleep with him, just to have the pleasure of not returning his call. She caught her breath and sat up straight.

"We know you're short, Jack," Cheryl said. "But I wouldn't make it so obvious you've never heard a woman choking."

The guys at the table roared. Andy had smiled, shaking his head.

"Stan isn't funny," Andy said, tapping his hands against the steering wheel. "So, why waste my breath?"

Cheryl looked at him in surprise. "Did you seriously just say that to me?"

"Am I supposed to worry that you're going to repeat it?"

"But you're . . . you're the new guy," Cheryl said, confused. Maybe it was her head injury but Andy just wasn't making sense. "You're supposed to kiss up to the boss. That's what new guys do."

Andy gave her a look. "This new guy's gonna do the work," he said. "Maybe that will be good enough."

"Good luck with that." Cheryl laughed. "What are you working on right now?"

"Pure. It's . . ."

As Andy started rambling on about his energy drink account, Cheryl listened closely, trying to figure out what made Andy tick. There was no way this kid believed it only took hard work to get ahead. Clearly, he was playing his cards close to his chest, which meant she really was going to have to watch out for him, which was incredibly annoying. Even though Cheryl had sealed her position at TurnKey years ago, she was always on edge. It was a boys' club and in spite of their casual amusement at her bawdiness, Cheryl would never be an official (ahem) member.

"Look, I'm glad I get to work with you," Andy was saying. "Your name was one of the reasons I came to TurnKey. It carries a lot of weight, especially in Chicago."

With anyone else, Cheryl would have retorted that it should, considering she developed TurnKey from a one-room marketing company into a full-blown necessity. The Midwestern advertising community couldn't live without it. But she only felt compelled to nod.

"I hope we get to work closer together," Andy said, looking over at her.

For a brief moment, their eyes locked and warmth spread through Cheryl's body. Irritated, she adjusted her seat belt.

"What's wrong?" Andy asked, immediately noticing her discomfort. He slowed the car, like he was ready to make a U-turn right back to intensive care.

"I'm fine," Cheryl practically shouted. "Just take me home already."

Andy's eyes widened in surprise. The rest of the ride was quiet, punctuated only by an assured mechanical voice neatly guiding them home.

Chapter Six

"DOUG, THIS PLACE IS JUST BEAUTIFUL," DORIS SAID, SETTING DOWN her purse and settling back into a white leather chair.

For their anniversary, Doug had surprised her with a table at Blackburn, one of the nicest restaurants in town. The lighting was low all around them and a harp player strummed softly by the fire. Bottles of Pellegrino sparkled on the tables.

"I thought you might like it," Doug said.

At the table next to them, a silver-haired gentleman and a distinguished real estate maven nodded a hello. After giving them an awkward smile, she leaned forward and whispered, "Are you sure I'm not underdressed?"

The light blue cotton dress Doris was wearing would have fit in just fine at the Outback, which is where Doris thought they were going, but not here. The real estate maven was wearing something low-cut and black, with a strand of designer pearls.

Doug gave her a quick glance. "You look fine."

Doris bit her lip. *Fine* was not the word she was looking for, but after twenty-three years of marriage, what did she expect? Tugging at her neckline, Doris said, "Well, then. Good."

A waiter with a pronounced upper lip swept up to their table. "Good evening, my name is Jonathan," he said. With a flourish, he handed both her and Doug thick maroon menus. "What are we drinking this evening?"

"A nice glass of red wine," Doug announced. "Doris?"

"Um . . ." Doris hesitated. Her hands fluttered around for a wine list.

"How about a nice champagne?" Doug suggested.

Doris smiled. "That sounds great."

The waiter whisked away. Doris's menu had already been opened for her, so she looked down at the heavy pages. The first thing she noticed was that there were only five options for dinner entrees. The second thing she noticed was that there were no prices.

"Doug, everything on the menu is free," she whispered.

"What?" Doug looked confused for a moment, then he looked at the menu and laughed. "In that case, I think I'll get two steaks."

"I'll get two chicken marsalas," Doris said, nodding. She set her menu to the side and admired the forks on the table in front of her. They looked like real silver. She wondered if anyone ever tried to steal them.

Doug reached across the table and stroked her fingers. Doris loved the way his gold wedding band seemed like a natural part of his hands. In fact, Doris couldn't remember a time she'd seen him without it.

"Are you stroking my fingers because you love me," Doris teased, "or because you want me to stop manhandling the silverware?"

Doug leaned forward. His voice dropped an octave, becoming low and suggestive in that way Doris had always loved. "What do you think?"

"The silverware." Doris nodded.

Doug's eyes grazed over her, settling on her ample cleavage. "I don't think it's the silverware."

Just then, Jonathan arrived with their drinks. He set a bulbous glass of red wine in front of Doug, a sparkling crystal flute in front of Doris.

Doris leaned back in her chair, lit up inside. It had been so long since she and Doug had connected like this. Thinking back to the incident at the mall with Katherine Rigney, Doris couldn't help but gloat inside. Katherine had been right. Doris *was* lucky.

"Are we ready to order?" Jonathan asked.

Doug raised an eyebrow at Doris. "We are," he said. "We'll have . . ."

Doris tuned out and looked around the restaurant. Couples leaned close together over intimate tables lit by candlelight. Over by the fire, the harpist was strumming with her eyes closed, the notes in rhythm with the crackling flames. The waiters rushed around in starched white uniforms, the utmost in respectful efficiency.

"Why haven't we ever come here before?" Doris said, as Jonathan scampered off.

"I don't know," Doug said. "Never thought about it."

"I'm glad you did."

"To us," Doug said, raising his glass. "Twenty-three years of . . ."

"Brilliantly wedded bliss." Doris smiled.

They clinked glasses. Doug's eyes held hers. Doris blushed, taking a sip of champagne. Light and bubbly, it left a pleasant finish in her mouth. "Yum. That's good."

"Mine is, too," Doug said.

Doris watched champagne bubbles float up through the gold liquid. It had been so long since she and Doug had actually sat down to dinner together, she wasn't quite sure what to say next. Most of the time, Mandy was the focal point, but Doris wanted to talk about something different, enjoy this connection she had with her husband, even if it was just for one night.

"Oh, I know what I wanted to tell you," Doris blurted out,

remembering. "I bumped into Katherine Rigney at the mall. At Macy's. It's hard to believe we're all so old, isn't it?"

Doug choked on his wine, spluttering loudly. The couple at the next table glanced over at them.

"Honey, are you okay?" she said, leaning forward. "Did it go down the wrong pipe?"

"Wrong pipe." Doug nodded, wiping at his mouth with a napkin. "Sorry about that. Oh, look."

Jonathan swept up to the table, moving the drinks aside to make room for the appetizers. With a flourish, the food runner laid out two dishes.

"Oysters Rockefeller," Jonathan said, pointing at a plate of baked oysters. "And the seafood salad." A shimmering display of calamari, shrimp, and baby scallops lay nestled between green olives and lemons.

"This looks great," Doris said, stabbing a piece of calamari with her fork. She brought it to her lips and took the first bite. To her surprise, it was rubbery and bland.

"How is it?" Doug asked.

Mouth still full, Doris nodded. After swallowing, she lied, "Really good. How are the oysters?"

"Try one," Doug said. "They're an aphrodisiac . . ."

Doris blushed. Even though Doug was always tired from work, there had been more than one occasion where he had turned the stereo in their room to jazz, splashed on some of that cologne she'd bought him years ago, and come at her with an awkward hug. Doris had been finding it hard to get excited about sex, mainly because of her weight. They hadn't been intimate in months but tonight, it was time to make a change. It was their anniversary, after all.

"An aphrodisiac?" Doris said. "Then maybe I should try one."

Doug passed her a forkful of steaming oyster. It was slimy and tasted like rotten fish, but Doris swallowed it whole and gave a big smile. "Doug, I think it's already doing something."

He grinned. "Really?"

Taking a deep breath, Doris slid her shoe off in an attempt to rub her foot against Doug's leg. After a moment, Doris realized the hard thing she was stroking was actually part of the table. Doris adjusted her position and thrust her foot out again. This time, it made contact with something soft.

"Ouch," Doug said, jumping. "Did you just kick me?"

"Sorry," Doris said, immediately drawing her foot back. "I was . . . my shoe fell off."

"Better put it back on," Doug said, plugging his nose and waving a hand. "You don't want to scare away the other tables with those stinky feet."

"Ha-ha," Doris said, fumbling for her shoe. Even though Doris liked it when Doug joked with her, sometimes his jokes were annoying. It wasn't like they were sixteen anymore. Who wanted to talk about stinky feet at an anniversary dinner?

Doug, of course, was clueless. He finished off the rest of his appetizer with gusto, while telling her some story about work. Doris sipped champagne, smiling at the punch line.

"Should we get more wine?" Doug asked when the busboys took the appetizer plates away and the food runners approached with entrees.

Doris glanced at her almost empty glass, surprised. "Um . . . sure."

On Doris's plate, a plump chicken breast swam in a light purple wine sauce with fresh mushrooms. Doris admired how neatly it was partitioned next to garlic mashed potatoes and grilled asparagus. Doug's steak also looked fantastic. Perfectly cooked, a solid brown heart cradled between green beans and garlic mashed potatoes. Fried onion strings decorated the top of the plate.

They ate in silence for a couple of minutes. "I'm in heaven," Doug finally said.

"Me, too." Doris nodded. After a minute, she said, "I can't believe it's been twenty-three years. Time goes so fast. You know, Katherine Rigney looked awful. She looked old. Do you think we look old?"

Doug took a long drink of wine. The color on his cheeks deepened, as though the liquid went from his mouth directly into his skin. He signaled to Jonathan to bring another.

"We look great," Doug said. "You look great."

Doris's heart leaped. "Really?"

Doug laughed. "Yes, really. We're in our prime."

"Well, *she* isn't," Doris said, biting into a piece of asparagus. "I felt bad for her."

Doug picked up a knife. Deftly, he cut through a bloody piece. After a minute, he set down the knife and looked at her. "Doris, what's this about?"

"Huh?"

"Why do you keep bringing up Katherine Rigney?" Doug asked. "I have no interest in talking about her, especially on our anniversary. I haven't even seen her in, what? Twenty years?"

Doris reached for another bite of chicken. Suddenly, she stopped. "Wait, what?"

Something on Doug's face changed. A muscle in his jaw pulsed. "What?"

"You haven't seen her in twenty years?" Doris repeated, watching him carefully.

Shifting in his seat, Doug stabbed a bite of steak. "Do you want some steak?"

"Doug, I asked you a question," Doris said, ignoring the approaching fork. "Katherine said she saw you."

"She did?" Doug said, his voice unnatural. "Oh, right. I guess I forgot about that."

The harpist hit a high note. Suddenly, the clinking of the silverware and murmurs in the restaurant seemed too loud. Doris wanted to run out the door, cover her ears, do something to stop the question she was about to ask. But she couldn't.

"Doug . . ." Doris said slowly. "Did something happen between you and Katherine Rigney?"

Doug dropped his fork with a clatter. He sat back in his chair, staring at her in shock. Immediately, Doris felt awful. Horrible.

What a stupid thing to say, on her *anniversary* of all days. So what if Doug had seen Katherine Rigney and then forgotten? Why on earth would he remember?

"I'm sorry," Doris said quickly. From her purse, Doris heard her cell's shrill ring. She fumbled for it. "Please forget I just said that."

"I . . ." The flush had left his face.

Doris fumbled for the phone, rambling, "It's just that you saw her, you know, at the mall and didn't tell me, so I thought that . . ."

"I . . ."

The ringing had stopped by the time she'd pulled out the phone. The real estate maven was now eyeing them angrily. "Probably shouldn't have my phone on in here," Doris muttered, embarrassed.

"I saw a movie with her," Doug said softly.

Doris gaped. "Huh?"

Doug looked up so quickly, eyes so panicked that something inside Doris went cold. She thought of the way Katherine was eyeing her in Macy's, chomping that gum like she had won a victory. Doris's heart started pounding. Her palms went wet.

"A movie?" Doris repeated. She barely had time to process this when her phone lit up, ringing again. Cheryl. Blankly, Doris watched the familiar name cross her caller ID. It could have been written in Chinese. "You saw a movie with Katherine Rigney?"

The phone kept ringing, vibrating in her hand. Doris ignored it.

"I bumped into her." Doug sighed. "I had intended to see it alone."

"Did you pay for her?" Doris asked, her mouth dry.

"Doris—"

"*Did you?*"

The ringing started again, loud.

"It would have been rude—"

"What was it?" Doris asked. "What movie?" She tried to picture Doug and Katherine walking up to the ticket counter, laughing about some R-rated film. They'd go get a bucket of popcorn, order a Coke with one straw, sit in a dark theater and . . .

"Turn off your cell phone," the silver-haired man at the next table boomed.

Doris looked down and sent the call to voice mail. But the ringing started again an instant later and Doug grabbed for it this time, pulling it roughly from her hands. "Yes, hello? . . . Yes. This is her husband."

Doris cringed at the word *husband*. What on earth did that mean? The chicken churned in her stomach.

"Okay. We're on our way," Doug said. He clicked the phone shut and handed it back to Doris. For a brief moment, their hands once again touched.

The real estate maven leaned over and said, "I hope someone is dying."

Doris froze, remembering the way her mother's shoulders had shaken with grief when she finally told them about the cancer. Doris could still remember the feeling of that thin frame in her arms, the fragile body like a little bird, heart beating sharply.

"It was Cheryl," Doug told Doris, ignoring the other couple. "She just has a concussion. Someone from work's driving her home now but she can't be alone overnight."

"A crash?" Doris whispered.

"No, honey. Just racquetball."

Tears streamed down Doris's face.

"Don't worry," Doug said. "She'll be okay."

Suddenly efficient, Doug pushed back his plate and stood up. He pulled several one hundred dollar bills from his wallet and threw them onto the table. Walking over to Jonathan, he said something and the waiter nodded. Doug came back, grabbed Doris's hand and pulled her up. He led her over to the real estate maven's table.

"I just paid for your meal," Doug told the couple. The man started to protest and Doug held up his hand. "Please. Let me finish. We disturbed your dinner so I wanted to take a moment to express my deepest apologies . . ."

The man nodded, dignified. His wife sipped her martini, a smug look in her eyes.

". . . that you married such a bitch," Doug finished. The woman's face went red with rage and her husband's bushy eyebrows shot up in surprise. Doris couldn't even muster a small giggle.

"Come on, honey," Doug said, straightening his shoulders. "Let's go see about your friend."

Doris clutched her husband's hand. He led her out of the restaurant.

Chapter Seven

"WHAT, THIS BEAUTY?" JACKIE CROONED INTO THE REARVIEW mirror. "I asked George to rent me a car and he thought this would be a scream—it was! I screamed."

Jackie fluffed her hair, then sat back against the springy seats, satisfied with her story. Crafting a lie ahead of time was a critical part of fooling Doris and Cheryl. She didn't want them to start asking questions when she rolled up in a car that was decidedly un-Jackie-like.

Even though the compact rental seemed perfectly efficient, it was oddly shaped and had gleaming chrome hubcaps and a cherry red paint job. The red paint looked like someone had taken an unattractive baby and dressed her in a prostitute's lipstick. Still, Jackie knew she was lucky to be driving out of the airport in anything at all.

After the flight, Jackie had made her way through customs, grabbed her luggage, and found the car rental counter. Eyeing the latest Mercedes pictured under the luxury models, Jackie crossed her fingers, pulled out a credit card and handed it to the young ticket agent. The girl was wearing a blue bowling shirt and dangly silver earrings with little balls at the ends. They made a jingling noise as she swiped Jackie's credit card through. A minute passed, then the credit card machine beeped.

"Hmm . . ." the girl said. "It doesn't seem to be going through. Got another card?"

"Yes, of course," Jackie said, fumbling through her wallet. "Here."

The girl gave a half nod, once again jingling the earrings. Jackie wondered if the sound gave her a headache.

"No luck," the girl said, after swiping it.

"Darling," Jackie said, resting manicured fingers on the dirty counter. "We simply must try again. My credit is quite fine."

With a sigh, the girl ran the card several times. Finally, she shrugged. "Declined, declined, and"—the girl held up the receipt the machine had just spit out, as though to emphasize the point—"declined."

Jackie's heart started to pound. Although her bank account had been drained, she had been counting on her credit cards to carry her through. If that option was gone . . . well, Jackie simply didn't know what to do.

"Well," Jackie said, desperately fumbling through her wallet and in the process dumping out a multitude of receipts from high-end French boutiques. "Try this one."

The agent stared at Jackie with unblinking hazel eyes. "But two of your cards have been declined. Several times."

"Please."

With a big sigh, the rental agent swiped the final card. The machine beeped. "Nope," the girl said. "I guess you had a little too much fun on vacation." Pointedly, she eyed the multitude of receipts and array of diamonds sparkling from Jackie's fingers.

Jackie forced a brave smile. "I don't think *fun* is the right word." Lowering her voice to a near whisper, Jackie said, "To tell you the truth, I was mugged." Her blue eyes pricked with tears. "The police found my purse by the Seine. I had no idea what cards to call in and report. It was a terrible experience but I . . ." She sniffled. "I was just happy to get out with my life."

"That's awful," the girl said, face flushed in excitement. It was clear she was torn between compassion and digging for details. "I'm so sorry."

Jackie let a single tear roll down her cheek. "The whole thing was a terrible ordeal," she said. "I'm not surprised some of it has followed me home. Anyway," she said, making a point of gathering her things slowly. "*Merci* for your trouble."

"Wait." The girl reached out a skinny hand and leaned forward, glancing around. "Let me help. I can give you a free promotion on one of our lower models if you bring it back in a few days. Just don't tell my manager."

"Free?" Jackie said, startled. She had only expected her performance to garner her a discount. "As in, gratis?"

The girl nodded, those silver earrings winking in the light. Jackie made a big show of rushing around behind the counter, arms outstretched. Gratefully and tearfully, Jackie accepted the keys.

Even though the car was a total hunk of junk, Jackie was grateful to have it. Thank goodness the girl had believed that ridiculous story. If it wasn't for her, Jackie would have had to hitchhike home. She felt a tiny pang for the deception but quickly shoved it aside. Survival was more important than guilt. Jackie had learned that a long time ago.

Turning the key, the car sputtered to life and something dusty shot out of the vents. After giving a slight sneeze, Jackie shut them off and pulled out of the parking lot. The car bounced along like a little red wagon.

"Only the best for me," she sang.

Hesitating at the turn, Jackie considered her options. Doris had a gorgeous spare bedroom, whereas Cheryl had most likely converted her spare room into a home office. Plus, Doris had time on her hands while Cheryl would have to be at the office all day.

Staying with Doris made the most sense. It would be seen as a delight rather than an imposition, but since Doris and Cheryl were fighting, it could also be tricky. Jackie didn't want Cheryl to think she was choosing sides. Maybe she should pick up the phone and explain the situation to Cheryl, just as a preempt.

"I'm only staying with Dori because you work too much," she'd say, leaving out the unnecessary detail about not wanting to sleep on a couch. "Waiting for you to get home would be ever so dull."

As Jackie was thinking this through, her cell phone rang. To her surprise, the caller ID said *Cheryl*. "You're psychic," Jackie screamed, snapping open her phone.

"Uh, hello?" a male voice said. "This is Stan, Cheryl's boss."

Jackie looked at the phone in confusion. "Is everything all right?"

"Cheryl's fine," Stan said. "You're on her speed dial but this number is European so . . ."

"Darling, it's Jackie," she drawled. "We've met." In fact, Jackie had met Stan several times. He was a thick, hairy sort of man. "What happened to Cheryl?"

As Stan explained the racquetball incident, Jackie couldn't help but think he sounded rather proud of the situation. Jackie hung up on him midsentence. Manhandling the car into a U-turn, she hit the gas and ten minutes later was pulling into Cheryl's driveway. Looking at the light blue shutters and stone chimney on her best friend's house, Jackie found it hard to believe that less than twenty-four hours ago, she had been in a French apartment, staring at a cheese wheel.

The lights were out, which meant Cheryl was still on her way back from the hospital. Turning off the ignition, Jackie rolled down the windows and breathed in the crisp, fall air. Somewhere down the block, one of Cheryl's neighbors was burning leaves. The smell was so perfectly October in the Midwest that Jackie wished she could bottle it and sell it as a perfume. A big smile stretched across her face.

"I'm home," she said softly.

Even though she was happy, it did feel a little strange to be sitting outside Cheryl's new house. In Paris, it had often slipped her mind that Cheryl had even moved from the two-story Tudor she'd shared with Sean. During one of their many transatlantic calls, as Jackie enjoyed a glass of Bordeaux on her wrought-iron balcony and chatted with Cheryl, she would picture Cheryl's life all wrong. She had imagined Cheryl in the wrong kitchen, using the wrong utensils, looking out the wrong window. Once, when Cheryl started talking about painting those shutters blue, Jackie had almost burst out with, "What an odd choice for a Tudor," before realizing her mistake. She had laughed out loud but refrained from sharing the joke. Cheryl wouldn't have appreciated the irony, considering how guilty she'd felt about the divorce. She would have just gone silent in that way she had.

When white headlights finally bounced down the drive behind her, Jackie leaped out, arms already open. Instead of Cheryl, Jackie saw the silhouette of a heavy, disheveled woman stumbling out of the passenger side of a Lexus. The woman's mouth practically dropped to the ground. "Jackie?"

"Dori?"

Before Jackie could stop herself, a hand flew to her chest in surprise. Doris looked like a completely different person from when Jackie had left town; she was at least thirty pounds heavier, and as she got closer, Jackie could see touches of gray at the roots of her light brown hair. Since the glare of the headlights was shining in Jackie's face, she was careful to mask her surprise. Pasting on a huge smile, Jackie rushed forward and engulfed her friend in a perfumed, busty hug.

"Mon chérie," Jackie cried. "I'm back! Finally, finally back."

"Please tell me I'm not dreaming," Doris said. She grabbed Jackie's hands and regarded her with those pretty eyes.

Doris had been voted Best Eyes for the high school yearbook, thanks to those thick black lashes that barely needed mascara and the way her blue irises shone like half moons. Still, she had kept her best feature hidden behind glasses for years. It drove Jackie and Cheryl crazy but no matter how many times they tried to get her to go for Lasik, contacts, or even blindness, Doris refused.

"You have the type of eyes that men go to war for," Jackie insisted.

"It's hard to picture Doug at war," Doris had said, laughing.

Tonight, those pretty eyes were rimmed in red. "Honey, what's wrong?" Jackie said, clutching her friend's hand. Doris looked back at Doug, then at Jackie. At her pained expression, it was obvious the tears weren't just about Jackie's homecoming. "Oh no," Jackie said. "Tell me everything."

Doris dipped her head and mumbled something but just then, a second set of headlights bounced into view. "I appreciate your help," Cheryl was saying, already half out the door. "See you tomorrow."

As the car backed out of the driveway, Cheryl stumbled toward them, hands to her mouth. She was dressed in a tiny gym outfit and looked tan and wiry, as always. "I can't believe it," she said. "This is the second time today I've thought I've died and gone to heaven." Then she squealed, barreling straight into Jackie's arms.

"Be careful." Jackie laughed. "You're injured."

"I'm fine," Cheryl insisted, holding her tight.

Jackie breathed in her familiar scent. Ever since they were kids, Cheryl had smelled like a cross between saltwater taffy and metal. Jackie liked to joke it was the scent of determination. "Oh, darling. I missed you," she said, affectionately stroking Cheryl's hair. The ends were brittle from all the highlights but masked with a thick hair serum. At the touch, Cheryl cringed slightly. "Oh no . . ." Jackie said, pulling back and eyeing her with concern. "Tell us where it hurts."

Cheryl lifted a limp arm and gestured at the general area of her head. "Eh."

The three friends stood silent for a moment. Then Doris gushed, "Jackie, you look *so good*. Cheryl, doesn't she look good?"

"Are you kidding me with this?" Cheryl demanded, whirling on Doris. "Don't just start talking to me like we're friends."

Doris's eyes widened and she took a step back.

Apparently, Cheryl and Doris had been avoiding each other for months, ever since Doris performed a "slut intervention" on Cheryl. The entire scene had been described to Jackie over the phone, blow by awful blow.

It had happened on a hot summer day when Doris and Cheryl had met for their biweekly lunch and pedicure date. Doris had shown up late, wearing some sort of a navy dress with large polka dots. It was too tight across the chest and kept gapping open, inadvertently exposing her humongous breasts to the other tables. Cheryl had teased her about it but instead of laughing, Doris had gotten more and more agitated. Halfway through lunch, Doris scarfed down a piece of bread, and then said, "I have to talk to you about something . . ."

"Don't talk about it," Cheryl joked. "Go in and demand a refund on that dress."

"You're sleeping with too many men," Doris blurted out.

Cheryl laughed. "What?"

"You heard me."

"Okay," Cheryl said, taken aback. "But who isn't?"

"I'm being serious," Doris said, attempting to spear a bite of salad. The tomato rolled across the plate and Doris's fork chased it until it was caught. "I don't really know why you're doing it, but it's pretty easy to see you're not happy."

"What makes you think I'm not happy?" Cheryl asked, gulping down her glass of Chardonnay. The entrees hadn't even come yet. Glancing at her watch, Cheryl wondered if they would be late for their pedicures.

"Well, you're drinking at lunch," Doris said, brushing a loose strand of hair out of her face. "Who does that?"

Cheryl indicated the tables around her. "Most of the restaurant."

"I don't know if they're happy either." Doris sighed.

"Are *you* happy, Doris?" Cheryl demanded, propping her chin on a hand and giving full focus to her friend. It wasn't a fair question. Ever since Doris's mother had died, Doris had become a completely different person. Gloomy, depressed, judgmental . . .

but Cheryl hadn't said anything because Doris had been a saint during the divorce. Even though Cheryl's affair had broken up their couples' circle, Doris had stuck by her side.

"Cheryl, I am being incredibly serious right now," Doris told her. "I need you to start thinking about your morals. Or I'll have to start thinking about our friendship."

Cheryl set down her wineglass, stunned. The pious look Doris was giving her should be reserved for drug pushers or animal abusers, not a divorcee in her late thirties trying to get a new lease on life.

Cheryl took off her sunglasses and took a long look at her best friend. "I'm sorry. Did you just . . . Are you giving me an ultimatum?"

Doris looked surprised at the label, but then nodded. "Yes. Yes, I think I am."

"Thirty years, Doris." Cheryl was aghast. "We have been best friends for thirty years. Are you seriously telling me you'd throw everything away because I'm having sex?"

Doris nodded, chin tilted up and nostrils flaring in that way they did when she felt threatened. "I stuck by you when you cheated on Sean because I didn't believe you were really that person. But since then, your morals have really gone out the window. Birds of a feather, you know. I don't want people to start thinking . . ."

Cheryl finished her wine in one gulp, stood up, and stalked out of the restaurant. She had not spoken to Doris since.

Now, Jackie was loath to witness the tension between them. Cheryl's fists were clenched and her face was all twisted up. Doris had wrapped her arms around herself and was shifting back and forth on the balls of her feet, like a fighter getting ready to dodge a hit.

"Girls, this is ridiculous," Jackie said. "I *just* got home."

Cheryl looked at her. After a moment, she nodded. "You're right. I'm sorry."

"Sorry, Jackie," Doris echoed, ducking her head.

"It's so good to see you," Cheryl said, touching Jackie's arm. "If you would have told me you were coming, I would have bought champagne or something."

"I have champagne," Doris said. "At my house."

"That sounds lovely," Jackie cried, smiling brightly. That worked out perfectly. She wanted to get them to Doris's as quickly as possible. It had been a long flight and a bed would be nice. "Cheryl must be freezing in that sexy little outfit so why don't we all pile into my hilarious little clown car . . ."

Cheryl took in the rental. "What the hell is that?"

"I asked George to rent me a car and he thought this would be a scream," Jackie recited. "And it was! I screamed." Her friends laughed and inside, Jackie gave a sigh of relief. "Listen, we're all going to sleep at Doris's tonight, so if everyone's ready . . ."

"I'd rather die," Cheryl said, "for the third time today," and started moving toward her front door.

Gently, Jackie reached out and grabbed her arm. "Darling, you're hurt," she said. "There's not room for all three of us to sleep over here and you can't be alone after a concussion. We're going where the beds are."

"I'm not interested in the three of us," Cheryl said, teeth suddenly chattering.

"I'm not giving you the choice," Jackie said. "We're going to Doris's."

"Please come," Doris begged. She looked at the ground. "I can't be alone with Doug. He . . . he saw a movie with another woman."

"*What?*" Cheryl said, clearly in spite of herself. "Who?"

"Someone we all know." Doris blushed, shifting her feet. "Katherine Rigney."

Jackie gasped. Katherine Rigney? Revisiting a high school girlfriend was certainly dangerous, regardless of how many hairstyles had changed since then.

"Damn," Cheryl muttered. She glanced at the hovering Lexus. Doug's silhouette was watching them patiently. "That's not good."

"He said he didn't sleep with her," Doris said, crossing her arms. "I believe him. I do."

"Absolutely," Cheryl said. She turned to Jackie and widened her eyes. "So. Are you here to stay or what?"

"Oui," Jackie said, trying to keep her tone upbeat. "It's time. And I'm . . ." Looking at her best friends, Jackie suddenly felt a rush of love mixed with a rush of guilt. Her eyes filled with tears. "I hope you will forgive me for the way I left."

When Jackie had left for Paris, the girls had planned to see her off at the airport. Jackie had deliberately given them the wrong flight time and called them as she was boarding, feigning embarrassment and stupidity. But the fact was, Jackie had needed her space, time to mourn her husband in her own way. The decision to bolt with no fanfare had been made the moment Robert took his last breath.

Jackie told her friends she was moving to Paris at the wake, Robert lying like a slab of ice beside her. As Cheryl and Doris absorbed this news, Jackie stared over their shoulders at the video of Robert's life. Robert's children were watching it and (finally!) noticing that the affection between her and their father was real. As if she hadn't (loyally!) been with him for ten years, for heaven's sake. It was interesting to watch his kids finally be nice to her but of course, that had ended a few days later, at the reading of the will. There, they learned what Jackie had already known. Robert had left his entire fortune to her. The kids were furious but what did they expect? They cut Robert out of their lives the moment he had left their mother.

Jackie did feel a twinge of guilt, now. Time had wrapped her story in ribbons but she still had to live with the fact that in her youth and naivete, she had stolen another woman's husband. At twenty-two, Jackie hadn't bothered to question Robert's claims that his wife was already out of the picture. Behind port and cigars, Robert's set whispered that his wife had been cheating on him for years. As Jackie got older, other women told her a different version of the truth. Robert's wife had always been faithful; he was the one who had always been on the lookout for something better. Jackie didn't know what to believe. Had Robert told her the truth? Or had she been set up by Robert's circle, a pawn in some game where youth won out over loyalty?

As for his children, Jackie didn't waste energy feeling bad about them. She hadn't affected their lives in any way, as they had been shipped off to boarding school and summer camps long before she arrived on the scene. The children still found a way to blame Jackie for Robert's death and their mother's misery. On bad days, Jackie couldn't help but wonder if they were right.

Looking around Cheryl's driveway, studying the faces she had known for so many years, Jackie thought about life and its many mysteries. So much had changed, so many miles had been traveled and yet, once again with Cheryl and Doris, Jackie could have been standing anywhere in time. High school, college, the marriage years . . . they all blended together. It was nice to feel that familiarity and have the knowledge that there were two people in the world who, no matter what, would always be her family.

"I missed you girls," Jackie said. "I'm glad to be back."

Cheryl let out a breath, putting her hand to her head. "After I got hit, Stan asked me who to call and I realized . . . you're my only friends. My real friends, I mean."

"Well, we all certainly hit the jackpot," Jackie said, adjusting her bag. She was beaming inside. "Shall we go?"

Doris eyed the leather purse enviously. "That's beautiful."

"The French." Cheryl nodded.

Jackie patted her purse. "My luggage is filled with all sorts of lovely things for you two. We'll have a gift session tomorrow. Now, I've got all our sleeping arrangements planned out. I'm sleeping with Doris in that memory foam, king-sized bed. Cheryl gets the guest bedroom . . ." Jackie paused for dramatic emphasis, then pointed at the hovering SUV. "Doug gets the floor."

Even though Jackie was trying to keep the situation light, she was furious with Doug. Things might have changed since Jackie had been gone but that was no excuse for chasing after someone like Katherine Rigney. Brushing a strand of hair back from Doris's forehead, Jackie thought back to when they were just teenagers.

Doris was lying in the hospital bed after the miscarriage, already married to Doug at seventeen and looking like her world just might end. Doug had forced her into that premature marriage; he best not ruin it now. Jackie might even have a word with him in private, if it was possible to get him alone.

"Momma Jackie's in town," she said, glancing once again at the SUV. "I'm taking care of you now."

For a moment, the three friends stood silent. They might be a triangle of broken hearts, broken heads, and—Jackie glanced back at the rental car—broken dreams, but at least they were together. Something Jackie had wished for less than twenty-four hours ago. *"Je t'aime,"* she said. "I love you guys. Let's go."

Chapter Eight

By six a.m. the next morning, Doris found herself standing in the middle of her kitchen, clutching a cup of coffee. She took a deep breath and smiled. The entire kitchen smelled like the Willy Wonka Chocolate Factory.

The night before, Doris had climbed into her marriage bed with her best friend instead of her husband. Considering it was her anniversary, Doris did feel a pang of guilt that Doug was out sleeping on the sofa with a thin blanket and lumpy pillow. But in the scattered moments Doris allowed his confession about Katherine Rigney to enter her head, she had to agree that he deserved it.

"Sweet dreams, my love," Jackie had said, turning out the light and curling up into a little ball. Probably because she was tired from her travels, Jackie immediately fell asleep.

Doris had wrapped the down comforter tightly around her and lain awake, thinking about the upset of her day. Not one moment of it had gone as planned. Doris's stomach flipped, remembering the way Doug had avoided her eyes at dinner, the sudden confession about Katherine. Doris couldn't get the image of Katherine's brassy highlights out of her head. What if Doug left her? Would he take Mandy with him? Doris tossed and turned, letting her mind take her places she didn't want to go.

Somehow, Doris started thinking about when Mandy was born. That had been the first time she had felt Doug cared for someone more than her and, Doris hated to admit it, she didn't like it. Doug had stared at their little baby so long and kissed her little face so lovingly that Doris finally had to remind him she was still lying there, bleeding. Doug had kissed her then and congratulated her for the miracle of childbirth or something but he hadn't taken his eyes off Mandy. Doug's priorities had shifted. From that moment on, Mandy was the center of his universe and Doris's role had changed, too. She was no longer just a lover. She was a mother.

This realization and all of the following emotions it brought up in her were scary. Doris didn't want to be one of those mothers, jealous of her daughter. Finally, she took her worries to her own mother, who had just laughed and said, "Oh, Doris. We all think terrible things. It's what you *do* with those thoughts that matters."

So, Doris had tried hard to accept her new role. She took a backseat to Mandy, committed to being the best mother she could be. Until the last year or so, she thought she had done all right.

"Mandy will be excited to see you," Doris had said to Jackie, when they'd all gotten to the house. Doris hoped that Mandy wouldn't turn on her best friend the way Mandy had turned on her. "I know you always had a good relationship but just be ready," Doris warned. "She's changed a lot."

"Everyone changes," Cheryl said, blowing into her hands.

Doug was juggling Jackie's two Louis Vuitton trunks and trying to unlock the front door.

"Is she beautiful?" Jackie asked. "I bet she is."

"She looks just like Doris at that age," Doug said, over his shoulder. "Minus the red hair."

When they had walked in, Mandy had glanced at her parents and given a half-wave from the couch. She was watching some reality show and fiddling with her laptop. But when she realized Jackie was there, Mandy pushed everything aside and leaped to her feet, shrieking, "Aunt Jackie?!" Like a gazelle, she shot across the living room and tackled Jackie in a huge hug. The heavy perfume of the two mingled together in a way that gave Doris a headache.

"Bonjour," Jackie had squealed, bouncing up and down. *"Bonjour, bonjour, bonjour!"* She had pulled back then, marveling at what a beautiful little grown-up Mandy had become. "Look at her," she'd gasped, turning to Doris with moist eyes. "She looks just like you."

"No I don't," Mandy said, outraged.

Doris blushed. The willowy beauty did have her blue eyes and full lips but Doris wasn't surprised she was protesting. Why would Mandy want to look like someone she hated?

"Mandy, you're gorgeous," Jackie was saying. "You're just perfect!"

Doris wanted to laugh out loud. If only Jackie could see the moody monster living just below the surface, she might change her tune. If Doris had been a worse person, she would have loved to expose it. Instead, she just hung back, feeling sweaty and uncomfortable in her heavy coat.

"Oh, Jackie," Doris said now, turning over in the sheets and facing her friend. "What am I going to do?"

Jackie's mouth opened and a rattling snore dropped out. In spite of herself, Doris smiled. For years, Jackie had denied her legendary snoring, even when Cheryl and Doris had gotten videotaped proof at one of their many sleepovers. At the thought of Cheryl, Doris's stomach tightened.

Cheryl had walked right past the reunion between Jackie and Mandy. She had gone straight to bed, stalking into the guest bedroom and slamming the door. Everyone had looked down the hallway in surprise, then Jackie had said, "She just got hit in the head. I think she's lost her mind."

Mandy giggled and had gone back to talking but Doris was

furious. She wished she had the guts to send Cheryl packing right then. Even if Doris had made her mad, Cheryl had no right to act that way. Besides, the conversation about Cheryl's promiscuity hadn't been easy on Doris either.

Maybe she hadn't handled the conversation well but how could anyone? The only reason Doris said anything to Cheryl in the first place was because the whole town was talking about it. The night before the fight, Doris had attended a particularly awkward PTA meeting where everyone had attacked her because of Cheryl's behavior. Apparently, Cheryl had slept with a freshly divorced father, whose ex-wife was on the board. The ex-wife had brought it up in front of everyone, knowing full well that Cheryl was Doris's best friend. Doris had sat through the woman's rant in silence, fidgeting uncomfortably in her plastic chair, hating that she was guilty by association.

"Tell her to keep it in her pants," the ex-wife had said, finally daring to address Doris directly.

Doris had flushed and nodded. What else could she do? Up to that point, she had always supported Cheryl, even when Cheryl had cheated on her husband, Sean. That ridiculous affair had been anything but discreet. Cheryl had paraded all over town with some pharmaceutical salesman until it became obvious that the only solution was a divorce. The day Cheryl's affair became a public scandal, Jackie and Doris had met at the Tea House to discuss their options.

"How could she do this?" Doris had practically sobbed to Jackie. "Sean and Doug are friends. We're all friends!"

"I know . . ." Jackie had mused, pouring some milk into her tea. "It's complicated."

"She should have just told Sean she wanted a divorce," Doris said. "Instead of this."

"Darling, this is Cheryl we're talking about." Jackie sighed, sitting back and breathing in the scent of the jasmine tea. "A divorce would be an admission that she made a mistake. And Cheryl doesn't make mistakes. Don't you know that by now?"

Doris had rolled her eyes, nodding. Cheryl had always been such a bullhead. "It's so embarrassing for him. Everyone will want to know why she did it. They're going to think there's something wrong with him."

"Exactly," Jackie said, stirring her tea. "Who in Schaumburg's going to believe a woman would just have sex because she wanted to?"

Doris bit into a sugar-covered scone. "I was really starting to believe she loved him."

"Sean was in the wrong place at the wrong time." Jackie shrugged. "He's just a casualty. Cheryl wanted to be married by thirty. It didn't matter to who."

They were quiet for a moment, and then Doris snorted. "Remember when she threw out their wedding dishes for those stupid plates?" Doris said. "The ones with the foreign women living in fabulous cities?"

Jackie laughed. "He should have known right then."

"But we're on her side?" Doris confirmed, going in for another bite.

"Always," Jackie said. "Unfortunately, loyalty can't go both ways."

To be fair, Cheryl did seem a lot happier the moment the ink on the divorce papers had dried. "I made a mistake," Cheryl admitted. "But at least I ended it now. Sean's still got plenty of time to find someone else. Get married. Be happy."

"What about you?" Doris had asked.

Cheryl shrugged. "I'm married to my work."

Although Cheryl's professional life did appear to be wild and glamorous—now that she had landed that big beer account, Cheryl was constantly running to Chicago to coordinate commercial shoots or going to parties with exciting people—Doris couldn't help but be worried about her friend. The lines under Cheryl's eyes had deepened. Alcohol was a part of every meal, even brunch. Doris was worried that if Cheryl didn't slow down and find someone she could love instead of someone she could make a story out of at a cocktail party, she would regret it.

"She's spent so much time proving she can take over the world," Jackie once said, "that sometimes, I think she's forgotten to live in it."

Not that Doris was perfect. She knew that. But at least she was willing to try.

Pulling the comforter tighter around her, Doris had forced herself to tune into Jackie's rhythmic rattle and try to fall asleep. She stared blankly at the dark hole of her closet. It seemed to go on forever but she kept her eyes fixed on it, knowing that when the sun rose there would be order waiting there to meet her.

Sure enough, when the sun came up, the answer to her marriage seemed to be hanging there, right next to the row of pastel sweaters. Doug may have seen a movie with another woman, but he was still her husband. Doris should do everything in her power to please him. Glancing at the clock, she saw that it was five a.m. Plenty of time to do something that would make Doug happy.

She climbed out of bed, careful not to wake Jackie, and sneaked out to the kitchen to bake snickerdoodles. They were Doug's favorite. By six, Doris had one batch of the cinnamon-coated cookies already in the oven and several more ready to go.

Pleased, Doris took a look around the kitchen and applauded her handiwork. The cookies were a good start. This afternoon she would order that bigger flat screen Doug had been talking about. Tonight, she would invite him back into their bed. She would turn off the lights, put on that nightgown and the sparkly powder, and throw herself at him.

Now, Doris's plump hands deftly sliced tomatoes for his salami sandwich. She made two lunches every morning, one for Doug and one for Mandy. Sometimes it seemed ridiculous to wake up when she did just to cook but staying in bed made her feel guilty. It was a luxury, and honestly, she hadn't done anything to earn it.

At half past six, Mandy walked in, stretching. Eyeliner was smudged in pools under her eyes. "It smells good in here." Mandy's voice was thick with sleep. "Are you making pancakes?"

"Cookies." Doris beamed. She wrapped Doug's sandwich in

foil, then pulled a sheet of cookies out of the oven. They were perfectly formed, tops firm yet puffy with cinnamon coating. Mandy grabbed for one, red hair flying.

"Don't get burned," Doris cautioned.

Mandy was sucking in air, trying to cool down the treat already melting in her mouth. "Mmmm . . ."

Doris's heart swelled with pride. She set the sheet down on the rack on the tile counter, placing another batch in the oven. There were ten batches altogether. Some of them she would freeze.

"Wait . . . Mom," Mandy said. Putting a hand to her mouth, those blue eyes widened. "*Gross*," Mandy cried. She drew back, spitting out the cookie from her mouth and throwing it on the table. "Are you trying to kill me?"

"What?" Doris's voice was high-pitched. She stared at the blob of chewed-up cookie on the table. "What happened?"

"These are disgusting!" Mandy's freckled face was twisted into maniacal laughter. Doug laughed like this sometimes. It was so ugly and she hated to see it mirrored in their daughter.

Doris stomped across the cold floor to the steaming tray of cookies. "I have been working on them since five. I'm sure they're quite fine."

"Try one." Mandy smirked.

Doris snatched up a cookie and took a tiny bite. At first, sweet cinnamon filled her mouth, but then her taste buds seemed to cringe and pucker. Startled, Doris grabbed for a napkin and spit the cookie out. Her eyes filled with tears. "I think I used . . ."

"Salt instead of sugar?" Mandy said. "No kidding."

The rows of cookies looked so perfect, lined up neatly on the cookie sheet. Doris looked at the huge wad of cookie dough waiting to be baked. Such a waste. It would all end up in the garbage disposal.

"Maybe if I added chocolate pieces . . ." Doris tried, glancing at her daughter for approval.

"The dream's over, Mom," Mandy said. "But I'll still let you make me eggs." She settled in at the kitchen table.

I may as well be a waitress in a diner, Doris thought. Maybe she should start carrying around a tiny notepad and a pen. She stifled a sigh. "How would you like them?"

"Salty."

"Mandy." Doris wiped a hand across her sweating forehead. Her patience had run out.

"Egg whites," Mandy said. "Scrambled hard."

Lately, Mandy had been obsessed with egg whites drowned in hot sauce. When she was younger, she'd loved poking in the yolks on sunny-side up eggs and watching the yellow liquid ooze out over her toast, just like Doris had taught her. Now, Mandy claimed to hate the smell of the yolk on her lips. Doris had a feeling Mandy's new favorite had less to do with how the eggs smelled and more to do with what the stars were eating. Mandy studied pop culture like it was her job, gobbling up those *Glamour* magazines almost faster than they came out, watching reality shows, and mimicking the way the girls talked, loving a brand of clothing one week and dubbing it "so passé" the next. Doris just couldn't keep up.

Carefully, Doris cracked two eggs into a mixing bowl. A tiny piece of shell fell in and Doris left it there. Mandy deserved a little crunch after making fun of her efforts. Doris finished the eggs, burning them only slightly, then poured a glass of orange juice and set everything in front of her daughter. Mandy drained the juice, wiped her mouth with the back of her hand, and belched.

"Mandy." Doris sighed. "That's really not polite."

"I can't believe Jackie's back," Mandy said, dousing her eggs in Tabasco and taking ferocious bites. "She's so cool."

"She's going to stay with us for a while," Doris said proudly. She was happy that Jackie had picked her and not Cheryl.

Mandy leaped to her feet, shrieking and dancing around. "Jackie's staying with us . . . Jackie's staying with us . . . I'm going to have her teach me French, how to put on makeup, how to do my hair . . ."

"Hush, Mandy, she's still sleeping!" Why did her daughter insist on loving everyone more than her?

Doug walked in then, flushed from his shower and trailing the scent of sandalwood aftershave. "Morning, ladies."

Doris rushed up and gave him a kiss on his cheek. "Good morning, honey."

"Good . . . morning, Doris," he said, drawing back in surprise.

"Yuck," Mandy muttered.

"Thank you for letting Jackie sleep in our bed last night," Doris said, too loud. "She really needed the sleep." Doris saw him get the message. She was trying to protect their daughter. "We'll have our bed back tonight," she promised in a rush.

"No problem," Doug said, avoiding her eyes. "Jackie can stay as long as she'd like."

"Would you like anything to eat?" Doris asked hopefully. Doug usually skipped breakfast but maybe if he would just let her . . .

"I'm good," Doug said. He rumpled Mandy's hair, got up, and grabbed his lunch. "You ladies have a good day."

Doris watched Doug as he left the house. As he shut the kitchen door, his eyes met hers once, briefly. They looked so guilty that Doris felt sick inside. She sank into a chair by the table, forcing herself to take slow, even breaths.

"What's wrong with you?" Mandy asked.

Doris shook her head. "Hurry up and get ready. You're going to be late for school."

CHERYL PEEKED INTO Doris's room, hoping for a ride from Jackie. Jackie was still fast asleep, those pretty blond curls like a halo around her head. Back in the guest room, Cheryl placed a call for a cab, then sneaked out the front door. She did not want to get stuck driving back to her car with Doris or, God forbid, Doug. That overgrown frat boy had been friends with her ex-husband for years and she knew he was still furious with her for leaving Sean.

They had not had a conversation since her divorce and Cheryl was not about to put herself in that position. She did know that Sean and Doug still played golf every Saturday at 6 a.m. Who knew how much "pissed-off" had been covered during the tee off?

When the cab arrived, Cheryl had given one more furtive look around, and then slid inside. Safe in the backseat, her driver loudly singing along with some soundtrack from Bollywood, it dawned on her that catching a ride with Doug might have actually been an amusing experience. She could have said, "So, Doug. *Seen a movie* with anyone lately?" and as he squirmed, added, "At least with Sean, I was decent enough to call it what it was."

As the cab pulled into the health club parking lot, Cheryl let out a little cheer. The BMW was still there even though she had half convinced herself it wouldn't be. Once she paid the fare and got out, she saw why the car was still in the lot. Someone had put a little sign on it that read, "Do Not Tow." As much as Cheryl hated to admit it, that someone had probably been Andy.

Once behind the wheel, Cheryl raced home. A sense of urgency had once again struck her. Stan still had her BlackBerry. Cheryl wanted to get to it and fast.

In spite of her hurry, she still felt that familiar rush of pleasure as she keyed into her pine-scented home. The sparkle had nothing to do with her and everything to do with her biweekly maid service. Sean had been so messy, throwing his wrinkled shirts wherever he felt like it—chair backs, the stair railing, the floor. It was so nice to come home to a clean house, knowing no one was there to mess it up.

Quickly, Cheryl tossed back two shots of espresso, checked her voice mail, took a two second shower, then threw on a tight black suit and three gold bangle bracelets. Eyeing her reflection, she nodded. Shrug or no shrug from some kid at the office, she looked good. She had to. Today was her yearly presentation with Fitzgibbon Ale.

Cheryl was excited to show up to the meeting fresh and prepared, simply because Stan expected she wouldn't. He had even left her a voice mail on her home phone, asking her to call him with the details of the presentation. Cheryl had chuckled at the message. Bob Turner was *her* client. There was no way she was letting him deal with Stan.

The son of old-time bourbon brewers, Bob was the creator of Fitzgibbon Ale, the beer that had changed her life. Cheryl had discovered it in Lexington, Kentucky, four years ago while in town supervising a commercial shoot. The crew had ducked into some dive bar for a bite and Fitzgibbon Ale was on tap. After just one sip, Cheryl wanted to know more.

The handsome bartender told her it outsold the big brands two to one. "Not just because it's local," he said. "Because it's good."

"It is good," Cheryl said, surprised. "It's great. Do you think you could tell me where the owner lives?"

The bartender was happy to help. Within minutes, Cheryl had directions straight to the owner's front door.

The next morning, she drove out to the country and gasped at the sight of Bob's estate. Like something out of a movie, the land stretched for miles; green grass waved in the wind and horses grazed in the fields. Historic stone fences lined the property. Suddenly nervous, Cheryl wiped her sweating palms on the skirt of her suit and wondered if this was the right approach. Then she remembered the taste and potential of that beer. Cheryl gunned her rental car straight up the drive, climbed the palatial steps, and knocked loudly on the front door.

It took at least five minutes to convince the servant to summon Bob Turner, but she finally succeeded. When Bob came to the door, Cheryl only had to take one look at his face to decide she liked him. He had bright, twinkling eyes that didn't take any crap and they were already studying her with amusement. After listening to Cheryl's praise for his product, Bob just laughed and invited her inside. Once in, Cheryl noticed he was dressed in some sort of a hunting ensemble. His high rubber boots squeaked as they walked across the wooden floors.

"So, it sounds like you know how to appreciate a good beer," Bob said, stopping at a long dining room table toward the back of the entryway. He pulled out a chair and Cheryl took a seat. "But what do you really know about it?"

Cheryl opened her mouth but Bob didn't wait for her answer. Instead, he went into the kitchen and came back out with an assortment of homemade beer. Apparently, Bob didn't just make ale; he experimented with lagers, stouts, and even cider.

"Let's have a beer tasting," Bob said, clapping her on the back. "Sound good?"

"I never knew there was such a thing."

The servant came out from the kitchen carrying bricks of dark chocolate, cured meats, and sharp cheeses and set them on the table. Bob bit into a piece of meat and poured himself a sip of beer. After tasting it, he passed it to Cheryl. She took a drink and noticed that the salt on the meat complemented the thick yeast of the beer. "Okay," she said. "I could get used to this."

Bob grabbed another pint and a piece of cheese, saying, "Good. Try this."

After each drink, the tastes became more exotic than the ones before. Finally, Cheryl pushed away a mug and got to the point.

"Bob, I like you," she said. "And I like your product. Let me manage your beer. My company can take Fitzgibbon Ale to the next level."

Bob didn't answer. Instead, he popped a piece of dark chocolate into his mouth and chased it with a stout. Cheryl set her lips together and didn't speak. Bob looked at her. The two stared each other down for at least two minutes.

"You ever been hunting?" he finally said.

Even though it wasn't always good business to speak her mind, Cheryl found herself doing it anyway. "In my opinion, shooting an innocent creature seems a little barbaric," she said, "especially when you could just call for takeout."

Bob had laughed out loud, slapping his knee like something out of a cartoon. "I might like you, too." He grinned, taking her arm. "Let's go for a walk."

As Cheryl ruined her shoes, swatted away mosquitoes, and let her makeup run in the sultry Kentucky sun, Bob cheerfully turned down her offer. He'd seen his family cater to the bourbon industry, mutating their product for market demand.

"I'm doing this for me," he said. "I want to stay local."

"But you could make millions," Cheryl argued.

"Look around you," Bob said. "Do you think I need any money?"

"But think of the tag lines," Cheryl insisted. "Fitzgibbon Ale, it's given me fits, it's the perfect fit, it keeps me fit . . . Wait," Cheryl said, stopping suddenly. She looked at Bob. "Your family name is Turner. If this is a family beer, why are you calling it Fitzgibbon Ale?"

Bob squinted into the sun. After a moment, he crossed his arms and said, "Rachel Fitzgibbon. She moved to New York, works for the U.N. She's the one who got away."

It was Cheryl's turn to throw back her head and laugh. Bob looked at her, confused.

"It's just so obvious," she said. "You're hanging on to this beer because you couldn't hang on to Rachel. But that's so selfish because, Bob, the world needs her."

"Young lady," Bob said. "You might just have a point there."

The leaves on the trees swayed around them like a million little green bills. Six months later, TurnKey had the account. Four years later, Fitzgibbon Ale was a multimillion dollar business, on tap throughout the country. Thanks to countless interviews asking Bob where he'd gotten the name, he had admitted the nature of his muse and won Rachel's heart. They were married and now lived together in both New York and Lexington.

Everything had worked out perfectly for Bob, Rachel, and TurnKey but not for Cheryl. The power of Bob's beer could have launched her very own advertising firm. Maybe if she hadn't been in the middle of a messy divorce, she would have listened to her instincts. Instead, she stayed at TurnKey because she needed some sort of stability during a tumultuous time. Now, instead of being a business owner, she was just another executive with a really great account.

At the memory, Cheryl shook her head and adjusted her suit. Oh well. What was done was done. One of these days, she would get the respect she deserved. It was just a question of when.

Chapter Nine

JACKIE CLICKETY-CLACKED HER WAY INTO GEORGE'S OFFICE, dressed to the nines in a tight black dress and her trusty mink coat. The coat was vintage, a great argument for anyone who cared to comment or ask her if she had ever heard of PETA.

"Inhumane?" Jackie had purred on more than one occasion. "For heaven's sake, it's vintage. They didn't know back then. It would be *inhumane* to not give the mink the respect it deserves for giving its life—I can't just hide it in the closet."

As a general rule, Jackie detested cruelty of any sort. But furs . . . old ones . . . she was a sucker for them.

At the sound of her high heels, George leaped up from his desk and bustled to the center of the room. Jackie briefly admired how his hair was now a dark black in spite of his age. It was pushed back, gelled into perfect uniformity. There was a hint of a five o'clock shadow and his upper lip still had that slight smirk that used to always make her smile, even if he hadn't said a word.

"Darling," Jackie cried, swishing her way into George's out-stretched arms. He squeezed her a little too long, a little too tight.

She felt him choke back a sob. "George, dear," Jackie said, her voice muffled against his lapel, "I *truly* hope you're not crying. On my mink."

Standing in this stately room, surrounded by brown leather, bookshelves, and that familiar dish of butterscotch candies on the middle of George's writing desk, she might as well have gone back in time. It was as though Paris had never happened and George had just finished reading her the will. That day, as the last "bequeath" left his mouth, George had burst into unabashed tears.

"A heart attack?" George had sobbed. "He was the healthiest man I know. He could lap me!" And Jackie had started crying right along with him. The two friends drank scotch late into the evening, turning the pity party into fun memories about Robert and the life and friendship they'd shared.

Now she pulled back and looked into George's handsome face. Sure enough, those dark eyes were swimming with tears. "George, you stop that," she ordered, feeling her eyes get wet. "We're not doing this again. If you want to drink scotch with me, you just have to ask."

"I apologize." George swiped at his eyes, then patted his pockets and found her a clean handkerchief. "You are absolutely right."

Jackie dabbed the starched material to her face. A feathered pattern from her mascara stained the white surface. "All right," she sniffed. "Now, you better say something nice to me."

"Jacqueline, my dear," George said, "you look beautiful."

"And so do you," Jackie scolded, really looking at him. When she'd left, George had been a bit portly, but now he looked sleek in dark slacks and a fitted gray sweater. "It looks like you need a woman to make you a sandwich. Just look at you, you're wasting away."

George beamed and spun around like Fred Astaire, hair falling across his forehead like in a moment from some classic film. "Ta-dum!"

Jackie giggled, reaching her arm out and grabbing his sleeve. This stopped him from another ridiculous spin. Voice deep and serious, she said, "Liposuction?"

George laughed. "Certainly not, my dear Jacqueline," he said, gently kissing her hand. "Diet and exercise. I spend an hour on my treadmill every day. Sometimes two."

"Hmm. Did the treadmill turn your hair back to black?" she teased. "Wasn't it a little . . . shall we say . . . saltier the last time I saw you?"

From under those dark eyebrows, George gave her an injured look and Jackie giggled. She wandered over to that hard leather sofa that she'd sat on so many times before and flopped down.

"Candy?" he offered. George knew she loved anything sweet.

Jackie held out her hand and let her fingers waggle. Her diamonds glistened in rainbow patterns across his hardwood floor. George threw her a golden-wrapped toffee and she flinched as it hit her in the face. "George, have you gotten clumsy in your old age?"

"Oh no, my darling," George promised, unwrapping another. "My aim is legendary. Arrows to the heart, all over town, you know."

"So you *were* trying to hit me in the face?" Jackie teased.

George rewarded her with a smirk.

"I believe it," Jackie said, shaking her head. "You've always been dangerous."

That day she had first met Robert, George had almost swept her away.

It had all happened at the Taste of Chicago festival, some fifteen years back. She'd been dragged to the summer festival by Cheryl, Doris, and Doug. That crew had looked like tourists in their khakis and T-shirts. Jackie, fresh out of her stint at the Art Institute, was inappropriately attired in a low-cut, black lace dress and ballet style leather shoes.

"You're wearing *that*?" Cheryl asked, as the group walked up to Jackie's brownstone. She had been waiting for them on the cement stoop. "You'll die. It's supposed to be really hot."

"I'll be fine," Jackie had said, hopping up and doing a little pirouette. But two hours into the hundred-degree heat, she had to admit Cheryl had been right. She was sweating profusely and the black lace was sticking to all the wrong places. Plus, festival people and men who must have been out on parole keep leering at her.

"This is a disaster," she'd muttered, tugging at her dress.

"But so fun," Doris had squealed, shoving a piece of fried dough into her mouth and squeezing Doug's arm. The couple had been having a wonderful time, gluttonizing their way through every food stand in the park. Cheryl had been enjoying herself, too. Halfway through the Italian section, she had started making out with a bartender who had been pouring them endless cups of Chianti.

"I don't know," Jackie said. "Do you want to go back?" But Doris had already turned to another vendor.

After bumping into yet another kid with a greasy face and hands smeared with blue cotton candy, Jackie ditched her friends and sneaked down to Lake Michigan. She was desperate to get away from the heady scent of diversity. At the water, she struck pay dirt. She stumbled in on an impromptu gathering of the Yacht Club.

The first time she saw Robert, he was on the upper deck of a yacht, carefree in a white linen shirt and leaning back in a chair in that way Jackie's mother had taught her not to. When Robert first saw Jackie, he had actually put up two hands—one to silence his friends and the other to shield his eyes from the sun. After a long moment, he'd beckoned to her, watch glinting. Jackie had blushed and preened. Then, like any self-respecting twenty-two-year-old, had gotten on board with the group of well-dressed men.

Just as Jackie climbed up the steps, thinking the situation couldn't get any better, the best-looking man she had ever seen came up from below the deck. He was holding a bottle of champagne and stopped to gape at her. "Who is this beauty?" he demanded.

"Hello," she said, turning her eyes to George.

"Welcome to my little tugboat." His eyes were dark and amused, already sporting fine lines at the corners. He was at least fifteen years older than she.

As though reading her mind, George said, "Just so you know, I'm too young to be hanging out with these geriatrics." The announcement was just loud enough for the other men on the yacht to hear. "It's a good thing you showed up."

The men burst out laughing. "He was in college when you were in diapers, sweetie," one of them said.

Jackie tossed her blond hair. "You don't look so young yourself," she told the man.

"See?" George said, setting down the champagne and putting a hand over his heart. "I swear I'm not as decrepit as this crew. I'm just a hungry lawyer, vying for their commission."

"Oh yeah?" one of the men shouted. The man was looking at them through binoculars and Jackie had the feeling his gaze was running up and down her legs. "Commission for what?"

"Estate planning," George cracked.

The men shouted and started pelting ice in their direction. Ducking, George grabbed Jackie's hand and swept her over to the other side of the yacht. After expertly pouring her a drink, George got her to talk. She told him about graduating from the Art Institute, her hope for the future, and whether or not she was talented at what she did (yes). George told her about his law practice, the time he'd spent in law school, and his success at making partner at his office in the Gold Coast. Soon, they had moved on to general interests and George was explaining sailing terms to her and making promises to take her out on the water.

Just as Jackie had almost fallen in love, leaning forward just enough to let this handsome, older man know it was okay to kiss her, another girl showed up. She was wearing a gold lamé bikini, and her fake breasts jutted out like the prow of a ship. Stomping over to George, the girl grabbed him by the ear and dragged him away from Jackie. She pushed him into a sun chair and practically straddled him, shooting rude looks at Jackie over her shoulder.

Mortified, Jackie turned to the water. Staring out, she clutched her drink and mentally recapped the false promises George had just made. Sailboat rides, dinner by the river, trips to Tiffany . . . The lavish attention had made her feel exotic and interesting; now she just felt ridiculous standing there in her tight black dress.

Setting down her empty glass on the rail, Jackie wondered where her friends were and whether or not the climb down the yacht's ladder would be possible in her half-drunken state. Letting out a little sigh, she decided to try. Turning around, she was startled to find Robert standing behind her. His hand was reaching toward her, as though to tap her on the arm. She jumped.

"Sorry to scare you," Robert said, dropping his hand. When Jackie didn't say anything, he reached up again, removing his designer sunglasses and tucking them into his shirt pocket. His eyes were the same metallic blue as the sky, but there wasn't anything cold about them. "And sorry about George. His girlfriend gets a little possessive."

"You're full of apologies," Jackie said, trying to sound brave. "Listen, it's okay. He . . . he said he was here with someone."

Robert studied her, forehead creased. "Interesting."

"What?"

"You're actually a really good liar," he said, laughing. "You must have a lot to hide."

Jackie glared at him, but after a moment her mouth tugged at the corners. "Tell me something I don't know."

Robert smiled, and then picked up the champagne bottle as though to pour.

Jackie shook her head. "I think I'm going to go," she said, sneaking another look at George. He was sitting by the girl, doing shots with her and some friends.

"Please. One drink," Robert said, refilling the glass. "I insist."

Irritated, Jackie took a long sip. The liquid was fizzy but cold and she shivered. Immediately, Robert grabbed a cable knit sweater from a nearby chair, draping it over her shoulders. Warm from the sun, the feel of the material was soft and heavy. It smelled like laundry soap and lemons.

"Thanks," Jackie said, surprised.

"You're welcome," Robert said. "George would have let you freeze to death. See?" George's girlfriend was shivering in her skimpy bikini, skin most likely crawling with gooseflesh. "Don't let your heart break over a rogue like him."

Jackie turned and faced Robert, really looking at him for the first time. With sandy brown hair and simple features, he wasn't anything that would have caught her eye at a party but there was something incredibly appealing about him. Maybe it was his kindness . . . or the direct way he'd called her on the lie. Whatever it was, Jackie was suddenly less interested in getting off the yacht and finding her friends.

"Shall we sit?" Robert asked, indicating the bench along the railing.

Jackie nodded. Once they were seated, she didn't protest when Robert put his arm around her. Snuggling into the crook, Jackie watched the colors of the sun begin to yawn over the horizon. Robert was silent, absently running his thumb over the inside of her wrist. When the sun finally dipped below the buildings and the night fell, Robert lifted her hand and brought it to his lips. They were warm against her skin. Jackie gave a little jump as he flicked his tongue across the sensitive area between her fingertips. Letting her hand drop, Robert winked at her. It was the first of many moments that would win her heart.

George liked to claim that the girl in the gold lamé bikini had ruined his life. "Jackie was in love with *me*," he always said, once she and Robert had become a couple. "Why did my date have to show up?"

"It wouldn't have mattered in the end," Robert would always say, turning to Jackie and giving her arm a gentle squeeze. "I'm much better looking than George. Right, honey?"

Dutifully, Jackie would nod. Everything between Robert and George was a competition, from the stock market to golf to women. Because of the way the two men joked, Jackie was always very careful to make certain her loyalty to Robert was clear. Neither of them took the conversation seriously though, because as Jackie fell deeper and deeper in love with Robert, she hadn't given George a second look. Still, as Robert's best friend, he was always present. In fact, George had taught her how to play golf, appreciate caviar, enjoy the symphony . . .

Sitting on this leather sofa and thinking back over her life, it seemed amazing to Jackie that two strangers who had once met by chance had experienced so much of life together.

"Oh, George," Jackie said now, shaking her head. "When did we get so old?"

"My dear," George said, straightening his cuff links, "*Nobody* in this room is old. If you disagree, please take me to pasture and have me shot."

After Jackie laughed, George folded his hands into a teepee and looked down at her over his glasses. The dark eyes turned serious. "I'd love to laugh with you but I have to admit . . . I am slightly furious with you for running away the way that you did."

"It was self-preservation," Jackie admitted, looking down at the floor. The tips of her black stilettos reflected in the polished wood. "I'm sorry if that hurt you."

"I lost my two best friends," George said, glancing at the picture of Robert perched on his desk. "It was . . . difficult."

Jackie twisted her wedding ring. "Yes. I know."

The room was silent, save the ticking of the clock on the shelf. An entire minute passed as George shuffled papers on his desk, ran his hand over the back of his head, and cleared his throat. "Anyway," he finally said. "That is the past. We need to discuss your future. My dear . . ." George looked up and another shadow passed over his handsome face. "It seems we have a problem."

"Yes, you've made it quite clear," Jackie said, forcing her voice to remain light. "I used all of my money and now will have to scrape by on a pauper's salary to pay off the debts. I understand."

"It's not just that," George said. Taking off his glasses, he folded them with a quick snap. "The economy crashed and although everyone adjusted accordingly, much was lost. That's nothing unusual, it's happened everywhere. The real problem is something a bit more . . . shocking."

Jackie adjusted her mink, waiting for George to continue. Instead, he unwrapped another piece of butterscotch candy and crunched down. "Okay," Jackie finally said, once it became clear George was not eager to share the news. "Shock me."

"We have a tax situation."

Jackie's heart froze in her throat. "Pardon?"

George picked up a large file from the top of his desk and opened it. Staring at the pages, he said, "It appears that . . . well . . ."

"Oh, just spit it out," Jackie cried.

"It appears Robert neglected to pay taxes on several of the properties he acquired in Arizona." George began flipping through the file in earnest, pulling out document after document and stacking them on the desk. "They were seized after his death and it was not made known to me or his accountant that there was anything wrong in the books. But Jacqueline, Robert owed in excess of a million dollars in property taxes."

Jackie nodded. The numbers were not new to her. Robert had been a very wealthy man. "But he's dead. Surely, I don't have to . . ."

"You do," George said, dropping the folder onto his desk with a bang.

Jackie put her hand to her mouth and visibly blanched. Immediately, George leaped up and bustled over with a bottle of water, then thought better of that and poured her a scotch. She downed both like medicine.

"Everything will be all right," George said, putting a hand on her shoulder. He hesitated for a moment, and then walked back to his desk. "Yes, you were overspending in Paris, but I thought we could retain the majority of the principal. However, the funds are simply not there. We must use the remainder of his estate to pay this debt. Then, the issue is closed."

"But I only *have* the remainder of his estate," Jackie said. "George, the car rental company wouldn't even let me use my credit cards."

"Your assets were frozen," George said. He shook his head. "I'm sorry, my dear. Had I known—"

Jackie held up her hand. George was an excellent lawyer. He would have fixed the problem yesterday had he known it existed. "Carl has to know something," Jackie said. Carl was the accountant who had worked with Robert for years.

George shook his head. "I spoke with him, formal deposition. He knew nothing about it. He knew the properties had been purchased but he can only work with the information Robert provided him. And in this case . . ."

Falling silent, George took off his glasses and cleaned them with a fresh white hanky. Jackie wondered if George had a hanky in every pocket of his suit.

"Robert was not honest?" she finished for him.

George hesitated. Finally, he nodded. "I'm disappointed in him, Jacqueline. This was not expected."

Jackie didn't know which part of the shock was greater—that she was completely bankrupt or that her gentle husband, the man who had promised her the moon, the stars, and at the very least, breakfast every day in bed, had portrayed himself as something he was not. Jackie stared straight ahead, fanning herself with a copy of the *Economist*.

"Whatever I can do . . ." George finally spoke.

"Oh, just toss me a candy, George," she said, throwing the magazine onto the table. "Just don't hit me in the face, this time. I can't afford the health care."

DORIS WAS STEAM cleaning the rug, listening to Windham Hill at full volume. She had her cell tucked into her sweater pocket in case Doug called. Ramming the steamer into the edge of the coffee table, Doris tried to get at a particularly difficult-to-reach area of the rug. On a normal day, she would have just moved all the furniture to make her steam efficient, but today was not a normal day. Jackie would be back for lunch at noon.

Doris sighed and wiped a hand across her perspiring face, glancing at her watch. Five minutes to go. Maybe she should just . . .

As though punctuating Doris's thoughts, Jackie burst through the front door, cheeks colored a bright pink. "And I thought Champs-Élysées was cold," she complained, shaking sparkling snowflakes from her mink. The scent of Angel perfume immediately filled the living room. "Why on earth is it snowing in October?"

Doris cut the power on the steamer, holding the vibrating handle as it sputtered to a stop. She blushed, watching Jackie survey the living room and take in the spotless silver picture frames and perfectly laid out flower arrangements.

"Darling Dori," Jackie said. "I simply do not know where you get your energy."

"Caffeine," Doris answered immediately. She wasn't trying to be funny but Jackie giggled anyway.

"Toss me your cell, love," Jackie said. "Let's call Cheryl for a little lunch on TurnKey."

"She might not pick up. She'll think it's me . . ." Doris hesitated but handed over the phone, hoping Cheryl wouldn't be mean enough to screen the call.

"Hi, Cheryl," Jackie said almost immediately, making a face at Doris. Doris felt relieved. Maybe their fight was finally over. Maybe she and Cheryl were . . . "Wait. Cheryl—are you *crying*?"

"She's crying?" Doris said, dread settling into her chest. Cheryl had no problem making other people cry, but Cheryl never cried.

"Where are you? Okay, we'll be right there," Jackie said. She clicked the phone shut and looked at Doris in surprise.

"What happened?" Doris said. "Is it her head? Is she back in the hospital?"

"I never thought I'd say something like this," Jackie puzzled, moving toward the couch and sitting down for a brief moment. "Cheryl . . . she . . ."

Doris broke into a sweat and put her hand over her mouth. "What?"

Jackie looked up, blue eyes wide. "She got fired."

Chapter Ten

SECURITY HAD ESCORTED CHERYL OUT OF THE BUILDING—HER building. Cheryl was screaming at Stan at the top of her lungs and he was blaming it on her head injury. That bastard!

"You violated my privacy!" she screamed. "You read my Black-Berry. I'll sue the shit out of you, you sneaky motherfucker!"

Stan stood against the background of TurnKey like some figure guarding a fortress on the cover of a war novel. Those dark eyes were hooded and Cheryl could not believe she had ever considered him an attractive, stable family man. He was a goon.

"I need you to leave immediately," Stan said, voice ringing out across the parking lot. "Or I will have you arrested."

"I gave you fifteen years," Cheryl told him, sucking in icy air and stomping her feet. "I *made* this company. I . . ." Cheryl lowered her eyes to the ground and called on every ounce of womanly theatrics she could find within her. "Come on, Stan . . ." she tried. "We've been friends forever. I don't want to lose you. Let's work this out."

In her heart, Cheryl wanted to bash his head in with a hammer, but this might just work. Stan could be a big old teddy bear—that was part of his problem. The fact that he had an online poker habit and had skimmed money off the corporate accounts was the rest of his problem. But just as she'd feared, he'd found the files she had on him and deleted the evidence.

"Stan, I wasn't going to say anything," Cheryl promised, inching forward. "I just wanted to protect myself. In case anyone blamed me."

Eduardo, the building's security, scuttled in front of her like a sand crab. He barked, "Stay back!"

Cheryl ignored him. "Besides, it's illegal to fire me without cause."

"Cheryl, I'm firing you for incompetence." Stan shrugged. "Period."

The parking lot was empty except for the three of them. Even in the wide open space with its big gray sky, Cheryl could barely find enough oxygen to fight the red wall of rage that threatened to overtake her. "Excuse me?"

"Cheryl, the presentation you lost for Fitzgibbon Ale could have cost us the client." Stan's bushy eyebrows were practically doing the rumba as he recited a script designed for Eduardo to hear and remember, just in case she tried to sue. "I think we both know that."

Cheryl shook her head in disbelief. On Stan's watch, she could see it was eight thirty-two a.m., less than forty-five minutes after she had gotten to work. She couldn't believe this had happened so fast.

When Cheryl had gotten to the office, everyone was watching her. She assumed it was because of the racquetball game so she made some joke that no one laughed at. Once seated at her desk, Stan came in and slammed down her BlackBerry. "So you bothered to come in," he said, glaring at her. "I need to see your presentation for Bob Turner. Now."

"Absolutely," Cheryl had said. Her voice was smooth but immediately, she started to sweat. Had he seen the information she kept on the BlackBerry? Those screenshots of the financial comparison

charts, her records versus the ones submitted to the board . . .
Carefully, she searched his face.

Stan stared back, expressionless. After a tense moment, Cheryl
convinced herself she was just being paranoid. Stan was probably
just irritated that she'd shown up for the presentation with Bob.
Stan had been trying to get in with Bob for years. He had probably
thought this would be his big chance.

"It's a good presentation," Cheryl said. "I think we'll get him to
agree to the Miami market and beach communities with this."

It was hard to keep the excitement out of her voice, in spite of
Stan's mood. The bikini promotion and commercial campaign she
had conceptualized was top dollar. It was a huge step away from
what Bob was used to, but it was time to sex up his campaign.
Cheryl had at least two hundred hours of work behind the charts
and figures. She had no doubt that it would make her case and
they'd finally convince Bob to expand. That would mean huge
money and, surely, a bonus for her.

"I'll pull it up," Cheryl told Stan. Manicured fingers clicked
in her computer password. "It's right . . ." she started to say, but
stopped.

The PowerPoint presentation was blank. Granted, she was not a
computer genius, but . . .

"Problem?" Stan said. He was leaning back on his heels, arms
crossed.

"Of course not," Cheryl said, clicking the mouse. Nothing.
Staring at her computer in confusion, she said, "You know what?
There's plenty of time. Bob's not even here until eleven. I'll show it
to you in a few."

"You've got five minutes." Stan turned on his heel and stalked
out of her office.

The second he left, Cheryl called tech support, eyeing her Black-
Berry with trepidation. She wanted to believe Stan had just woken
up on the wrong side of bed but when tech sent up Blake to paw
through her computer, her worst fears were confirmed—the presentation for Fitzgibbon Ale was history. Stan had wiped her

memory, she was certain now. Her computer records showed the file deleted yesterday, while she was still in the office. But that was impossible, of course. It had been the last thing Cheryl had looked at before grabbing her coat and heading to racquetball at six.

Cheryl bit her lip and turned to the computer tech. "Blake, is there any way to prove the file could have been deleted at a different time or . . . ?"

"Your dates would have to be off on your computer." Blake glanced at something on her screen. "No, everything's current." Blake pushed back her desk chair and stood up. He was one of those computer guys with stooped shoulders and an appreciation for kindness.

"You're the expert here," she persisted, touching his hand. "Tell me this. Could someone have changed it?"

Blake blushed. "That's real tricky to do. You couldn't have done that by mistake."

Cheryl nodded. "That's what worries me."

Stan was at her desk the second Blake left. "So?"

"Stan, it's gone," Cheryl said. She settled back in her chair and waited for the storm to break. "But I think you already know that."

"You mean to tell me you do not have the report for our top client that will be here . . ." At this point, Stan already sounded as though he were reciting from a script. The way he looked at his watch confirmed the setup. "In three hours? If you can't produce it, we might have a serious problem."

Cheryl leaped to her feet, got in his face. "And what's that gonna be?"

Out of the corner of her eye, she saw Jack, Chad, Sam . . . all of them, heads poked out of their offices.

"You'll be fired."

"Don't be ridiculous," she hissed. "You have no grounds."

"Wanna bet?" Stan pulled two warning slips from his pocket. They were in reference to Cheryl's other snaggles with the computer—always presented to her as a joke. Cheryl grabbed one and really looked. They were on official company letterhead.

"You're not the only one who was playing chess," Stan said quietly, tapping her BlackBerry. "I need to see that presentation, Cheryl. Or you're out."

"Nice work, Stan," Cheryl said. "Nice work."

He nodded. And that's when she went ballistic.

Now, Stan and his rent-a-cop stood watching her. TurnKey loomed over her lowly position on the steps and the two men stood ready to cut her off at the knees if she tried to take back what was rightfully hers. Cheryl drew her thin wool coat close around her, looking up at the impressive building.

Its windows were tinted a sleek black, an elegant contrast to the light tan of the brick. All of its surrounding hedges were uniformly planted with trees placed here and there, creating a touch of friendly accessibility. Cheryl had been the one to find this building, when the client *she* landed made the company so big that an office upgrade was required.

"I am going to fuck you up, Stan," she finally said. "I will put you out of business. I don't care how long it takes."

"Good luck with that." Stan gave her a scornful look, then clapped Eduardo on the back, like they were poker buddies at a game. Stan walked up the steps and used his key card to get back into her building. Eduardo trotted faithfully behind him.

Cheryl climbed into her vehicle. She could hear the rhythm of her heart pounding in the back of her head, right next to the part of her brain that had been bruised by the misguided hit. Cheryl pulled the car door shut behind her, slamming it with a loud bang. She sat in silence for a long moment. Taking a deep breath, she dropped her head to the steering wheel and started to cry.

"I SEE HER," Doris proclaimed, spotting the hunched-over form of their friend. Cheryl was facedown against her steering wheel, highlighted hair sticking up in all directions.

"I'll drive her car," Jackie said, hopping out of the passenger's side. "Follow us to your house."

Doris watched as Jackie rapped on the car window. Cheryl's freckled face lifted slowly, etched with grief.

"It'll be okay, Cheryl," Doris called, leaning forward and waving at her. Cheryl didn't even respond.

"Slide over, honey," Jackie said softly. "We're taking you home." Opening the door, Jackie climbed in.

Back at her house, Doris dug out a pair of snug microfleece pajamas for Cheryl to change into and pulled a frozen eye mask from the freezer. She ran it under warm water to soften it, and then brought it to Cheryl.

"Put it over your eyes," Doris instructed, then went back to the kitchen to heat up a rice relaxer.

The rice relaxer was a long tube of material made to be popped in the microwave for a few seconds, then draped over the shoulders, nice and warm. Doris had this comfort system of fleece, ice, and warmth down—she'd gone to it so many times after her mother died.

"Better?" she said, smiling at Cheryl.

Cheryl nodded, her chin thrust out. Squinting through the holes in her eye mask, she dialed Bob Turner. Jackie settled in next to her, a comforting hand on her knee.

Doris fluttered around, setting up a pot of ginger tea and her best china, along with a box of chocolates. She wanted to do everything right, happy to have her best friends back in her home. She was only half listening to Cheryl's phone call with Bob, but turned to look when she heard shouting from the other end of the phone.

"Thanks, Bob," Cheryl was saying. "Yup, I know. I appreciate it. We'll talk soon." Cheryl hung up.

"What happened?" Doris asked.

"Bob's livid," she reported, reaching for a truffle. Her tiny hands hovered over the box for a moment before selecting a dark chocolate lined with coconut. "He's on the first plane to New York and his lawyers."

"Do you think he'll be your client?" Jackie asked eagerly. "You could go out on your own, open your own office. Cheryl, this could be big for you . . ."

"That would be great," Doris tried, settling on the edge of the sofa.

"His contract's watertight," Cheryl cut them off. She rubbed her forehead vigorously. "Even if they found a loophole, Fitzgibbon Ale couldn't work with any other marketing company for three years."

"How on earth do you know that?" Jackie marveled.

Cheryl sighed. "Who do you think drafted it?" She took a sip of tea and winced.

"Too hot?" Doris grabbed for the cup. She would have taken it back to the kitchen to drop in a tiny ice cube, but Cheryl deliberately held it out of reach.

After a moment, Doris sat back and fiddled with a string on a throw pillow. There was silence and Doris wished she could blurt out something to make Cheryl feel better but the Xanax she'd taken was making it hard for her to focus. The shiny set of silver tea set tongs were captivating her attention, as Jackie used them to drop three sugar cubes into her cup.

Doris pushed her glasses up her nose and the motion seemed to jog her brain. "Stan," she cried, suddenly. Everyone looked at her in surprise and Doris blushed. "I mean, why do you think Stan did all . . . I mean, why did he . . . ?"

"Stan was always a bit of a weasel," Jackie scoffed. "He's wanted to push Cheryl out for years."

"But why, if she's good at what she does?" Doris was having a hard time understanding. It wasn't just the Xanax. It was her lack of experience in the corporate world.

"It doesn't matter," Cheryl said. "It's over. I was playing hardball and I struck out."

"That's enlightened," Jackie said.

Cheryl snorted. "I'd still car bomb him if I could."

"Or blow up his house."

"Or shit-bag him."

Jackie and Cheryl cackled, setting down their tea to keep from spilling it.

Feeling left out, Doris stirred hers, the tiny spoon clinking against the rim. "Cheryl, why *were* you keeping accounts on Stan?" she finally asked.

"I wanted to take over the company." Cheryl's answer was short. "What do you think?"

"Oh, Cheryl." As soon as Doris heard her voice, like some kindergarten teacher scolding a kid for writing on the walls, she wished she could take it back. It wasn't how she meant it, but of course, now both Jackie and Cheryl were staring at her like she was some monster. Shit.

"Doris, you are really unbelievable," Cheryl shouted, tugging at the face mask like she was going to remove it and throw it at her. "Just when I think . . ."

"Honey, stop," Jackie said. Her many diamond rings sparkled as she grabbed Cheryl's hand. "Don't get upset. The trick is to figure out what you're going to do now."

"There's nothing I can do," Cheryl said, obviously irritated. "Jackie, I've had enough. Grab your stuff and come stay with me. I'll need someone to play nurse so . . ."

Suddenly, Windham Hill blasted over the speakers. Everyone jumped and Doris fumbled around underneath her for the remote control. Sitting on it had been a happy accident. Doris certainly didn't want Cheryl to leave and take Jackie with her. If Jackie stuck around, maybe some of her glamour would rub off on Doris. Doris smiled at the thought but then cocked her head in confusion. She was hearing a low rumbling. Was the stereo still on? She looked up and the tiny blue lights on the dials were dark. The rumbling got louder.

"Do you guys hear that?" she asked, looking around in confusion.

"It's a motorcycle," Jackie squealed, leaping up. "Hottie alert!" She bounced to the bay window. "When did Doug start riding a bike?" Jackie said, disappointed.

"It can't be Doug," Doris said, not trusting her own voice. "He doesn't ride motorcycles."

Just like he didn't see movies with other women.

Jackie nibbled on a piece of chocolate and gestured at the front lawn. "He does now."

Doris raced to the window and sure enough, her husband had just pulled into the driveway on a roaring death machine. His thighs were wrapped around it and he was struggling to pull his helmet up and over his head. The chin strap seemed to be stuck under his neck.

Doris rushed to the front door, shoving her feet into a pair of boots and pulling a sweater around her shoulders. She stumbled outside, saying, "Dougie? What on earth . . . ?"

Doug had finally gotten the helmet off and tiny spikes of brown hair stuck up like sharp little thorns, all over his head. Mashing his lips together, Doug stared at her for what must have been a minute. The yard was filled with the smell of gasoline and suddenly, Doris felt cold and afraid.

"Doris," he said, "I need to tell you something." Doug's familiar eyes looked past her as he started to speak, to some point far away on the horizon. "When I married you, I made you a promise. But we were young and I didn't know someone else would come along and make a liar out of me . . ."

Instead of looking at Doug's eyes, Doris found herself staring at a piece of dry skin that hung from his nostrils. In a gesture of intimacy that did not match up with the words coming out of Doug's mouth, she ached to reach out and brush it away as her husband admitted to having an affair with Katherine Rigney.

Time might have skipped forward then because before Doris knew what was happening, she found herself down on the driveway, pummeling her husband's body with her fists. Her knuckles were contacting his fleshy face with a force she didn't know she had in her. As Doug tucked his knees to his chest and tried to grab for her hands, Doris grabbed for the bulbous helmet dangling from his hand. The coarse strap cut into her skin as she wound up, getting ready to swing it at his head.

Doug rolled to the side just in time and with a sharp *thwunk!* the heavy plastic made contact with his shoulder. He yelped. "Doris!"

"You pansy piece of dog doo-doo," she screamed, pulling back for another hit.

Doug leaped up and started to run. Doris chased after him, swinging the helmet like a machete. She slipped, falling face first on the ground, the helmet tumbling from her hand.

As Jackie rushed to help her up, Doris cried, "He slept with Katherine Rigney. He slept with Katherine Rigney!"

"*Why?*" Cheryl said, facing Doug. There were two red indentations from the face mask along her freckled nose. "Oh, I know," Cheryl said, voice thick and sarcastic. "Because you like to set standards but not live up to them. Isn't that right, Doug?"

Doug glared back at Cheryl. "Could I have some time alone with my wife?"

"No," Doris sobbed, desperately stretching her arms out. "Please don't leave me. Don't leave me . . ."

Jackie engulfed Doris in her arms. Smoothing her hair with one hand, she patted her back with the other. "It's okay, honey," Jackie told her, voice soft and soothing. "It's going to be okay . . ."

As Doris sobbed, her thoughts were no longer on her bastard of a husband but on her mother. Her mother could have fixed this. Her mother had fixed so many things with Doris's father; making sure he was comfortable and happy in their little home, cooking his meals and raising their child. That man had loved Doris's mother with a lifelong devotion. The type of devotion Doris had always assumed she had from Doug.

Opening her eyes, Doris saw that Doug was clutching his helmet, jingling his keys, and looking from the house to his wife back to the house. Just as he looked ready to make a run for the house, Jackie demanded, "What's with the bike, Doug? Couldn't pony up for a midlife Corvette? Or a midlife . . ."

"Miata," Cheryl volunteered.

"He s-s-saw *Wild Hogs.*" Doris sniffled, remembering what

Doug had been saying just before dropping the bomb about his affair. "He wants to go—go f-f-find himself."

Cheryl whipped her head toward him. "You have *got* to be kidding me."

As Doug shifted his weight from one foot to the other, Doris remembered the first time she and Doug had kissed. It was after school, they were only fifteen. There were kittens behind Doug's parents' house and he invited her over to see. Together, they walked behind the garage. Doug pointed into an abandoned dog house, where the furry little bundles lay huddled up next to their mama. The cat eyed the two teens, tail batting with protective concentration. When Doris finally turned away from the sweet sight, ever so gently, Doug took her mouth with his.

At the memory, Doris wailed. "I loved you," she cried, pointing at him. "How could you do this to me?"

Jackie, pressing her hands deep into her pants pockets, stepped protectively in front of Doris. "Doug, you need to leave," she said.

"I need to get my things."

"You need to get the fuck out," Cheryl said.

Doug took a long look at everyone. Realizing he was outnumbered, he shook his head and hopped back on the motorcycle, yanking his helmet back on. The engine roared to life and Doug sped out of the drive, without even a glance behind him. The neighborhood was silent in its wake, its giant houses looming.

"Well, the weather's not great . . ." Cheryl mused. "At least there's hope he'll crash."

WHEN THE GIRLS were thirteen, the crash had changed their lives. It happened when they were in junior high, on a Tuesday night, the second week into soccer practice. The entire team was crammed into the "kidnapping van," that white carpool monstrosity that had no windows in the back and worse, no seat belts. The van smelled like Plumeria deodorant, dirty socks, and sweaty teenage girls; their very own locker room on wheels. When the accident happened, the majority of the team had already been dropped off so the only ones left were Peyton Henderson, Cheryl, Doris, and Jackie.

Jackie, with her fluffy blond hair and upturned nose, was the most popular girl in school. The girls in her clique hadn't joined the soccer team so this gave the girls hoping to break into the in-crowd their chance. They swarmed around Jackie on the soccer field and in the van, desperately trying to find a friendship or at least a conversation starter. Jackie enjoyed the attention, but the only girl on the team that really interested her was Dori, the lanky dark-haired girl who always sat across from her in the van, sucking on that bottle of Gatorade.

Dori had nabbed Jackie's attention because she was outrageous. She was known for performing keg stands with the Gatorade jug in the middle of a game or tearing off her dirty socks in victory, waving them above her head like helicopters and tossing them out to the stands. Dori got away with all this because she was fiercely talented with the ball, able to do outrageous stunts and hit goals that seemed impossible. Everyone expected her to act a little crazy on the field and she didn't disappoint them. Jackie wanted to ask her for lessons or something but interacting with Dori was impossible because she came prepackaged with (puke) Cheryl.

Cheryl was Dori's neighbor and apparently, her best friend. They were always together, so it was impossible to get to Dori without bringing that girl into the mix.

Cheryl annoyed Jackie and her friends to no end, with her shrieky, high-pitched laugh designed to get anyone and everyone's attention. To add insult to injury, Cheryl wasn't even that pretty. She had a freckly face and plain, strawberry-blond hair, but all the boys were crazy about her. It wasn't uncommon for Jackie's friends to "accidentally" spill sodas down Cheryl's back in the cafeteria or steal her homework and change all the answers. Consequently, every day after practice, Jackie had to feel Cheryl's dislike for her from across the van.

In all her junior high superiority, Jackie wanted to tell the girl to lighten up; it wasn't her fault the popular kids picked on Cheryl. But maybe it was. Jackie had the power; she could have told her friends to stop at any time but a little tension kept school much more fun. If the price of that was chatting with Peyton on the last leg of the carpool, so be it.

When the drunk driver T-boned the van at an intersection, the sound was all movie magic and grinding metal and screaming tires. The elbows and arms and feet banging against warm flesh were something not noticed at the time but remembered later in nightmares or therapy. Jackie eventually remembered that Peyton had gotten thrown across her lap, then into the ceiling, just before Jackie was pitched forward onto Cheryl. Cheryl had already been pushed halfway into the console between the front seats and was lying on top of Dori, whose body was pinned to the floor. Everything was moving in slow motion and Jackie felt the van spin three times before halting suddenly, crashing into a tree with a mind-numbing thud.

As cold air spilled in above them, Jackie wondered how windows had appeared in a windowless van before realizing the van had been split in two. Out of the corner of her eye, she saw Mrs. Lewis, their driver. Mrs. Lewis was slumped over the wheel and motionless, a trickle of blood running down her cheek. Cheryl and Doris were moaning, and suddenly Jackie processed the fact that they were lying underneath her. She stopped herself from flexing her limbs, remembering something she'd read once about how to avoid paralysis after a car crash.

"Hold still, okay?" Jackie had said. "We could be seriously hurt and if we move, it'll be worse, okay? So I won't move if you don't."

"I can't breathe," Doris cried, muffled somewhere beneath her.

"Hang on. Just wait, like, five minutes," Jackie had begged, already hearing sirens in the distance. She could see someone's hand and gently, she took it and squeezed. "Who is that?"

"Cheryl," a voice sobbed. "Jackie, I can't move my leg."

"It's just 'cause I'm on you," Jackie lied, forcing her voice to be perky. She learned later that her statement was true but at the time, she'd made it up to keep Cheryl calm. "Hang in there, okay?" Then she'd called for Peyton, but didn't get any answer. The only things they could hear were the sirens getting closer and the radio still belting out "Achy Breaky Heart."

"Why does Mrs. Lewis always have to play country music?" Jackie tried to giggle but she was having a hard time keeping her voice steady. Her heart had started to race and tears were rolling down her cheeks. Suddenly, she felt pressure on her hand. Cheryl.

"You're okay, Jackie," Cheryl promised. "We're all going to be okay."

"Not if we have to keep listening to this song," Doris said from below, voice muffled. "Country music sucks," and the three burst into giggles.

In the hospital, they all sat together on gurneys trying to piece together what had happened. It was hard to believe that they'd gotten out with barely a scratch. Doris was the only one with a long red cut on her leg. The cut wasn't from being thrown—it was because she'd landed on the soccer equipment. As they'd lain there in a pile, a cleat had dulled its way through her leg. They overheard a doctor say that Mrs. Lewis had broken her arm and needed stitches. Then came the choked, hushed whispers about Peyton—she had been killed.

The next day, back in the junior high cafeteria and after the grief assembly, Jackie's friends were saying that Peyton should not have died; that it should have been Cheryl. Without a word, Jackie picked up her peanut butter and honey sandwich. She marched over to Cheryl and Doris, squeezing in beside them. From that moment on, she never left their sides. Every year, the three of them held their own memorial service for Peyton, the quiet girl they had barely known.

More than twenty years later, snuggled safely in bed, Jackie was once again grateful that she had made the friendship choice that she had. After all, Doris offered such a cozy guest room. Who knew what type of sheets her former best friends would have picked out?

After Doug's announcement, Jackie and Cheryl had gone into the house and spent hours consoling Doris. When she was finally calm but wanted to be alone, Jackie had lain down for a quick nap. Stretching luxuriously, she eased her eyes open and glanced at the clock. The red numbers flashed five o'clock.

Screeching, Jackie bolted out of bed and tore into the kitchen. Doris was moping at the kitchen table. She was wearing the blue eye mask and staring glumly into a cup of hot chocolate.

"Sorry I took such a long nap," Jackie apologized. "It's the jet lag. Are you okay? Where's Cheryl?"

Doris pointed toward the living room. Cheryl was lying on the sofa with the rice heater draped over her shoulders. Looking from the rice heater to the blue face mask, Jackie had the urge to laugh but didn't. The situation was too dire.

"Doris, how are you doing?" Jackie pressed. "Are you feeling any better?"

Doris considered the question, squinting through the slits in the mask with puffy red eyes. Instead of answering, she licked whipped cream off a spoon.

Jackie turned to Cheryl. "What about you?"

"Oh, just fabulous," Cheryl said, then shook her head. "Congratulations, Jackie. You are the only one left standing."

"What do you mean?"

"You are the only one who hasn't completely, utterly, and totally fucked up her life."

"That's not true," Jackie pleaded, searching for the right words to tell them the reason for her return. "My life is not . . ."

"Oh please," Cheryl half-laughed. "You don't need to play small for us."

"I swear," Doris said, "if you weren't here to give us hope, I think we'd . . . we'd . . ."

"There would be a mass suicide," Cheryl finished for her. "No doubt."

Doris nodded, vehement. The blue face mask jiggled.

Jackie's heart sank. Pressing her fingers under her eyes, she squared her shoulders and took a deep breath. "Well, then," she said. "I'll do what I can to help."

Jackie walked toward the fridge, thinking. If her friends needed her to play the part of the fabulous friend, she would. There would be time to tell them the truth later. Until then, she would just have to focus on helping them to make it through. Dramatically, Jackie turned toward them and put her hands on her hips.

"Girls!" she cried. "I have an idea . . . Doris, tell Mandy to stay at a friend's house tonight."

"Why?" Doris said.

"You'll see . . ." Jackie sang. Reaching into the fridge, she yanked out a carton of orange juice and a bottle of champagne. As she poured three mimosas, she said, "Cheryl, I want you off that couch in thirty seconds. We're going to have a toast. Then, off we go."

Her best friends stared at her blankly. "Where?"

"Chicago," Jackie sang. "Chi-town, *méchant!*"

Cheryl buried her face in a couch pillow. "Sounds like a blast," she grumbled.

"Aargh," Doris agreed, shifting slightly. She took another sip of hot chocolate.

"We're leaving in twenty minutes," Jackie said, handing out the cocktails. "Get it together, ladies. Or so help me, I will go to the spa without you. And Doris, you'll need to give me your credit card because Doug's paying for it."

At that, Doris's eyes lit up. Fifteen minutes later, the three women were in the car, talking excitedly about how they were going to bankrupt Doug in the Windy City.

Chapter Eleven

IT HAD TAKEN THREE TREATMENTS AT THE SPA, FOUR MARGARI-
tas, and an intimate Mexican cantina with colored lights and cac-
tus cutouts to make that switch inside Cheryl flip from heartache
to rage. One moment she was feeling sad and tipsy, wondering
where she'd gone wrong, and then suddenly, that image of Stan
looking like some bloated version of Donald Trump in the boardroom would sear through her head. The very thought made her
pound her fist on the table.

"This can't be legal," Cheryl said. "I'm going to sue him for
everything he's got. I *built* that company. That has to count for
something!"

Brief memories of creative campaigns and client presentations
and company meetings flashed through her head, reminding her
that everything she once loved was gone—all because of one stupid, sneaky man.

"Are you guys *listening to me?*" Cheryl demanded.

Doris was hunched over the appetizer tray like the sole survivor
of some violent crime. Jackie was fiddling with her straw.

"We're listening, honey," Jackie said. "You have every right to be angry."

"I'm angry," Doris said, shoveling chips and salsa into her mouth with the rhythm of a salsa dancer. "In fact, I think I'm going to kill Doug."

"Oh, really?" Jackie covered her mouth to hide her smile. "How are you planning to do that?"

"A circular saw," Doris said. "Or a nail gun. Something from his tool kit."

"*Mame* him or kill him?" Cheryl wondered.

"It's all the same, isn't it?" Jackie said, giggling.

"Kill," Doris insisted, biting down hard on a chip. "He is my husband. How could he *do* this to me?"

Cheryl knew the answer. In fact, it was pretty obvious. Doug had done it because Doris had let him. The same way Cheryl had let Stan walk all over her.

"Stan didn't know a good thing even when it was staring him in the face," Cheryl said. Shaking her head, Cheryl took a long drink of her margarita and once again reflected on her defunct career. It was amazing. She had always thought she was a savvy person, a woman in charge, but look how that had turned out. She should have opened her own firm when she'd had the chance.

"Men suck," Doris said.

"Yup," Cheryl had to agree. "They're good for sex and that's about it."

Jackie grinned. "Isn't there a male strip club around here?"

Cheryl looked at Jackie in surprise. "I think so. Why?"

"Let's go," Jackie said. "We'll hoot and holler at them. Degrade them, for once. It'll be fun." Jackie folded her hands, somehow managing to look like a guest at the Four Seasons instead of someone suggesting a night of debauchery.

Cheryl felt a rush of love for her friend. "I am *so* glad you're back. Let's do it."

Doris turned gray. "No." She grabbed for the basket of chips and held on to it like an anchor. "Absolutely not."

"Let's vote," Cheryl said. "Who wants to go?"

Both Cheryl's and Jackie's hands shot up. Laughing, they hopped to their feet and grabbed their purses. When Doris didn't move, Cheryl let out a huge sigh and said, "Please don't make this difficult." But of course, she did.

It was a physical battle to drag Doris outside the Mexican cantina. She wouldn't budge, babbling on about morality and sexually transmitted diseases, and finally, Jackie had to grab Doris's purse and race out the door. Doris had no choice but to chase her two doors down to the dingy male strip club. Once there, a red-faced Doris panted, "If you ever do that again . . ."

"You'll call the police?" Jackie said. "Good. I love a man in uniform."

The doorman pushed open the metal door and Doris was ushered inside. The moment they walked in, a blond Adonis wearing nothing but a Speedo sidled up to them. His muscular form reminded Cheryl of the statue of David. She squeezed Jackie's arm and whispered, "This is the best idea you've had yet."

"Hi, ladies," the stripper said, flashing a perfect smile. "Now, who's this goddess?"

Automatically, Jackie had fluffed her hair and batted her eyelashes, assuming he meant her. Instead, the blonde pushed past both her and Cheryl, grabbing for Doris's hand. Doris's eyes went wide like saucers.

"What's your name?" he asked, smiling at her.

"I'm . . . I'm Doris," she said.

"You're beautiful," he said, then escorted her to a front-row table, right by the stage.

Jackie and Cheryl stood stock-still, mouths dropped to the floor. "Can he smell a sucker or what?" Cheryl finally said.

"Well, whatever it is," Jackie said, leading the way to the table, "I have a feeling this will be good for her."

Three margaritas later, Cheryl couldn't help but agree. Doris was watching her sculpted stripper gyrate on stage with rapt attention. The straw from her fourth margarita was plastered to her mouth and her fist rhythmically pumped at the air in time to the pulsing bass of the music. She was clutching a handful of crisp bills and giggled like a schoolgirl as her stripper steadily removed them with his teeth. The moment her hands were empty, Doris moved back to her bag and refilled her stash.

"Does she have an ATM in there?" Jackie said, watching the transaction in confusion.

"If she does, her PIN is *c-o-c-k*," Cheryl said. Pounding her fist on the table, Cheryl shouted, "Tequila shots!"

A scantily clad Puerto Rican sidled up. His hair was slicked with some sort of gel, making him look like he'd just eased his way out of a hot tub. After thanking her in a thick Spanish accent, he held her gaze and gave a sensual lick to her hand. His tongue was soft and warm and even though Cheryl should have been disgusted, she was too entertained to care.

"Ew," Doris cried, tearing her eyes away from the stage. "He licked her. Jackie, did you see him lick her?"

Jackie nodded. "I sure did."

The waiter grinned. As he strutted away from the table, Cheryl looked him up and down. He wasn't bad. His skin was smooth and dark. Those broad shoulders tapered down to a thin, cut torso where a pair of brown leather pants hung low over powerful hips and a bulging crotch. "That man can lick me anytime," Cheryl said, "and anywhere."

"That's disgusting," Doris told her, before turning back to her dancer.

Eyes narrowed, Cheryl formulated a plan. The moment the waiter returned, sloshing a tray of tequila shots onto the table, Cheryl cried, "Hey, Doris! Watch this." Pushing back her chair, she beckoned to the waiter. Without a moment of hesitation, the waiter straddled her.

As Doris looked on in dismay, the stripper pressed his hard body against Cheryl's. He smelled like alcohol, cigarettes, and hair product. Deliberately, she lowered her shoulder and leaned in. The waiter came in even closer, then slowly nibbled the exposed flesh just underneath her ear. Cheryl made a big show of gasping and squirming beneath his touch. For a moment, Cheryl even considered letting the hot lips grazing her body come in for a kiss but thought better of it.

Instead, she whispered, "Thank you, that's all I need," and pressed twenty dollars into his palm. As he winked and writhed away, Cheryl pressed a glass of ice to her heated neck and then smiled big at Doris.

"I can't believe you did that," Doris practically shrieked. "You could have caught something."

"*Boire*," Jackie said, getting up and walking over to Cheryl. "This should kill the germs."

Taking a glass of tequila from the table, Jackie brought it to Cheryl's lips. The spicy tequila burned down the back of her throat.

Watching them through slit eyes, Doris swayed unsteadily and grabbed for a shot. She downed the ounce of gold liquid and reached for another.

"Slow down, sweetheart," Jackie purred, sliding the next one out of the way.

"Let her," Cheryl said, pushing it back. "Drink up, Dori."

"She's a lightweight . . ." Jackie's voice tinkled.

Doris downed the tequila and gave her the finger.

Cheryl screamed with laughter. "*VIVA LAS MUJERES*," she cried, pounding her chest like an ape. The women around them cheered and hooted. "Oh God, this is so incredibly trashy," Cheryl laughed. She half-wished her former coworkers could see her.

Through a blurry haze, she took in the wide variety of shapes and sizes of women in the strip club. There was a table of sorority girls wearing matching sweatshirts and blond ponytails, pretending to blush over the raunchy display. There were several tables filled with women who obviously had money, dressed in expensive outfits and sipping at martinis. There were even old ladies with blue hair, fat pearls, and open wallets.

"This place is making bank," Cheryl said in surprise.

"As long as there are women like our Doris in the world, the strippers will clean up," Jackie said. "*Non*. Look at her now."

Cheryl turned and stared. With that last tequila shot, Doris's remaining inhibitions had flown out the window. "Funky Cold Medina" was blasting through the club speakers and Doris had ripped off her light pink cardigan and was waving it in the air. Through the thin shirt covering her, Cheryl could see the outline of Doris's bra straining against those huge breasts. They were shaking like maracas in time to the music.

"Doris, are you stripping?" Jackie called over the din.

Doris nodded earnestly and undid her belt. With a quick motion, she pulled it off and twirled it over her head. Ducking, Jackie scampered over and pulled Doris back down into the chair, taking the belt and smoothing her hair.

"But I wannna dansssh," Doris slurred, trying to get back up.

"This is a *male* strip club, honey. No one wants to see you naked," Jackie said. She shot a helpless look at Cheryl.

"I wanna get naked! I'm shhhhexy . . ." Doris insisted, struggling to get to her feet. She stood up. Confused, she started to lift her shirt.

"TAKE IT OFF," Cheryl cheered, pounding the table. She grabbed her cell and cued up the video camera, eager to document this moment. At the very least, she could torture Doris by threatening to put it on YouTube.

"Cheryl, stop it," Jackie pleaded, pulling Doris's shirt back down. "Darling, you can get as naked as you want back at our hotel room, okay?"

Another round of tequila shots arrived. Cheryl looked at the waiter in surprise. "But we didn't order these."

"From her dancer," the waiter said, nodding toward Doris.

"Thankshhh, lover," Doris cried. She could barely hold the glass but threw back the liquid like an oyster at Mardi Gras. "I'm show happy," she sang, pushing past Jackie to stroke the legs of a tanned and beefy waiter. "This is why Doug goeshhh to Hooterssssh. We need a male Hootershhh," she shouted with a slur.

"That's right," the girl at the next table shouted. Her friends cheered in agreement.

"Oh my God," Cheryl marveled. "Why didn't I think of that?" She surveyed the room, calculating totals in her head. "If every woman in here was having dinner . . ." Cheryl turned to the ladies at the next table. "Would you really go?"

"Russshhhh the ssshhhhttage," Doris begged, tugging at her arm. "Russshhhh the ssshhhhhttage!"

"I'm in the middle of a focus group," Cheryl said, shaking her off. "Would you guys go? To a restaurant with male strippers?"

"I'd go," an older lady said, taking a satisfied drink of her frozen piña colada. "And bring the sisters in a heartbeat." Her friends hooted in agreement.

The dancer on the platform did a series of pelvic thrusts, thinking he was inspiring the cheers.

Doris hit the table, yelling, "Russshhhh the ssshhhhhttage!"

"Oh, Doris," Jackie sang. With a big smile, she set down her drink and stood up, pushing a chair next to the wooden platform. "Did someone say rush the stage?" she said, hopping up onto the platform. Cheryl scampered over to the chair and boosted herself up, carefully copying Jackie's salsalike moves under the bright, hot lights. She prayed she wasn't so drunk that her depth perception was off and she'd fall and crack her head open. Again. For a brief moment, the half-naked dancers looked panicked at the breach. Then they seemed to realize the full potential for their performance.

A baby-faced stripper with torn, frosted jeans grabbed Jackie, bent her over, and started slapping her ass. A dirty-hot dancer wearing a cowboy hat, chest dripping with sweat, thrust his way across the stage and pressed up against Cheryl. His sculpted body gyrated wet against hers, hips rocking with the rhythm of the bass. The crowd went crazy.

The theme music from *Top Gun* started to play. Men of all shapes and sizes began filing onstage. They wore white thongs fitted over swollen packages and sea caps cocked jauntily on their foreheads.

Doris jumped up and down with glee. "Chhhharrggghshe!" she shrieked, arms over her head. At Doris's command—and the sight of this unabashed naval erotica—women surged forward. All shapes and sizes threw down their purses and hurried to the stage, desperate to climb onto the tiny platform.

Clearly proud to be the mastermind, Doris looked somewhat confused that she wasn't climbing onstage, too. She eyed the wobbly chair, fumbled, and steadied herself.

"Cheryl, we need to help her," Jackie said, pulling Cheryl out of the grasp of a dancer. They hustled to the edge and peered down at Doris. Extending a hand, Jackie said, "Come on."

"I . . . I . . ." Doris covered her mouth with one hand and held up a wobbly finger with the other. Taking a deep breath, she hiccuped and then cringed, eyes widening in surprise.

"What's the problem?" Cheryl demanded, peering down at her. "We've got to dance with the strippers. Get up here."

Doris's face flushed bright red. As women continued to claw, push, and scratch their way onto the platform, Doris dove for her Coach bag and fumbled with the shiny latch. The purse burst open just as Doris did, filling her purse with rejected tequila.

"PLEASE CALL AN ambulance," a voice moaned from underneath a stack of feather pillows.

At that, Jackie put down her newspaper and stood up with a stretch. "*Debout, debout,*" she chirped.

An old friend of Robert's owned the hotel they were staying at. He had been more than happy to give them a suite overlooking the high-end shops Jackie used to patronize on a regular basis. Delighted to find herself in luxury yet again, Jackie was already up, showered, and thumbing through the room service menu. There was little she liked more than a stay in a sumptuous hotel.

"Get up, girls," she said. "We need to figure out if anyone had promiscuous sex with a stripper."

There was movement under the blankets on Cheryl's bed. When her pale face poked out, Jackie cringed and suggested, "Ooh. Just ease it back down to a steady horizontal."

"Can you call an ambulance?" Doris repeated, arms flailing.

A tiny crack of sun, white like bleach, poked through a slit in the heavy curtains.

"I know what you two need," Jackie decided, padding over to the curtains. She threw them open, revealing harsh white sunlight and an expansive view of Michigan Avenue. At the unexpected light, Doris shrieked like a vampire.

"Who's hungry?" Jackie sang, holding out the room service menu. "Pick something out, then let's talk about Doris's idea. I placed a call to George and he's looking into logistics."

"For . . . ?" Cheryl asked, rubbing her eyes.

"Why, the male version of Hooters," Jackie said. "We can pull it off. It's a wonderful idea."

"Are you kidding?" Cheryl demanded.

Jackie shook her head. "Totally serious. It's hilarious."

"It's horrible," Doris protested. "Men serving food half naked? It's completely inappropriate."

"Wait," Cheryl argued, struggling up onto an elbow. "Women serve food in their bras at Hooters. TurnKey takes *clients* there. Why is that okay?"

"That's different," Doris said, voice husky from a night of debauchery but somehow still prim. One hand rested against her head while the other reached for the glass of water Jackie had placed on the bedside table. At Cheryl's outraged look, she said, "Cheryl, it's a man's world. You know that. If you can't accept it, then you're setting yourself up for disappointment."

"If it's such a man's world, then why can't Doug bang Katherine Rigney?" Cheryl demanded. "And anyone else he wants?"

"That has nothing to do with anything!" Doris's face went red with rage, and then she lowered her head, moaning.

"I think we've *all* had a little bit of disappointment this week, haven't we?" Jackie spoke quickly. "And maybe we should get mad at the disappointment instead of each other, don't you think?" At their silence, she picked up the phone and placed an order for pancakes, eggs, fruit, and a large pot of coffee. "The male version of Hooters," she laughed lightly, setting down the receiver. "I guess it is silly . . ."

"It's not silly," Cheryl argued, pushing off the covers and stumbling out of bed. She fumbled around in her purse and pulled out the crumpled-up strip club brochure. It was covered in promotional photos of half-dressed firefighters, naval captains, and businessmen. Waving the brochure at Doris, Cheryl muttered, "It's brilliant."

Jackie's eyes widened, innocent. "Well, then . . ."

"Toss me that notepad," Cheryl said, forcing herself into a sitting position. "We've got some plans to make."

Chapter Twelve

THE WEEKEND IN CHICAGO FLEW BY. PAMPERING AT THE HOTEL spa, fabulous meals on Rush Street, and little trinkets courtesy of Doug's credit card did much to put the women back in good spirits. When they returned to Doris's house two days later, Jackie felt much more capable of figuring out the next step to put her life back on track. But Cheryl had beaten her to it.

The morning after they returned, the doorbell chimed at five a.m. Jackie pulled the pillow over her head, hoping the noise would stop. The bell kept ringing.

"Son of a bitch—somebody answer the door!" Mandy shouted.

Jackie climbed out of bed, pulling on a silk robe around her pink pajama set. Fluffing her hair, she headed out into the hallway.

Doris was already dressed and rushing down the staircase. "Maybe Doug came back," she whispered, hopeful. Jackie followed her downstairs, not wanting to point out that if it were Doug, he would have just used his key.

Doris fumbled with the locks and threw open the door, then

seemed to wilt against the door frame. "It's just Cheryl," she said. "What are you doing here?"

"Did I wake you?" Cheryl asked. Without waiting for an answer, she pushed her way inside. Her arms were filled with papers, her face heated and manic.

"What are you doing here so . . . so early?" Doris asked, biting at her lip. She peered past Cheryl as though Doug might still be standing there like she'd hoped, waiting to surprise her.

"Early bird gets the worm," Cheryl said and held up a drawing of a penis.

Jackie shrieked. Ceremoniously, Cheryl plunked an armload of similar drawings on the kitchen table. Bustling back out to her car, she called back over her shoulder, "Hang on, girls, I've got lots of surprises."

After her next few trips, the kitchen table was full of papers, a laptop computer, breakfast sandwiches, and coffee. "Well? Where are the plates?" Cheryl asked. "I'm starving."

Doris sprung into action, setting the table with the finest china. Jackie poured coffee for the three of them, then walked over to stand behind Cheryl, cradling the mug in her hands. Cheryl turned on her Mac and slid on a pair of reading glasses. "All right, here we go. I spent a lot of time working on this stuff so you guys better like it."

Peering at one of the graphic designs on the screen, Jackie squealed. It was a man wearing a banana hammock, carefully placing cocktails on a table. As Cheryl clicked through the drawings, Jackie burst out laughing.

"What?" Doris said, setting down her breakfast sandwich. Jackie beckoned, and with a sigh, Doris walked over and peered at the computer. "This is obscene," she finally said.

"Which one?" Cheryl asked. "There's more on the table."

Together, Jackie and Doris sifted through the other papers. Doris held up a drawing and said, "This one." Jackie burst out laughing. Cheryl had cut out one of the firefighters from the strip club brochure and glued a tray of food to his hands. A hose was hanging out of the front of his pants.

"If obscene means cha-ching," Cheryl sang, grabbing the paper from Doris and laying it back on the table, "you're so right. After our little brainstorming session in the hotel, I came up with a few ideas."

"You mean, there's more?" Jackie said, looking around in surprise.

Cheryl smirked and opened a PowerPoint presentation. "Girls," she said, "get comfortable."

It took about ten minutes for her to blow through the rest of the drawings and mock-ups she'd spent hours creating. Cheryl had laid out an entire plan to open a restaurant with a focus on the male package. "And there it is," she finished, glancing at her friends for approval. "Look, it's about time somebody did it."

"What's on the menu?" Doris demanded. "Bratwurst?"

"No, no," Cheryl grinned, taking a gulp of coffee. "Normal food but it's all served by men that look exactly like the one Doris funded the other night."

A bright red blush crept over Doris's cheeks. "That's inappropriate," she mumbled.

Jackie was eyeing the plans, dollar signs starting to form in her eyes. "This could be huge."

"I know it's huge." Cheryl nodded.

They heard a giggle. All three heads swiveled to the door where Mandy stood, listening. "Huge," she repeated. "Get it?"

"Mandy," Doris admonished. "Go back to bed."

"Wait," Mandy said. "I have a name. If you're serving fast food, it could be called Speedy Dicks. Or if you did, like, breakfasts, you could call it Early Risers."

"If we had outdoor seating," Cheryl added, "we could say, Welcome to Eat Outs."

"And if you had a long line or something, your dudes could say, 'It won't be schlong,'" Mandy said, then collapsed in giggles.

"Enough," Doris cried, hitting the table. Her sausage sandwich bounced.

The room went quiet for a minute. "What is your problem?" Cheryl demanded.

"We're not . . . we're not setting a good example," Doris said.

"What's new?" Mandy said.

Mother and daughter locked eyes.

"What if we . . . What if we just called it The Whole Package?" Doris finally said, looking away. "The name doesn't have to be dirty. It can be about anything." Cheryl looked at her in surprise. Doris bowed her head. "Maybe that's stupid. Sorry."

"No, it's great," Cheryl said, writing it down.

"If you guys really do this," Mandy said, "can I watch the dancers?"

"Like mother like daughter," Jackie sang and Doris turned beet red.

"Do I smell bacon?" Mandy asked. She took a few steps into the room. Doris threw her arm across the drawings Cheryl had made.

Jackie held up the bag of breakfast sandwiches and waggled it. The teen dove forward and grabbed two. Hands full, she started to head back for her room, then stopped and said, "Mom, when's Dad back from Albany?"

"The company hasn't told him yet," Doris said.

The question—Jackie quickly realized—had been a setup. Like any good poker player, Mandy hadn't even looked at Doris, but had watched Jackie and Cheryl for a reaction. Before thinking about it, the two of them swiveled their heads to Doris, mouths open in surprise. Mandy's eyes instantly brightened with tears and she slammed her way back to her bedroom.

"Doris," Cheryl admonished, looking at her friend in amazement. "You have to tell her Doug left."

"I'll tell her what's going on," Jackie volunteered, getting up from the table. She and Mandy had a good relationship. Maybe Mandy would take the news that her father had left better from someone other than her mother.

"She's not your child," Doris said. The kitchen chair scraped back and Doris stood up. "I'll go." Wiping her eyes, she swept by Jackie, down the hallway and to her daughter's room.

Jackie and Cheryl looked at each other. Cheryl took another sip of coffee. After a moment, she said, "We need investors. Got any?"

GEORGE MET WITH Jackie and Cheryl about the restaurant, pro bono. Cheryl said it may as well be pro boner by the way he kept leering at Jackie.

"He *is* making a fool of himself, isn't he?" Jackie whispered. She was surprised; George was blushing and acting very un-George-like.

From the moment the two women breezed into his office, George would not stop staring at her. To be fair, it *was* partially her fault. She was deliberately radiant in a stunning, clingy white cashmere sweater and a gray pencil skirt. After all, if George was going to help them she could help him; those were the rules of the world. But she didn't realize the sight of her was going to help him so much.

Before setting the appointment, Jackie had spoken to George about maintaining the secrecy of her financial situation. Since Jackie hadn't told the girls she was flat broke, she certainly didn't want them to learn it from George.

George was concerned. "They are your closest friends," he had said. "Are you sure not telling them this is wise?"

"My dear, I don't have a choice," she said. "They're going through some things right now and they really need me to be . . . me. And to be honest with you, I have always kept secrets from my best friends. There's a lot of things they don't know about me. That's just who I am." Jackie's words surprised her. She did not typically confide such personal details to anyone. Nervously, she twirled her wedding ring.

George was silent for a moment. Then, he cleared his throat and said, "You can trust me, Jacqueline. Besides, it's law. Everything I know about you is confidential. I could not share it without your consent."

"Well, then . . ." Jackie said, forcing her voice to be light and fun. "It will be our little secret." She could almost hear George smile on the other end of the phone. "But what about the tax issue? If this is a success, wouldn't the IRS take this from me, too?"

"Jacqueline, you do not owe anything else," George said. "The issue used the remainder of Robert's estate but has been entirely resolved. Case closed. Thanks to a certain brilliant lawyer, of course."

"Of course," Jackie said. "Thank you, George. You'll never know how much I appreciate you."

"I know, my dear," George said. "I do."

Now that they were in his office, Jackie was trying very hard to dispel the intimacy that phone conversation had created between them. She avoided his kiss when she walked in and looked away whenever he tried to make eye contact. The fact that George was clearly admiring Jackie's outfit was certainly not helping the situation.

"Jacqueline, you look wonderful," George told her. "Cheryl, doesn't she get even more beautiful as the years pass?"

"I like to think that *I* get even more beautiful as the years pass," Cheryl laughed.

He winked. "I didn't want to be too forward, but now that you've mentioned it . . ."

Jackie cleared her throat. "George, thank you for taking the time to speak with us. What can you tell us about the process of opening a restaurant?"

"Before we get started, may I offer you something to drink?" he asked. "I have coffee, sparkling water, tea . . ."

"Coffee, please," Cheryl said.

"Jacqueline?" George asked.

"Fine," Jackie said with a sigh. "Coffee." She sat on the couch and crossed her legs.

George went into the side room and returned with coffee on a silver tray. Carefully, he poured it into china cups. His hand brushed against Jackie's as he set hers down. Irritated, Jackie took her hands and folded them tightly in her lap.

"Will Doris be joining us?" George asked, about to set out a third cup.

"Doris doesn't have a sense of humor," Cheryl said, taking a sip of coffee. "She doesn't want to be involved."

"Ah," George said, ducking back out of the room. He came back in with a tray filled with tiny cakes and cookies. "That's unfortunate. I had purchased enough for three. Enjoy."

"You got this for us?" Cheryl squealed, grabbing a chocolate-and-macadamia-nut cookie. "I think I like it here!"

"Darling, can we please get started?" Jackie asked, irritated. "I do have somewhere to be."

Cheryl looked at her in surprise. Jackie ignored her, selecting a cake with pink icing. She took a tiny bite.

George settled into his desk chair and folded his hands. "Of course. Allow me to take you through everything you will need to know . . ." He launched into a lecture about investors, food preparation laws, potential permits, and the risks associated with opening a restaurant.

Cheryl asked question after question and Jackie took copious notes. They were there for more than an hour.

Jackie avoided his eyes the entire time.

IN THE ELEVATOR, Jackie studied her reflection in the mirrors. Puckering her lips out, she hunted for laugh lines. "Do you think I look old?" Jackie asked.

"Are you crazy?" Cheryl said. "You're in your prime."

That may be so, but Jackie knew a woman who had fallen on hard times and literally aged overnight. At a cocktail party, with a heavy exhalation of cigarette smoke and the ultimate in French candor, Marie had lamented that since her divorce, her hair had betrayed her—sneaking in strands of gray at every turn—even down *there*. This was from a woman who always wore eye-catching red silk skirts; a French muse of black-and-white nude photography; a character guilty of riding a pink motorbike and singing at the top of her lungs as she drove through the cobblestone streets. The signs of age could happen to anyone.

"I might get Botox," Jackie said, puckering up her face.

"Great. You'll always look interested in what I have to say," Cheryl said, stretching luxuriously. "So, when did George turn into such a hottie?"

Jackie's stomach dropped right along with the elevator. She turned away from the mirror and gave Cheryl her undivided attention. "What?"

"He's gorgeous." Cheryl grinned. "And you never mentioned that he was madly in love with you. Is that why you were being so rude to him?"

"*George*, of all people?" Jackie said. "He's not in love with me. He's . . . just George. He was flirting with you, too. He just flirts. It's what he does."

"I think . . ."

"He's also my dead husband's best friend," Jackie said, indignant.

"Still . . ."

"*Qui l'aurait pensé!*"

Cheryl pressed her lips together. Jackie pulled out a tube of Chanel lip gloss and dug in the dredges for the last drops of shiny pink goo.

"Oooh, we might have to go shopping," Cheryl said.

Jackie turned beet red and shoved the telltale tube back into her purse.

"It's good that he likes you," Cheryl continued, oblivious. "He'll be motivated to help. He can put the feelers out for investors, and did you hear when he started suggesting those lawyers for my wrongful termination suit? He wouldn't do all that if he wasn't crazy about . . ."

"I'm so happy you're suing Stan, by the way," Jackie said, deliberately changing the subject. "You simply *must* tear that whole company out of his fat little hands. After all, you made him a millionaire. What do you have to show for it?"

Under the harsh lights of the elevator, Cheryl seemed to wilt. "I know," she said softly. "I can't believe that fuck-face fired me."

"You'll be all right."

"Absolutely. I'll get him," Cheryl said, squaring her shoulders like a soldier. "And I've got all the time in the world to spend on my case. I don't have anything to do in the meantime."

"Until we open The Whole Package," Jackie chirped. "Then you'll have plenty to do."

"Wouldn't that be nice," Cheryl said. "But I'm not going to hold my breath."

"Why not?" Jackie demanded. "George thinks it's hilarious. He's contacting investors right away. I think it's quite brilliant. We've got a good shot."

Cheryl still looked skeptical. "We'll see."

The elevator pinged. They were at the bottom.

"Have some faith," Jackie said, sneaking one last look at her reflection and finding it to her satisfaction. She pointed at the lit numbers on the elevator wall. "We've got nowhere to go but up."

Chapter Thirteen

THE CALL CAME FROM GEORGE EARLY MONDAY MORNING.

Jackie was in the kitchen, trying to decide if she should bother to boil an egg. She was aching for some form of the breakfast she'd been eating for the past two years—a gently salted soft-boiled egg served with a cappuccino and followed by a chocolate croissant—but nothing Doris had quite fit the bill. The cappuccino machine had spit out something grainy, and even though she and Doris had stopped at the bakery and picked up some croissants, they weren't quite right. The bread was crusty and they tasted like butter and gasoline. Plus, there wasn't even a drizzle of chocolate on them.

"Jacqueline?" George said when she picked up the phone. "George here. Do you have a moment?"

"I don't know," Jackie said absently, peering into the fridge. "I'm in the middle of a food crisis. Do you think I could create a chocolate croissant if I smashed a chocolate bar into a roll? Doris has enough chocolate in here to stock an army platoon."

"Missing the good life, are we?" George laughed. "Listen, I have some things to discuss with you . . ."

Jackie selected a vanilla bean yogurt and peeled off the thin, silver foil cover. Since talking about her financial disaster was the last thing she was in the mood for, she said, "No, thank you. Why don't you mesmerize me with news on the restaurant instead?"

"You'll be happy to hear that is indeed why I am calling," George said.

Jackie set down the yogurt in surprise. "What?"

"I have some gentlemen interested in The . . . The Whole Package," he said, giving a little laugh. "Was that the name you girls decided on?"

"George," Jackie grabbed the receiver, clinging to it like a life raft. "Already? You're lying to me."

"No, no," he laughed. "Apparently this is an attractive idea. I've acquired the investment capital you were hoping for. There is a . . ."

Jackie laid down her cell phone and danced her way across the tile, squealing. She was going to be rich. Rich! *Again!*

"Jacqueline? Jacqueline? Do we have a bad connection?" George was worried, talking to dead air.

She picked up the phone. "No, darling. I'm here. Just dancing."

"Ah. Very good." George chuckled. "Now, as we discussed, they will require that initial amount from you, Cheryl, and Doris. How soon can that—"

"Darling, hold on," Jackie cut him off. "Doris isn't involved. Cheryl and I . . . we don't . . . What about getting a percentage for the concept? For running it?"

"A percentage of zero is zero, Jacqueline," George said gently. "Per our discussion, you must have the initial amount or these investors will not move forward."

Jackie's dreams crashed to the floor. "I don't have any money," she reminded him, cheeks flushed. "You of all people should know that."

"You will not be left out," George said, formal. "I am funding your part."

Jackie's mouth dropped. It wasn't like she and Robert hadn't paid him that tenfold over the years but . . . "George," she said softly. "I can't accept that."

"Robert was my best friend. I will not stand by and . . ."

"This is too much."

"No," George told her. "It is not. And it's not up for negotiation, either." She could practically see him with his arms crossed, that nautical necktie blowing back in the breeze from his tiny desk fan. "You will need to match the investors' amount or the deal will fall apart," he continued. "We have to make this work. How can I bill you by the hour if that doesn't happen?"

Jackie smiled. "So, really . . . you're doing this for you?"

"Certainly."

"You are so wonderful, George," she said, touched. "And I'd pay you back every cent but it won't work. We still won't have enough. There's no way Doris will do it." Jackie dipped the spoon into the smooth top of her yogurt, thinking. "Can't we try luring in more people, so the whole thing is paid for?"

"Impossible. Cheryl will have to cover the remainder."

"I don't know if she'll have enough," Jackie said. "Cheryl only has her savings and the severance package. Plus, she has a mortgage." Jackie heard George chomp down on a piece of butterscotch candy, but he didn't say anything. "There's nothing we can do?" She was desperate. "We really can't . . ."

"Jacqueline, getting this commitment was extremely difficult." George sighed. "It will be practically impossible to create additional capital if the business owners are not primary holders."

"What does that mean?" Jackie cried, but she already knew.

They needed money. Or they were through.

WHEN THE GIRLS were in high school, coming up with money for school events had never been a problem. If the class wanted to take a day trip to the museums in Chicago or even have an outing to a theme park, Jackie, Cheryl, and Doris could always figure out how to do it. Organizing car washes or bake sales was a cinch with the soccer team or the cheerleading squad behind them, but the girls quickly grew tired of the typical. As time went on, they got more and more creative in their fund-raising pursuits.

One day, Cheryl had been lying across a table during one of their student council meetings, fiddling with a frayed part of her jeans. "We should auction off all the guys on the football team," Cheryl suggested absently, "for, like, the weekend or something. Maybe then somebody could land Johnny May."

Johnny May was the quarterback. With his Paul McCartney eyes and dark curly hair, he was the quintessential high school hottie. He'd always dated this older girl named Stephanie but had just dumped her or gotten dumped for some college guy, depending on who you asked. Cheryl had already made out with him behind the school, Doris had French kissed him at a party, and Jackie had had a nice conversation with him after school on a bench, but the handsome quarterback wasn't willing to commit to anyone.

"You mean, buy him for the whole weekend?" a freshman girl asked, her eyes wide.

The silence in the room was deafening, then the girls started squealing and chattering. The only boy on the student council piped up with, "Now, wait a minute . . ." until Jackie pounded her gavel from her position at the front of the room.

"Order!" she called. When the girls in the room fell silent, their student body council president fluffed her blond hair and said, "Cheryl, do you think you can coordinate a fund-raiser like that?"

Realizing she'd piqued everyone's interest, Cheryl had sat up straight and grinned. "Absolutely."

The auction brought in $3,046—a record for fund-raising at their school. At first, the guys hadn't wanted to participate, but when Cheryl presented them with a signed petition from every girl in class, their egos couldn't say no. Within two weeks, Cheryl had the football players strutting across the stage in their boxer shorts, arms raised to the sky.

Johnny May brought in the highest bid. Even though every girl wanted him, the high school students simply did not have the pocketbooks to compete with the young and pretty geometry teacher who upped the bid every time someone dared go against her. By the time Jackie finally dropped the gavel at the auction, shouting, "Sold!" Cheryl and Doris were fuming. They didn't have a chance.

When asked by the school board how the weekend with Johnny May had been spent, Ms. Kramer said, "Oh, it was so nice to have a strong boy to fix things around my house."

The rumors swirled for years. Although Johnny May had refused to confirm or deny any of the whispered allegations, everyone had to wonder. For a boy who wasn't that bright, he'd certainly done well in geometry that year.

WHEN JACKIE CALLED her, Cheryl rushed right over. The two friends stood in Doris's living room, staring at each other.

"What can we do?" Jackie finally spoke.

"You can put up more than me," Cheryl said. "It's okay if you're a bigger partner. I would do more, but this is everything I . . ."

"I can't," Jackie said. "George looked over my finances and . . ."

"What do you mean, you can't?" Cheryl demanded. "Robert had millions."

Jackie paced around, setting out the scented candles she'd found in Doris's cupboards and methodically lighting them. "Everything's tied up," she lied, shaking out a match. "George said it would cause problems because of early withdrawal penalties, tax implications . . . it's not a viable plan."

"What about some of your art?" Cheryl suggested. "Your paintings? Jackie, let's gather them up, sell 'em and . . ."

Jackie regarded her friend in amazement. "Darling, I'm a *failed* artist. I barely sold *any*thing in Paris. And I only sold stuff here because Robert's friends felt sorry for me."

"Your work's amazing," Cheryl said, wrinkling her forehead. "You could open a gallery and . . ."

"Are we trying to get funding for a penis restaurant or some artistic fantasy?" Jackie said lightly. "Because if it's the fantasy I'm really not that interested." She knew that Cheryl wasn't trying to hurt her, but Jackie had let go of the dream a long time ago.

Looking around Doris's living room, Jackie took in the dark impressions of wildflowers that dotted the walls. Some artist somewhere had painted those. Once upon a time, Jackie could have done it so much better.

As a student at the Art Institute, Jackie had always received praise from the teachers and guest artists. Her bold work had attracted envy from even the most levelheaded artist in the room. At the time, she had believed a successful future was only a brush stroke away, but Jackie had never been clear on what she wanted that future to look like. Did she want to be a commercial artist? Own a gallery in New York? Create commissioned pieces for high-end clients? She couldn't decide. As her fellow students followed the paths they had set for themselves and eventually surpassed her, Jackie continued to flounder.

Some saw her marriage to Robert as an opportunity; Jackie found it limiting. Although many of his friends commissioned her work, the art they wanted to buy was very safe and conservative. Jackie accepted this, hoping that one day her creativity would have the chance to rebloom. When she decided to go to Paris, she was certain that she'd have some sort of a personal renaissance but, instead, spent hours on clichéd landscapes. Eventually, she just shoved her easel into a closet; paints shriveling up like butterflies trapped in jars.

"What are our options?" Jackie said. "How do we get more money?"

"I'm not sure." Cheryl sighed. She perched on the edge of the couch. "I don't want to open a restaurant with a bunch of strangers. It has to be ours—our heart, our soul, our money. Otherwise, what's the point of even doing it?"

"Yes," Jackie said, swallowing a lump in her throat. "You're right." Cheryl would freak out if she knew George was funding Jackie's part. She would call off the whole project.

"You know . . ." Cheryl said. "There's always Doug's money."

Jackie lit another candle and shook out the match. A delicate wisp of smoke danced its way up to the ceiling. Nodding, Jackie said, "It's not like they don't have it. These are forty-dollar candles, never used."

"Are you kidding me?" Cheryl demanded. She stalked over to a candle and picked it up, checking the price tag stuck to the bottom. She slammed it back down on the table. "That's just ridiculous."

When Cheryl and Sean were still married, they had constantly complained about the stacks of money Doug's family came from. Every time Doug would buy a new computer or buy a box at a playoff game or debate about taking some safari that he and Doris were never motivated enough to take, Sean would buckle down and try to work even harder. It was a pathetic picture: Sean's greasy hair bent over the drafting table in Cheryl's kitchen, wearing some sort of shirt that looked like it came from the Goodwill.

"At least he's not trying to compete with Robert." Jackie would sigh when Cheryl told her about it. "He could never catch up with him."

"He can never catch up with Doug," Cheryl said, exasperated. "Their house is paid for. Mandy's college education is paid for. Doug could retire today, if he wanted to. No matter how hard Sean works, he will never pass him. Ever. I don't know why he tortures himself. It's masochistic."

Now, Cheryl sank onto the cushions next to Jackie, shaking her head. "It's amazing. Doug's money could totally fund the rest of this thing but there's no way Doris would do it. She'd let some weird moral standard get in the way." Cheryl rubbed her hand against the couch cushions. "We are going to miss out on the greatest opportunity of our lives because Doris has her head up her ass."

"What did you just say?" a voice demanded. Doris was standing in the door of the living room, her fists clenched.

"Oh, hi," Jackie said brightly. "Welcome home."

"Why does Cheryl think I have my head up my ass?" Doris

demanded. Her glasses were foggy, face red. "And who lit my candles?"

"I did," Jackie said quickly. "Listen, we have potential investors for The Whole Package . . ."

"That's great!" Doris's mood changed immediately. She lit up, clapping her hands. "Good job, you guys."

"But we can't afford to match them so the deal will fall apart," Cheryl said.

"Oh." Doris took off her coat and started to walk toward the closet. She hesitated, then draped it neatly across a chair. "How much are you guys short?"

"Two hundred fifty thousand dollars," Cheryl said, throwing a pillow across the room. The pillow crashed to the floor, taking out a tiny decorative with it. "It's a *throw* pillow," she said quickly, at Doris's look.

"It's mine," Doris told her, setting it back on the sofa. "Please don't throw my things."

"Just . . . Can you two please . . . ?" Jackie said, then blurted out, "Doris, we need you to be a partner. Please. We can't do it without you."

Doris looked at her in surprise. Lips pressed together, she perched on the edge of the sofa, folding and unfolding her hands. Unconsciously, Jackie did the same thing. They were dry and cracked from the cold. No matter how much scented lotion she lathered them with during the day, they always felt like cardboard in the winter. Jackie would have liked to go back to sleeping with moisturizing gloves but the lotion she liked was too expensive.

"What would a partner *do*, exactly?" Doris finally asked.

"Create the restaurant," Jackie said, voice bright. Convincing Doris would change everything. "It could be whatever we wanted— like planning a party! We'd make up the decorations, design the menu, hire the dancers, think up advertising . . . decorate the place with our gorgeous selves . . ." Jackie's hands gestured wildly; she was giving such a great performance she may as well have tap danced across the coffee table. "We'd be the glamorous mavens who revolutionized Schaumburg and we'd be the most famous women business owners ever."

Doris was silent. "It sounds like a lot of work," she finally said.

Cheryl threw up her hands, exasperated. "Are you out of your mind? Of course it's a lot of work."

"I didn't mean that in a bad way," Doris protested. "I just . . . I would have loved to have a career," she said, looking down. "You know that. Doug was the one who wanted me to stay home and take care of him and the house and cook and clean and . . ." She looked around the living room. It was pristine. "I hope you'll let me do it," she said softly. "I would really like to be a partner. It sounds . . . fun."

Jackie's stomach dropped. She and Cheryl looked at each other, eyes wide, before turning to Doris and screeching, *"Really?"*

Doris was staring down at her lap. "Really."

"Wait," Cheryl said, hands on her hips. "You do understand we're talking about a male version of Hooters, right? You seriously want to put your name on a restaurant about a penis?"

"Cheryl," Jackie snapped.

"I'm sorry but there are things to think about," Cheryl insisted. "What about when Doug comes back? How long will it take for her to rethink it all and back out of the deal?"

"I won't back out," Doris argued, getting to her feet. "If I say I'm going to do it I'm going to do it."

"Girls, this is ridiculous," Jackie seethed. "George is on a deadline. I need to know whether or not this is something you're both interested in. Or I have to tell him it's off."

Doris fidgeted, looking from Cheryl to Jackie back to Cheryl again. "I'm in," she said softly. "I am, if you'll have me."

"You have no business experience," Cheryl warned. "I hope you know enough to know that you could lose everything."

Doris's chubby cheeks stretched into a bitter smile. She rubbed her hands on her size 16 jeans. "If I did," Doris said, nodding, "Doug would deserve it. He owes me at least that much." Then she blew out a candle and stomped out of the room.

The girls were silent for a moment, and then Jackie came to her senses. Cheryl had to make up with Doris. Otherwise, everything could still fall apart. "Go make up with her," Jackie said. "Now."

Cheryl's eyes widened. "No way. Just because we're business partners does not mean we have to be friends."

Jackie got to her feet. She put her hands on her hips and her nose in the air, the same stance she'd had as the captain of the cheerleading squad. Back then, there had been more than one instance when Jackie had been forced to mediate for bickering cheerleaders. One time, she'd had to stop practice for an hour until one girl finally apologized to another for sitting in her boyfriend's lap at a party. "You need to go talk to her," Jackie said, in the same tone she would have used back then. *"Do it."*

"We're not sixteen," Cheryl reminded her. "You can't just tell me what to do."

"You know what? You've been picking on Doris since I've been back," Jackie said. "And I get it. She hurt your feelings but it's time to move on. Right now, you're the one who looks like the bitch."

Cheryl ran her fingers through her hair. "I'm not so sure about that."

"Look, you've been the head of marketing for years," Jackie said. "You should know better than anyone else—you don't bully a top investor when there's money on the table."

When Cheryl didn't say anything, Jackie pursed her lips and said, "Well, well, well. Maybe Stan had the grounds to fire you after all."

Jackie walked down the hall and slammed the door to her room. Once there, she stood and waited. Sure enough, she heard Cheryl let out a big sigh, then walk down the hall toward Doris's room.

CHERYL FOUND DORIS lying facedown on the bed, pressing one of Doug's shirts against her face. She drew back in surprise. She had done that with Sean's clothes, even though she had been the one who had told him to go away.

Cheryl cleared her throat. "Doris . . ."

Doris didn't move. She looked like a beached whale against the starched shirt and mound of white feather pillows.

"Jackie's making me apologize to you," Cheryl told her. "So, I'm sorry."

"I'm sorry, too," the muffled voice said.

Cheryl stared at Doris, surprised. "What?"

"I know you're mad at me for what I said that one time." Doris rolled over and looked at her, blue eyes bright. "That was stupid of me and I'm sorry."

"Thank you," Cheryl said, feeling her voice catch. The last thing she had expected was for Doris to apologize. The cold pain that had been sitting in her chest for months seemed to break apart and thaw. Cheryl let out a deep breath and sank onto the edge of the bed. "I love you, Dori," she admitted. "We're like sisters. I think because of that, sometimes we . . . we don't think it's permanent when we fight. I let it get too far and I'm sorry."

"You wouldn't even call me back," Doris said, twisting the sheets around her finger. "You just cut me off."

"I know," Cheryl said, putting her head in her hands. "I was busy with work and before I knew it, all this time had passed and . . . I was embarrassed. About what you said. It's no excuse, but the thing that happened with Sean wasn't easy on me, no matter what everyone thinks. I felt so stupid after you talked to me. I felt like a whore."

"I didn't mean it like that," Doris said, touching her hand. "Well, I guess I did at the time, to be honest, but I've been thinking about it and thinking about it and I was wrong. You're my best friend. I should be there for you. Not judge you."

"Look, I get it. When those women were talking about me, it must have been embarrassing for you," Cheryl said, picking at the edge of the white duvet cover. "It was embarrassing for me, to hear about it. But it's not fair. It's a double standard, and honestly, I always thought you'd be on my side, no matter what."

A tear ran down Doris's cheek. "I am, Cheryl. I'm sorry."

"I'm sorry, too," Cheryl said. "I'm sorry I reacted the way I did." Cheryl grabbed a tissue from the bedside table and handed it to Doris.

"Do you think Jackie's going to stay?" Doris said, sniffling. "I really want the three of us to be together again."

"I don't know," Cheryl said. She'd been wondering that herself. Lowering her voice, Cheryl said, "She hasn't said anything about buying a house, so I just don't know. I bet she's planning on going back to Paris or opening an art gallery in Maui or New York or something."

"She'd stay if we open the restaurant," Doris said, wiping her glasses. "She'd have to."

"For a while, at least." Cheryl nodded.

"I wonder why she came back." Doris folded Doug's shirt and slid it under a pillow. "Have you asked her?"

"I did," Cheryl said. "And she gave me some line of bullshit. You know how she is. She's so secretive. But if she's a partner . . ."

The idea hung between them. Finally, Cheryl stood up and stuck out her hand. Doris took it, lumbering to her feet. They looked at each other for a long moment, not letting go. Cheryl felt her eyes fill with tears. Quickly, she blinked them back.

"Promise me we'll never fight like that again," Doris said.

Cheryl nodded, not trusting herself to speak. The two shared a smile, then after a long moment, filed back out to the living room. Jackie was back out there, sitting on the couch Indian-style and fiddling with the clasp on her watch. Seeing them, she lit up and leaped to her feet. "Friends?" she beamed.

Cheryl and Doris grinned, awkwardly putting their arms around each other. "Friends."

Chapter Fourteen

CHERYL WAS ON A MISSION. NOW THAT THEY HAD THE MONEY they had to get the location for The Whole Package and fast. They planned to open the restaurant right around Thanksgiving. Even though Cheryl had never opened a restaurant before, she knew some things about the business from market research and others just from living in the world. For example, the days leading up to Christmas were the best for restaurants and the days after were the worst.

Every Christmas, Cheryl saw friends and acquaintances race against the clock, trying to bake cookies, buy presents, and still look amazing at every social gathering. Women would band together for the shopping portion, hitting department stores with a hunger rarely seen throughout the year. For Cheryl, Christmas was the only time she really liked to shop. There was something about the Christmas tunes playing in the background, the smell of warm coffee and candied almonds, and the constant hum of energy through the stores that put her in the spirit.

After shopping, there was nothing she loved more than

stepping into a restaurant to exchange gifts with friends. Cheryl had always loved toasting Christmas bonuses with a starter of sparkling champagne and to keep the cheer up, ordering bottle after bottle of ruby red wine. After a hard day of shopping, feasting on a gorgonzola-encrusted filet or an overpriced piece of fish was the height of decadence, not to mention finishing off a meal with a piece of mixed-berry tart. Diving into its nutty crust and creamy center, she would giggle with whoever she was with and excuse the gluttony by saying, "Why not? It's the holidays. It would be rude *not* to have dessert." No, Cheryl had never seen a restaurant near the shopping district that wasn't packed all through December. It was only after the holidays, when the credit card bills rolled in and the tax clock started ticking, that the waiters started peeking out windows, searching for anyone willing to spend money. Business people with expense accounts still showed up for ahi tuna salads and lamb chops but otherwise, the restaurants were empty until Valentine's Day.

Knowing all this, Cheryl was determined to get The Whole Package up and running as soon as possible. Finding the perfect location was step one. Thanks to the help of an overeager Realtor named Betsy, the right spot dropped into their lap like a gift from Santa Claus.

"You need a place for a restaurant?" Betsy squealed, slamming a folder onto her already crowded desk. "The *best* spot opened up, right in the center of town. Old Millstines just closed."

Jackie, Cheryl, and Doris were all sitting in a row by Betsy's desk, waiting to see the options she'd have available for them. They certainly had not expected this.

Cheryl's heart jumped. "You're kidding," she finally said.

"This is fate," Jackie agreed, nodding.

Doris took off her glasses and wiped them nervously.

"Good news, right?" Betsy said, beaming.

It wasn't good news, it was great news. Cheryl could not believe their luck. Millstines was smack dab in the middle of the downtown shopping district. This was one of the main parts of their sleepy little town, right in the center of everything. At Christmastime, with the proximity of the mall and other theme restaurants like Medieval Times, the location for Millstines would pay for itself.

Millstines had been around forever. It was an upscale, popular place—a mom and pop, but with style. There was a bar in the center, fireplaces to the side and plenty of room for big and small tables. The way it was set up, they wouldn't even have to remodel for The Whole Package; they would just need to build a stage for their dancers. Even though Betsy's high-pitched voice had already given her a headache, Cheryl almost leaped up and hugged her.

"The Millstines want to retire, you know," Betsy gushed. "They plan to head to Florida, just like all old people do. To be honest, I'll probably do the same when I'm that age. Florida's *beautiful*."

Betsy gestured at the calendar of tropical locations hanging over her desk as though to emphasize the point. The calendar hung next to magazine cutouts of male celebrities and a large sticker of a cartoon bunny. Jackie giggled.

"They will be *sooo* excited to have another restaurant open. It'll be like carrying on their legacy. Do you think your restaurant will be open by Thanksgiving?" Betsy pressed. "They can stop by before they leave for Florida."

"Um . . ." Doris hedged, looking around Betsy's office as though there were video cameras recording the exchange.

"Betsy, let's just keep those little details under wraps," Cheryl suggested, leaning forward in her chair. "We should make an offer and close first because our restaurant probably won't be the Millstineses' thing."

Betsy cocked her head and picked up a purple ink pen. She started clicking it. "Why? They're not Kosher or anything."

Doris turned beet red, shoving her hands deep into her coat pockets. "It's a theme restaurant . . ." she tried.

"Like a theme party? My friends and I just had an eighties theme party. I wore Electric Youth perfume and, like, a Cyndi Lauper wig. Blue and yellow. It was hilarious. What's the theme?"

"Betsy," Jackie gushed, gesturing toward the celebrities on Betsy's wall. "Imagine attractive men, partially clothed, serving your meals in style."

Betsy whipped her head back toward the pictures. "*Really?*" She was transfixed for a moment, as though imagining George Clooney swathed in a silky thong and feeding her bonbons. She turned back to the three women, grinning. "You really mean, like, half-naked?"

Cheryl and Jackie nodded.

"That's so hot . . ." Betsy breathed. Her entire body relaxed, as though she'd had a massage.

Doris ducked her head and opened her purse. She pulled out papers, tissues, and lipstick tubes. Mindlessly, she began sifting through them, dumping certain things in the tiny trash bin in front of the desk.

"Whenever this place opens, I'm bringing *all* the girls and telling *every*one," Betsy promised, snapping back into action. "I'm gonna IM my best friend, Jenny, but I won't give away the location or anything. Naked men . . . that's so cool." Betsy pulled out her keyboard and started typing away, repeating, "It's just hot."

Cheryl shifted in her chair. The clock was ticking. "Let's go ahead and . . ."

The young Realtor nodded, giggling and pointing at her computer. "Jenny just wrote LOL."

Jackie and Doris looked at each other, confused.

"Acronym," Cheryl translated. "Laugh Out Loud. You guys seriously don't know that?"

When Jackie and Doris shook their heads, Cheryl groaned, "You guys are old. So, listen, Betsy. We want to make an offer . . ."

"Wait." Doris panicked. She shoved everything back in her purse and tossed it on the ground. In the process, she bumped into an organizer on Betsy's desk and knocked it to the floor. As Doris scrambled to pick up the colored paper clips, Post-it notes, and staples, she said, "If we're partners we have to decide together whether or not to make an offer."

Betsy watched them, hands poised but twitching over her keyboard.

"Doris is right," Jackie said, fluffing her cotton candy hair. "This is our first big decision as a group. If we're partners, everything has to be thirty-three, thirty-three, thirty-three, *oui?*"

Cheryl's face flushed. After this, Betsy would know that they were amateurs and, therefore, suckers. Even though she wanted the location for Millstines more than anything, they were going to have to lowball whatever offer the Realtor gave them.

"Exactly," Doris said. She placed the organizer back on Betsy's desk and leaned back in her chair. Folding her hands, she looked pointedly at Cheryl.

Cheryl sighed. "Okay, great. Girls, are we gonna do this Millstines thing or "—she shrugged to prove she could go either way—"shop around?"

"Well," Jackie said, fluffing her hair again, "the location's darling. People associate it with a successful restaurant already but that could be a problem. What if people walk in wanting Millstines? What do you think, Doris?"

Doris fiddled with her watch. "We need to look at it before we decide anything. We need inspections and appraisals before we even think about making an offer. What if the kitchen is a mess?"

Cheryl hated to admit it, but Doris did have a point. The girls knew nothing about the condition of the inner workings of the place, even though they'd sat in the dining room countless times. Suddenly, she felt nervous. What if their dream location was a bust?

Betsy nodded, her dark curling hair bouncing in the light from the window. "You're absolutely right. Then, if everything's to your satisfaction we could probably get the offer approved and papers signed within a week or two. The Millstines are super motivated."

Cheryl waited. "Any other objections?" she said but the girls were silent. "They're super motivated," she repeated. "We should get on this and figure it out."

"Sounds divine," Jackie said. "Doris?"

Even though Doris nodded, her face said she'd rather be doing just about anything other than opening a restaurant centered on a phallic symbol. "Sounds good," she said weakly.

"Should we start the inspections?" Betsy was suddenly total efficiency, pushing back her keyboard and hopping to her feet. "We'll run down there and take a peep."

Cheryl burst out laughing. "Perfect phrasing, Betsy. Let's go."

Chapter Fifteen

"Jackie, I'm tired," Doris said, handing her the remote control. "I think I'm going to go to bed."

Jackie looked at Doris in surprise. After they had checked out Millstines, Cheryl had gone home to do some paperwork and now it was just the two of them, camped out on the sofa. They had been watching reruns of *Sex and the City*. Another episode was about to start, Jackie giggling as she always did at Sarah Jessica Parker getting her tutu wet, staring at the bus that drenched her with loving chagrin.

Before Jackie had left for Paris, the girls used to get together to watch the episodes every Sunday night. They'd snack on cheese and wine, arguing over who got to be what character, even though it was pretty obvious. Jackie was Carrie, Cheryl was Samantha, and Doris was Charlotte. The girls only bothered to claim Miranda if they were in a bad mood.

"Doris, think it through," Jackie said, grabbing the remote and pausing the television. "What would Charlotte do? Would she go to bed at eight thirty?"

Doris was sprawled out at the end of the couch, stuffed into some atrocious flannel get-up and snacking on a box of chocolates. The box was empty, except for the raspberry ones Doris hated. Those were broken in half, mixed up with the paper candy holders. "If she was tired," Doris said, "yes, she would."

"No wonder you're tired," Jackie said, indicating the candy scraps. "You need to start eating better."

"I know, but . . ." Doris waved her hands around, as if to say she wouldn't know where to begin; they would betray her and grab for the candy anyway.

"If you're bored with this we can order a movie or something," Jackie tried, clicking on the Menu button. Hundreds of channels popped up and Jackie laughed, clapping her hands and pointing at the list in delight. She was two years behind on American pop culture, proving that exotic travel did not always come without consequence.

"No," Doris said softly. She had dark circles under her eyes. "I really need to go to bed."

"Then let's just talk," Jackie pleaded, switching off the television. The prospect of being alone with her thoughts and worries was not appealing. She needed Doris to stay up with her. "What do you think about the offer we made on Millstines? I hope it goes through. If it does, we can *do* something with our lives!"

"I *am* doing something. I'm raising a daughter," Doris recited, "and that's enough for me." She glanced at the clock above the mantel. "Speaking of, she'll be home from volleyball practice soon. I want to be in bed before she gets here."

Jackie sighed. "You two still aren't getting along?"

"No," Doris admitted. "And it just keeps getting worse."

Out of the three of them, Jackie had always thought Doris would make the best parent. She had such a close relationship with her mother that when they found out she was having a little girl, they had all assumed history would repeat itself, but it didn't turn out that way. Probably because Doris hadn't wanted to be a mother in the first place, but somehow, it just kept happening to her.

The first time Doris had gotten pregnant, they were seniors. The night she found out, they were all supposed to go to a party at Casey McAvoy's house. At first, Doris said she wasn't feeling well and tried to cancel, but then she decided to be the designated driver instead. Once there, she spent the evening in the corner with Doug, whispering in his ear and clutching his hand. Neither of them drank a drop. On the ride home, Cheryl and Jackie were giggling and slurring that they should stop for snacks when Doris pulled her mother's car over to the side of the road.

"We can't get snacks here," Jackie had said, peering out the window. "I want some candy. Come on, let's go."

"Doris, what are you doing?" Cheryl said, pulling down the lit passenger's-side mirror and inexplicably applying fresh lipstick. "The cops might think we're making out and, like, shine that vicious light on us so they can see some naked skin."

"I've gotta talk to you guys for a second," Doris said, swiveling in her seat to face them. "I'm sick of secrets. It's time to clear the air."

Jackie sobered up immediately, wondering how Doris had learned that Jackie's father had a court date in the morning. Jackie had been so good at keeping her problems a secret that she couldn't believe they were coming out now. Nervously, she tugged at her bustline. She was wearing a pretty little red-and-white gingham bra that gave her great cleavage. "I love this bra," Jackie tried, desperate to change the subject. "We should go shopping this weekend and get some more. Okay, let's go."

"Doris, come on," Cheryl said. She rolled down the window and poked her head out. The night air floated into the backseat and Jackie thought it smelled like rain and tree frogs. The dark woods twisted above them, the trees creaking in the wind. "I bet there's some serial killer in there," Cheryl said, cringing, "just waiting to—"

"I'm pregnant," Doris said.

All of the air seemed to leave the car.

In a rush, Doris added, "That's why I wanted to be the driver tonight and that's why I wasn't at school on Tuesday. I went to the clinic to be sure. I'm sorry I told you guys I had the flu. I didn't want to lie but . . ."

The news was too much for Jackie to process in her intoxicated state. She started to cry. It was a mixture of relief and despair. She couldn't believe what Doris was saying.

"You have to get an abortion," Cheryl said, turning to Doris with wide eyes. "You have to."

Doris's jawline set in the muted light of the moon. "No. Doug and I have to take responsibility. He proposed at the party." She held up her left hand and showed them a tiny silver ring with a turquoise heart. "We're getting married."

"You're in high school," Cheryl cried. "You can't do that! Don't fuck up your life."

"What am I supposed to do?" Doris demanded. "Kill my baby?"

"Be responsible," Cheryl said. "What about your scholarship? You can tour with the soccer team after college. You can *do* something with your life."

"Not anymore," Doris said, bowing her head. Her permed hair fell in a messy sheath, blocking her face. "I made a mistake and now I have to live with it."

In spite of how brave Doris was pretending to be, Jackie knew how much this mistake hurt her. Brushing blue mascara-ed tears off her face with one hand, Jackie had touched Doris's hair with the other. The three friends sat in the car for an hour that night, silent, as the spring evening settled around them.

Doris went forward with her plans. When the recruiters found out her situation, Doris lost her scholarship, just like they knew she would. As Jackie packed her bags for the Art Institute and Cheryl for the University of Michigan, Doris started buying items for a nursery and coordinating married housing. She and Doug got married at the courthouse.

When the miscarriage happened, Doris had been devastated at first and then giddy with relief. She was up and out of the hospital bed within the day, back on the phone with recruiters, making plans to head to Florida State for the second semester. Jackie and Cheryl sat in the apartment she shared with Doug, watching as Doris packed her things.

When Doug came home, he had looked at Doris in surprise. "What are you doing?" he asked. Without answering, Doris set down her bag, went into the bathroom and shut the door.

A half hour later, the families arrived. Jackie and Cheryl left then, but not before realizing that Doris might have gotten herself into something she couldn't get out of. Doug's family had their son's future mapped out. Whether Doris liked it or not, her name was on his marriage certificate and some accountability came with that.

Later, Jackie learned that their perception had been all wrong. It hadn't been Doug's family who had made Doris stay in the marriage. Doris's mother had convinced her to go through with it. Holding her sobbing daughter, she'd said, "Doug loves you and he wants to take care of you. What's so wrong with that?"

"I want to play soccer," Doris had wailed, "and have a fun life."

Smoothing Doris's hair, her mother had said, "You have to be smarter than that, Doris. Women get old. I know you don't believe me now but you'll get cellulite on your legs, and your breasts will sag and your face will get fat. Would you rather have five years of adventure or a lifetime of security?"

"That's the most old-fashioned crock of shit I've ever heard," Cheryl cried when she heard the story. "A woman doesn't just have to rely on looks. What about the brain in her head?"

Either way, Doris's bed was made. So she lay in it—with Doug—and was pregnant again by twenty-four. When they went shopping for baby stuff together, Doris seemed thrilled with her new life. She had grabbed for every cute decoration within reach: little ducky murals, a blue and silver star mobile and fuzzy white baby blankets. "After this we're getting cheesecake," Doris cried, arms full of baby paraphernalia.

"Cheesecake?" Cheryl repeated, pulling up her own shirt and patting her tight stomach. "Really?"

"Absolutely," Doris said. "You two might get to have exciting lives, but I get to get really, really fat!"

Now, Jackie sneaked a peek at her old friend and shook her head. Doris had achieved her goal. Even though she wore the weight well, she looked a lot older than her thirty-nine years. There were tiny grays peeking out from the areas around her ears and a worry wrinkle had set up shop right in the middle of her forehead. Jackie half-expected the glasses to fall forward and rest like grandma lenses on the tip of Doris's nose.

"*Quel dommage,*" Jackie said, giving it up. She stretched, adjusting her fluffy pink socks. "I can't force you to have fun but just so you know, I'll just be out here all night, sneaking sips from your liquor cabinet."

Doris grinned, nudging her with her foot. Jackie took the opportunity to leap across the couch and pull Doris into a hug. "*Bonsoir,*" she said affectionately. "And, darling, just let me know what I can do for you. I understand you might be mad that I left for so long but . . ."

"No," Doris's body stiffened and she pulled back, grabbing Jackie's hands. "I'm so happy you're back. I just . . ." A key turned in the door.

"Is that Mandy?" Jackie cried, leaping to her feet.

Doris's face fell. "Good night," she said quickly, racing out of the room just as her daughter bounced in, red hair flying.

"Look how fun you are," Jackie said, admiring her. The child beamed and spun around. She was wearing a cute little blue T-shirt with tiny light blue horses scampering across it, accessorized with five different necklaces of assorted beads, charms, and colors. "Did you have fun at practice?"

According to Doris, Mandy was on the volleyball team, a member of student council, debate club, Spanish club, forensics, theater, and who knew what else. Like mother, like daughter . . . like all three of them when they were her age.

"Come, come." Jackie pulled Mandy to the couch and plunked her down, grinning from ear to ear. Mandy was the closest thing to a child Jackie was ever going to get. She and Robert had considered having children once but figured there would always be time. "What were you listening to?"

Mandy passed over her headset and Jackie pushed the silver buds into her ears. Since Mandy was watching her, Jackie made a big deal out of rocking out to the beat of the pulsing music. Mandy burst out laughing. After a minute, she reached over and pressed the Pause button, helping Jackie extract herself from the cord.

"I'm going to take dance in the spring," Mandy gushed, stretching out her long legs. "I can't believe I haven't done it before. Boys love dancers."

"Do all the boys love you?" Jackie teased.

Mandy nodded but her face went serious, red hair flopping over one eye. She looked around the darkened room. "Look, did my dad leave?"

Jackie's heart sank. "I thought your mother had a conversation with you about that."

Mandy pursed her lips, just like Doris always did. "Mom's been avoiding me. I haven't gotten any real answers out of her in weeks."

Jackie felt a little thrill, hearing Mandy form such an adult sentence. She could still remember when Mandy was waddling around this house in diapers, red hair sticking up all over her head. She loved to hunt for electrical outlets, reaching her chubby hands toward childproofed plugs and muttering, "Touch."

Now, the grown-up version persisted, "So, he left?"

Jackie held up a hand, listening. She could hear water running in Doris's bathroom.

"*Je ne sais pas.* He's just . . . finding himself again."

There was silence and then a jingling sound. Mandy was rhythmically thumbing a silver charm that hung from her bracelet. "Huh," she said.

"You okay?" Jackie tried to catch the teen's eye.

Mandy shrugged. "I mean . . . it's not like it wasn't a matter of time or whatever. My mom's crazy."

"Do not talk about your mother that way," Jackie said sharply.

Mandy's eyes filled with tears. "Oh, baby," Jackie said, immediately feeling bad. "I'm sorry, but your mother's going through a hard time right now . . ."

"What about me?" Mandy cried.

"I know," Jackie assured her, pulling her in for a hug. "But arguing with her over every little thing will just make things worse. Darling, I could've told you years ago that your father would have some midlife crisis and take off. They got married so young. He just needs a little time, then he'll come back."

Mandy sniffled. "Are you sure?"

"Positive," Jackie lied. "Now, let's talk about *you*. Why are you having a hard time?" Jackie asked, wiping away the young girl's tears.

Mandy hesitated. "Mom's in bed, right?" When Jackie nodded, Mandy said, "I thought I was pregnant."

"No," Jackie cried. Déjà vu all over again. Lowering her voice, she said, "But . . . you're not, right?"

"No. That was a while ago. A month or two," Mandy said in a rush. "I was scared. Mom doesn't even know I have a boyfriend. She'd flip her shit."

True. Doris wouldn't want Mandy to make the same mistakes she had, but Jackie doubted Mandy even knew about that mistake. It was hardly something her parents would advertise.

"How did this happen?" Jackie said. "What were you using?"

"Condoms."

"Yikes," Jackie cringed. "Not super reliable. Is that what you're using now?"

Mandy studied her jeans. "We stopped doing it. Since then. But it's so hard."

"Why don't you get on the pill?" Jackie said. "I mean, you'll have to use a condom, too, but . . ."

Mandy looked at her like she had nine heads. "How? I need permission."

"I'll give you permission," Jackie said. Before she knew what was happening, Mandy had her arms back around her and was sobbing again. "Oh, honey," Jackie said, patting her back in confusion. "I don't understand. What's the matter now?"

"I'm just . . . It's so easy with you. You don't judge me," Mandy told her. "Mom is just so . . . we fight all the time . . ."

"I know, but she's your mother," Jackie said, patting her back. The young girl was heaving with sobs and Jackie was reminded of how important everything is at that age. So much emotion. The slightest trouble felt like the end of the world. "It's her job."

"She just doesn't understand," Mandy hiccuped. "I really wish she did."

Jackie reached her hand forward. "I bet she would. Give your mother time," Jackie suggested. "I can talk to her."

"Not about this!" Mandy panicked, drawing back.

"No, no, no," Jackie promised. "But you need to be nicer to her and she . . . she probably needs to be a bit nicer to you." They sat in silence for a minute. "Should we listen to music again?" she tried.

Mandy leaned back against the couch cushions and nodded. Handing one ear bud to Jackie, she stuck the other in her ear. The two friends listened to the pounding music in silence, sitting side by side.

DORIS WAS LYING awake in her bed, fighting off panic attacks. She had run out of the living room because she didn't want to witness Mandy drooling all over Jackie. Plus, Mandy would press her with more questions about Doug. She hadn't wanted to lie to her daughter but Doris didn't know what response to give. She didn't know if and when Doug was coming home. Claiming he was on a business trip was just going to have to do for the time being. The idea that Doug might never come home repeated itself in her mind. Another wave of panic washed over her, as excruciating as childbirth.

Doris fixated on the ceiling, intent, taking measured breaths. She really wished Jackie hadn't taken it upon herself to throw out the Xanax. That morning, she had fumbled around for it everywhere but it was nowhere to be found. When she finally went into the guest bedroom, hands on hips and sweating, Jackie had looked up from the book she was reading and said, "The Xanax? Yeah. Flushed it," and Doris had slammed out of the room.

In the morning, Doris would call her doctor and get a refill. Doris hated to imagine the silence that would meet her request. It would certainly raise some eyebrows, considering the most recent bottle had been prescribed last week, but Doris didn't care. She would tell him the truth and if that didn't work, she'd figure out a way to get another bottle somehow. At this point, Doris would do anything to stop the images inside of her head—the movie frames of Katherine on the back of her husband's motorcycle, Katherine touching his body, Katherine undressing him with those overly made-up eyes . . . If the doctor could see all that, he'd probably prescribe her a *truckload* of Xanax, no questions asked.

Lying in bed, something new dawned on Doris. For the first time, she wondered if Doug had been lying about going on a road trip. She hadn't called his office to see if he'd cashed in all that vacation time he'd saved up. Maybe the road trip was an alibi and in truth, her husband was living at Katherine Rigney's right now, having the time of his life. Maybe they were both laughing at poor, stupid Doris for ever believing her straightlaced husband would actually go on a cross-country trip. Maybe they were sitting on that motorcycle, peeling off layer after layer of trashy lingerie . . .

Doris shot straight up in bed. She shook the images from her head. It was time to stop whining and take some action. She was going to find out what had happened to her marriage. Either way, Katherine Rigney was going to pay.

Chapter Sixteen

THE VIBRATION OF CHERYL'S CURSED BLACKBERRY JOLTED HER out of a half-sleep. She cracked open her eyes, looking around the den in confusion. She hadn't even made it to her pint of ice cream, simply dozed off on the couch three pages into Hillary Clinton's biography.

Hopefully, Cheryl glanced at her phone—maybe the offer on Millstines had gone through. She hoped so. Cheryl was desperate to get to work on something. Lying around her house all the time just wasn't cutting it. "This is Cheryl," she said.

"This is Andy," a deep voice echoed.

Cheryl yanked the phone away from her ear and stared at it as though it were a snake.

"Hello?" he spoke into her silence. "Did I lose you?"

"Hello, Andy," she said, voice like a glacier. "What can I do for you?"

Cheryl had no problem being rude to Andy. She felt an unreasonable flood of anger at this guy she barely knew because:

1. He had infiltrated her health club, worn distracting gym shorts, and ultimately, thrown her off her game enough to get hit in the head with a racquetball.
2. He had allowed Stan to steal her BlackBerry, had not stolen it back, and had basically abetted Stan in seeing the files that had caused her to get fired.
3. He had not bothered to call and apologize for setting into motion the chain of events that, ultimately, he was completely responsible for—thanks to those stupid, distracting gym shorts.

Completely oblivious to her rage, Andy's voice came out smooth as sugar. "I was calling to see how you're feeling."

The Hillary biography fell off her lap with a loud thud. "Thank you so much," Cheryl said, matching his tone. "Do you mean my feelings about *getting fired*? Something that happened well over a week ago?"

"Look, what happened at TurnKey was wrong," Andy said. "I'd like to take you out to dinner and talk about it."

Cheryl glared at the receiver. "Not interested," she told him. "But thanks so much for calling." Deliberately, she pressed End and tossed her phone to the other end of the couch. She eyed the screen, challenging it to light up with a call-back. It didn't. That was the end of that. Fired or not, Cheryl was still in control.

Ding-Dong.

Cheryl jumped. Was that the doorbell? She wasn't expecting anybody. Nobody would dare drop in on her except . . . Jackie! Oh, good. Before Cheryl had fallen asleep, she had been thinking about calling Jackie anyway. They could have some wine and make plans for the restaurant and Cheryl would have to give her the dish on the audacity of this Andy character.

Taking the steps up to the living room two at a time, Cheryl turned on the porch light and peeked out the peephole. She drew back, gasping in surprise. *He* was standing there, wearing a heavy black wool overcoat and clutching a bouquet of . . . she peered again through the door . . . roses?

Ding-Dong.

Damn. She'd turned on the porch light, so pretending she wasn't home was a useless prospect.

Ding-Dong. Ding-Dong. DING DONG.

Was he insane? A serial killer? Cheryl threw open the door, hand firmly planted on her hip. "What the hell are you doing here?"

"It's freezing outside," Andy complained, pushing his way into her home.

"I didn't invite you in," she cried, but he'd already moved past her, into the living room by her fake fire, rubbing his hands together in earnest. The flowers had been unceremoniously dumped on her leather sofa.

"Freezing," he repeated, stomping his feet. "This is the coldest October I've ever dealt with in all my life."

Cheryl watched him, dumbfounded. "Stop getting snow on my floor," was all she could think of to say.

Immediately, Andy looked at the tracks of moisture he'd left and said, "Whoops. Sorry." He took his shoes off and carried them back to the foyer. There, he set them down, toes pointed neatly at the wall, right next to her high-heeled black boots.

"Andy, not to be rude," Cheryl said, "not that rudeness is something you're aware of, considering you've just *stomped* your way into my home . . . but I am going to ask you nicely, before I call the police to have you physically removed, what the hell are you doing here?"

As she spoke, Andy walked through the room, picking up her framed photographs and studying them one at a time. "Ha," he said, pointing at one. "Your hair is long. Looks good. Listen, it's freezing out there. Do you have anything warm to drink?"

"No."

"Bummer," Andy said, setting down a photograph. "Well, it's probably best not to drink before getting on the road. I made us a reservation at Blackburn, which we can make . . ." Andy glanced at his watch, "if we leave here in ten minutes. Can you do it?"

For a moment, Cheryl thought he was joking, but at Andy's

earnest expression, she couldn't help but burst out laughing. "I can't believe this. You got stood up. That could be the only explanation for you standing here in my house, uninvited, telling me I'm having dinner with you."

"That's not true," Andy said, rushing to the sofa and picking up the roses. "By the way, these are for you."

"You definitely got stood up." Cheryl nodded, crossing her arms. She made no move to take the flowers.

"Think what you want," Andy said, grinning until his dimple showed. "But I really did buy these for you. Not a big deal. These were on sale at the gas station for, like, four bucks. Just a 'Sorry you got fired' kinda thing."

Cheryl recognized the sheer red paper around the stems of the bouquet. The flowers were from Bramble's, an exclusive greenhouse down the road. The wrapping alone cost more than four dollars.

"I'll just leave these here," Andy said, setting them back down on the couch and unbuttoning his coat. He was wearing a black cashmere sweater and tailored slacks. That same woodsy scent she smelled before fainting at the Racquet Club wafted toward her. For a moment, the two stood still, evaluating each other. Then, Andy's eyes roved over her body. Cheryl was wearing a pair of rose-colored velour sweats.

"I see you're not dressed for dinner," he said. "I would have told you to put on something nice , but your phone cut out."

"It didn't cut out, I hung up on you," she said.

Andy grinned. Glancing pointedly at his watch, he said, "Cheryl, we really gotta go."

Cheryl looked at him in disbelief, turned on her heel, and stalked up the stairs and into her bedroom, slamming the door. There, she took a couple of deep breaths, then ran to the mirror and checked her reflection. In spite of the sweats, she looked good. Eyes bright, skin glowing from a peel she'd given herself the night before . . . maybe her eyebrows were a little too thin . . .

"What am I doing?" she said out loud. "I'm not going to dinner with that little weasel."

Clapping a hand over her mouth, Cheryl looked toward the door and wondered if Andy could hear what she had said all the way from the living room. She half hoped he had. It was the perfect description. Andy was a weasel. He'd weaseled his way into her company and stolen her job. Now, he had weaseled into her home and was trying to force her to go to dinner. What did he really want?

"Who cares?" she finally said out loud, remembering her favorite mantra. "What do *you* want?"

Suddenly, an idea popped into her head. Cheryl stood stock-still, then burst out laughing. She had thought of just the thing to wipe that cocky grin right off Andy's face.

Throwing open her closet door, Cheryl started digging for a pair of red stilettos and her most scandalous dress.

Chapter Seventeen

DORIS SNEAKED OUT OF THE HOUSE THE MOMENT SHE HEARD THE guest bedroom door shut. Jackie was going to bed. Doris was going for revenge.

Waiting patiently had not been easy. Once Doris had come up with her idea and gotten dressed in black from head to toe, she had waited by her bedroom door, breathing heavily. After what felt like two hours, Jackie and Mandy said their good nights and headed off to bed.

The second the doors clicked shut, Doris shot out of the bedroom and scampered down the stairs. Stealthily, she grabbed supplies from the refrigerator and the storage cabinet. Taking one last look around, she darted into the garage.

There, she piled everything into the trunk of her car and pulled a stocking cap onto her head. As she backed her Lexus out of the garage, Doris glanced at herself in the rearview mirror. She looked like a criminal but it was necessary. If things got harried, she could just pull the mask over her face like a bank robber. And if she actually did get caught . . . well, it wasn't like Jackie couldn't afford to post bail.

The arsenal of revenge supplies crashed against each other in the cargo area as she drove toward Katherine Rigney's. Doris decided that it was the five cans of shaving cream that were so loud. She was grateful she had thought to wrap the carton of eggs in bubble wrap and settle the package in between the six rolls of toilet paper. The last time Doris was at Sam's Club, she'd debated about keeping her membership. Now she was a firm believer.

Doris's heart pounded as she navigated the evening streets. Maybe she should have asked for Jackie's help with the prank, but Jackie would probably consider this particular felony a little beyond fun and games. As she drove, Doris noticed that most houses around town were dark; she pictured married couples safely asleep in their beds. Another flash of Katherine and Doug plowed through her mind and Doris hit the gas.

When she got to Katherine Rigney's neighborhood, Doris realized it was in a sketchy part of town. This did not surprise her. No one waltzed around with her chest out that far if she wasn't looking for something better. Driving past the beat-up vehicles parked on the side of the street, Doris suddenly realized the Lexus was a tactical error. In this neighborhood, it was about as discreet as a twenty-four-foot Ryder truck.

The address she'd scratched into her notepad matched the plain brick house to her left. Doris sank low into the front seat and slowed the car to a crawl and stared. A chartreuse Camaro sat idle in the garage. Its pink, fluffy mirror dice seemed to be advertising for Katherine like something out of Amsterdam's red-light district. Doug's motorcycle was nowhere in sight but that didn't mean anything. It could be parked on the street, hidden behind the house, or even left behind at a bar somewhere, for all she knew. There was still a chance he was there, and for that, Katherine Rigney was going to pay.

Several hundred feet down the block, Doris eased to a halt. She parked under a weeping willow tree that half-concealed her vehicle. Getting out, she furtively looked around. There was no sound. Everyone seemed to be asleep. The only sign of life was the distant barking of a dog. The snow had stopped falling a day or two ago and had it been daylight, Doris could have seen the warning signs of additional neighborhood dogs in the yellowed and burnished snow. But it was pitch-black, so she went straight into her mission without a fair assessment of What Could Go Wrong.

Doris grabbed supplies from the cargo area, breathing heavily. Everything seemed louder in these heightened circumstances—the hatch clicked like a gunshot, her boots crunched across Katherine's driveway like it was made of broken glass, and her heart pounded louder than a car outfitted with ghetto-bass. Doris stopped suddenly, wondering if Katherine might be watching her from the window or if she was in bed with Doug, chomping gum and moaning into his ear.

That was just the thought Doris needed to swallow her fear and commit her crime. Furiously, she ducked into the garage and got to work cracking eggs. The yellow liquid drizzled all over the hood of Katherine's car and dripped stickily into the vent openings. When summer came, Doris wanted that unexpected, sulfuric stench to blast through the heater as a reminder that everything about Katherine stank. Doris also counted on the egg eating away the paint job, lightening the cheerful chartreuse to a pukey pea green.

Shaking the can of shaving cream, Doris thought back to the time her friends had used shaving cream to paint "Just Married" on her parents' car, after Doris and Doug got married at the courthouse. They even tied aluminum cans to the back tailpipe and covered the car with silly string. Doris and Doug had held each other, laughing hysterically, so young and in love. Doris wished she could go back in time now and tell that young version of herself not to be such a sucker; not to give up her dreams for some man who would eventually break her heart.

A sudden shuffling sound broke through the memory and Doris

froze. Looking at her gooey hands and the work she'd already completed, she had a sickly moment of knowing she was about to get caught red-handed. Should she run? Try to escape? Doris's legs went weak. It was like one of those nightmares she'd had as a teen, where the soccer field was made of quicksand as she stood in the middle of it, naked.

"Hello?" she dared whisper, looking around. She gripped the cold can and got ready to swing. It wasn't much, but it could serve as a weapon if she needed it. "Who's there?"

A low growl cut through the garage. The hair on the back of her neck stood up. Slowly, Doris peeked over her shoulder. She squealed in terror. A large dog with yellow eyes was staring right at her.

Chapter Eighteen

Sitting in Andy's car, Cheryl waited until he pulled out of the driveway before she removed her coat. From the corner of her eye, she saw Andy do a double take at her shocking attire.

Cheryl's dress was skintight, electric blue, and maximized her A cup to its full potential, especially with the water bra she had put on. Her red stilettos laced up and over her calves like something out of a dominatrix video. Instead of wearing lace stockings, which would have been more appropriate, Cheryl was sporting bare legs and outrageous underwear. Of course, Andy was not in on that part of the joke, but Cheryl thought the fire-engine red thong that matched her shoes was hilarious.

"Great pick on the restaurant," Cheryl said. Her voice was flip and sarcastic, barely her own. "My friend Doris got dumped by her husband at Blackburn."

"I'm sorry to hear that," Andy said, sneaking another look at her outfit. "Why don't we go somewhere else?"

"Not a chance," Cheryl said. She cranked up the radio.

"Take It on the Run" blasted through the speakers. Cheryl

reached over and pressed the button on her window, lowering it all the way. Icy air shot in and she sang at the top of her lungs, laughing inside as Andy reached over and turned up the heat. She knew every word and even drummed her knees with wild abandon. She and Andy didn't speak the rest of the way there.

When they pulled in, Cheryl hopped out and gave a huge smile to the valet. Skipping ahead of him, she walked up to the hostess stand and said loudly, "TurnKey Marketing. Andy has a table."

Andy came up behind her, smiling apologetically at the hostess. Cheryl tossed her coat at him and allowed Andy to take in the full effect of her dress for the first time. To his credit, he did not blush at her ridiculous appearance. He just smiled.

The hostess led them to a far corner, taking them around the back of the restaurant instead of through the center. "I've never been this way," Cheryl gloated. "I must be a total eyesore."

"You must be trying to be," Andy said, pulling out her chair.

Cheryl flopped down and dropped her purse on the table. "Well?" she said.

"Well, what?" Andy took his time picking up the wine list, read it through, and finally studied her over the top of it. Once the waiter came over and the wine order was placed, Andy said, "Cheryl, I know you're angry. I'm sorry about what happened at TurnKey."

"What happened at TurnKey?" Cheryl asked, fiddling with a tiny corner of her cloth napkin. It had been folded into some shape and she deliberately pushed it until it collapsed.

"I didn't know what Stan was up to," Andy insisted, leaning forward. His green eyes were bright, with hazel speckles. Cheryl remembered when she had passed out, waking up to find herself looking into those eyes. "I had actually left for a family thing that day . . ."

Cheryl turned away. Snapping her fingers loudly, she gestured at a waiter. He bustled right over. "Hi," she said. "Could I get an appetizer?"

"What would madame care for?"

"You're paying, right?" she asked Andy. At his nod, she said, "Whatever's most expensive." The waiter nodded and ducked away from the table. Turning back to Andy, she said, "Continue."

"I know you're furious, Cheryl," Andy said, "but there's no point in taking it out on me. I'm on your side. You built that company up and Stan . . ."

"Excuse me," Cheryl snapped her fingers again. After a busboy registered polite surprise on his face, he set down a bottle of water and came running. "This music is too loud," Cheryl said sweetly. "Can we kill it? Thanks."

The table next to Cheryl and Andy had been half-listening to Cheryl's demands. At this one, they peered up toward the speakers as though there was something wrong with their hearing. Cheryl almost laughed out loud. The music really was at such a low decibel that it could have been mistaken for someone's ringtone, but she planned to draw as much unsatisfactory attention to her and Andy as possible.

"You didn't mind loud music in the car," Andy pointed out. Cheryl let a beat pass and just as Andy opened his mouth to continue his speech Cheryl shrieked and jumped up on top of her chair.

"Oh, no! A mouse," she cried, gesturing at the floor. A panicked hush swept over their area of the restaurant. Cheryl peered at an area under the table and said loudly, "Whoops. Sorry . . . sorry . . . it's just someone's handbag. Sorry." She climbed down, deliberately letting her dress creep up. Andy stared at her in dismay.

The sommelier cleared his throat, approached and displayed the bottle, which happened to be from one of Cheryl's favorite vineyards and a very good year. She took a deep breath, calling on all of her inner theatrics. The second the ruby red liquid flowed into Andy's glass, she snatched the glass, took a swig, and spit the wine in her napkin. "Send it back," she proclaimed, waving her hands dramatically. "It's like vinegar. Send it back!"

All the tables surrounding them were now staring openly. Andy's eyes had darkened slightly and he nodded at the waiter, who went away to get a different bottle of wine. Running his hands through his hair, Andy glanced up toward the heavens as though for strength.

"Tell me something," he finally said, leaning forward and speaking in a hushed tone. "Are you acting this way to prove that you are still in control? That getting fired from the job you loved didn't affect you?"

Cheryl shrugged. "This is out-of-the-office Cheryl. Don't assume you know her."

"Don't assume I want to."

She blinked. Ouch.

Cheryl decided to squelch her performance for a minute; the element of surprise and all that, a critical part of war. Ladylike, she folded her hands. "Do you want to leave?" she asked primly.

Andy's shoulders had slumped slightly. He was fiddling with his silverware, scraping the fork across the tablecloth as though it were part of a Zen garden set. For a reason she didn't even begin to understand, Cheryl yearned to reach out and stroke the light stubble that lined his jaw. She was being hard on him. Regardless of what Stan said about Andy's promotability, her firing had nothing to do with him and she knew it.

"We can go," she conceded. "This is stupid. Let's go."

"Nah," he said. "I like the food." Andy cleared his throat and adjusted the sleeves of his sweater.

Cautiously, the sommelier approached the table and presented another bottle of the same wine. Andy tasted it, then amazingly, offered the glass to Cheryl. The tables around them tilted forward in eager anticipation but she shook her head, declining the sip. The sommelier flashed his teeth in relief, pouring. Andy took a long drink.

After a tense moment, she tried hers. "That's really good," Cheryl admitted, in spite of herself. "Good choice."

Andy brightened. "It's my favorite. Sorry the first bottle was bad."

It wasn't, she thought. *I was.*

A waiter approached then, with a steaming whole lobster on a platter. Its claws were raised to the sky, as though in surrender. "What on earth is that?" Cheryl gasped.

"Your appetizer, madame?" the waiter said nervously.

Her mouth fell open. She met Andy's eyes. At the sight of the ridiculous appetizer, they both burst out laughing.

"This'd better be good." Andy chuckled, and they dug in.

Chapter Nineteen

THE YELLOW DOG BARED ITS TEETH, GROWLING ANGRILY. IT WAS wearing a black collar with little silver studs, looking like the canine version of a motorcycle thug. Fitting.

Doris was frozen with fear. She couldn't believe her life had come to this, culminating in a dog tearing her apart limb by limb in Katherine Rigney's garage. As she thought this over, the dog let out another low, deliberate growl.

I don't want to die, a little voice inside of her whispered.

Doris was surprised. Her life had taken on such a gray pallor that she may as well have one foot in the grave. To be honest, there were times recently when she *had* wondered if she wouldn't be better off dead.

DO something, the voice insisted. *Change something. Just please don't get torn apart by a wild dog!*

"I won't. I don't want to die," she said, as though it were a revelation. "*I don't want to die.* Hey, doggie. Please . . . Doggie, doggie, doggie . . ."

The words sounded very similar to "Dougie, Dougie, Dougie."

At that thought, hot tears smarted against the backs of her eyes. The dog moved forward, slightly. A tuft of scraggly hair stood up on the back of his neck like a misplaced Mohawk.

"Nice doggie . . ." Doris fumbled around her supplies, until she found an almost full carton of eggs. "Yummy, yummy," she tried. "Hey, doggie, here you go . . ."

She tossed a couple of eggs onto the pavement, as far away from her as she could. The eggs broke, yellow yolks oozing like molasses in the forty-degree weather. The dog sniffed the air, looked at Doris suspiciously, then whimpered slightly.

"Come on, doggie. Yum yum . . ."

The beady eyes softened. With Olympic dexterity, the dog pounced on the broken eggs. Razor-sharp teeth tore into the meal, shells and everything. Doris didn't wait. With a trail of toilet paper streaming behind her, she took off at a full run, praying her boots wouldn't slip on the icy ground.

It took a few precious moments for the dog to realize what had happened. By that time Doris was halfway across the yard. She'd always been a fast runner. Back in the day, she and Cheryl used to have sprinting contests after soccer practice and Doris would always win. Doris was relieved she still had the ability when it counted. At the first disgruntled yelp, Doris quickened her pace as those strong paws thundered on the ground behind her. The dog came at full speed, barking and snapping angrily at her heels. Smelly breath panted hot and heavy just behind her. Doris screamed and flailed her arms as she ran. The lights in the neighborhood turned on one by one.

Doris leaped into her car, slamming her door shut just in time. The large, hairy body leaped up against the window, its teeth snapping dangerously. Doris stared at the dog, dumbfounded. Then, she peeled out from under the weeping willow and down the street, the dog racing behind and barking furiously.

"Thank you, God, thank you, Jesus, thank you, automatic locks," she panted.

As she drove by Katherine's, Doris swiveled her head to see if the lights had come on. They had. As Doris sped by, she watched Katherine throw open her door and walk out onto her porch, pulling a sweater around her bony shoulders. Doris's heart leaped. He was not with her.

Katherine was all alone.

Chapter Twenty

WHEN THE WAITER SET THE BILL ON THE TABLE, CHERYL GAVE A tiny frown. Reaching for her purse, she tried to pull out her wallet.

Andy said, "What do you think you're doing?" and yanked the calligraphy-written check out of her hands. "No way," he scolded. "Dinner's on me, just like I promised."

"I was horrible," Cheryl said. "I'm paying." She reached for the bill again but he held it out of reach, its white leather holder glistening in the candlelight. "Andy, let me at least pay for the appetizer. Give it to me or I will . . . ooph . . ." Cheryl tried one more good grab. Finally, she gave up and leaned back in her chair. "Thank you."

"Thank *you*." Andy grinned, slipping an American Express into the bill jacket.

Cheryl chewed the inside of her cheek. Her mind was working overtime. The dinner had been way too much fun, once she'd stopped punishing Andy. The conversation between them had been fantastic, and Cheryl had to admit, Andy deserved to be the cocky guy he was. He was well educated, well traveled, and (as she'd seen in his gym shorts) well endowed. He'd spent several years in New York City and regaled her with various stories of battling the subway system through his three internships.

"I think I had at least five boyfriends," Andy said, tallying the memory on his fingers. "There were these homeless guys who loved me. Whenever I'd get on the train, they'd bypass everyone else and come sit by me. I was felt up. Many times."

Cheryl could relate to city life. Her early years had been spent in Chicago, navigating the subway system and doing everything possible to avoid the ridiculous wind chill. "I moved there after college," she told him. "I was so poor. My diet consisted of Ragu. Breakfast, lunch, and dinner." She went on to admit that the only apartment she could afford was right by the El train. "It served as a surrogate child, waking me up every fifteen minutes. I didn't sleep for four years."

"What about your family?" Andy asked. "They couldn't help you?" Cheryl opened her mouth to speak but Andy held up his hand. "Oh, wait. I know. You wanted to do it on your own."

"Of course," Cheryl said. "My family wasn't rich or anything but yeah, they would have helped if I'd asked. I didn't, so in the end I think my overall exhaustion is what made me say yes to my ex-husband's marriage proposal."

Andy gawked, straightening his napkin. "*You* had a husband?"

"Yeah," Cheryl felt a smile pull at the corners of her mouth. "I know it may shock you but we gave it the good old college try. We even joined a couples' golf league."

Andy's green eyes sparkled. "He must have been a bad player."

"Actually, *he* was a team player," she admitted, chewing the inside of her mouth. Cheryl remembered how she had brought another man to their bed during her lunch hour. At night, she'd sometimes look over at Sean's curled-up form and wonder if he could sense it. "But I wasn't," she admitted. "I'm not proud of that, just in case you're wondering."

Cheryl dipped her spoon into the remainder of her crème brûlée. It was a perfect blend of custard and fresh berries, with burned sugar crusted over the top. Closing her eyes, she savored the last bite and let the sweetness salve her old guilt. When she opened her eyes, Andy was watching her with a knowing smirk.

"Glad we ordered that after all," he said.

When the waiter had come over with the dessert tray, Cheryl had attempted to claim she wasn't a dessert person. She said she would only have a bite of whatever Andy ordered. He had nodded seriously and then ordered two.

"Did you get enough?" Andy said, pushing his dish forward. Half of his dessert still remained. "It's all yours."

Cheryl shook her head and took a sip of her coffee. "You are truly insane if you think I'm going to eat that."

The waiter returned with the bill and Andy glanced at it, not batting an eye. He signed and pocketed the receipt, pushing the leather holder to the side of the table. After drumming his fingers for a moment, he leaned forward.

"Cheryl, can I ask you something?" Andy wondered. Cheryl nodded, waiting for him to ask if she was seeing anyone or if she still had feelings for her ex-husband. Instead, he said, "Do you think you're going to sue Stan?"

Cheryl choked on her coffee and took a long sip of water. "Excuse me?"

"I'm sure you feel that you were wrongfully terminated," Andy said. "Do you think you're going to go after him?"

Cheryl's eyes were steely as they met his. "Newsflash—the first thing I told Stan was that I was going to sue his fat ass."

"Oh." Andy nodded, face blank. "When are you doing it?"

Cheryl set her face into a calm mask. "Well, I have appointments set with a couple of lawyers but I'm curious to see if I even have a case. Stan had official warning papers. To be honest, I don't have anything other than a track record of impeccable employment and a paper trail of a million dollars worth of clients I obtained, but whatever. The official papers might carry more weight." Cheryl stared Andy down. "So, are you supposed to get back to Stan on this tonight or tomorrow?"

"I'm not getting back to Stan on anything." Andy chuckled, stretching. "If I was in your shoes, I'd be doing the same thing. If you already told him, then he knows you're doing it anyway."

Cheryl studied Andy for a moment. His green eyes were sincere but she still didn't trust him. Even if Stan hadn't sent him directly, Andy was definitely trying to figure out some tidbit to bring to her former boss. For fun, Cheryl decided to throw him some information; just enough to really freak Stan out.

"To tell you the truth, Stan should be worried." Cheryl leaned forward onto her elbows to display just the right amount of cleavage. "I will be able to prove my computer was tampered with. Someone is planning to sneak me out the hard drive."

In reality, Blake had sneaked her out the hard drive just two days after she'd been fired. Blake had recommended the best computer wizards he knew so that she could determine exactly when her presentation for Fitzgibbon Ale had been deleted. But if Andy really was a rat, it was fun to let him think he still had a chance to stop the hard drive from leaving the office.

Andy's eyebrows shot up. "That's too dangerous. That person could get caught. He could get fired!"

Cheryl smiled. "Stan only fires people who bring the company millions of dollars in business, remember? Besides, he won't get caught, because what I'm telling you is confidential."

Andy shifted in his seat, then nodded. "I know what you're thinking and you're wrong. Stan didn't send me, I'm not going to run back with a report on you, and I won't tell him anything you said, even if he asks. Okay?"

Cheryl ran her finger around the edge of the coffee cup. When she looked up, Andy was still watching her, intent. He gave a little smile and Cheryl looked down again, suddenly confused.

What if he *hadn't* been sent by Stan to spy on her? Either the guy was an exceptionally good liar or this *was* supposed to be a date. If so, it was the most unusual one she'd ever been on. Cheryl couldn't believe he'd brought her flowers. That was something Sean, in all the years they were together, had never done.

Every time Cheryl thought about her ex-husband, she felt sick. The thoughts were always so petty. It was almost as though her mind was on a continuous campaign to convince her that the quiet, kind man she'd once pledged her life to had been a bad guy. That way, Cheryl wouldn't have to go through the rest of her life with a noose around her neck for ruining a marriage that most people would have been fine with. She couldn't believe her love had been dictated by something as foolish as a foam finger. That foam finger had started and finished her relationship.

It had all begun at a Cubs game, back when she was still living in Chicago. It had been one of those hot summer days when even the lakeside breeze was lazy, refusing to push away the dust and humidity of the city. The only way to handle the heat was to cool off with icy beer. So, Cheryl met up with Sean and a group of friends for a morning of drinking in Lincoln Park. Slowly, they worked their way toward the game in Wrigleyville.

That day, Cheryl had gone into their date ready to cut Sean loose. Sean was a fine enough Mr. Right Now, with his thin brown hair, lanky body, and obvious interest in her, but there wasn't anything special about him or his mediocre ambition as a draftsman. There was another guy in the group Cheryl had her eye on, someone as loud and as ambitious as she was. By the end of the day, she planned to be rid of Sean and stumbling home with Charlie. As she tucked her long hair up into a ponytail, shimmied her body into a tight Cubs T-shirt and saggy jean shorts, Cheryl practiced her exit speech. "It's not you, it's me," she recited. "I just need some time to myself."

When she and Sean were drinking at the bar in Lincoln Park, there was a quick moment when Cheryl almost said it but something stopped her. Maybe it was the bartender telling them a story about a couple of regulars who had just gotten married or . . . no. Cheryl remembered now. Sean had told some joke that everyone laughed at so hard and for so long that he was on cloud nine for an hour. Unwilling to burst his bubble, Cheryl threw back a few shots and decided to dump him at the baseball park. But by the time they finally stumbled through the gates at Wrigley Field, she was smashed. When Sean bought a blue foam finger from a vendor and held it up, everyone around him cheered. Cheryl looked on in surprise, then cried, "That's my boyfriend!"

From the start of the national anthem through the final pitch, Cheryl became transfixed by that fucking foam finger, and even more, by the way it transformed her date. Every time Sean raised that #1 for the crowd to see, the people around them would go nuts. Suddenly, she saw him as a warrior striving for greatness, the #1 symbolizing a mighty sword. That night, instead of getting "It's not you, it's me," Sean got Cheryl's first ever "I love you." As the years went by, Cheryl realized her mistake. The warrior she had seen in Sean that day had been a product of wishful thinking. Maybe it had been the beer talking or heat stroke but Sean could never live up to what she'd seen in him. Through no fault of his own, the Sean she had fallen in love with that day didn't exist.

Looking across the table at Andy, Cheryl wondered what would happen if she shared that story. She'd never told it to anyone before. At the sudden impulse, she set down her coffee and pushed back her chair. She and Andy weren't even friends. What on earth was she thinking?

"You ready?" he asked and she nodded.

From under her lashes, she sneaked a peek at him. Their eyes met. Lightning. Cheryl shivered, looking back down at her coffee.

"How's your head?" Andy said.

Cheryl gaped. "My *head*?"

Andy's eyes widened, realizing that his innocent question did sound graphic over the low murmur of the intimate restaurant. "No! I mean, your injury, your *cabeza* . . ." At Cheryl's smirk, he chuckled. "Never mind."

At the hostess stand, Andy helped her with her jacket. As she shrugged into it, Andy's hands accidentally brushed against her skin and Cheryl jumped. All the way to the valet stand, she relived the moment. Her skin was still hot, as though he'd branded her.

When the car pulled up, Andy raced to her door. He opened it and closed it behind her, then headed back to his side to pay. When he slid into the vehicle and clicked on the ignition, eighties funk blasted out of the speakers, full volume.

"I can't believe the valet didn't turn that off," Cheryl groaned.

Andy smiled. "It probably rocked his world."

The drive home was quiet. Lit jack-o'-lanterns smiled from windows and bright stars dotted the late night. When Cheryl finally turned to look at him, it struck her how masculine and firm Andy's profile was in the muted light. When they reached her house, Andy pulled up the driveway and shut off the ignition. He sat for a moment, then turned to her. Once again, their eyes met. After a long, silent moment Andy got out of the car and walked around to her side. As she got out, he took her arm.

"Don't want you to fall in those heels," he said.

His scent was already familiar. Cheryl breathed it in like pleasant cologne and walked as close to him as she could, enjoying the heat of his body. She wondered what it would be like to kiss him. At her front door, Cheryl waited.

And waited.

This was the moment the guy always did *something*, tried to con his way through her front door and into her bed. Andy wasn't trying anything. He was just standing there patiently, hands now stuffed into the pockets of his overcoat. The inaction was getting humiliating, so Cheryl crinkled up her nose in confusion, poking around in her purse. She found her keys and took them out as slowly as possible. Should *she* make the move? Invite him in?

No way, she decided. Guys came on to *her*.

"Well, thanks for dinner. That was a nice . . . gesture," she finally said, smiling up at him.

"You're welcome," Andy said. "It was good to see you."

Good to see her? What about seeing her naked? Cheryl bit her lip. "Okay, well . . ." She stuck her key in the door and turned it, looking over her shoulder with a seductive smile. He smiled back. Suddenly, she blurted it out. "Did you want to come in for a drink or anything?"

It hung in the air, awkward.

"I . . ." Andy looked away, back toward his car, then at the windows of her house. A light was still on in the den, from when he'd first arrived. "I really should go."

"Really?" she said, knowing she sounded like a total girl.

"Really." Andy nodded.

Then *shrugged*.

"You certainly like to shrug," Cheryl practically shouted, hands on hips.

Andy cocked an eyebrow. "Sorry?"

She let out a huff. "Skip it."

What was with this guy? Every other male on the planet wanted to bed Cheryl. Why was he . . . ? Suddenly, she froze in utter disbelief. In all of her admiring, glancing, openmouthed stares she had forgotten to check for one thing—the ring. Andy's hands were deep in his pockets.

"Are you married?" Cheryl demanded.

Andy's mouth fell open and he actually started laughing. It echoed long and loud through the starry night. "Why would you care about my marital status?" He chuckled, rubbing his gloved hand across his forehead.

"I don't, I . . ."

His eyes flickered over her body. "You got a little crush?" he whispered.

Cheryl drew back, speechless. She wanted to punch him but at the same time . . . "*No*. I just . . . I . . ."

Andy pulled his hands out of his pockets. He crossed his arms, the left hand deliberately on top. Cheryl glanced down and gasped. He was wearing gloves. They were thick leather, which made it impossible to see an imprint of a ring.

"Asshole," Cheryl said, stomping into her house and slamming the door in his face.

She could hear him laughing all the way back to his car.

Chapter Twenty-one

"I REALLY CAN'T STOMACH A DINNER RIGHT NOW," JACKIE LIED. "American food just isn't working for me these days."

When George called, Jackie had been about to shove a grilled cheese sandwich into her mouth. It was made out of white bread, butter, and an orange substance pretending to be cheese. A handful of salty Pringles lay on the plate next to it, alongside a crunchy dill pickle. Even though her meal was as American as it could get, the lie was necessary. She couldn't risk having a dinner date with George.

"Well, that's fair," George said.

Jackie let out a deep sigh of relief. She selected a chip from her plate and chewed it softly.

"What about the art fair?" he suggested. "We could find some holiday presents?"

"Little items made out of Popsicle sticks?" Jackie crooned. "How gauche."

"A play?"

"*Non.*"

"The symphony?"

"Oh geez, George," Jackie said. "You're not going to let up, are you?"

George agreed that no, he did intend to spend time with her. "You're one of my best friends," he insisted. "And we need to celebrate the successful acquisition of your new property."

The offer on Millstines had been accepted the day before. Jackie, Cheryl, and Doris were scheduled to sign off on the property the next morning. George had helped them negotiate the deal.

With a huge sigh, Jackie agreed to go out with him on Friday. It was only polite, considering all George had done for them, but she would certainly draw the line if he tried to kiss her. There was a big difference between being indebted and being a prostitute.

ON THE WAY to the signing, Doris could not stop worrying. "What if something happens at the last minute? What if everything goes wrong? What if we are making the biggest mistake of our lives?"

Cheryl was driving, careening her BMW through the streets with a speed that made Jackie want to throw up. Sliding low into her seat, Jackie put on her sunglasses and cracked the window open. "The only thing that could go wrong," she finally said, "is if we end up in jail for reckless driving."

"There are lots of things that could go wrong . . ." Doris started to say and Cheryl gave her a withering look in the mirror.

"Did you get more Xanax from your doctor?" she asked.

Doris nodded, clutching her purse and shooting a guilty look at Jackie. "Yes," she admitted.

"Take it," Jackie and Cheryl both chorused. The only sound for the rest of the car ride was Doris fumbling through her purse for her bottle of pills.

At George's office, the girls were met by an efficient secretary. She took them into a boardroom. Stacks of contracts glistened from the table, pens placed neatly beside them. At each seat, there was also a fresh cappuccino next to a plate with strawberries and a chocolate croissant.

"The croissants were imported from Europe," the secretary said.

Jackie gasped, then clapped her hands in delight.

Betsy bustled into the room then, in a burst of perfume and curly hair. "Good morning, ladies," she sang, taking a seat at the table. "Ooh, who got us treats?"

George walked in, looking handsome in his gray suit. "Guilty."

"Hi," Betsy practically squealed, rushing over to shake his hand. "I'm the Realtor." She stared up at him googly-eyed and Jackie felt an odd sensation in the pit of her stomach.

"George darling," she said, batting her lashes in spite of herself. *"Merci de le chocolat."*

"Anything for you, my dear," he said, smiling at her.

A disappointed Betsy flounced to her seat and said, "Shall we get this party started?"

George went to the head of the table and began reading through the closing contracts. It was quite dull and Jackie wasn't paying attention, simply enjoying the flaky croissant and its rich chocolate. She hoped George had more than the ones that had been on the table. Knowing him, he had probably ordered a whole case. Both he and Robert had never been shy about spending their money on the pleasures life had to offer. That was something Jackie had loved about both of them. Halfway through her reverie, Betsy's cell phone rang and Jackie jumped.

"It's the Millstines' Realtor," Betsy said. "We better take this."

After a friendly exchange, it became clear that Betsy was on a three-way call with both the Millstines and their Realtor. Suddenly, Betsy's face changed. "Uh, hold on just a second," she said. Carefully, she put the phone on mute and set it on the table.

"What's wrong?" Cheryl said quickly. "Are they backing out?"

"It's a routine call," Betsy said. "They just wanted to find out if we'd signed off yet but they just asked what type of restaurant it will be," she said, yanking at a curly strand of her hair. "What do I say?"

"Lie," Cheryl said. "Lie!"

"Do not lie," George said, tapping a pen against his cheek. "The information is irrelevant. They have no legal right to it."

"But it could slow down the closing if I don't answer," Betsy said. The strand of hair she had twisted around her finger was turning her finger purple. "They are motivated, but nervous. They might relook at everything."

"We have to think of something," Jackie said. Rapidly, she fanned herself with her hands, half standing up from her chair. She searched for the right words. "Tell them The Whole Package will primarily focus on women, giving them a fun place to go with their friends."

George shot her the thumbs-up sign. "Tell them that."

"Sure thing." A flustered Betsy took her phone off mute. As she opened her mouth to speak, Doris shrieked, *"Just tell the truth. I don't want them to sue us!"* At that, Betsy's eyes widened and she blurted out, "Mrs. Millstine? The buyers would like you to know the food will be served by scantily clothed men."

George put his head in his hands. Jackie grabbed her purse and hit Doris with it, hard. Cheryl slammed the papers on the table and started to lunge for the phone. Betsy held up her hand and said, "Okay, great! We'll sign the papers right now."

Betsy hung up and gave the thumbs-up sign. After a tense moment, the entire group turned to Doris and stared.

"What?" Doris said, taking a sip of her cappuccino. "Honesty. It's always the best policy."

George chuckled and went back to reading the contracts.

An hour later, the girls stood in the middle of Doris's living room, champagne flutes raised. Doris's heart swelled with pride. They had signed their papers, gotten everything in motion, and for the first time in her adult life, Doris felt like part of a major project and responsibility. It felt good.

"To my girls, *bonne chance*," Jackie declared, raising her glass and looking at her friends with affection. "In spite of Doris's ridiculous obsession with the truth . . ."

Doris giggled.

"Together," Jackie said, beaming, "we are The Whole Package."

Doris clinked the fragile flute against her friends' and took a long drink. The bubbly liquid was sweet in her mouth and she felt another rush of pleasure. Things were going well for now and Doris hoped that would last. At some point, she was going to have to deal with Doug and his opinion on what she had done with their money. Every time the phone rang, she jumped.

One of these days, he was going to notice that their accountant had liquidated all of their stocks and transferred them to some fund he'd never heard of. In a normal situation, Doug watched their money like a hawk. Given his silence, Doris would have been worried that he was dead or something but she knew he wasn't. Doug had been in contact with Mandy, on her private cell phone. Her daughter had confessed this the night before.

"Dad called," she announced, hopping onto Doris's bed and crossing her legs.

Doris froze. "Oh? Did he . . . say anything?" Instantly, she found herself wringing her hands, ready to reach for her new bottle of Xanax. She'd stashed it in her bedside drawer in a hollow book, a place Jackie wouldn't think to look.

"About . . . ?" Mandy said. It was almost as though Mandy was enjoying Doris's discomfort. She was always punishing her for something.

"Where is he?" Doris pleaded.

"Arizona, New Mexico . . ." Mandy said dreamily, leaning back on the bed. "He's living the life of a cowboy."

"Shooting people?" Jackie said from the doorway.

"Just living free," Mandy said. "By the way, thanks for telling me, Mom."

"He wanted a vacation," Doris tried. "He had years of vacation time stacked up."

Doris thought this line might carry some weight. After all, even Doug's parents had no idea that there was a problem in the marriage. When Doris finally got brave and called them, they asked how Doug was doing on his little road trip. In her heart, she had taken that as a good sign. If he'd told them he was coming back, maybe that's what he was planning.

In spite of the way Doug had hurt her, Doris missed him. She missed his wry humor, the scent of sandalwood in the morning, and the occasional kiss he would plant on her forehead right before they fell asleep. Maybe the whole thing was all her fault. Maybe she had lost sight of him due to her depression and been too cold, too self-absorbed. If Doug would just come back, she would . . . she would . . .

"When *does* he plan on breezing back in?" Jackie asked, smoothing down her silky blouse. Even though her tone was light, Doris knew she was concerned. If Doug came back before The Whole Package opened, he might try to stop Doris from being a partner.

"He's not going to stop us from opening the restaurant," she said. Doris picked a silver hairbrush up off her dresser. She polished it with a tissue, then ran it through her hair. "I might not even take him back," she said, even though it was the furthest thing from the truth.

Mandy snorted. "Whatever, Mom."

"A woman needs time to forgive," Jackie said, nodding. "He left her, you know."

"Mom." Mandy sat up on her elbow. "You wouldn't do that, would you?" Doris's jaw pulsed and her daughter practically shrieked, "*Mom?*"

"No," Doris admitted. She set down the hairbrush and studied the lines in her face. The furrow between her eyes got deeper when she thought of what had happened between her and Doug. Unable to face her reflection, Doris finally moved away from the mirror. "Of course I'll take him back. He's my husband."

Back when Sean and Cheryl had separated, Doug had taken it as a personal offense. It was like Cheryl had wronged him, not just his friend. "Marriage is forever," Doug had said, from that chair in front of the television. He set down the remote control with a crash. "Are you planning on leaving me anytime soon?"

Before his outburst, Doris had been pawing through their bookshelves. She was trying to figure out whether or not they should send some of their leather-bound classics to a halfway home. Walking over to Doug, she gave a big sigh and rubbed his shoulders. "Honey, Cheryl's always been wild."

Doug eyed her. "So were you."

Biting her lip, Doris leaned forward and kissed the top of his head. "I love you," she'd said. "That will never change."

"Doris," Jackie called now, waggling her champagne flute from across the living room. "Come back to planet earth. You need to keep drinking or our toast will be cursed."

Doris looked at the full champagne flute in surprise. Jackie and Cheryl had each already finished theirs and were tipsy, thumbing through the plans for The Whole Package. They had interviews scheduled for the waiters and the two were fantasizing about what they could get away with making them do.

"We will pick the best-looking ones," Cheryl said, "and put it in their contract that they have to come home with us every night if we want them to. They'd be our employees. They have to do whatever we say."

The doorbell harmonized with their laughter and Doris looked up in surprise. Who could be ringing the bell this late? She got up to answer it, half hoping it was Doug.

Throwing open the door, her knees buckled at the sight of two police officers. They were standing on her front porch in full uniform. One was short, one was tall; both looked very serious.

"Where's Mandy?" Jackie shrieked, leaping to her feet. "Where is she?"

"Volleyball," Doris said, voice calm. This visit wasn't about her daughter. "Won't you come in, Officers?"

"It's Doug," Jackie cried, bustling to Doris's side. "Doris, sit down. There's no reason for you to panic, but please take my hand."

"We're here on a vandalism report, ma'am," the tall one told Jackie. "Not a fatality."

Doris could have told them that. She stared at the carpet, feeling her face get hot. Cheryl's relief was painted on her face, especially after what she'd said about it being snowy and hoping Doug would crash and all that. Since all eyes were on Doris, she cried, "Oh, thank God. My husband's okay," like some soap opera star in a hospital scene.

Jackie's and Cheryl's eyes narrowed.

"Mrs. MacLean, where were you on the night of October twenty-seventh?" the tall officer asked, opening his notepad. A large gun dangled from a leather holster on the side of his navy polyester pants. Doris stared.

"She was hanging out with Jackie," Cheryl said quickly. "Right?"

Doris looked at her in surprise. Feeling a glimmer of hope, she nodded. "We watched *Sex and the City*."

"I had a date that night," Cheryl said. "At least, I think it was a date. He didn't even try to kiss me. Can you *believe* that? Don't you think that if a guy shows up at your house, brings you flowers, and takes you out on a date that he should at least *try* to kiss you?"

"What?" Jackie said eagerly, fluffing her hair. "You didn't tell us that. Who was this guy?"

"Andy." Cheryl grimaced. It was obvious that even saying the guy's name got her blood boiling.

Doris ran through the catalogue of men they knew, trying to figure out who Cheryl was talking about. "Who's Andy?" Doris asked. "I can't place him."

"That guy I used to work with," Cheryl said. "The one who drove me home after I was in the hospital. I can't *stand* him."

"Excuse me just a moment, ladies," the short one interjected. "Can we stay on topic? Who here is Mrs. MacLean?"

Cheryl took a sip of champagne and pointed at Doris, who raised her hand.

"I am," Doris said. She took a deep breath. "Like they said, on October twenty-seventh I was with my friend Jackie here. We watched television and then we . . . gosh, we . . ."

"Painted," Jackie said quickly, "but not graffiti-style or anything, so don't think we vandalized anyone. We were painting indoors."

"The vandalism was not graffiti," the tall officer said, eyeing Doris.

"Then *do* share your dirty little secret," Jackie said. "What happened? We would love to know."

"We'd *love* to know," Cheryl repeated, sneaking a look at Doris. "We're surprised we haven't heard about it already."

"Those details are confidential," the short officer said. "But Mrs. MacLean was on our list of inquiries. Ma'am, do you drive a silver Lexus?"

"Yes. Yes I do." Doris nodded.

"Did you and . . ." The officer glanced at his notepad, "Jackie . . ." She waggled her fingers. "Leave the house for any reason that night?"

Jackie stood up on her toes like a ballerina, looking around the room for inspiration. Her eyes settled on the champagne bottle. "Alcohol run," Jackie said quickly, prancing over to refill her flute. "We are so rude. Officers, would you like some champagne?"

The short one looked like he just might go for it but the tall one shook his head. "We are on duty, ma'am."

"My heart is officially broken," Jackie said. She smiled big and the short officer blushed, clearing his throat. "Don't be dull," she pressed, letting the bubbly liquid fizz into her glass and bubble up to the top. "You simply *must* tell who was vandalized."

"Yes." Doris nodded, finding her voice. "What happened? Who was it? What did they do?"

The officers eyed the three women staring back at them as though waiting for a scoop. They glanced at each other.

"They're going to tell us," Cheryl cried, clapping her hands.

Doris almost fainted with relief as the tall one shook his head and closed his notepad.

"That's all we need," he said. "Thanks for your time, ma'am. Sorry to bother you," he apologized.

Doris nodded primly and saw them out the door, amid cries from Jackie and Cheryl of: "Come on! Just tell us . . . Pretty please?"

Once the door was tightly shut, Doris squared her shoulders, waited a moment, and then turned to face her friends. They were both staring at her, arms crossed.

"Naughty, naughty," Cheryl said, voice tinged with admiration. Doris blushed. She hadn't heard that tone since high school.

"What did you *do?*" Jackie whispered.

Doris turned to the bay window as though expecting the officers to come busting through. Pushing back the curtain, she waited until the cop car had pulled out of her driveway. Only when she was sure the coast was clear, Doris burst out laughing. She laughed so hard that she had to take off her glasses to wipe her eyes.

"Let's just say . . ." Doris finally gasped, "Halloween came early for Katherine Rigney this year."

Chapter Twenty-two

As Jackie dressed for her outing with George, she took a moment to watch the reflections from her sequined gown dance their way across the ceiling. Even though he was forcing her into going out to the symphony, Jackie had to admit she was excited. In Paris, there was art on every corner. Here, there was Starbucks.

Jackie preened in the mirror, enjoying the sight of her reflection. The dress was low-cut and flattered her body in all the right places. Her blond curls were swept up into a neat chignon and accessorized with her favorite earrings, delicate diamond drops. Bankrupt or not, she looked the very picture of success.

A light knock sounded at the guest bedroom door. "Come in," Jackie called, spritzing on some Angel perfume.

Mandy stood in the doorway. "Just wanted to check," she whispered. "How late will you be out?"

"Your mother's not here, you don't have to whisper," Jackie said. "I'll be gone until ten thirty but your mother will only be at her meeting until ten. Please use discretion. You should have him out of here by nine thirty, just in case. And have him read you some poetry," she added as an afterthought. "Or play guitar. You deserve to be romanced."

Against her better judgment, Jackie had agreed to help coordinate Mandy's alone time with her boyfriend. The teenagers had been having most of their make-out sessions, including the pregnancy scare, in the back of her boyfriend's car. Jackie thought it much more practical to let them have some private time in a safe environment instead of risking their lives to any psycho that wanted to sneak up and attack. Jackie figured what Doris didn't know wouldn't hurt her, as long as Mandy didn't get caught . . . or pregnant.

"Thanks, Jackie." Mandy beamed. "You look beautiful."

"Listen, if you do anything more than cuddle," Jackie said, shaking her head. "Please . . ."

"I started taking the pill. We'll double up if we do anything," Mandy promised.

Jackie's stomach turned at the thought of the girl having sex at such a young age. When Jackie was in high school, she had not done anything more than kiss. Granted, she would have loved to have done more but didn't dare get that close to anyone.

Growing up, Jackie had been a genius at hiding her problems from her girlfriends. To explain why she could never invite them over, Jackie made up an entire life for her father that he didn't have. She told everyone he got up at the crack of dawn to manage a branch at an industrial plant, so inviting anyone for a sleepover was impossible. He couldn't be kept awake by a bunch of giggly girls.

In truth, her father was a drunk. He downed Jack Daniels from the moment he woke up to the moment he passed out. Luckily, he got the majority of his rage out at the bars; Jackie had only had to lock herself into a bathroom twice, shaking and sweating, wondering if she should call the police. Of course, he'd been in and out of jail several times. When Jackie was in college, he cracked a man's head open and was in there for the same amount of time it took Jackie to get a degree. That had been slightly distracting but nothing new. On the rare occasions her father was sober, Jackie would take the opportunity to show him off and squelch any suspicion that anything was wrong. She would have her friends meet them at some local restaurant for dinner, which her father always paid for. Those nights, he was charming and witty, flirting with her friends and patting Jackie's arm with affection.

Jackie's father had loved her something fierce. He called her his "little bunny," as her two front teeth were pushed slightly forward when she was young. Jackie loved hanging out with him. When he was sober, he was fun. He would pull out his guitar and serenade her like a rock star or take her to places like Baskin-Robbins or the arcade, no matter how old she got. But good intentions aside, the man just didn't know how to be a father. Jackie learned that in the fifth grade, when he tried packing her lunch for the first time. Happy to be like the other kids, Jackie dumped the contents of her brown paper sack onto the lunch table and was instantly mortified. Her father had given her a peanut butter and jelly sandwich and a warm can of Miller Lite. Luckily, none of the kids knew what the can was and she dumped it in the garbage before any of the teachers noticed.

Jackie survived her childhood by deflecting—being popular, being perky, and being fun, signing herself up for as many friends and activities as possible. The constant busyness of her life kept her away from home. Once in a while, it dawned on her that she should be angry at the hand she'd been dealt, but she wasn't. Jackie loved her life. Plus, she'd been given a consolation prize for not having a family. Jackie was gifted at art and everyone knew it. While Doris and Cheryl spent their time messing around with boys, Jackie protected her privacy by perfecting her craft. But even back when Cheryl and Doris were going all the way, they had certainly seemed a lot older than the young girl standing in front of her now.

"Mandy, are you sure you're ready for all this?" Jackie said. "Hearts are so fragile when you're young. Shouldn't you be hanging out with your girlfriends or . . ."

"Volunteering at a shelter or something?" Mandy was sarcastic, but her eyes were sparkling. "I see my friends all the time. Jackie, it's really cool that you're helping me."

"My goal isn't to be cool." Jackie sighed, adjusting her décolletage and dabbing on some sparkling powder. "My goal is to keep you safe." Her cell lit up. George. "*Bonsoir*. Have a good night."

Mandy nodded. "Will do."

Jackie shook her head as Mandy closed the bedroom door. "*Will do.*" How old was this child?

GEORGE'S TOWN CAR was waiting out front, a sleek black ride complete with a driver and tinted windows. Jackie floated up the drive and climbed in, smiling at George in the dim interior. He was leaning back against the plush leather seats, and the moment the driver pulled out, he cracked open a bottle of cognac. Jackie held up her hand. "George, wait. I have to tell you something."

Jackie planned to excuse herself from any thoughts or illusions George might have about their visit to the symphony. *Nothing* was going to happen between them and she wanted him to know that. Even though Cheryl was correct in her earlier assessment—George was still a very good-looking man, with his dark eyes and intelligent face—he had to remain Just George. The alternative was just too unsettling.

"I have to tell you something, too," George said, before she could finish her thought. "You look beautiful, Jacqueline. Truly radiant."

"Thank you, darling," she said nervously. "Listen—"

"Tonight will be grand," he interrupted. "We're primarily seeing Tchaikovsky. The conductor is that young man who's been receiving such favorable press."

"Really?" Jackie lit up. She had been interested in the conductor for quite some time, but he had not toured while she was in Paris. "That sounds lovely," she admitted.

"I've been looking forward to it," George said. He settled back in the seat, suit rustling softly. "The tickets were not easy to come by. It should be a pleasurable evening."

Jackie eyed him. There was nothing lascivious in what he said or the way he was looking at her. Maybe she should save her speech. George was a music lover and probably just wanted company. After all, he had been the one to convince her and Robert to get a subscription to the symphony, so long ago. When the violins sang their mournful song, George would always close his eyes, minutely conducting the music with his fingers. Jackie used to mimic him; miming the action and making Robert laugh. It was hard to believe that, so many years later, they were headed out for a night on the town without her husband.

"Jacqueline," George said. "I know this is hard on you. It's hard on me, too." Suddenly, George's hand was on hers, warm and comforting. "If you don't want to go . . ."

The question lingered in the air and she turned to him, surprised. "Maybe it's too soon," George said honestly, shrugging. "This has to be a bit unusual for you, having an outing with me. You probably half expect us to pick up Robert at the office. I know I do."

Jackie looked down and studied the way her hand looked in his. George's hands were smooth and moisturized, the skin slightly tanned. Hers looked slight and sparkly, her rings and manicured nails glistening prettily.

"I can see you struggling," George said. "You tell me what you need and I will try to help."

A tear had formed in the corner of her eye and she blinked it back. How could she explain to George that the problem was completely different from what it should have been? In Paris, Robert had become an idea and seemed to be around every corner, even while she was dating another man. Now, back in this town where they had shared a life together, Jackie could barely picture his face. She hadn't even reached out to any of his other friends. Granted, they were a lot older than she was and she no longer had the money to keep up with their lifestyle but still . . . shouldn't she miss him more than she did?

I'm angry with him, she realized with a start.

Angry that he had cheated on his finances and not even shared the secret—that type of deception made her wonder what else Robert had been dishonest about. Was there a Katherine Rigney out there for him? Some other family on the side? Jackie had dealt with enough secrets in her life. Promises made, promises broken. But for that to come from Robert . . . it was a surprise.

"I like this cognac," George was saying. Gently, he removed his hand from hers and poured them both a bit of the amber liquid. "It's quite smoky," he said. "It would be even nicer with a cigar."

Jackie debated telling George some of the questions on her mind but decided against it. It was not the time. Instead, she picked up her drink and admired the color of the liquid in the dim light. Taking a deep breath, Jackie said, "Shall I sip it?" She already knew the answer, but also knew George loved teaching her things. It had always been his role, teacher to student. Returning to that familiar place might just even out the confusion pounding through her head.

George nodded, then stuck his nose in the top of the glass and breathed deeply. Jackie laughed. The sound was a light tinkle.

"Yes?" George looked up, ready to be amused.

"I was just thinking how funny it would be if the driver hit a bump," she admitted, smiling. "It would be all over your face."

"Ah." George winked. "That's a very sly way to sneak alcohol into the symphony. I could just chew on my bow tie, yes?"

"You're a criminal," Jackie said.

They sat in companionable silence. Jackie sipped on her drink, feeling her body unwind for the first time in weeks. She watched the cars zoom past them on Lakeshore Drive.

"Thanks for inviting me," she finally said. "This is lovely."

"I'm really glad to hear that," George said, his dark eyes holding hers.

"Well, it's been two and a half years, George," she said lightly. "I can't ignore the symphony forever."

Chapter Twenty-three

THE MORNING THEY PLANNED TO HIRE THEIR WAITSTAFF WAS A beautiful day. The slush had cleared, the sun was shining, and the girls were giddy with excitement. As they walked into the conference room they'd rented at the Westin hotel, they giggled at the prospect of hiring someone simply because "eight-pack" appeared on his resume.

"Maybe this is too demeaning," Jackie said suddenly, hesitating at the door. She was suffering a brief moment of conscience, loath to hurt anyone's feelings. "Who am I to tell"—she flipped open her notebook and ran her finger down their list of appointments, stopping on a random name—"Marco O'Donnell that he needs to work out a bit more? Get a tan? Trim his gnarled body hair?"

"You're right," Doris said. "It's not very nice."

"What are you two talking about? We're turning the tables," Cheryl said. She stalked into the room and flipped on the overhead lights. "Women go through this every day. We get evaluated just for going to the grocery store."

"Speaking of," Doris said, "do you guys think I look stupid?"

She tugged at her new suit and turned her pretty blue eyes on them.

"Doris steps in to illustrate the point," Cheryl sang. "Doris, if you want to be a career woman you have to act like one. That means strong and confident. *We're* interviewing *them*, you know. Not the other way around."

The night before, Doris and Jackie had spent two hours flipping through Doris's perfectly organized closet, trying to find the combination that would make her look high-powered yet attractive. Nothing worked. Finally, they just ran to Talbots and picked up a formal navy suit and a white silk shirt to put on underneath it. She ended up looking very put together but she definitely smelled like new clothes.

"You look very glamorous," Jackie approved.

"Come on, let's get set up," Cheryl said. She started moving chairs to the conference table, putting three at the front of the table and one right across from them. She also carried five out into the hallway, setting them up in a neat little row. "For the early birds," she explained, as Doris studied the setup with confusion.

The hotel had supplied them with a pitcher of ice water and some chocolate candies. After a moment, Doris moved the pitcher of water over to the table, then brought over three heavy crystal glasses. Jackie followed with the dish of colorfully wrapped candy, then set out some paper and pens.

"Looks good," Jackie said, dusting off her hands and taking a seat.

Cheryl walked in and gave the room a once-over. "Maybe it's a little cold in here. The hotel said they'd send someone up to check on things, so we'll ask them to turn up the heat." In a whisper, she added, "We don't want shrinkage."

Doris pursed her lips in disapproval. "Gross," she said, but after a moment, blurted out, "I hope they're handsome."

The girls burst out laughing. Doris lit up and they all took their seats around the table, Cheryl glancing at her watch. "The first one will be here in five minutes. If he's ugly, you better believe I'm chasing him out of here with a stick."

"Maybe this *isn't* legal," Jackie said. "Should I call George?"

After mentioning his name, she blushed. They'd had a nice time at the symphony. He had been a perfect gentleman, not crowding her in the tight auditorium seats, no arm "accidentally" coming into her space or anything. After the concert, they went to Hugo's on Rush Street, Jackie's choice. George had been entertained by her narration of Parisian life and Jackie embellished the stories wherever she could, trying to make him laugh out loud at her colorful descriptions. She had left out mention of Christian altogether. Not that she cared what George thought about her private life, but for whatever reason, she felt it should be kept just that—private.

Lingering over Irish coffees and cake, George told her about the trips he had taken while she was gone: an international cruise through the islands of Greece, a river ride down the Nile, and another to the top of a mountain in Africa. His stories were outrageous and Jackie refused to believe that pampered George had camped in a tent in Africa, then trekked his way up to the top of a mountain. No matter how many times she implied otherwise, George insisted, "No, I was not airlifted in." Their night had flown by and Jackie found herself wondering why she'd been trying so hard to avoid spending time with him.

On the car ride back from their evening, Jackie had let her head rest against the window. Eventually, she drifted off into a comfortable sleep. She was not worried about any type of good-bye at the door. When they were at Doris's and Jackie got out, he simply said "Thank you for the lovely company," and didn't even offer to walk her up, just waved at her like a good friend.

"Jackie, I'm sorry," Doris interrupted her thoughts, "when you say the interviews might be illegal . . . ?" She popped three pieces of hotel chocolate like they were medicine.

"She's joking," Cheryl promised, flipping through resumes. She looked radiant in her bright melon-colored suit. "As long as we're hiring these guys as models, it's not considered discriminatory. And yes, I checked all this out with the almighty George and he cleared it. I'm fired up, ladies. This is a billion times better than anything I ever did for TurnKey."

"How's your lawsuit coming?" Jackie asked, delicately reaching for a piece of candy.

"It's a pain in the ass." Cheryl sighed. "I have to give it to Stan, he's kind of a genius."

Cheryl explained that, after spending several frustrating days interviewing lawyers, she learned that Stan's move with the documented warnings was perfect. He'd set her up good. It made the plan to take him down with corporate embezzlement look like child's play.

"In a perverse way, I'm glad," she admitted. "It gives edification to my time at TurnKey. Who wants to admit their boss was a total loser, especially considering the time I put in?"

"But doesn't that make it harder to find someone to represent you?" Doris asked.

Cheryl nodded, thinking back to some of the meetings she'd already had with lawyers.

"Okay, if wrongful termination won't work, what about sexual harassment?" Cheryl had tried, just two days before. "I cannot tell you how many times TurnKey . . ."

"Do you have documented harassment incidents on file?" This particular lawyer looked like a horse, with wide eyes and a long nose. She fingered a double-stranded pearl necklace, legs crossed comfortably. She was eyeing Cheryl like a patient at a counseling session instead of someone seriously investigating a million-dollar lawsuit.

"No, but . . ."

"As your former boss demonstrated"—the Horse Lady yawned—"That would have been the appropriate course of action. Without evidence, you won't be able to make a strong case that you were the victim of harassment."

Cheryl wanted to cut off the woman's head and slide it into Stan's bed, pearl necklace attached.

"Why didn't you tell her you have proof that Stan tampered with your computer?" Jackie asked.

"Because I decided against the woman altogether and slammed out of the office," Cheryl said. "I can't wait to see if Andy tells Stan that I have that information," she admitted. "I'm curious to find out if he really is a rat."

"Wait, wait, wait," Doris said, listening as Cheryl explained it all. "But what if Andy does tell and Blake gets fired? Cheryl, that's a risky position to put him in."

"I didn't mention names and besides, Stan couldn't prove a thing," she scoffed. "Not until we are in court. If that happens, it would be a little late for him to go after Blake because Blake would have the grounds to go after Stan."

Doris shook her head, totally confused. "I have another question on a different topic. When you talked to George about legalities for the restaurant ... um ..."

"Yes, Doris," Cheryl sang, already knowing what she was going to ask. "All the permits came through. The health department gave us the go-ahead."

"That can't be right," Doris protested.

Jackie laughed. The Health Department was the one denial Doris had been counting on. If they were turned down by the Health Department, Doris suggested dropping the whole idea and just opening a cozy place with good food that the three women created together.

"Oh, honey," Jackie giggled. "It will be okay. The men aren't *really* going to be serving food naked. They'll be wearing something."

"But ..."

"Seriously," Cheryl demanded. "How is this different from a woman wearing a miniskirt? Serving dinner in a sports bra?"

Doris looked stricken.

"Have you *been* to Hooters?" Cheryl asked.

Doris didn't answer. Instead, her jaw practically hit the table. Jackie turned to see the first male model poking his head inside. He was like an overgrown, male version of Swiss Miss—all blond hair and milk-white teeth.

"I heard you need a package," he said in broken English.

"Let the games begin," Jackie chirped, fluffing up her hair.

The man sauntered into the room and stood in front of them. Without any prelude, he made a move to unbuckle his pants.

"Wait!" Doris cried and the man looked at her in confusion.

Cheryl held up her hand. "Hold on a second . . . Christoph. Please remain clothed. Before we get into all that, why don't you tell us a little about yourself?"

Christoph cleared his throat and Jackie watched him with interest.

"I think he really wants to take his pants off," she whispered to Doris.

"Well . . . I am a model," Christoph explained, flashing his teeth. "I am eighteen. I am here on a work visa . . ." As he talked, it became clear that he had no idea what to do with his hands. First, he tucked them in his belt buckle. Then, he spent two minutes running them through his hair. Finally, he just let them hang out midair, which made him look like a goalie for some German football team. "My visa will run out in two month unless I get job. I need to work so I think I work for you. I show you my package now." He reached down to unbuckle his belt once again.

Jackie rested her chin in her hand.

"No," Doris practically shrieked and the blond giant jumped back in surprise.

"We *really* don't need you to take off your pants." Cheryl grinned. "Not yet. Maybe not ever. You gave us your comp card. I think that gives us a good idea what you look like in a thong."

Jackie grabbed for the composite postcard Cheryl was holding, a collection of Christoph's modeling pictures. In one he was shirtless, riding a horse; in the next he was in said thong, surfing; in the next he was oiled up, riding a bicycle . . .

"I think," Jackie mused, studying the card, "I just don't have enough information."

"Jackie," Doris said, pinching her under the table.

Jackie slapped Doris's hand away and cleared her throat. "You know what, Christoph. It actually would help us with our decision-making process if you would just drop your pants."

The model gave a big smile, undid his belt buckle, and let his pants drop to the floor. He was wearing a bleached white pair of Calvin Klein underwear, which cupped his package perfectly. It was well formed and very appealing.

"Uh . . ." Cheryl cleared her throat. "Wow."

"It is big." Christoph nodded. "Like a snake."

Doris let out some sort of strangled cry.

"Okay," Jackie laughed. "That will do."

Christoph pulled up his pants and gave them another big smile.

"Thanks so much for coming in," Cheryl said. "We'll be talking to you soon."

The model turned and strutted out the door, smiling at them one last time over his shoulder. The second he was out of sight, Jackie and Cheryl bounced up and down in their chairs, squealing. Doris was silent, but after a minute, she looked at them with a slight gleam in her eye.

"He was good-looking," she said. "Should we hire him?"

"Abso*lutely*," Cheryl said.

"*Magnifique*," Jackie agreed. "He seemed a little shy, though. How on earth are we going to get him to show the customers his package?"

The girls were still giggling when the man with the gray mullet and comb-over walked in.

"Great," Cheryl said, hopping to her feet. "Thanks for checking in. Can we get the heat turned up just a touch and maybe a bit more water?" She held out the pitcher, smiling graciously at the man from the hotel.

"My resume already says I've waited some tables in my time," the man drawled, amused. "Do you really need me to prove it?" Seeing Cheryl's confusion, he pointed at the next resume on the table. "Henry Durrett."

"Oh," Cheryl said, baffled. "You're . . . not with the hotel?"

There was an awkward silence.

"I think he's our next interview," Doris whispered, glancing at her list.

"Oh, here's his picture," Cheryl said, voice high-pitched. Sitting down, she slid the photo over to Jackie and Doris. They peered at the picture on the table for several moments, while Henry stood in front of them clearing his throat. His leather biker jacket seemed to crinkle with every breath.

"*Je regrette, mais . . .*" Jackie looked up at him, then back down to the photo again. "This is you?" she finally asked.

Henry grinned. "That's the *real* me," he said proudly.

"I think this is . . ." Cheryl peered closer at his photo. "Isn't this Robert Redford when he was younger?"

Jackie grabbed for the picture, squealing in delight. The man took that opportunity to drop his pants, showcasing a red Speedo ensconcing an incredibly large member. He tilted his chin back proudly. "What do you ladies think of that?"

"We'll call you," Doris said hurriedly and practically dove under the table, pretending she'd dropped a pen.

Henry nodded and pulled up his pants. Giving a little wave, he walked out. Doris shot back up from under the table, a bottle of hand sanitizer in her hand. Like a woman trying to put a fire out, she doused her hands with it.

Jackie waggled her fingers. "Here please."

"Squirt it in my eyes," Cheryl begged. "They feel dirty." When the group had nearly depleted the bottle of sanitizer, Cheryl said, "Hey Doris, don't you think it gave him the wrong impression when you dove to your knees?"

Jackie laughed until she cried.

Even Doris managed to crack a tiny smile. "Good lord," she said. "I wonder who we'll have next."

Six hours later, after going through countless interviews and peep shows, they'd found the majority of their . . . "Staff?" Cheryl cracked.

"Please don't say that word," Jackie groaned. Her interest in the male genitalia had waned after the tenth interview. "I've never seen so many men in my entire life."

"I hope Doug never comes back," Doris said, rubbing her eyes. "I never want to see a penis again."

They had stopped off at a local diner for dinner. Doris and Jackie had each gotten a chicken salad. Cheryl had ordered a chocolate shake, a burger with fries, and a large bowl of corn chowder on the side.

"Forgive the indelicacy but . . . are you pregnant?" Jackie marveled, after their tired waitress dumped the entire spread onto the table and Cheryl dug in.

Dipping a fry into her yellow soup, Cheryl laughed. "That would be the immaculate conception, wouldn't it?"

Truth be told, she had been sleeping with a Dad-type actor she'd met through one of TurnKey's commercial sessions. Cheryl didn't want to mention that, considering Doris's recent judgment of her sex life. As for pregnancy, though, Cheryl really doubted it. The only thing she was really worried about was her inability to do anything physical without fantasizing about Andy.

"Remember that guy Andy?" Cheryl said. It gave her a little thrill to say his name out loud. "He hasn't called." In fact, she had heard nothing since their dinner, not even a thank-you for her time.

Jackie tried to suggest that perhaps, just perhaps, her bad behavior in the beginning of the date had put him off.

"I bet he thinks you hate him," Doris agreed, chomping on a piece of chicken.

"I asked if he was married." Cheryl bellowed this so loudly at least three people in the diner turned and looked. She lowered her voice. "How do you get *I hate you* out of that?"

"Just because you want to sleep with him doesn't mean you like him," Jackie pointed out, stealing a fry and nibbling at it.

"What do I care?" Cheryl said, morose. "He was setting me up. I know it. That whole thing where he was asking if I was gonna sue Stan? Does he think I was born yesterday?"

Cheryl grimaced. There was something stuck in her teeth. This was why she never ordered burgers; she inevitably ended up with some piece of gristle lodged somewhere. Grabbing for Doris's purse, she rooted around until she found a circle of Oral-B.

"Do it in the bathroom," Doris scolded.

Cheryl stood up, lingering. "I think I liked him," she admitted. "I don't know if it's because he didn't seem to like me or what . . . but it was just the first time in years I've really even felt anything for a guy."

"Give him the benefit of the doubt," Jackie said, swiping at the whipped cream on Cheryl's milkshake. "Maybe he didn't kiss you because it was the first date."

Cheryl rolled her eyes. "Doubt it."

"Maybe he had a cold sore on his lip," Doris considered. "Did you check?"

The two friends turned to her, aghast.

"What?" Doris said, blinking. "It's a fair question."

"Well, it *is* a practical question," Jackie laughed, going in for more whipped cream. "Doris, you never fail to surprise me."

When Cheryl got back from the restroom, she waved away further questions about Andy and turned the conversation back to The Whole Package. "All right. We've decided on our musky little waiters," she said, pulling out a notebook where they had made a list of the men they wanted to hire. "So, what are we going to do about the managers?" She had envisioned two men running the show, the best looking of the bunch. Although the guys they had decided on today were gorgeous, there wasn't anyone who was quite hot enough for the position she had in mind.

"They were all good-looking," Doris said, crumpling over the table like she'd run a marathon. "How are we going to decide this? What are we looking for, exactly?"

Cheryl wanted someone who looked like he didn't belong in Schaumburg. "You know, like that dancer you were all over at the strip club. Somebody that will make women come back again and again."

"I don't know . . ." Doris hedged. "Let me see the list. Do you have the pictures? This could take some time to figure out."

"We are opening in less than a month," Cheryl barked. "We have to make some decisions tonight!"

"Travis was perfect," Jackie said. Cheryl rifled through the comp cards and pulled out his picture. Travis had a face like a soap opera star and the body of a beach volleyball player.

"He'll leave us for L.A. within a year," Cheryl promised. "Remember when we talked about hopes and dreams?"

Jackie nodded glumly. Travis did want to be a soap opera star. Or a beach volleyball player.

"Maybe another round of auditions," Doris suggested. When everyone groaned, she said, "Fine then. Let's just hire the strippers." Cheryl and Jackie turned to her, surprised. "We'd have to pay them a lot, but my blonde really was cute."

"And our waiter," Jackie said, snapping her fingers. "The one who licked Cheryl."

"The waiter had an accent." Doris sighed, folding her napkin. "That's always good."

Jackie and Cheryl once again stared at her in surprise.

"For heaven's sake, I was drunk." Doris threw up her hands. "I wasn't blind or deaf."

"Hire the strippers," Cheryl said, begrudgingly. "It's so obvious. Why didn't I think of it?"

"Nice work, Doris," Jackie said.

Cheryl nodded. "You might be good for this business after all."

"Well, we'll see," Doris said. She ducked her head and took a long drink of water. Behind the rim of the glass, Cheryl could tell she was smiling.

Chapter Twenty-four

ON THE SAME DAY THAT THE PAPERWORK FOR MILLSTINES WAS processed and Betsy delivered the keys, the girls held the interviews for their managers. Since it was their first time setting foot in the restaurant, Doris ran around the room with a spray bottle and dust cloth, wiping the place down. The Millstines had left everything in great condition, but there was still a lot of work to be done and Doris was eager to get started.

"We *are* hiring cleaners," Jackie told the stripper with the accent, "in spite of what it looks like."

Jackie, Cheryl, and the stripper sat in the office, watching Doris. She was on her hands and knees, ample bottom pointing at them. Were she wearing a polka-dotted skirt, she easily could have been mistaken for one of those lawn ornaments designed to titillate passersby.

Jackie whispered, "She likes playing Cinderella."

The sexy stripper laughed. Leaning back in his chair, he said, "Good for her. Listen, I think this is a gorgeous space. A gorgeous space. Perfect location for a restaurant."

Cheryl looked up from her clipboard in surprise. "Anthony, where's your accent?"

Jackie regarded him with interest. Had he been faking it?

Anthony shrugged and stretched. As he did, the tight black T-shirt he was wearing crept up and exposed his perfect abs. "I'm from New York," he admitted. "I'm an actor. Was. Women like accents. So some nights, I have one."

There was a sardonic tone to Anthony's voice, a slight lisp. "Darling man, are you gay?" Jackie asked.

"Don't answer that," Cheryl hissed, glaring at Jackie and smiling too big at Anthony. "We're sorry, Anthony. She's been living abroad and forgets that asking questions like that in an interview is *illegal.*"

Fluffing her hair, Jackie pursed her lips and sat back in her chair. She was just making conversation. Half of her friends from the art world were gay, and she'd lost touch with so many of them. Anthony even looked a little like Mathieu, one of the gorgeous men she used to hang out with. He had driven Robert batty with jealousy.

Just like Anthony, Mathieu had black hair shaved close to his head, a strong jawline, and dark eyes. He was a tortured artist who read poetry, smoked cigarettes by candlelight, and danced with her on his roof. Robert hated that Jackie would let another man hold her close but she just laughed, saying, "Give me a break. He's really not getting anything out of it."

At the question, Anthony smiled. "Nice call," he told Jackie, winking. "You nailed it."

Jackie beamed, pulling a pack of pink bubblegum out of her purse. After offering some to Cheryl (who declined), then Anthony (who accepted), Jackie unwrapped a piece and popped it in her mouth, chewing softly. She was already starting to like this man.

Deliberately, Cheryl cleared her throat. When Jackie looked at her, Cheryl raised her eyebrows and made a chewing motion. It was clear Cheryl thought that gum chewing should be saved for non-interview times. Jackie waved her off and popped a tiny bubble.

Turning her attention back to Anthony, Cheryl said, "You *are* Latino, though." When he shook his head, she sighed. "Are you even foreign?"

"No. I'm just from New York," Anthony said. He ran his hands up and down the tops of his thighs. "I'm a dancer by trade but I won't do what they do onstage. Could choreograph it for you, though. I'm a choreographer. Studied it for years. The strip club's packed. Every night. Every night it's packed," he said. "But if you want to do a restaurant you'd have to do sexy. Not raunchy. Women don't want to see that when they're eating."

"Hmm . . ." Jackie considered. She hadn't really thought of that, but now that Anthony mentioned it, he might be right.

Doris had sneaked in and was leaning on the office door, face red and perspiring from her cleaning duties. "That's what I've been telling them."

"We don't want raunchy," Jackie explained. "We just want sexy."

"But there are still many things that haven't been decided yet," Cheryl said, voice extra brisk and professional. "Tell us," Cheryl said, leaning forward like she was conducting a television interview. "Why did you agree to meet with us in the first place? I imagine the money's good where you're at now."

Jackie popped another tiny bubble and Doris leaned forward. They were all dying to know. Why would someone want a managerial position with long, thankless hours, if he was already making so much money where he was?

"Why do you think?" Anthony said, sadness flashing in his dark eyes. "I didn't imagine this for my life. I didn't imagine it. Being a manager is better than being a waiter. If you pay me enough, I'm yours."

Jackie clapped her hands. Cheryl shot her a look, shaking her head. Jackie widened her blue eyes as though to demand *What?*

"So . . ." Anthony said, throwing Jackie a perfect smile. "What's it going to be?"

"We'll call you," Cheryl said sharply, closing her notebook.

Anthony looked surprised. He nodded abruptly and jumped

up. He shook their hands quickly, moving with the grace of a dancer. After the pleasantries, he bolted through the office door like he couldn't get out of there fast enough. Waiting, Jackie listened for the front door. It practically slammed shut behind him.

"Cheryl, you were incredibly rude," Jackie scolded. "He was *your* waiter. I thought you liked him."

"When he was licking me at a club and I was intoxicated," Cheryl said, reaching for a piece of gum.

"You guys, I hate gum-chewing noises," Doris said, fiddling with her dust cloth. When they ignored her, she added, "And Cheryl, you were kinda mean to him."

"Was I?" Cheryl sighed, running her hands through her hair. "Well, maybe that's because I don't like the sound of gum chewing either, especially in the *middle of an interview*." Jackie popped another bubble. "And why on earth were you cleaning, Doris? You guys, if we want to be taken seriously, we have to . . ."

"Why didn't you like him?" Doris demanded.

Cheryl's throat tightened. "It's just . . . He's too slick, he's too fast."

"*Non, non,*" Jackie marveled, eyes bright. "He's great. *Tres* mysterious. The women will love him."

"Will you knock it off with the French?!" Cheryl exploded. "We don't understand half the shit you're saying."

Jackie pursed her lips and looked at Doris. After a moment's hesitation, Doris grabbed for Jackie's pack of gum. "I loved Anthony," she said, shoving two pieces into her mouth. Gingerly, she started to chew.

"But he's not going to take direction," Cheryl argued. "He . . ."

"*Je ne crois pas,*" Jackie emphasized. "Which means *I don't think so,* for those of us who do not know French." She hated to torture Cheryl, but sometimes it was necessary.

Doris giggled. Looking over her shoulder at the notebook in Jackie's lap, Doris gasped. Rather than taking notes during the interview, Jackie had made a sketch of Anthony. "Jackie, that's really good," she said, leaning in closer.

"Look," Jackie said, ignoring the compliment. "Anthony is sexy, direct, and he knows what he wants. He'd be a great manager."

"I wonder what he's doing in Illinois?" Doris said.

"Definitely running from something," Jackie guessed, quickly moving her pen across her drawing. She wanted to capture the pain that was hiding just behind Anthony's dark eyes.

"A broken heart." Doris nodded.

Cheryl groaned. "He's . . ."

"Perfect," Doris and Jackie chimed together.

Cheryl shut her notebook in defeat. "You're right," she finally said. "Anthony can do the job. He's competent, confident . . ."

"Then why don't you like him?" Doris demanded.

Cheryl was silent for a long moment. "He's too confident. And I've *really* had it with cocky men."

Jackie nodded. That was easy enough to understand.

Chapter Twenty-five

THAT EVENING, JACKIE SWEPT INTO GEORGE'S OFFICE WITH HER typical bustle, carrying a tray of coffees and a waxy white doggie bag. He looked up from his computer, then mock-slumped over in relief.

"You are a lifesaver," he said, getting up from behind the desk. After kissing her cheek, George took the doggie bag from her hands and peered into it with excitement. "What did you bring me?"

"The best food you'll ever taste," Jackie said.

After their interview with Anthony, the girls had worked all day, making plans and setting appointments. They'd coordinated a cleaning crew, a painting crew, graphic designers, and menu printers. The day had ended with a decadent sampling of dishes cooked by their new chef.

Greg had been referred to them by their Realtor. Apparently, he had been the lunch chef at Millstines and was desperate to move up. When Greg learned that Millstines was up for sale, he'd begged Betsy to pass his name on to whoever bought the space. True to her word, she had. Cheryl was skeptical at first, but Greg drew up an entire menu plan that not only fit in their budget but incorporated the type of food women might like, instead of just the typical burgers and fries fare usually associated with a theme restaurant. Intrigued, the girls scheduled a tasting.

Greg started them with delicate shitake mushroom puffs, the pungent mushrooms ensconced in delicate phyllo with melt-in-your-mouth cream centers. He served them a spinach salad, salty yet sweet with its gorgonzola cheese, fresh cut pears, and pecan shards. Then there were fresh scallops, grilled to a perfect consistency and topped with a light vanilla bean and champagne glacée. They were served alongside blackened asparagus and grilled vegetables. The skirt steak with the cheese sauce was sampled along with braised lamb chops and a chicken cooked in lemon sauce. At the very end of the meal, Greg finished them off with a hard-shelled chocolate mousse: cold, light, and perfectly creamy.

"Good find," Jackie whispered to Cheryl, nibbling delicately at a braised lamb chop.

As they wrapped up the huge dinner, Jackie called George to brief him on their progress. She was shocked to discover he was still at the office and hadn't eaten anything since breakfast. Immediately, she packed up a box of leftovers for him and headed over to his office.

"This is fresh from The Whole Package," Jackie sang, sliding out of her mink and handing over the bag of food.

"You underestimate the cringe-worthiness of that phrase," George said.

Jackie swatted at him, peering over his shoulder at the food. She had brought grilled vegetables, slices of skirt steak, and some of the chicken. A container of gorgonzola cheese sauce was neatly packaged to the side.

"You would have gotten chocolate mousse but Doris got there first," Jackie said, grinning.

"You're an angel," George said. Those dark eyes seemed to drink her in. "I would have starved without you."

"Aren't you precious," Jackie said, quickly moving away. Darting behind the desk, Jackie peered at his computer screen. There were windows and windows of material on the screen that Jackie didn't even want to understand and she flicked the monitor with her rose-tinted nails. "I've always been so curious what it is you do, exactly. I know you're a lawyer but how do you justify staying at the office until ten in the evening?"

"Lots to do, not enough time to do it," he said.

"Well," Jackie said, "I have to say, looking over the designs for my penis restaurant seems a lot more fun. That's what we did all day. I have some copies of the mock-ups . . . I think that's what Cheryl called them . . . in my purse."

Grabbing some sparkling water from the bar, George headed over to the couch, saying, "Then let's have a look." They positioned themselves at the table by the sofa, George diving into his dinner as Jackie spread out pages of designs and drawings. They seemed tacky and out of place in George's serious office.

"This one's the cover for the menu," Jackie giggled, pointing. An erotically posed man had a kitschy bubble over his head reading, "Hungry?" George shook his head, peering over his glasses, clearly uncertain whether to praise or scold. Methodically, he went through the various mock-ups with their loud colors, bright lettering, and random pictures of sexy men in aprons. The men were serving apple pie, suggestively opening bottles of champagne, and even straddling the letters that read, "Big Appetite?"

"I hope Schaumburg's ready for this," George finally said. "Darling, did you draw any of these? I feel like your work could . . ."

"We hired a graphic designer," she said brightly. When George tried to say more, she cut in with, "Tell me what you worked on today."

"The case that will never end," George groaned, neatly biting into a piece of asparagus. "I'd tell you all about it, but I don't want you to run screaming. It's late at night and you're in my office—we don't want people in the building to get the wrong idea." Jackie laughed and George wiped his hands on a napkin, saying, "The food's quite good but tell your chef he needs to marinate the vegetables more."

"Oh, he'll love that," Jackie said, rolling her eyes. "Advice from a lawyer on how to cook. He'd throw a tantrum and storm out."

Even though the girls were in love with Greg's food, Jackie had to admit she was a little worried about Greg's ego. When Greg was in the kitchen, he threw around pots and pans like some contestant on a reality cooking show. At one point, Doris suggested Greg put a lid on the noise and he threatened to sauté her. Doris had run from the kitchen, squealing and carrying on like he had come after her with a knife.

George chuckled at the picture of Doris and her near escape. "I have something for you," he said. "I keep forgetting to give it to you but . . ." His voice had taken on an unreadable tone and Jackie looked at him in surprise.

"If it's a summons for debtor's prison, I don't want it," she said.

Without answering, George bustled over to a closet. Pulling open the paneled doors, he reached in and took out a wooden box, measuring about a foot long and a foot wide. The wood was dark and rich, perfectly complementing the mahogany of the room.

"Darling, what on earth is that?" Jackie said, squinting. Her voice was perky but her stomach had turned. She really hoped George wasn't going to ruin their friendship by trying to give her presents—unless it was something too pretty to refuse, of course.

"This belonged to Robert," he said, carrying the wooden box over and carefully setting it on the table.

"It doesn't look familiar." Jackie studied the wooden artifact, surprised. It looked like something purchased at that art fair George had wanted to take her to. Jackie ran her fingers over the carved wood, then looked up, confused. "Why are you giving it to me?"

"I was holding it for him," George said, wringing his hands. "Hiding it. Your birthday present is inside, so *bon anniversaire*. Your birthday present from a few years back."

Jackie's hand flew to her chest, shocked. She thought back to all the times she'd searched for the birthday or Christmas presents Robert would get her. She'd shake them and sometimes even slit the tape open, just to get that first glimpse at whatever piece of jewelry or trinket was lying inside. One birthday, she had hunted everywhere for her birthday present and had almost given up. Just as she pulled a sapphire necklace out of his sock drawer, Robert walked into their bedroom. He had come home early from work.

Jackie seduced her way out of that one, marching up to Robert and saying in a pouty voice, "I'm a very bad girl. What are we going to do about this?" Then she'd taken his hand and pressed it against her firm breast, enjoying how quickly Robert forgot about the necklace. Breath coming fast, Robert picked her up, carried her to the bed and swatted her playfully on her taut bottom. As she squirmed and protested, he pinned her arms behind her back, flickering his tongue in and out of the sensitive area of her ear until she'd squirmed, begging him to let her go.

"This is your punishment, my dear," Robert had laughed.

That night, he explored Jackie's body in ways she had never allowed. There was little she could do to fight him off—her arms stayed pinned gently behind her back—so Jackie just endured the sweet torture, just letting out tiny little startled gasps. When he'd finally had enough, Robert had made love to her, the sapphire necklace draped over her neck and falling across her breasts like something out of *Titanic*. After that day, regardless of how pleasurable catching her had been for the both of them, Robert had gotten much more ingenious about hiding her presents.

"Giving it to George was cheating," Jackie said out loud, as though Robert were watching the transaction.

"Let's end the suspense," she said to George. "What's inside?"

Folding her hands neatly in her lap, Jackie waited. She did not make a move toward the box even though in the old days, she would have dived right in.

"I don't know," George admitted. "The IRS did look through it. They determined its contents were not fiscally related."

"If it's already been opened," Jackie mused, "it's technically a re-gift. I don't want it."

Her voice shook, revealing a confusion she didn't want to feel.

"I'm sorry I can't tell you what it is, Jacqueline." George took off his glasses and set them on a table. There were lines on his nose from the metal rims. "But the gift was for you, not me."

"You didn't snoop?" Jackie said. "I would have snooped." She looked up at George from under her lashes.

At the slight flirtation, he blushed and Jackie laughed out loud. Teasing George was much easier than dealing with this unexpected trifle.

"Robert was your best friend," she said, poking at him. "You weren't dying of curiosity?"

George shook his head. "I imagined it was personal."

They sat for a long moment. Jackie thought back to all the presents Robert had gotten her. Her favorite had been a poem commissioned from a local artist she knew, painted in calligraphy over the top of her caricature. Robert had given it to her as a joke, and then followed up with yet another piece of jewelry. He didn't understand why she only oohed at the Hawaiian pearl bracelet but then went straight back to the poem, giggling at its beautiful juxtaposition over her cartoon face.

"Are pearls no longer satisfactory to my queen?" Robert asked. He dropped a series of kisses onto the top of her head and touched the Hawaiian bracelet.

"No, it's divine," Jackie assured him, "I just think this drawing is hilarious."

Robert had pouted, taking the poem and flipping the paper over. Then, he took the bracelet and presented it to her again. "This, my dear, is for you."

"And I adore it," she said, picking up the bracelet and hooking it around her thin wrist. "Look how iridescent those pearls are." The moment Robert seemed satisfied Jackie turned her attention back to the paper with the poem.

Light, like a bird is her laugh. Strong, like a breeze is her flight.
Willful, like a crown to a queen
stands my one and only Jacqueline.

"I really love this poem," she said again.

Robert tore it from her hands, shouting, "It's just a joke! The bracelet is your gift."

"And you just turned it into a handcuff," she said. Grabbing the poem, Jackie stomped into their bedroom and slammed the door.

At the memory, Jackie shook her blond curls and pushed the intricately carved wooden box far away from her. It had been rare for her and Robert to fight but when they had, the fights had certainly been memorable.

"You're really not going to open it?" George asked, gazing at the box in confusion.

Jackie shook her head. "Not tonight," she said. "It's been waiting for me for years, hasn't it? Do a few more days really matter?"

"I couldn't have said it better myself," George said. Clearing his throat, he stood up. "I must get back to the grind," he said. "Thanks so much for dinner, my darling."

Jackie turned to the box. Picking it up, she silently cursed how heavy the wood was. It would be a struggle to carry that weight with her. "Good night, George," she said.

George nodded, watching her carefully. "Good night, Jacqueline."

Chapter Twenty-six

DORIS REFUSED TO COME TO THE ASSISTANT MANAGER INTERVIEW for her blond stripper. "He'll recognize me," she fretted.

"He sees hundreds of women every day," Cheryl said. "No, he won't."

"I'm busy," Doris said. "I'm making banana bread." Just then, she dropped her wooden spoon on the floor. Quickly, she snatched it up, rinsed it, and continued stirring the dough.

"Ew," Mandy said, chin on her hand.

Jackie, Cheryl, and Mandy all leaned against the counter at Doris's, entertained as always by her attempts to cook. Like the setup for a comedy skit, eighteen banana peels, six broken eggshells, and three empty bags of flour lay on the counter next to a big mixing bowl. So far, the bowl held a glumpy mixture of flour, two hard sticks of butter, and mashed-up bananas. Doris was trying to stir this with a wooden spoon, sweat beading on her forehead.

"This is painful," Cheryl said. Sweeping past Doris, she opened drawers until she found an electric mixer, and then practically threw it at Doris. "Use this. You're driving me bananas."

Mandy cracked up, indicating one of the banana peels on the counter.

Shaking her head, Doris pushed the electric mixer aside and explained that she'd read dessert tasted better if the whole thing was made by hand. "It has something to do with the connection of energy to the food," Doris said. "I didn't really understand it, but I think it made a lot of sense."

"Mom, no one will even know," Mandy protested. It was Mandy's turn to bring snacks for the debate team. "Just use the beater."

"I want to infuse the bread with my love," Doris said, beating harder. "Because I love you."

Mandy rolled her eyes. "Puke."

"I'm making a cappuccino," Cheryl said, slamming the cupboards until she found a can of espresso. "Who wants one?"

Cheryl needed the caffeine because, in truth, Doris's clumsy motions had grated on her last nerve. More than that, Cheryl needed to get pumped for this interview with the blonde. He had sounded hesitant over the phone and Cheryl was frightened that he might say no to the opportunity altogether. They needed him. Otherwise that Anthony character would be running the show.

"Doris, I really think you should come to this interview," Jackie said. "It will be very informal. After the way Cheryl freaked out during Anthony's interview, I'll definitely need you for some levity."

Doris nodded. "You do make a good point . . ."

Cheryl turned the milk frother on full blast, eyeing her friends. They had already ganged up on her about Anthony; now they wanted to tell her how to handle Gabe?

"Look," Cheryl said, pouring the froth over a shot of espresso. "I have been in the corporate world for years. You need to recognize that I am a fountain of information. You should learn from me instead of discounting my knowledge. Because it's vast."

"We're opening a penis restaurant," Jackie said. "It's meant to be fun."

"It will be," Cheryl said. "After all, we're holding our interview at a coffee shop, of all places. If you pull out a dollar to tip the waitress, our future manager might get confused and . . ."

"My daughter is standing right here," Doris shrieked, slamming the mixing bowl on the counter. She ran her fingers through her hair, the flour settling in like a bad case of dandruff. Mandy took the opportunity to dip her finger into the batter to taste. "How is it?" Doris asked, pulling her hair up and off her neck. Flour rained down.

"Wow, Mom," Mandy said. Casually, she meandered over to the cupboard and grabbed for a glass for water. Doris watched her do this, alarmed.

"Is it . . . ?"

"No comment," Mandy said, swishing the water in her mouth.

"The consistency will probably mellow out when it's baked," Jackie said, peering suspiciously at the thick concoction.

"I hope you're right." Doris sighed. "Okay, listen. When you do the interview, remember that we are offering this man a professional position. I don't want him to think we're bringing him on for any reason other than his . . ."

"Perfect abs, hot body, and large schlong?" asked Mandy, batting her eyes. She grabbed a soda out of the fridge and scampered out of the kitchen before her mother could scold her.

"Doris, just come with us," Cheryl said.

"She doesn't have to," Jackie said.

Cheryl threw up her hands. "Okay. And when I don't feel like coming to work, I won't show up either."

"We shouldn't hire him," Doris said, setting down the wooden spoon. "I know he'll remember me. It's going to look bad."

"Honey, I'm sure he'll appreciate the attention," Jackie said. "Besides, we're giving him an opportunity to do something with his life."

"He was probably doing plenty right where he was," Cheryl said. Doris's blue eyes widened, so she added, "I'm just kidding. It will all be very professional. That's why you should come. As a business owner, you need to get experience at this type of thing."

"No, that's okay," Doris said, flinging banana peels into the trash. "Just . . . don't say my name or anything."

Cheryl regarded her with amazement, pulling on a fleece-lined leather jacket. "How would he know your name?"

"The bouncer checked my ID," Doris said, face mournful. She was looking off into the distance, obviously reliving the entire night at the bar. When she cringed, Cheryl assumed she'd remembered the part where she threw up.

"Stop worrying," Jackie said.

"There's nothing to worry about," Cheryl said. "If he's too pretty to talk, we won't hire him—we'll just fuck him."

Picking up the car keys, she headed to the door.

"Don't do that," Doris begged, chasing after them with the wet wooden spoon. It dripped across the floor.

Outside, the sun was bright. Cheryl took a few deep breaths of the crisp autumn air. The car door dinged as they climbed in, Cheryl's silver keychain glistening in the sunlight. After pulling the door shut behind her, Cheryl looked at Jackie. Her lips twitched.

Widening her eyes and looking slightly panicked, she said, "Don't do that." It was a perfect impression of Doris. The two friends erupted into laughter. Tears ran down Jackie's cheeks and Cheryl banged her hand against the steering wheel until it hurt.

Wiping her eyes, Jackie said, "We can't hire him. We'll find him tied up in her bedroom with his sexy little ankles broken!"

Gasping, Cheryl opened the window to let the air cool her face. "Doris is scary. If she got away with vandalizing Katherine Rigney, that woman can get away with anything. I'm warning this guy to stay far, far away."

"Should we raise the bet on the banana bread?" Jackie said. "I say she's going to the bakery the second we pull out."

"No way," Cheryl said. "She'll keep trying until the house burns down. Of course, she might get confused. You know, start pulling out the dollar bills when the firemen arrive."

The friends cracked up. Cheryl pulled out of the driveway, Doris waving hopefully from the window.

Chapter Twenty-seven

IN SPITE OF HER CONCERNS ABOUT GABE, CHERYL FELL IN LOVE with him the moment he opened his mouth.

"I remember you ladies," he said, easing his handsome form into the booth.

The coffee shop where they met him was halfway between Chicago and Schaumburg. Over the phone, Gabe had explained that since he lived in the city, he had to borrow a car to get to the interview. At the time, Cheryl had thought, *Unprofessional.* Staring at his gorgeous face, she thought, *So forgivable.*

Gabe was like a tanned statue of David. Curly blond hair wisped around his cherubic face. His eyes were wide and the color of the ocean at a vacation resort. The man really was gorgeous—it wasn't the tequila goggles that had made them think that.

"Where's your friend?" Gabe asked, looking from Cheryl to Jackie. "The one who had the flu?"

"You *remember* her?" Jackie burst out laughing. She put her hand to her mouth. "I'm sorry. God, she'll be thrilled."

"You're very sweet," Cheryl said. "But I think we all know it wasn't the flu."

Gabe's eyes sparkled and he adjusted the collar on his fur-lined jean jacket. "Never would have guessed it."

Cheryl pulled out her notebook and ran through the same questions they'd asked Anthony. Halfway through, Cheryl realized she was being as informal with Gabe as she had been formal with Anthony. This wasn't her intent but Gabe's aquamarine eyes and dimpled chin made it impossible to be professional. After learning Gabe had an MBA from Northwestern, Cheryl stopped short and said, "Gabe. Why are *you*, of all people, a stripper?"

Gabe blushed. Turning a packet of Sweet'N Low over and over in his hands, the young man seemed at a loss for words. A golden lock of hair fell over his forehead, and suddenly, Cheryl felt like she and Gabe were out on a porch somewhere, sharing secrets over a glass of wine. *That's his gift*, she realized with a start. Gabe had a way of creating immediate intimacy, even though he was a perfect stranger.

"Gabe, don't answer that," Jackie said. "It's probably illegal to even ask a question like that, isn't it Cheryl?"

Legal or not, it was certainly uncalled for. Cheryl started to apologize but Gabe cut in with, "No, I understand why you're asking. It's a tough question. I ask myself that all the time and, in the end, I try not to get too introspective about it." Cheryl almost melted. The should-be model had uttered a four-syllable word without even batting his beautiful lashes. "But I guess the answer is . . ." Gabe hesitated, then looked right at them. "Women love me. They always have, they always will. I know it sounds cocky and I'm sorry, since you ladies are women, but I may as well make a living off of it."

Jackie nodded. Cheryl noticed she had her chin in her hand, admiring Gabe like some exhibit at the art fair.

"You'd be a great serial killer," Cheryl said. "I'd get in the car with you."

Gabe narrowed his eyes and glared. "Try it. Just see what

happens to you," and the three burst out laughing. "I am, in a way," he admitted. "I kill 'em with kindness, every day."

"Gabe, if you did us the honor of working with us we'd pay for your move to Schaumburg but you'd be on salary. It wouldn't be nearly as much as you make right now or even a corporate position," Cheryl apologized. "But we'd get you out of that sleazy club," she said. "However, you'd be the co-manager and . . ."

"Are you the manager?"

Gabe's gaze seemed to penetrate her and Cheryl couldn't help but think the most inappropriate thoughts. She blushed all the way down to her freckles. "No, no. We hired . . . someone from your club, actually. Anthony."

Gabe turned pale. "Oh."

"What's wrong?" Cheryl demanded. Quickly, she said, "I can fire him."

Jackie elbowed her. "Cheryl."

The waitress arrived just then, a skinny little thing with black dyed hair and painted-on red lipstick. As she laid out the food, a slow flush crept up the back of her neck. Handing Gabe his hamburger, she turned beet red as he said, "Thanks, doll."

The young girl practically ran from the table. Hiding behind the host stand, she giggled behind her hand with another waitress. The other server was about eighty, wearing sensible shoes and a no-nonsense light blue dress. Even she squinted toward their table to get a better look at Gabe. Oblivious, he picked up his burger and started to eat. Cheryl and Jackie stared, fixated on the way he handled the bun.

"So . . ." Cheryl finally said, taking a sip of ice water. "Talk to us about the problem with Anthony."

Gabe set his burger down and added more ketchup. "He doesn't like me. I'm not sure why."

Jackie made a high-pitched noise and Gabe looked at her sharply. Digging into her salad, she started rattling on about their plans for the menu. Gabe relaxed and started asking questions about the restaurant and then, Schaumburg. When they had finished eating, Gabe kissed both of their hands and promised to think over their offer.

"What was all the squealing about?" Cheryl asked the second Gabe was out the door.

"I'm sorry to tell you this ..." Jackie said, staring at Gabe through the restaurant window. He was loping across the driveway like a young cowboy heading out to rope a steer. As his taut form slid behind the wheel of a white Volvo, they both sighed in admiration. "But that man is gay."

"*No*," Cheryl bellowed, mouth dropped to the table. She peered at Gabe through the windowpane, pressing her nose to its steamy surface. "Are you kidding me? I already mapped out my future with him and everything. We're getting married in the spring. Honeymoon is somewhere we can be naked. All the time. You really think he's gay?"

"Absolutely," Jackie mused, smearing on some lip gloss. "And the sad thing is . . . he wishes he were straight more than anything in the world." She snapped her compact shut with a flourish.

Grabbing for the container of salt, Cheryl sprinkled a large quantity on her hand and tossed it over her left shoulder, insisting, "No way. Didn't you see the way he was looking at us, at the waitress? He remembered *Doris*, of all people. He likes the vagina."

Jackie hummed a little tune, smiling prettily. It was obvious she thought she'd spent more than enough time in the art world to have her gaydar in check. "I think he and Anthony are a couple," she whispered. "In a lover's quarrel."

"Stop it," Cheryl pounded the table, half in resistance, half in glee.

Gabe drove past the window, waving and beeping his horn.

"And if they're not," Jackie considered, eyeing him and waggling her fingers, "they certainly should be."

"GABE REALLY ASKED about me?" Doris repeated, for the tenth time. Her eyes were bright and starry and she was clutching a steaming pot of tea. A tell-tale bakery box lay on the counter instead of a batch of banana bread and Jackie's heart swelled with love for her friend.

"For God's sake, give me that," she said affectionately, grabbing the teapot from Doris and setting it down with a plunk. "He's gay."

"You shouldn't joke about that," Doris said, sitting at the kitchen table and adding a sugar cube to her tea.

"Gay people exist, Doris," Jackie said. "Believe it. There is more to the world than Schaumburg."

"Just because I haven't lived in Paris for the last several years does *not* mean that I am unfamiliar with the layout of the planet," Doris said, slamming down her mug and splashing some green tea onto the table.

Jackie giggled. It was fun to make Doris angry. Whenever she got mad, she'd lean forward and bare her teeth like a bulldog ready to attack. This had always been effective on the soccer team so many years ago, but now it was simply entertaining.

"I like it when you get mad," Jackie said. "It's much better than that even keel the drugs put you on."

"They help me," Doris said.

"They *helped* you," Jackie said, "get through a depression. But do you want to be on them forever?"

Shaking her head, Doris said, "No. But . . . I just want to wait until I'm sure. Okay?"

Jackie squeezed her hand. "Okay."

Out of the corner of her eye, Jackie noticed her name on the schedule board. She'd written it up in red marker to help Mandy better manage her trysts. "I put myself up there," she said guiltily. In the bright red ink, Jackie's name stood out like the scarlet letter.

Doris looked up at the schedule board and brightened. "Good, Jackie. That looks good. Now we can all keep track of each other."

Trying to fight away that twinge of guilt, Jackie clicked her manicure against the counter. Her nails were looking ragged. It might be time to pawn off another piece of jewelry so she could afford those little necessities like mani/pedis. Jackie considered the sparkling rings decorating her hand. The emerald was way too precious, the solitaire from Tiffany too sentimental, and the pretty pink cocktail diamond . . . not a chance. Jackie was going to have to dig into her regular jewelry stash and sell off pieces like that bracelet from Hawaii. The thought made her feel sick.

"You're thinking about Gabe," Doris guessed, grabbing a gingersnap off the plate set in the center of the table. "Isn't he beautiful?" Jackie nodded. He really was. "I can't believe he remembered me. What if he's my soul mate?" Doris fantasized. "What if the restaurant is a huge success and we become ladies of leisure . . ."

"You're already a lady of leisure," Jackie said, perching on the edge of a chair.

"What if he wants to run away to an island together?" Doris chewed on a cookie, her thoughts a million miles away.

"He'd have to wear a swimsuit the whole time," Jackie said, grinning.

Doris shook her head and took a sip of tea. "I couldn't leave my family. I wouldn't go."

"Oh, we'd be fine," Jackie said. "And if Doug bothered to come back, I'd make him sleep outside where he belongs." Jackie could have kicked herself. She'd gone too far, actually saying his name out loud. There had been a silent understanding in the house since the day Doug left—the only one who mentioned his name was Doris.

Doris's face immediately went splotchy. She set her tea down with a clatter. Instantly, tears streamed down her face.

"Honey . . ." Jackie said. Jumping up from her chair, she walked over to Doris and put an arm around her shoulder. "Where is this coming from?" Jackie was amazed that someone could go from happiness to devastation in less than ten seconds. Doris was teaching her all sorts of new emotional tricks these days.

"I miss him," Doris said, sniffling. "I haven't even talked to him."

"*Bien sûr*" Jackie repeated, patting her friend's back each time. "*Bien sûr* . . ."

"I just don't understand it," Doris said. "What did I do?"

Jackie pulled Doris's chair out from the table. Taking Doris's face in her hands, Jackie stared into her eyes and said, "Listen to me. You didn't do anything. He's just going through a midlife crisis, angel. Men do that. *Women* do that. It's not personal."

Doris hiccuped. "Maybe I should have been nicer to him," she admitted, taking off her glasses and wiping her red-rimmed eyes. "He thought that I hated everything he did."

Jackie shook her head. "Doug was not perfect either," she said firmly. "Look at me." Doris's eyes were watery. "Marriage is work. If Doug was unhappy, it was his job to talk to you about it. You don't have a slew of psychic powers I don't know about, do you?"

"No."

"And if he would have told you he was unhappy, you would have done something to fix the situation, right?"

Doris nodded. Building up steam, Jackie gave a whole speech to convince her that Doug could have done something to change their situation. He could have done anything other than leave. He had options like communicating or communicating or communicating . . .

Doris finally gave a tiny smile and shook her head. "I would have done anything he'd asked. I love him."

"I know you do," Jackie said.

The two friends were silent for a minute, then Jackie grabbed a ginger cookie and leaned forward eagerly. "Now, let's have some fun. Tell me how you're going to seduce Gabe on that island."

Chapter Twenty-eight

As it turned out, Doris did not have to make an effort to plot and pander for Gabe's attention. From the moment he walked through the door of Millstines for staff orientation, in all of his blond glory, he was on Doris like a piece of oversexed Velcro.

"My beauty," he exclaimed, rushing forward. Gabe practically bowed to the floor, covering her hand with kisses. Clearly, Doris loved the attention. She was more animated than she had been in weeks, gesturing with her hands, laughing, and even flirting.

"This could be really good," Cheryl said, watching the scene. "Maybe he's, like, the fairy godmother who can turn her back into Dori."

"Just don't call him a fairy," Jackie twittered. "I think he'd get very upset."

The staff orientation was a training designed to teach Anthony, Gabe, and the waiters what would be expected of them at The Whole Package. Earlier in the day, Cheryl had set up the main area like a conference room. Now, groups of handsome men were camped out at the tables like models at a runway show. As the women walked through the crowd, perfectly gorgeous faces swiveled their way. Many of them gave flirty waves.

"This is like heaven," Cheryl whispered behind her hand.

Jackie nodded, giggling. "We. Are. Geniuses."

Cheryl nodded, looking around the room. "Everything is falling into place."

The waitstaff wasn't the only thing ready to go. The storage room was stocked with kitchen supplies, plates, tablecloths, and decorations. The marketing materials they had selected were all at the printing company and in two days, the sign for the door was scheduled to arrive. MILLSTINES—PIES AND PEOPLE would be replaced with THE WHOLE PACKAGE—COME HERE. This slogan would appear over a caricature of an oiled-up man, beckoning erotically to the general female population.

"I almost forgot to tell you," Cheryl said, pulling out her notes and setting them onto a banquette table. "The Almighty George was asking about you."

"*Oui?*" Jackie said, straightening her décolletage and smiling at one of the waiters. "What did he say?"

"Just wanted to know if you were all right," Cheryl said, glancing through her notes for the training. "I think we'll start in ten minutes. Sound good?"

"Of course," Jackie said. "Is that *all* he said?"

"Yup."

At Jackie's silence, Cheryl crossed something off her notes. Looking up, she raised an eyebrow and said, "He talked my ear off about you for an hour. I can't believe you didn't tell me you went on a date with him. When were you going to mention that?"

Jackie adjusted her earrings. "It wasn't a date."

"You two might be really good together," Cheryl suggested.

"You've already mentioned that," Jackie said, suddenly angry. "Do I have to hear it again?"

Cheryl giggled, assuming Jackie's rage to be a joke. When her fair-haired friend actually stood there with fists clenched and eyes blazing, Cheryl backpedaled in surprise. "Jackie, I'm sorry. I thought . . . I just . . ."

"*Why?*" Jackie demanded. "His best friend was my *husband* and now that he's out of the way, George thinks he can just have me? I loved Robert."

Cheryl was genuinely confused. "Of course you did. What does that have to do with anything?"

Doris was looking over toward them, probably trying to see what all the commotion was about.

Jackie lowered her voice. "I am never, *ever* getting involved with George."

"Relax," Cheryl said in an equally hushed tone. She smoothed down a strand of hair. "Jackie, you're making a scene. I didn't mean to . . ."

"Everyone thinks we'd be so perfect together," Jackie said, practically getting in Cheryl's face. "But it would be a huge mistake."

Since Jackie rarely showed her cards, Cheryl didn't know what to think. Did Jackie really have feelings for George? It wouldn't surprise her. Even though George was older, he was distinguished, worldly, and crazy about Jackie. The combination of her and George really wouldn't be that far-fetched.

"I'm sorry," Jackie said after a moment, pressing her fingers into her temples. "I'm sorry, Cheryl. It's just been a . . ."

"It's okay," Cheryl said, cautiously squeezing her friend's hand. From the corner of her eye, Cheryl could see Anthony watching them. He was sitting over in the corner, dressed all in black. His muscles were well defined underneath his cable-knit sweater, and his hair glistened under the light. "Well, you look good," Cheryl finally said. "Anthony was staring."

Jackie turned her blue eyes to Anthony. He gave a little nod and went back to reading the management training manual Cheryl had put together.

"I'm going to go talk to him," Jackie said. "Okay?" Without waiting for an answer, Jackie trotted over to the gay man.

Cheryl shook her head. Typical Jackie. The moment things got personal, she ran away.

Standing alone, Cheryl considered the room. The waiters were seated at several tables throughout the room, talking among themselves. Many of them had brought notebooks, just like Cheryl had instructed. That was a good sign; her staff would follow directions.

Considering that both Jackie and Doris were hanging all over their two managers, Cheryl wondered if now would be an appropriate time to give a speech about sexual harassment. Unfortunately, even thinking about that word made Cheryl remember her time at TurnKey and the fact that she would have sexually harassed Andy on the copier, Stan's desk, the stairwell—anywhere he'd asked, if only he'd asked. But of course, he never had.

Cheryl put her hand to her head, remembering. The night before, she'd made a huge mistake. She was at home alone and had had one too many espressos. After putting in four hours on the paperwork for The Whole Package and her lawsuit against Stan, Cheryl was restless. She wanted to do something exciting . . . Two seconds later, "exciting" turned into "dialing Andy's number." Pressing Send was like having an out-of-body experience. Cheryl gritted her teeth and held the phone away from her ear, wondering what she would say if he actually picked up. After four rings, the call went to voice mail. It was only as she heard his message echo in her ear that she'd glanced at the clock. Two a.m. So, thanks to caller ID, Andy now knew that Cheryl had been thinking about him in the middle of the night. The very thought made Cheryl flush with embarrassment.

"Attention, everyone," Cheryl announced, clearing her throat and straightening her skirt. "Let's talk about what it means to be The Whole Package."

"GABE WANTS TO go shopping with me," Doris said eagerly. The meeting was over and they had piled into Cheryl's car. "He said my shirt wasn't as flattering as it could be for such a . . ." Doris clapped her hand over her mouth and looked out the window, embarrassed, as though the passersby could read her lips.

"For such a . . . ?" Jackie prodded.

"Nice figure," Doris mumbled.

"Big rack," Cheryl said, pulling out of the drive. Doris had always been blessed with the bazookas. She just hid them under those grandma sweaters.

"Well, that's inappropriate," Doris said primly, folding her hands. "I don't think that's what he was trying to say."

"So are you going to go?" Jackie asked. "Shopping with him?"

Doris paused, and then nodded. "Yes. But I told him it couldn't be a date."

Cheryl coughed to cover her laughter. "And how did he take that?"

"He was fine. He knows I'm married."

Of course it was fine, Cheryl thought. He's *gay*.

"When is this fun little excursion?" Jackie asked, putting down the rearview mirror and applying some lip gloss.

"Tomorrow." Doris beamed. "He's picking me up at ten."

"Don't buy him anything," Cheryl said. At Doris's glare, she added, "He likes you, he's not using you but . . . it's too early to hand over the credit card."

"I'm not stupid," Doris said. "But thanks so much for the warning."

WHEN CHERYL DROPPED them off, Jackie and Doris piled out of the car and Jackie immediately complained of a headache. Inside, Doris bustled to the cabinet over the kitchen sink. Throwing it open, she eyed a row of pills. "Do you want some Vicodin?"

Jackie burst out laughing. "No! What is wrong with you? Darling, I didn't take a bullet, I have a headache."

Doris looked confused and Jackie smothered another giggle. "Thanks, honey. I think I'm just going to turn in early."

"I think I'll read," Doris said, wandering over to the cupboards to hunt for a snack. She was humming to herself and for a moment, Jackie wanted to tease, "Doug? Doug who?!" but thought better of it.

Instead, she sneaked off to the guest bedroom and pulled the door shut behind her. She didn't have a headache at all, just needed some alone time. The things Cheryl had said about George had really gotten under her skin. It was time to nip this thing in the bud. Settling into the down duvet, she took a deep breath, picked up the phone, and called him.

"Hello, Jacqueline." George answered on the first ring, clearly pleased to hear from her. "How did the meeting with the waiters go?"

"We have to stop having these conversations." She said it cold and clear, like an executioner.

There was silence on George's end of the phone. Then he cleared his throat. "Had I asked you about the waiters before? I'll try to stop being redundant."

Jackie was sitting on the bed, legs dangling over the edge like she was in high school, calling a crush. Out of the corner of her eye, she could see the wooden box George had just given her, perched on the very top shelf of the closet. She still hadn't opened it.

"George, don't be coy," Jackie said. "You were Robert's best friend. I was his wife. I loved him."

"Yes."

"So . . ." Jackie twisted the phone cord around her wrist, then looked at it in surprise. Who on earth had phone cords anymore? Only Doris, because this was a princess phone that perfectly matched the ivory princess decorations that made up the room's decor. Jackie smiled in spite of herself.

"What am I doing with my life, George?" she asked, lying back on the bed. "I'm camping out in my friend's guest bedroom, which is something out of the *Princess Diaries*. Plus, I'm having a conversation that borders on intimacy with—"

"Jacqueline," George interrupted her, gentle. "I do not mean to rush you. Take all the time you need. But I think my intentions for you are quite clear."

Her heart skipped a beat. "You have intentions?"

George didn't answer.

"*Why?*" she said, voice fearful.

"Why what?" he wondered.

"Why do you have feelings for me?" Jackie asked. "Why are you so kind to me? What have I done to deserve it?"

With Robert, the answer had been clear. When they had met, Jackie was a young, gorgeous woman amazed at his opulent lifestyle. She had made him feel like a man. With George . . . George had always had more going for him than Robert had. He could have had his pick of women, one much younger than she was now. Why was he interested in her?

"I'm sorry this is confusing for you," George finally said. "It is not my intent. I have always enjoyed your company, Jacqueline, and I made it quite clear to Robert that if he ever left you, I would snatch you up. Of course, I had meant that in quite another way," he said, somber. "Please do not think that I am happy with the turn of events."

Jackie stayed silent, hugging a pillow to her chest.

"The affections have been here for years," George said. "I apologize if it seems as though I am not respecting Robert, but he loved you and he loved me. This is not like he is still here, Jacqueline, and I am trying to speak with you behind closed doors."

Jackie thought back to all those times they had been on double dates. George would make jokes and while his date smiled politely, Jackie would be the one laughing out loud. Once in a while, her blue eyes had met his dark ones for a moment too long. She'd avert hers in confusion, certainly misreading his intent.

"You mean you've always had a thing for me?" she asked, kicking at the bed with her stocking feet.

"Not a thing, Jacqueline," George complained. "Please do not be base. I have admired and respected you for years. That's all."

A tear rolled down Jackie's cheek.

The first time Jackie realized her feelings for Robert might be fiscal, not physical, was the first time Jackie introduced him to one of her artist friends. Kimi had graduated with her from the Art Institute and had become a successful sculptor. A beautiful girl adorned with facial piercings, Kimi was someone always experimenting with things like colored extensions and dreadlocks, even well into their "adult" years. She had missed Jackie's wedding due to a fellowship in South Africa, so Jackie was excited for her and Robert to finally meet. At least Jackie had thought she was excited, but on the way to the restaurant, she and Robert had fought, something they rarely did.

The fight had started because Robert insisted on showing up to dinner in a three-piece suit, his typical style of dress. Jackie had begged him to consider the audience—cool Kimi and whatever exotic lover she'd attached herself to this time. She didn't want him to look so . . . well, old.

"Jacqueline, there is nothing wrong with wearing a suit to a nice dinner," Robert said, smoothing his hairline in the rearview mirror. "Only the little people don't take the time to bother with good grooming."

"The little people," Jackie echoed. "Wow, Robert. You certainly can be a judgmental asshole, can't you?"

Jackie rolled down the window, letting the breeze blow back her hair. For about the billionth time, Jackie was grateful that Robert still believed she was an orphan. When Jackie was a child, her father had stumbled around in the same grimy pair of Levis and the same light blue, button-up shirt every day. When the stains got too bad, Jackie would steal his clothes and run them through the wash, her father yelling, "Where'd my pants go?"

Good grooming was one thing, but that didn't mean dressing for a cocktail party at all times. So, instead of feeling proud to introduce Robert to her friend, Jackie felt shame as she walked into the casual restaurant with a husband old enough to be her father and dressed like a board member of the New York Stock Exchange.

Surrounded by loud music, plentiful tapas, and waiters fluent in Portuguese, Robert seemed even more formal and out of place. Of course he was pleasant to Kimi and Jumar—a luscious Egyptian archaeologist—but since the two smelled like weed and sported especially wide pupils, Robert seemed amused by the experience rather than a part of it.

"Let's get them a big bottle of water," Robert whispered to Jackie, behind his manicured hand, "to wet down that dry mouth." Instead of making her laugh, this irritated her even more. The fact was, Jackie had dived into every outing Robert had ever taken her to, no matter what she thought of his friends.

The minute Robert excused himself to go to the bathroom and was out of sight, Kimi had clapped her hands in reverence. "Brilliant. You found a patron," she said. "Now, you focus on your art."

"Kimi," Jackie scolded, ducking her head.

The other artist gave her a knowing smile. Years later, Jackie realized she had never denied the statement.

"Jacqueline?" George said now. "Are you still there?"

"Yes," she said, staring across the room at the wooden box. "I care for you, George. But I don't want to care for you because of what you *give* me. I'm poor, I'm desperate, and I'm lonely. That's not a good combination in a woman."

George chuckled loud and long. "Jacqueline, anyone who takes one look at you can see that's not true."

"Maybe they should look a little further," Jackie suggested. Once again, she wrapped the cord around her finger. She watched as the skin turned a bright purple.

"Then I will take you at face value," George finally said. "I do not want for you to love me for anything other than me."

"Love," Jackie repeated. Her voice was weak. "Who said anything about love?"

"Good night, Jacqueline," he said. "I'll speak with you tomorrow."

Jackie bit her lip and set down the receiver, hating herself. She was already looking forward to his call.

Chapter Twenty-nine

CHERYL WAS OUT RUNNING ERRANDS WHEN HER PHONE LIT UP. Easing her car around the corner, she pressed the button on her earpiece. "This is Cheryl."

"Was there any particular reason you called me at two in the morning?" The voice was warm, masculine.

Andy.

"Hit the wrong button," she lied, her body in an immediate fervor.

"Interesting . . ." he said. Cheryl cringed, tightly clutching the steering wheel. "Do you want me to stop by?" he asked. "I imagine you must. I've just finished dinner with a client, so if you had something you wanted to talk to me about . . ."

"Why would you *imagine I must*?" Cheryl demanded. It had been so long since they'd spoken that she'd forgotten just how infuriating he was.

"Well, you called me at two in the morning." There was a smile in Andy's voice. "You must have had something you wanted to get off your chest."

Cheryl checked her reflection, desperately wiping at the mascara melted around her eyes and trying to remember where she was in her waxing cycle. She took a deep breath. "Well, I don't know why you're even *asking* if you can stop by. Last time you just did."

"I think you made it clear that wasn't the correct approach."

Cheryl almost ran a red light. Desperately, she tried to slow her heart rate and remind herself she was behind the wheel of a powerful vehicle. Without proper handling, it could kill her and everyone around her.

"Don't be ridiculous," she practically shouted. "But I really did just . . ."

"Dial the wrong number?" Andy said. "Well, nice to hear from you. Oh and thanks for calling to thank me for dinner, by the way," he finished. "I appreciated that."

Andy hung up. Furiously, she hit the callback number. He picked up on the third ring. "This is Andy."

"The woman does not call the man to thank him for an evening out," Cheryl spat. "The man calls the woman to thank her for going out. So thank *you* for not calling *me*."

Cheryl careened into her driveway, slammed the car door, and stomped inside, switching on the lights in the kitchen. The room was empty, clean and sparkling. Just the way she'd left it. She stomped into the living room, threw her phone on the sofa, and then flipped on the fake fire, wishing she could throw Andy over the logs.

I imagine you must.

What an ass!!!

Cheryl paced the living room angrily, picking up her phone a thousand times, almost calling him back just to tell him what a complete and utter bother he really was. Suddenly, she saw the reflection of headlights bounce across her living room walls. Heart in her throat, Cheryl looked toward the window. The 4Runner was parked in her driveway and Andy was barreling up the walk.

Immediately, Cheryl opened the door and put her hands on her hips.

"You are really unbelievable!" she told him.

He pulled off his leather gloves and gently threw them in her general direction. She let them land in the snow by her feet. "You worked with me for how many weeks and never bothered to find out if I was married?" he demanded.

She sneaked a glance at his finger. Bare.

"You think you don't even have to call me if you want to go on a date?" Cheryl shouted back.

"Just because we have dinner you think it was a date?" Andy stooped down to grab his gloves, brushing past her into the house.

Cheryl pulled the door shut behind them, hands shaking. Andy turned, his woodsy scent filling the room, the fire flickering behind him.

"We have to get something straight," Andy told her, voice low. Pulling off his shoes, he threw them toward the door and started moving toward her. "There's really very little about you that I like."

Cheryl gulped. Andy was dangerously close. She backed up until she was pinned against the door. Deliberately, Andy reached forward, placing his hand just above her left shoulder. She could not move without their bodies colliding. Her chest heaved.

"So, why don't you tell me," he whispered, green eyes penetrating hers. "Why did you call me last night?"

"I don't . . ." He moved forward, lips parted. "I think you should . . ." Cheryl could barely speak.

Slowly, Andy lowered his hand, gently touching her hair and tracing his fingers over her lips. "Yeah?" he challenged. "What did you want to talk to me about that was so urgent?" He pressed his body forward so that it was lightly touching hers. Cheryl's knees actually buckled.

"This," she admitted breathlessly.

Andy pinned her against the door and grabbed her face in his hands. His mouth crushed hers with a hot intensity, and then slowly, deliberately, ran his tongue over her lower lip. Gently, he took it in his teeth. "Oh . . ." she begged, straining toward him.

Finally, Andy kissed her. Pushing her up against the wall, Andy plunged his tongue deep into her mouth. Cheryl's body ached as she buried her mouth in his, finally becoming part of this man she had yearned for. Tasting his minty breath, she melted into the warmth of his kiss. His hands were everywhere, running up and over the back of her skirt, around the tiny curve of her waistline, and up and under the softness of her shirt. His touch was firm and possessive, searing her skin as he cupped her breasts, sliding his hands back down and behind, holding her up against him. Roughly, Andy lifted her. She wrapped her legs around him, and quickly, he carried her into the living room. Her foot knocked into a lamp and it crashed to the ground with a tiny spark. Andy pushed her onto the rug by the fire, hand gently cradling her head. Andy lifted her skirt and expertly stroked her body, while unbuckling his pants with one hand.

"You sure about this?" he asked, voice hoarse. Cheryl took advantage of the moment of hesitation and flipped him over, desperately trying to push herself onto him. He chuckled. "Oh no."

Deftly, Andy grabbed her arms and guided her back to the ground. She gazed up at him, longing for his touch. Andy took his time; kissing her neck, slowly tasting every inch of her body. Then Andy held her gaze, letting the desire build between them with every excruciating second.

"Please . . . " she begged.

Cheryl didn't have to ask a second time.

Chapter Thirty

DORIS WAS SITTING AT THE KITCHEN TABLE BY SEVEN A.M.,
getting ready for her "date" with Gabe. She had set up a display of
makeup and a light-up mirror, and was heating up curlers that
may have been from the seventies.

"He's not picking you up 'til ten," Jackie groaned, shuffling past
her to the fridge. "What on earth are you doing?" Although it was
nice to see Doris taking an interest in her own appearance, this
was a little ridiculous.

Jackie opened the fridge and selected a vial of face lotion from
her stash in the meat drawer. She needed something for her eyes.
She'd been up half the night, crying. At least seven times she'd
almost opened the damn box from Robert, then finally put it away,
his gift still a mystery.

"Why do you keep that in the fridge?" Doris wondered, watching the pearly liquid shimmer against Jackie's skin.

"Cools on contact. That reduces pore size, encourages collagen
productivity and tone enhancement. Would you like to try?"

"No, I . . ." Doris hesitated, glanced at the blue tube.

"Oh, just put it on," Jackie said, squeezing out a pearly dollop.

Dutifully, Doris removed her glasses and let the lotion be massaged into her face. She peered into the mirror. Her face brightened.

"Wow," Doris said. "My face looks shinier. Younger."

"The magic of the French face cream," Jackie said. She rummaged through the cupboards until she found the coffee press, filled it with water, and put it on the stove.

"It smells like roses," Doris said, touching her face with her hand, and then sniffing it.

Jackie settled at the table and watched as Doris picked up a pair of tweezers and attempted to pluck her eyebrows. This was a task that could take hours. Doris's eyebrows were thick, perfectly in fashion back in the day when Brooke Shields was all the rage. Jackie considered mentioning a good wax, but decided to save her breath. Instead, she went in for another sensitive topic.

"Doris, did you tell Mandy?" Jackie asked.

Doris's face fell. She set down the tweezers and blinked. "Tell Mandy what?"

"That you're going on a date with a man that's not her father," Jackie said. If Gabe showed up here without Doris saying anything to Mandy, the poor kid might have a heart attack.

"It's not a date," Doris insisted, picking the tweezers back up.

"Because he's *gay*," Jackie drawled. "But do you know that?"

Doris pursed her lips in annoyance. "He is not gay."

"Well, seriously. Don't give him any money." Jackie sighed. "Remember how you like to throw him those bills."

"Jackie, you're being rude."

Jackie nodded. Sometimes the best remedy for failing at your own life was to interfere with someone else's. "I'm just saying," Jackie said. "If he's picking you up you should tell her . . ."

"Mandy will be at school."

"Mandy is standing right here," a voice said from behind them. The two women jumped.

"Good morning, sweetheart," Doris said.

"You're going on a *date*?"

Doris threw her hand over her mouth, actually turning pale.

"Oh settle down," Jackie said, then turned toward Mandy. "No, it's not a date. The man is gay."

"Not gay," Doris said, through her fingers.

"And he works for The Whole Package," Jackie said, voice dismissive. The trick was downplaying the situation. She didn't want Mandy to freak. "He's our employee."

"Huh . . ." Mandy's face was working. It was clear she was still deciding whether or not to be entertained or upset.

"He's just taking your mother shopping," Jackie said, hopping to her feet and ruffling the teen's red hair. "And he's *gay*."

"Well, that's good," Mandy said. She walked into the kitchen and grabbed a box of cereal. "Maybe he'll come in and sweep her shitty wardrobe."

"*Mandy,*" Jackie and Doris exclaimed at the same time.

Mandy laughed, slamming around for a bowl. "I'm joking."

"That was not kind." Jackie stared her down. "I have about had it with the lack of respect in this household. Do you want me to change my schedule?"

Mandy cringed and studied the floor.

"No, don't," Doris was oblivious. "I'll be back by the time Mandy gets home from practice. And yes, Mandy, maybe we will throw away some of my . . . old stuff."

Doris turned back to the mirror, tugging on her bangs. Jackie waggled a finger at the teen. Mandy slunk on down the hallway, her Rice Krispies crackling away.

"Doris, you have to teach your child some manners. You're doing her a disservice, letting her say whatever she wants," Jackie said, walking over and putting her arms around Doris's shoulders. In the makeup mirror, their reflections stared back at them, shimmery-skinned. Jackie laughed. "We look like we're made of tinfoil."

"I like it." Doris smiled, leaning forward and finding an eye-shadow brush. Carefully, she applied brown shadow to the creases over her eyelids, then swiped on the tiniest amount of mascara. After applying a light lipstick and a touch of blush, she spun away from the mirror, arms out.

"How do I look?" she asked.

"Tempting," Jackie said. Then she said seriously, "Take it slow, honey. You don't know what Gabe wants from you."

"Jackie, have a little faith in people. Not everyone's out to get something," Doris said. "And if somebody needs something bad enough to try and trick me, they probably need it pretty bad. I really don't have a problem sharing."

Jackie blushed and looked at the table. It was as though Doris could see right through her.

GABE BROUGHT DORIS a bouquet of violets and even opened her car door. She put her hands to her chest and looked around nervously, feeling like she must be on some sort of a prank show.

"These are really for me?" Doris asked, leaning down and smelling the fragrant purple buds. "Thank you."

Carefully, she slid into the passenger's side, pulling the door shut behind her. Gabe stood at the window for a moment, confused. Blushing, Doris realized why he was still standing there— she was supposed to let him close the door for her. When he loped around to the driver's side and ducked into the car, she apologized, "I'm sorry. My husband hasn't opened a car door for me in years. I forgot what to do."

Gabe laughed with her. He waggled the keys before putting them in the ignition. "You're one of the first to have the honor . . ."

"Is this your new car?" Doris squealed.

As part of his contract, Gabe had negotiated a new car. The women had included a lease in his contract. Doris was pleased to see he had picked something so nice.

"You have good taste," she said.

Gabe clapped his black leather gloves together, turning to her in excitement. "Yes, isn't it marvelous?"

It was a white Volvo, just like the one he'd driven to the interview. Gabe explained that, after years of borrowing his friend's car, he knew exactly what he wanted. When Doris teased him softly about his lack of creativity, Gabe shook his head.

"You're right. I am a total creature of habit," Gabe admitted, tucking his light blue scarf into his jacket. Doris admired the way his blond hair curled neatly around it. "But I love Carolyn's car so why take a risk? Plus, look what it comes with—seat warmers."

Doris flipped them on, sighing in relief. Her bottom had been cold against these hard leather seats. "Gabe, I think I'm spoiled," she admitted. "I haven't been in a car without warmers for who knows how long."

"That's okay," Gabe said, brushing a lock of hair from his eyes. "There's nothing wrong with knowing what you like. Now, let's put on some music. What do you listen to?"

Doris beamed, settling back comfortably. "Oh, who knows? Whatever you like, Gabe."

His cell phone rang then, vibrating against the console. Out of the corner of her eye, she saw the picture of a pretty woman show up on the caller ID. "Speak of the devil." Gabe smiled, reaching over and sending it to voice mail. He turned to Doris and said conspiringly, "Carolyn would not be happy to learn that I am shopping with another woman."

"Is she your . . ." Doris's tongue seemed to thicken on the word, "girlfriend?"

Gabe grinned. "Well, she is a girl and she *is* my friend. Oh, I almost forgot," he said, indicating a tall Starbucks cup perched in the coffee holder. "I got this for you. Do you like mocha?"

Doris giggled, grabbing for it. "Somebody told you!"

"No, just guessed." He smiled, easily pulling out of the drive.

A comfortable silence fell over them and Doris enjoyed the soothing smell of new car, cologne, and warmed chocolate. Gabe looked so handsome, bundled up to her left. Doris wasn't sure how she felt about the way he'd avoided questions about this Carolyn, with her matching Volvo and pretty cell-phone ID, but Doris decided it was okay. If Gabe wasn't comfortable sharing his romantic life, then it wasn't her business. Besides, it wasn't like she and Gabe were on a date—although Doris did wish she could give that impression, snapping a picture of the two of them and texting it to Doug. She laughed out loud, imagining the expression that would cross his chubby face.

Gabe looked over and smiled. "What's so funny?"

"I don't know . . . " Doris suddenly felt her palms go clammy. She didn't know what to say.

"Should I bore you to tears?" Gabe said. "Tell you all about me?"

Doris nodded eagerly. After all, what would she tell him about her life? That she had a teenage daughter who treated her like a servant? A husband that thought he was a cowboy in some western, skipping town on a modern-day version of the horse? She looked at Gabe with appreciation, grateful that he was so good at making friends.

As Doris listened to his story, she suddenly understood why. Gabe's parents were diplomats, so he'd traveled from country to country as a child. He was raised in American embassies. "It was hard," he admitted. Now that Gabe had made a life for himself here, he avoided travel at all costs. He rarely saw his parents, even if they were in the country. In a sense, he admitted, this had been ideal, as they had no idea he was a stripper. They would be absolutely scandalized. His mother would cry, his father would shout, and they would leave as quickly as they'd arrived.

Gabe shook his head, navigating his car through the Schaumburg streets. "I don't think it's a big deal. The only time I do think it's a big deal is when I start thinking what my parents would say if they walked into my club," he admitted. "But they never would have, so it was a stupid worry."

"Will you miss . . . stripping?" Doris asked. She knew he and Anthony had turned in their notice on Friday. "You were . . ." She colored, then mumbled, "You were really good at it."

"Now, how could I miss stripping when I have the chance to

spend every day with you, Cheryl, and Jackie?" Gabe asked, touching her arm with affection.

Absently, Doris put her hand to the part of her body Gabe had touched. She wanted to fantasize that the handsome, model-esque man had used it as an opportunity to be near her but the truth was, the contact reminded her of how Cheryl's brothers used to touch her—friendly and casual with no sexual intent whatsoever, except for that one night she'd seduced David. To this day, Cheryl still didn't know about that.

Maybe it was for the best if Gabe just saw her as a buddy. Reaching for her mocha, Doris took a long drink. She was still a married woman. There was absolutely no reason she should even wish Gabe saw her as anything else. It was just that . . . Doris sneaked a peek out of the corner of her eye. Gabe's profile was beautiful, like an angel in the soft morning light. Adjusting her bottom in her heated seat, Doris felt a rush of attraction. Gabe was just so incredibly handsome.

Chapter Thirty-one

CHERYL CRACKED AN EYE OPEN AND PEEKED TO THE OTHER SIDE of the bed, where Andy was stretched out. The sheet was halfway down his chest and his eyes were closed, a slight smile lingering on his handsome face. While his eyes were still closed, Cheryl took the opportunity to study the soft trail of fuzz on his chest, that tiny mole just under his left arm, the stubble along his jaw. She yearned to reach out and run her tongue against it.

Cheryl had been shameless the night before. What else could she do? There was something about seeing Andy in her home, in a position she'd imagined him in so many times, that was the height of eroticism. Having him against her blue-and-white-striped pillowcases was an image she never wanted to forget. She half wished she had a camera, imagining how funny it would be if Andy woke up to Cheryl and a tripod. "For the Christmas card, honey," she'd say. Cheryl had a feeling Andy would grin at the joke, even striking hilarious poses for the camera, whereas Sean would have gotten crabby and buried himself under the sheets.

As they got older, Sean had started to hate jokes of any kind, up to and including practical jokes, knock-knock jokes, wordplay, physical comedy . . . He started to become a very serious guy, only finding amusement in "stupid people." Sean had defined "stupid people" as anyone entertained by Britney Spears, *USA Today*, or mindless daytime television—basically, everyone. Cheryl had eventually redefined "stupid people" as "Sean." Just as she started breathing angrily at the memory, Andy eased open his green eyes and looked at her. Cheryl pulled the sheet up to her chin, immediately shy.

Andy reached out his hand. Tenderly, he ran it across the soft skin on her face. "Good morning."

"Hi." Cheryl squinted at him. "You stayed."

"Did you want me to go?" Andy said. "My wife might be really mad, you know."

Cheryl batted at him.

"I can't believe you thought I was married." Andy grinned, stretching luxuriously. One hand slid under the sheet and started stroking her thigh.

"Of course I thought you were married," Cheryl said, leaning into his touch. "You didn't even try to kiss me after dinner."

With the other hand, Andy reached forward and poked her nose. "That's because you were a nightmare. You needed to be punished."

"But I was wearing a very sexy dress," Cheryl protested, grabbing his hand and kissing it. Andy ran his fingers over her lips, momentarily slipping through them into the warm wetness of her mouth. "I thought we had a nice time."

"Of course we did," Andy said. "Right after I decided I wouldn't touch you with a ten-foot pole."

"Really?" Cheryl smirked. "But would you touch me with a . . ."

Andy raised himself up on one elbow, turning toward her. "You really gonna say that?"

As he got closer, Cheryl breathed in his scent of earth and spice. Wrapped in the force of his gaze, her heart pounded and her mouth went dry. Cheryl clutched the sheet in her hand, suddenly worried about her breath.

Andy leaned forward, dangerously close. "Hmm?"

Running his tongue down the length of her neck, he gave it a soft flicker right above her collarbone. The sensation was like a match to a stack of dry love letters—her entire body lit. Cheryl slid toward him. Entwining her legs in his, she took his mouth in hers.

"I'll say whatever you want," she said.

"Yeah?" Andy's hands were everywhere.

"Andy," she begged, breathless.

"That's not very convincing." Andy's hands wandered farther below the sheets, finding her firm bottom and cupping it. His fingers slid between her thighs.

"*Fuck*," she gasped, bucking against him.

With that sexy little wink, he ever so slowly ducked his head under the sheets.

Chapter Thirty-two

AFTER MUCH PERSUASION, GABE HAD ACCOMPLISHED WHAT Doug, Jackie, Cheryl, Mandy, and the entire state of Illinois could not and had not been able to do for years—he had convinced Doris to trade in her clunky glasses for soft contact lenses. This was a remarkable achievement, since the biggest style change Doris had ever experienced was back in 1986. She had gotten a spiral perm, which had given her a shaggy, wild mane.

Gabe made his move the moment they got to the mall. Pretending it was an afterthought, he grabbed Doris's hand as they walked by a contact store. Doris was so busy blushing at his touch and trying to figure out if her hand was clammy that she missed where they were headed until it was too late. "What are we . . . ?" Doris asked, looking around at the rows of glasses in confusion.

Gently, Gabe slid off her glasses. "Your eyes are like something from a fairy tale," he said. "Why are you keeping them hidden?" He was so close Doris could feel his breath on hers. Her mouth went dry, heart pounding at the idea of him moving in just another half inch, taking her lips in a kiss.

"It might break my heart if you don't buy contacts," Gabe said, turning to a soft lenses display. "Maybe you could just try on a pair and see how they feel. If you hate it, we walk away."

It was hard to say no to a man who looked, even when he was blurry, like a supermodel. Dumbly, Doris nodded her head. If she passed out from the pain, maybe he would revive her.

In spite of what everyone thought, Doris *had* tried contacts. Her mother had taken her to the mall at Cheryl's urging. "If someone kicks a ball at your face," Cheryl had said, "you're gonna get all cut up. If you want to play soccer, you have to ditch the glasses."

Excited to try contacts, Doris was dismayed to find that the thin plastic felt like a razor slicing through her eye. She'd actually dropped to the floor in pain, ripping it out of her eye and throwing it across the room. That was the first and last time she tried them.

At the memory, Doris trembled. Gabe stood by with fingers crossed, the optometrist moving forward with the thin contact rested innocently on the tip of his finger. Just as Doris flinched and tried to duck, the doctor slipped it in. If it wasn't for the chart behind him suddenly sharpening into focus, Doris never would have known. She didn't feel a thing.

"When did you invent these?" Doris marveled, touching the thin skin around her eyes.

The optometrist looked puzzled. "About forty years ago."

"But I tried them," Doris said, glancing at Gabe. "They hurt."

"Hmm," the optometrist said. "If you can feel them, there's some sort of problem. Maybe there was a piece of dust caught in them or a tear."

"Well, they don't hurt now," Doris said, giggling. "These feel great."

"You look beautiful," Gabe said. "Your eyes are your best feature."

Doris nodded, mesmerized by her reflection. It appeared slightly blank without the protection of her glasses. Gabe promised it would be fabulous after their makeup excursion.

"I'm not going to Macy's," she practically shrieked.

Confused, Gabe agreed that Nordstrom might be the better choice. As they headed for the department store on the opposite end of the mall from Macy's—and Katherine Rigney—Doris felt foolish for her outburst. Silently, she perched in a chair and squeezed her eyes shut against her new lenses. A male makeup artist deftly brushed color on her lids and lashes. With every stroke of the powder brush against her face, Doris imagined it was Gabe's lips. When the makeup artist finally spun her toward the mirror, Doris opened her eyes and they filled with tears.

"Don't let the mascara run," he pleaded, hovering behind her.

"See?" Gabe gushed. "What did I tell you?"

Doris nodded, awestruck. Her skin had been smoothed with a light foundation, blending those harsh patches of red around her nose. The plump apples of her cheeks had been filled in with a soft coral. Around Doris's upper lashes, a subtle brown liner drew attention to the suggestive, hooded arch of her bedroom eyes. A frosty pearl highlighted her brow bone and a smoky gray shimmered along the fold. Doris's lips were lush and sparkling.

Doris didn't know if it was the gorgeous man whispering in her ear or the actual palette highlighting her face but she felt more beautiful than she had in her entire life. Insisting on adding some hand creams and cologne for Gabe, Doris laid down her worn Nordstrom card for everything the makeup artist recommended.

"Time for clothes," Gabe sang, swinging her bags. "Where shall we go? You are my project and you are shaping up nicely. We're about to put you at one hundred ten."

Doris suddenly felt too hot in her heavy sweater. She stopped walking and fiddled with the handle on her bag.

"What's wrong?" Gabe asked, immediately noticing her expression. He put a warm hand on her shoulder.

Doris squinted at the mall in confusion, as though not understanding how she had gotten there. "I don't want to be your project," she finally said, turning to him. "Did Cheryl and Jackie put you up to this?"

"Oh, I didn't mean it like that," Gabe said, grabbing her hands.

"You're stunning. Everyone in the mall keeps looking at you," he practically whispered.

Doris blushed, sneaking a glance around at the bustling shoppers, wanting to believe him.

"Let's just look for clothes here," he suggested. "It's probably the most efficient. I'm thinking more in the vein of what Jackie wears. Some nice cashmere, sleek skirts, something with flair . . ."

"I don't really like skirts," Doris said, hating herself. She didn't want to disappoint Gabe, but she'd been wearing slacks for thirty years. Getting rid of both slacks and glasses in one day would be too much. Her heart had started to pound, and suddenly she craved a Xanax. "I'm sorry," Doris whispered. "I need . . . I need a minute."

Gabe got serious, looking around the store for a bench. There was one over by a large fake plant and a waterfall. Gabe led her there and sat her down. Doris took deep breaths, eyes darting around like a trapped animal. "I'm sorry," she said, voice catching. "This is so embarrassing."

"No, no," Gabe said, cracking his knuckles. "You're having a panic attack, right? I used to have a problem with that, too."

Doris reached in her purse and wrapped her fingers around her trusty bottle of pills. Absorbing his words, her grip softened. She looked at the gorgeous man sitting next to her. "You did?"

"Unfortunately, yes." Gabe bit his lip, then explained. When he was younger, traveling from country to country, he had struggled with anxiety all the time. "I literally felt like the walls were closing in on me," he said. This didn't go over very well in his parents' straightlaced world. They had put him on medication. It had taken a year with the anxiety drugs for him to feel like himself again and another two for him to get weaned off. "In retrospect, I'm glad I went on the medication," he said. "But at the time, I was really angry they made me do it."

"Wow," Doris breathed, nodding. "Do you know why it happened in the first place?"

"Yeah." Gabe flopped into the seat next to her. "My therapist said it was triggered by stress. Jackie mentioned you're going through a hard time right now?"

Doris nodded. Absently, she picked at the fake wood on the bench. "My husband left me to ride a motorcycle across the country. He saw *Wild Hogs*."

"Well, I'd panic at that, too." Gabe laughed, tapping his hands against the bench.

"And my mother died a few years ago," Doris blurted out.

Gabe was silent. After a long moment, he said, "I'm really sorry to hear that."

"Yeah." Doris nodded. "I'm sorry, too."

"Do you need some water or something? A soda?" Gabe put a comforting hand on her knee.

Doris's senses leaped to life. She half wished she had fainted dead away during her panic attack. That way, just like in the stories, Gabe would have had to kiss her to bring her back to life. Her heart pounded at the thought. After a long moment, Doris turned her attention to the pill bottle in her hand.

"No, I don't need any water," she said, sliding the bottle back in her purse. "I think I'm okay now. Gabe . . . thanks for talking to me."

"You bet," Gabe said, removing his hand and running it through his hair. "Thanks for listening to *me*. That's not something I tell people."

"Me neither." They sat for a moment, silent. All around them, people were bustling in and out of stores, chattering happily, carrying heavy bags and sipping on coffees. "Look at this place," Gabe said, considering. "Christmas seems to start earlier and earlier every year, doesn't it?"

Doris nodded. "We're hoping it'll be good for The Whole Package. It's right down the block."

Wickedly, Gabe pointed out a particularly uptight woman, her bleached blond hair pulled back in a tight bun. She was wearing a navy St. John's suit and cufflike gold jewelry. Had they been sitting closer, they probably would have caught a heavy whiff of her perfume. "There's your first customer," Gabe teased. Doris's mouth tugged at the corners. Gabe hopped up and extended his hand. "You good now? Ready to shop?"

"Ready." Doris grabbed his hand, bouncing to her feet. Every woman in the vicinity noticed, sneaking sidelong glances at Gabe. Guiltily, they then linked arms with their husbands. "People aren't staring at me, Gabe," Doris said, proud to have this man next to her. "They're staring at you!"

Gabe grinned. "Gosh, I don't know. So . . . If you hate skirts I'll make you buy a whole bunch of sexy sweaters and we'll partner them with slacks," he said. "You're gonna look great. You already do," he promised.

They ducked into the nearest store and went straight to the women's department. In moments, an entire dressing room was filled from top to bottom with sleek cashmere sweaters and slacks. Gabe perched on a chair in the waiting room and it was Doris's job to come out and model for him. Every time she spun out of the dressing room, she was floored that such a handsome man was paying attention to her.

"You look just like a movie star," she told him, shyly. "I keep thinking that."

"Look at *you*," he exclaimed. "You look amazing!"

Doris looked in the mirror, blushing. Gabe and the saleswoman had dressed her in a tight sweater with delicately puffed sleeves and a thin, seventies-style string belt around the waist. It highlighted her curves, but was cut just right. For the first time in months, Doris didn't think she looked fat.

"Gorgeous," Gabe told the saleswoman. "We'll take white, black, and gray. You need classic colors," he explained to Doris. "Then we can partner everything."

"Have you worked in a clothing store before?" Doris asked in awe, watching him assemble an entire wardrobe with all the pieces they'd picked out.

"No," Gabe said, shaking his head. "But Carolyn loves to shop."

Doris was dying to cry out, "Who is this Carolyn?!" but instead, she primly adjusted her sweater. When they got to the checkout counter and the lady was ringing up her purchases, Gabe said, "Now, will you please explain to me why you didn't want to go to Macy's?"

Doris fumbled with the gourmet candy display in front of the register, adding two chocolates to their purchase. After a moment, she finally mumbled, "My husband had an affair with a lady that works there." She looked at the blond employee at the register. She was young, about twenty and most likely not friends with Katherine Rigney, but there was no telling.

"Your husband's an idiot," Gabe scoffed. "He doesn't know what he's missing."

When the saleswoman gave her the total, Doris blanched.

"It's okay," Gabe said. "You deserve it. Your husband deserves to pay."

Doris laughed as she laid down Doug's card. "That's not the first time I've heard that."

"Now," Gabe suggested, grabbing all her bags before she could. "We can go into Macy's if you want. Give her a show?"

"Nah," Doris said. When they were walking away from the counter, she added in a whisper, "I already vandalized her house."

Gabe squealed with laughter. "Stop it! We'll peep in a side door," he insisted, "and you must, *must* show me which one she is."

Chapter Thirty-three

WHEN GABE CARRIED DORIS'S BAGS INTO HER HOUSE, MANDY—who was back from school and mixing up a gooey batch of Rice Krispie treats—almost dropped a sticky spoonful on the floor. She watched in dumb silence as Gabe left the bags in the foyer and hugged Doris good-bye. He flashed Mandy a quick smile before leaving.

"Who was *that*?" Mandy asked. She ran to the window to watch him drive away.

Doris beamed. "My friend," she said proudly.

"The gay date?" Crunching down on her spoon, Mandy viewed Doris with something bordering on respect. She scrunched up her pretty face and rubbed her eyes. "Mom . . . what on earth happened to you?" she asked.

Doris's hands fluttered to her face. "What? What's wrong?"

"You look . . ." Mandy moved forward, appraising her. "Beautiful."

Doris moved toward the sofa and sat down, hard. She was so touched—and shocked—at her daughter's compliment. Grabbing a stack of mail from the end table, she flipped through, embarrassed. It felt funny to be able to read the tiny print without constantly pushing her glasses up the bridge of her nose. She felt naked without them. But she also felt thinner, somehow, in the black pants and black sweater.

Mandy came over and perched on the sofa. After a minute, she leaned against her mother and Doris held her breath, so unexpected was this sudden affection. "How is everything, honey?" Doris said carefully, setting down a stack of bills. It was so rare her daughter was kind to her, she wanted to make it last as long as possible. "How is school?"

"Good." Mandy nodded. She smelled like apricot hair product and Dial soap. She must have showered right before Doris got home. "We won all the debates last week. I got a lot of points. Mom, I . . ." Mandy was biting her nails nervously. "Can I tell you something?"

"Anything," Doris said, heart full.

In a burst of excitement, Mandy announced, "I think I'm in love."

Doris's heart emptied. Mandy was not allowed to be in love. She wasn't even allowed to date. This was something she and Doug had decided on a long time ago.

"I really want you to meet Will," her daughter was rambling on. "I've been going out with him for . . ."

"Mandy," Doris said. "You are not allowed to date! You're too young."

Her daughter looked as though she'd been slapped. "Can't I just tell you about . . ."

"No, you may not," Doris said. "This is not okay."

Mandy leaped up from the couch. Doris got up, too.

"What is wrong with you?" Mandy demanded.

Doris had been Mandy's age when she and Doug had started dating. Look where it had gotten her. She tried to picture the young girl standing in front of her giving up all of her hopes and dreams just to make out with some boy named Will.

"Mandy, you know you are not allowed to see anyone until you're sixteen," Doris said desperately. "That can't change just because your father is not here."

"But I love him," Mandy screamed. "Don't you even care?"

"You're too young," Doris insisted. "I don't want this to continue, do you hear me?"

Mandy's hands were planted on her hips. Her eyes were slits, filled with hate. It was a look Doris had faced so many times before. "Daddy would let me," she said.

"Your father would not let you," Doris said, suddenly hating Doug for leaving her in this position. "He and I made up that rule together."

"Then you should have stayed together," Mandy shouted. "You can't tell me what to do. *I hate you and so does he!*"

This last part she screamed at the top of her lungs. Thundering up the stairs, she slammed the door to her room three times for emphasis. Doris jumped with each one, certain the door would break off its hinges. With her daughter's hate ringing in her ears, Doris curled up on the sofa sobbing, feeling her new contacts harden under the salt of her tears. Eyes aching, Doris wondered where she'd put her glasses. She wondered why she'd dared trust the world would give her a good day.

HAD JACKIE KNOWN she was walking into a war zone, she might have stayed out a bit longer. That morning, she'd stopped into a sleazy pawnshop and sold off her sapphire necklace and that pearl bracelet from Hawaii. They weren't pieces she cared about, so she didn't feel much disappointment when the foreign woman refused to give her more than six hundred dollars. Jackie just ran to the spa as quickly as she could, eager to treat herself for the first time in weeks.

Once she was out of her appointments, dazed with relaxation and smelling like lavender and white lilies, she tried to call Doris—just in case. She didn't really think Gabe would be pawing her in the back of the car somewhere but Doris was vulnerable and Gabe was a handsome stripper. Anything could happen.

When Doris's cell rang and rang, Jackie raced home. A transformed Doris stood in the living room, crying into a cell phone. Makeup was running down her cheeks, leaving tracks as black as motorcycle oil.

"Oh no. What happened?" Jackie whispered, rushing forward.

"I can't do that, Doug," Doris said, "I won't do that."

"Give me that," Jackie snapped, grabbing for the phone. "Doug? Hello, darling. This is Jackie."

"Jackie, let me talk to my wife." Doug was in a bar, the jukebox blasting country music. She could practically see the cowgirls in their tight Rocky Mountain jeans, stomping peanut shells and trying to master the two-step.

"Well, at least you're in the South," Jackie applauded. "Maybe someone will write a song about you. *I left my family, left my home because I wanted to get on a bike and roam,*" she sang this part loud and off-key.

"Are you behind all this?" Doug's voice was angry. "My wife went shopping with a stripper? She will *not* be opening a strip club. Not if I have anything to say about it."

"Now, why on earth would you think she was doing that?" Jackie asked, fumbling for time.

Doris watched the exchange tearfully, hand over her mouth.

"My daughter told me," Doug railed. "So help me God, if you humiliate our family name . . ."

"Oh, please," Jackie hissed, reaching out and grabbing Doris's plump hand. The skin was sweaty, but cold. "You had an affair with Katherine Rigney, of all people. I really don't think you're worried about your family's reputation. We are opening a restaurant, Doug, not a strip club. It is divine. You will be very proud of your wife, who looks beautiful right now, by the way."

Doris sniffled, mouthing, "Thank you."

Jackie lowered her voice, "Doug, when are you coming home?"

"Put my wife on the phone," he ordered.

"You really need to rethink your priorities," Jackie spat. Practically throwing the phone at Doris, Jackie swore a blue streak in French and then headed straight for Mandy's room. The scent of patchouli greeted her before she even got there. Was Mandy smoking pot? Jackie wouldn't be surprised. The teen was sitting on the bed, pretending to read a magazine.

"Did you tell your father about The Whole Package?" Jackie demanded, hands on hips.

"Is that against the law?" Mandy asked, blinking.

"Mandy," Jackie mirrored the attitude the teen was throwing at her, "Why would you do that?"

"She wouldn't listen." The teen's face was mutinous. It was moments like these when Jackie realized Mandy really was just a kid. "I tried to talk to her. I tried to tell her about Will and she went crazy."

"Do you understand that The Whole Package is important to me and Cheryl, not just your mother?" Jackie demanded. "I know you wanted to hurt your mother, but if your father interferes with this, it's going to affect me, too. And as unbelievable as this may sound, I don't have anything else to do with my life. This restaurant is my last chance to do something great."

Mandy turned pale. "Jackie, I . . ."

"*Non, non, non!*" Jackie put her foot down, impatiently wiping away a tear that was not meant to be part of her performance. "This time, we are not having a conversation like mature adults. You need to go out there and let your mother know you support her and that you support us. If you don't, I'm really going to have a hard time understanding why I ever supported *you*."

At that, Jackie swept down the hallway. Slamming her bedroom door, she picked up the princess phone and dialed George. When he picked up, she didn't even give him a chance to say hello.

"Hello, darling," she said. Jackie was so wired, she hadn't realized her hands were shaking. "I'm calling from crazy town. Please come get me out of here."

Chapter Thirty-four

AFTER AN ECSTATIC MORNING EXPLORING EVERY INCH OF EACH other's bodies, Andy and Cheryl finally ventured out to the kitchen for some food. Andy opened her refrigerator and drew back in surprise.

"If something moves, just kill it," Cheryl said, padding up behind him. She liked to tell people the refrigerator was where she kept her pets, Mold and Moldier. Cheryl stocked up on containers of prepared entrees from Whole Foods every two weeks. Since the lag time was so high, most of them went bad before she had a chance to eat them.

"You don't throw anything away." Andy was baffled, sifting through the putrid cartons. "I'm calling the Health Department. No wonder you're so thin."

"There's vodka in the freezer." She giggled, pulling out an icy bottle of Ketel One and waggling it at him. She tossed it back in and shut the door, wrapped her arms around his muscular body, and peered into the lit white space of her refrigerator. It had been a while since she'd been shopping but there were some survivors—

a promising chunk of Parmesan, some German chocolates, a carton of eggs, and a half bag of spinach.

"You are the ultimate bachelor," Andy chuckled. He turned around, kissed her lightly, then put his hand on her bottom and gently pushed her toward a chair. Rolling up his sleeves, he threw away the rotting cartons, and then pulled out the Parmesan and the carton of eggs.

"Warning," Cheryl laughed, making an alarm sound. "Watch the eggs."

Andy got into a wide stance, as though getting ready for a fight. "Checking for an expiration date . . ." He peered at the stamp on the carton. "Clear!"

Cheryl gave an exaggerated wipe to her forehead. "Whew. How close?"

"We just made it. Now, talk to me about spices," Andy said, swiftly cracking eggs into a frying pan. Cheryl watched with interest. His strong hands were gentle but firm with the fragile shells.

"Truffle oil. In the cupboard."

"Not a spice," he lectured, "but promising nonetheless."

Andy reached up and rummaged through her shelves. Cheryl was enjoying the sure way he grabbed for things—the bottle of truffle oil, a can of shitake mushrooms, that box of instant biscuit mix. It was impressive what he was finding. Andy might be a nice person to have around during a war.

Humming and whistling, he made his way over to her dish cupboards. With a little effort, he found a large mixing bowl. Of course, it was covered with a thin layer of dust. "My sisters would freak," he said, up in arms. "Are you sure you're not a man?"

"Sexist remark," Cheryl sang, pulling out a chair from the kitchen table and drawing one knee up to her chest, a spectator. "Please note you're the one cooking right now."

Andy smiled, deftly rinsing out the large silver bowl, then adding cinnamon, sugar, water, and a tiny dash of olive oil to the biscuit mix.

"I can't believe you have three sisters," Cheryl said, picking at a hangnail. "I have three brothers. They all left me to move to California."

"Mine are in New York." Andy nodded, stirring. After a moment, he lifted up the spoon. It was covered in something that actually resembled batter. "Voila!"

"Nice." Cheryl applauded. "I am truly amazed." She was. Andy was sexy *and* handy in the kitchen. She didn't realize such a breed existed.

"So," Cheryl said. "A couple weeks ago you said you went to a family thing. Reunion?" She didn't want to be nosy, but she was curious. She wanted to know everything about him.

Methodically, Andy spooned batter into the pan, forehead wrinkled in concentration. "My grandfather died," he admitted. "He was ninety-seven. I'm bummed but I guess it was time. My grandma died ten years ago, so he was kinda lost without her."

"I lost both sets in my twenties," Cheryl said. Losing her grandparents had happened in a year when it had seemed to be happening to everyone. Sean's grandma died first, then Doris's, then Cheryl's grandpa and finally, someone at TurnKey lost a set in a head-on collision. That odd period had brought Sean and Cheryl closer. They had lain in bed, staring at the stars out the window and talking about it.

"It's a lost generation," Cheryl said. "My grandma used to make five-course meals, breakfast, lunch, and dinner." She thought back to the times she and her brothers would crowd across the table, marveling that the tiny bent lady they called Grandma had made such a feast.

"Your grandmother was a good cook," Sean said, pressing his cold feet against hers, "and a sweet lady. I always thought mine was too mean to die."

Cheryl laughed, picturing Sean's cantankerous Italian grandmother. Natalie had sported a heavy black purse and a hard cane. She frequently used both as weapons. Her Eldorado was a threat to the neighborhood, trolling down the middle of the road like some teenage gang car looking for trouble, her hunched-over figure peering out from behind the wheel.

"Isn't it strange," Andy said now, sliding a pan into the oven, "to be at the age where losing our parents is more common than losing our grandparents?"

Cheryl nodded. "My friend Doris just lost her mom."

"Rough," Andy agreed. "I've got both of my parents, thankfully. They're in Boston. It's not easy being so far away but it is what it is."

"Why didn't you get a job there or in New York?" Really, Cheryl was asking in Girl Speak if he was ever going to leave her for New York. Good to know these things in the beginning of . . . whatever this was.

"New York's too much for me," Andy said, brushing his hands off on his boxers. "Besides, I think I like it here." He tossed Cheryl a dimpled grin.

Feeling warm, Cheryl was suddenly grateful for her fake tan. Her tendency to blush was part of the reason she'd gotten caught up in the spray-tan fad in the first place, no matter how much Doris tried to tell her the chemicals were just as poisonous as the sun. Cheryl's fair skin and freckles had made her readable in a way that she much preferred to hide.

She eyed Andy in his button-up shirt and white boxer shorts. The crisp cotton shirt was only half buttoned, exposing his muscular abs. She eyed the fit of his boxer shorts, toying with her light blue camisole. Cheryl smiled, remembering the struggle she'd faced trying to find something to wear down to the kitchen. For all her sexual exploits, she had never had a need for the morning-after outfit. She usually insisted on going out to breakfast instead of hanging around. But here it was three o'clock in the afternoon, Andy was still in her kitchen—and she was surprised to find herself dreading the moment he would leave.

That morning she had asked him, "Don't you have to go to work? *You* didn't get fired." Andy had called in sick to TurnKey, lying to Stan right in front of her.

Cheryl made little fists with her hands, clenching and unclenching, watching as Andy navigated her kitchen. The way he moved his body was aggressive, like a tiger taking on a cage that wasn't big enough. But in bed, he'd been a perfect mix of gentle and aggressive, always maintaining just the slightest level of control. She shifted in her seat, thinking of it. He gazed over at her, green eyes glinting.

"If you're trying to read my thoughts, you'd better like stories that are X-rated," she said.

Andy gave a final evaluation to whatever he was preparing, then carried it across to the table. He set down a plate and Cheryl laughed. On it, there was a perfectly formed truffle oil omelet, mandarin orange segments, and fresh-baked cinnamon bread.

"Did you go for takeout when I wasn't looking?" she said, taking a big bite of bread. "Wow. That's actually good."

Andy grinned and grabbed his dish. Settling in across from her, he reached forward and brushed a crumb off her lip. Quickly, she took his finger in her mouth, biting it playfully.

"No, no," he scolded, pulling his finger back. "What you're doing there just isn't fair."

Cheryl grinned, leaning forward slightly to give him a clear view down her top. His green eyes followed her every movement and the moment they were finished eating, he threw their dishes in the sink and led her to the rug by the fire. They made love against her collection of colored throw pillows.

After they were through, gasping for breath and gazing at each other in amazement, Cheryl hopped up and lit some candles. A nice cinnamon scent wafted over them and she flipped on her stereo, blasting music from the Bing Crosby Christmas collection.

"Hope you like Christmas music," she said, dancing seductively to the first notes. Pulling her down to the rug with strong arms, Andy kissed her again as she ran her hands over his hard stomach. "You must do Pilates, Jane Fonda, or hot yoga," she accused him.

"I'd do anything to get your attention," Andy said, touching her face.

Cheryl snorted. "You had it from day one."

"No way," Andy said, sliding his hands under her lacy shirt and running a thumb over her bruised nipple. "I was just the new guy. You didn't even notice me. Until I rescued you at racquetball."

Gently, Cheryl pummeled his chest with her fists, and then rolled on top of him. "You didn't notice me!"

"Oh, really? Let's talk this through," Andy said, sliding his hand up her thigh. "I wanted to rip your skirt off when you were unconscious on the floor at the Racquet Club. Take you on the table when you licked salt off your margarita that day at lunch . . ." He cupped her backside and pressed her against him. Lips tickling her ear, Andy whispered, "And I *definitely* would have enjoyed a little going down that day in the elevator."

"You *shrugged*."

"It worked." Andy grinned. "You should have seen your face. You wanted me bad."

Cheryl laughed. Rolling off him, she snuggled into the crook of his arm.

"I'm dreaming of a White Christmas . . ." Andy sang, staring at the fire.

Cheryl froze inside, so surprised was she at the feelings his resonant baritone brought up in her. Sean had had a terrible voice and because of it, never sang. Cheryl's voice wasn't great but she could carry a tune. Still, whenever she would sing along with a song on the radio or something, Sean would sneak irritated glances her way, turning up songs he didn't even like just to drown her out. Now, probably as some sort of a test, Cheryl took a deep breath and started singing along with Andy. He looked over at her, gave the thumbs-up sign. Laughing, the two belted out the Christmas carol, arms wrapped around each other. Cheryl's heart leaped. *This* was the type of guy she should have married.

The idea of growing old with someone had been very appealing to Cheryl, especially since her parents had such a fun time together—cooking dinner, running two miles every day, happily raising their boisterous brood. Cheryl had always planned to find the perfect guy by thirty. Of course, once the deed was done, she had spent as many nights away from dreary Sean and their dull little home as she could. If only she had picked someone like Andy instead . . .

Looking over at him, Cheryl noticed the way his lashes threw shadows over his handsome face. Cheryl's stomach knotted. She didn't know if it was the warmth of his body or the pleasant hum of Christmas tunes or simply getting older, but Cheryl found herself once again wondering what it would be like to grow old with someone by her side. She couldn't help but think—what would her life be like if . . . say . . . this man was singing to her next year at Christmas and the next and the next, for years and years to come?

Chapter Thirty-five

JACKIE WAS IN THE OFFICE OF THE WHOLE PACKAGE, WORKING ON some paperwork George had requested they turn in. She was irritated because, for the first time in her life, she was the one doing all the work. Doris's day was booked with beauty treatments and Cheryl had stopped picking up her cell phone, probably holed up with some guy. So Jackie was stuck filling out forms she had no real idea how to complete. As she studied the contracts in front of her on meat shipments and vegetable orders, she wanted to bang her head against the table.

"Is it too early to start drinking?" she bellowed.

Anthony laughed. "I won't tell," he called back. Anthony was out in the main room, sifting through boxes of point-of-sale items, making sure they'd gotten everything that appeared on their extensive tracking list.

Jackie rested her chin on her palm, watching as he sliced open a packing box, then started counting through one hundred laminated menus. That looked easy enough. Why wasn't she doing that?

Anthony stood up and stretched, glancing at his watch. "Jackie, the boys will be here for dance rehearsal in a half hour," he called. "I'm going to finish up here and then go grab a quick bite. Want anything?"

Just as she was about to request a latte, a key turned in the lock. She watched as Anthony looked at the door in surprise, and then leaned forward in anticipation as Gabe bustled in, dressed in a leather jacket and a pastel scarf. The scarf was light blue, probably meant to accent his china blue eyes. Spotting Anthony, Gabe jumped.

"Hi," Gabe said, shifting from one foot to the other.

Anthony looked over at Jackie and she pretended to read her paperwork. Turning his back to Gabe, Anthony deliberately ignored the greeting. He continued checking inventory against the boxes on the floor.

Gabe sighed and came into the restaurant, navigating through packing materials. He accidentally stepped on a piece of bubble wrap and it popped like a pistol. After a moment, he took off his coat but left on his blue scarf.

"Sorry I'm early," Gabe ventured. "Thought I'd stop by before rehearsal and get some things done. I have to check the inventory on the —"

"I'm already doing that," Anthony's tone was sharp.

Jackie jumped, surprised. That was the type of tone she and Robert would use with each other after a fight, not the way you'd speak to someone you worked with. Jackie peered at the scene from behind a paper with interest, dying to see these two interact. After the awesome makeover Gabe had done on Doris, she was 1000 percent sure he was gay. Now, she just wanted to know what was going on. She'd tried asking Anthony, but he had breezed over the topic and started chatting about good restaurants in Chicago.

"Actually, *I'm* supposed to do inventory for the bar," Gabe corrected, standing in front of Anthony with hands on his hips. "Make sure all the alcohol came in."

"Already did that." Anthony was brusque.

Jackie smiled to herself. The tit-for-tat would typically happen when Jackie did something deliberate, like throwing a towel on the floor. Robert hated messiness of any kind, so if she was feeling passive-aggressive, Jackie had fun strutting around their bedroom in sexy lingerie, drying her wet hair with a towel and then letting it drop.

Robert would never scold her directly, though. He would do things like pick up the towel and say, "We need to schedule maid service this week," and Jackie would respond with a gleeful, "Already did it."

"Thanks, then," Gabe conceded, hands up in the air. "I guess you beat me to it."

Jackie studied Gabe. He reminded her of a golden retriever, all hair and friendliness, but like Anthony, there was something vulnerable there. Her womanly instincts wanted to get to the bottom of that—whatever *that* was.

Gabe's boots echoed across the floor. Anthony's back actually stiffened as Gabe slunk up to him. "Let me help you with *something*," he pressed, putting an arm on Anthony's shoulder.

Robert had also used touch to try to soften Jackie up. After one of their snippy little exchanges about buying new toothpaste—"squeeze from the bottom"—or remodeling the bathroom—"just put the toilet seat down!"—or taking a spa weekend with the girls—"I can't stand you anymore, why don't you just die," Robert would sidle over and run both hands up the back of her arms. He'd bury his face in her hair, breathing in her sweet and spicy scent. "I love you, sweet angel. No more quarreling," he'd say, just before spinning her around and crushing her mouth in his.

Jackie touched her lips at the memory. She lowered the paper she was holding and shifted in her seat, trying to get a better view of the boys.

"If you want to help, show up for rehearsal at the time I give you," Anthony muttered, shaking Gabe's arm off and stepping away.

"What is your problem?" Gabe marveled. "What did I do?"

Anthony whirled on Gabe. Jackie held her breath as the two men stared at each other,

Anthony's jaw set. After a long moment, some of the anger in the room seemed to dissipate and they both turned away.

"You know what you did," Anthony finally said, shoving his clipboard into the box and picking it up. "But don't worry. It will never be a problem again." He swished out of the main room into the stock room, slamming the door behind him.

Jackie nodded. That was how most of their fights would end. She would endure a kiss from Robert, and then place her hands on his chest, gently pushing him away. "I need some fresh air," she'd say, stalking out of the room and "accidentally" slamming the door behind her.

When Gabe sank into a chair, mindlessly chewing on a nail, Jackie felt it was time to make her presence known. She yawned loudly, standing up. Gabe looked over at the office in surprise, so she made a big show of squinting into the dark restaurant and saying, "Who is that?"

"Hi, Jackie," he said, standing up and smiling. "It's Gabe."

"I thought you were Anthony," Jackie lied, walking out and giving him a peck on his beautiful cheek. "Doris looks amazing these days. Nice work."

"Can you believe I got her into contacts?" Gabe grinned. After a moment, he confessed, "Jackie, I think Anthony hates me."

Jackie's blue eyes widened. "Tell me more."

Gabe went on to explain that he always hated confrontations. He liked to think of himself as a generally nice guy.

"So what happened?" Jackie begged.

"Anthony made a pass at me, and of course, I turned it down. I'm not like him," Gabe said, deliberately letting his eyes wander over Jackie's body. "But I wish there was a way he and I could still be friends. It doesn't have to be like this."

At Gabe's earnest expression, Jackie ached to smile. In spite of Gabe's best intentions, his gorgeous body was not putting out even an iota of sexual chemistry. Gabe was *exactly* like Anthony, he just didn't want to admit it.

Jackie thought back to her close friendships with these types of men. Mathieu hadn't been the only one Robert had been jealous of. At parties, the majority of her male friends would hang all over her until Robert snapped the stem of his martini glass in frustration, guiding her out to some balcony or another to "talk."

"You have let that guy hang on you all night," Robert would complain, running his hand over a steamed brow. "Everyone's noticing. Why would you do this to me?"

"Darling, he's gay," Jackie laughed. "*Everyone* knows it. Are you out of your mind?"

Robert had crumpled up a napkin from some appetizer and flicked it onto an ashtray. "Bullshit. The man has stared at your breasts all night."

Jackie had no desire to explain the psychology of a gay man to her husband. "Relax," she said. "He just likes pretty things. If it really concerns you, I'll tell him to stop."

Once back inside the party, Jackie would have to roll her eyes and gesture her thumb at Robert. Whatever friend it was would pout for a moment and then almost instantly find another beautiful woman to attach to his side.

"See," Robert would say in triumph, "He'll take anything he can get."

Now, Jackie looked at Gabe affectionately. She reached out and ran her fingertips over his sculpted face. "You're so handsome, *mon ami*," she said. "One day you and Anthony will be good friends. I promise."

"You think so?" Gabe asked, nervous.

"I know so," she said, nodding. Taking his hand, she led him to the bar. "It's evening in Paris. Let's get ourselves a drink."

Chapter Thirty-six

ANDY'S GREEN EYES STUDIED CHERYL WITH CONCERN. IT WAS late in the evening and they had just finished a pizza and were finishing off a bottle of red wine. The '98 Barbaresco had been an anniversary present for her and Sean, something they'd been saving for a special occasion. Sean had forgotten all about it and Cheryl only felt a slight twinge of guilt as she slid out the cork.

The wine was rich and potent, quickly loosening Cheryl's tongue. It had only taken one glass to inspire her to tell Andy about The Whole Package. At the reveal, Andy's eyes had widened. Without saying a word, he listened to her description of their marketing materials, the menu, and the hilarious process they went through to hire the waiters.

"I have to interrupt," Andy finally said, as Cheryl attempted to describe the waiter uniforms: sexy little bottoms made out of spandex. "Did you girls do market research on this idea?"

"Market research is for assholes," Cheryl said. At his look, she grinned. "Of course we did. We went to a male strip club."

Andy shook his head. "Cheryl, this type of thing has never worked before." The tone Andy was using was one he had used during client presentations at TurnKey. Back when Andy was a sexual fantasy, his tone was a pleasant distraction. Now, it was only succeeding in pissing her off.

"First of all," she said, setting down the glass of wine with a crash, "we are not in the boardroom. We are in my kitchen, so you can lose the tone." Her home was not a place for her to be questioned. "Second, it's not critical to perform market research for every little thing you do. The Whole Package is a no-brainer. Everyone goes to Hooters—with *clients*, I might add—and if you haven't noticed, Hooters is a hotbed of cash. What's the big, scary difference? Women should have an option, too. Are you scared they'll lose control and start raping every man in sight?"

"There are demographics to consider," Andy insisted. "I'm sorry if you think they're lame but . . ." Andy started rattling off additional concerns, and Cheryl tuned out, pointedly sipping her wine and staring out the window. "This is making you mad," he finally noticed. "Look, I'm sorry. I'm just being honest with you. Women aren't going to take their clients to a place called The Whole Package. It's not gonna happen."

"Women have sexual fantasies, too," Cheryl said. "If you are too big of a Puritan to understand that, then I may have to review your prowess."

Andy grinned. "I will be more than happy to accept that challenge. But listen, I just want to say one more thing. This type of restaurant will work for a girls' night. No question." He reached for her hand. Cheryl hesitated. Letting him take it, she squeezed him just a little too hard. "*Ow*," Andy said, pulling away. "But they'll only go once. It's a novelty. Dudes might bring their friends to Hooters all the time, but that's because they're going to watch the game or grab some wings . . ."

"Or grab some tits."

"That's not true," Andy said. "Please tell me you're offering more than . . ."

"Service with a schlong?" Cheryl sang. "Look, I think we all know a big hard dick is nothing to be afraid of. So, just stop."

Even though Cheryl was sassy and gloating on the outside, Andy's concerns were making her nervous. He wasn't the first person who had insisted they were off-base. Not one of her brothers had thought it was a good idea. *But those were men*, Cheryl argued with herself. *They don't want to be objectified any more than we do.* Women, on the other hand, loved the idea—Betsy, case in point. Shaking her head, Cheryl thought back to Doris's performance at the strip club. That night out had helped Doris. It gave her the freedom to transform from a mundane housewife to a wild vixen twirling a sweater over her head—minus the incident with the vomit, of course.

"You're wrong," Cheryl said, voice final. "*I* would go there. And I'd go with clients. I'd come again and again," she drawled, kicking her legs up on the table. "And again . . ."

Andy's face brightened. He ran his hands up and down her smooth skin, fingers kneading the soft area inside her thighs.

"Look," she said, touching his hand. "I don't mean to be so protective about this but it's a little late for stage fright. We open in a few days."

The long green tentacles of her spider plants were dangling behind his head. Cheryl realized they looked a little peaked. Reluctantly, she removed Andy's hands from her body, hopped up, and started digging around the cupboards for a pitcher. Her cell phone ring cut through the kitchen. It was sitting on the counter, vibrating and beeping away. Cheryl hadn't looked at it all day.

"I'll bet that's one of the girls," Cheryl said, voice guilty. "They are going to kill me for disappearing for the past twenty-four hours."

"If it is them, tell them I said the concept's interesting," Andy said. He gave her a cute little look and Cheryl smiled. If he was trying to charm himself back into her good graces, it was definitely working. "And if you're hiring male dancers . . ."

"We will audition you tonight," Cheryl laughed. "That is . . . if you were planning on staying?"

"Absolutely," he said.

Cheryl's heart leaped.

Looking at her phone, Cheryl couldn't believe how many calls she'd missed. "Thirteen," she laughed, holding it up. "I'm popular."

Cheryl scrolled through the numbers on her caller ID. Jackie . . . Jackie . . . Doris . . . her parents . . . David . . . TurnKey actor (Cheryl blushed—she'd better delete him) . . . Jackie . . . Jackie . . . some number she didn't know . . . the same number she didn't know . . . the same number she didn't know . . . the same number she didn't know . . .

"Who on earth is that?" Cheryl puzzled. "Hey, let me check my voice mail. I've got five calls from the same number. Maybe it's about The Package."

Andy's eyes twinkled. "I think the idea is growing on me."

Cheryl elbowed him and then punched in her pass code. She stood behind Andy, absently running her hands over his starched shirt and broad shoulders. She skipped the messages from the people she knew and went straight to . . . Blake.

"It's Blake," the voice practically whispered. "Sorry I called so many times but I wanted to try and get a hold of you. Andy's a rat. Stan has been storming around the office, trying to figure out who stole your hard drive, which means Andy told him everything . . ." Cheryl's insides went from sugary, liquid love to rock-hard, subtemperature hate. She stared at the top of Andy's head, wondering how many years she'd get in the slammer for bashing it in with a cell phone. "Andy wasn't at work today," the message continued, "but when I see him I will . . ." The phone dropped from Cheryl's hand and fell with a clatter to the floor.

Andy looked over in surprise. "Hey . . ."

"Get out." Her voice was like cool steel.

Andy swiveled around in the chair, baffled. "What?"

"*Get the fuck out.*"

Everything was moving in slow motion. Although something inside was playing out a video with her in a wedding dress, ripping off her veil, screaming and hitting Andy with all her might, Cheryl managed to keep her tone even and her face blank. The handsome face in front of her changed from confusion to guilt. Clearly, Andy knew she had discovered the truth.

"Cheryl, wait." Andy got to his feet and reached for her. "I can explain . . ."

Cheryl jumped back. She stood poised but alert, as though facing an intruder. "Get out of my house," she repeated.

Even though Cheryl had suspected the dinner with her had been a setup, the time spent with Andy had convinced her otherwise. He'd said he wanted her since day one. If that was true, there was no way he would ever have taken her out to dinner just to get information for Stan. Clearly, everything that had come out of Andy's mouth had been a lie.

"I had to tell Stan," Andy said. "He was . . ."

"*NOW.*" The veneer finally cracked.

Still, instead of breaking every dish in the house, Cheryl managed to stand stock-still as Andy went upstairs, got the remainder of his clothes and walked back down to the kitchen. He stood in front of her for a moment, face working, probably trying to think of a good excuse for taking her out to dinner that night not because he wanted to, but because he'd been sent to gather information. Cheryl looked right through him. With stooped shoulders, Andy finally showed himself out of her house.

Cheryl raced up the stairs to her bathroom, barely glancing at the rumpled sheets on her way past the bed. She turned the shower on full force. The handle squeaked and steaming water hissed furiously out of the faucet.

She soaped herself thoroughly, scrubbing any memory of Andy out and off her body. Opening her mouth, Cheryl turned the water to scalding. She let the heat wash away the taste of that wine she'd been waiting to enjoy for so long. How could she have been so stupid? Andy was definitely not her special occasion. He was nothing at all.

Chapter Thirty-seven

JACKIE RESTED COMFORTABLY IN GEORGE'S LIVING ROOM, THUMB-
ing through old photo albums. Vanilla and tobacco scented the
room as George puffed away on his pipe, working on a deposition.
A fire popped and crackled. Classical music played softly in the
background.

"Darling, perhaps you should invest in a hound," Jackie joked,
taking in the picturesque scene. "At this moment you are
Mr. Darcy, in his most ravishing form."

George smiled, half listening. Jackie took in the airy sitting
room with appreciation. George really had such elegant taste. His
home rested on the top of a hill, situated on at least forty acres of
land. The style was a grand Tudor, something Jackie would never
have liked for herself but could always admire for its classic com-
ponents. It was pleasant being there.

The night before, after she'd called him to rescue her from the
loony bin, they'd gone to see a play at a local theater. Afterward,
she stayed over in his guest bedroom. The situation was perfect;
Jackie didn't even see George for the rest of the night and she

certainly felt no need to turn the lock on the door. After that one phone conversation about their "relationship," George had backed off entirely. He was now completely focused on being a friend. This was not to say that if Jackie were to dive across the room and push the paperwork from his hands, George would not be thrilled, but for now he seemed willing to bide his time. For that, Jackie was grateful.

She went back to turning album pages. The pictures of her husband and George made her laugh. There was a whole section on their collegiate summer abroad. George had a beard, which was so unlike him now. Back then, he resembled a hobo caveman.

The ring of his cell cut through the room. "George, here," he said gruffly, getting to his feet and starting to pace. He glanced at Jackie. "Hello, Doris."

Jackie waved him off. She had left a message on the answering machine letting Doris know she'd be back sometime tonight but didn't want to deal with her until then. Jackie knew her friend had probably needed support after that volatile call with Doug but Jackie was spent. Her own problems were really starting to take a toll. She needed some space.

One thing Jackie valued more than anything was alone time. Being fabulous around other people had its perks but there was something to be said for a cold Chardonnay, a lilac-scented bubble bath, and the knowledge that, unless she felt like it, no one had a right to her time. Jackie needed those moments in order to stay who she was. Without them, she had nothing to give.

"Were you looking for Jacqueline?" George asked.

Jackie waved at him earnestly, shaking her head.

"Ah, you wanted to talk with me," he repeated, glancing at Jackie over his glasses. George listened, letting out a few grunts here and there. "I see," he finally said. "However, this was a joint bank account, yes?"

"Oh no . . ." Jackie whispered, heart catching in her throat. She set down the photo album and leaned forward in her seat.

"Yes, yes," he said. "Well, if he decided to pursue the issue, he could claim partial ownership and force you to pull out but that would take some time. How do you propose to handle it?"

Jackie wrung her hands.

"Pulling out as a partner would be complicated," George blustered, clearing his throat and looking at Jackie. "Have you talked to the girls about this yet?" He nodded. "I see. I see. Well, yes, you certainly must speak to them before you make any hasty decisions. Yes, yes. Good-bye." George placed his cell on the side table and took out a handkerchief to wipe his glasses. After a moment, he set them down and turned to Jackie.

"My dear," he said, "we may have a little problem."

CHERYL WAS DOWN in her basement, angrily sorting through Christmas decorations. Her entire body ached from her activities with Andy. Plus, the thought of sleeping in the same bed he'd been in the night before made her want to drag the mattress outside and light it on fire. The pain of betrayal was starting to transition into rage, which was good. Get mad and get him out of her system— that was the key.

Cheryl pushed through some dusty boxes of ornaments to get to the artificial tree. Decorating for the holidays would be a welcome distraction and the only way to get through the night. Hopefully, she'd wear herself out enough to fall asleep on the couch downstairs and if not, there was always the option of a midnight jog. Maybe that would get her blood pumping and strengthen her resolve to crush Stan and TurnKey like a bug.

Spiders scurried out from year-old cobwebs on the tree and Cheryl let out an involuntary shriek. She hated spiders. Her brothers had ribbed her for it her entire life. Cheryl looked at the top of the basement stairs as though someone from her family would be there, dressed in a football jersey and clutching an eggnog, laughing.

Cheryl took a deep breath. She missed her family. It had been so long since she'd seen them. After the lawsuit was over and The Whole Package set up and running itself, maybe Cheryl would finally have the time to get away. As she'd told Andy, her entire family had fled to the West Coast several years back, claiming intolerance for cold weather. She'd just shook her head, claiming intolerance for slow pace. Her visits to California had been quickies. In and out for business, sneaking joyous hugs with her nieces and nephews and admiring her brothers' lucky wives.

Cheryl breathed in the musty scent from the basement, remembering how close she used to be to her brother David. Only two years older, he had been her confidant and teacher for most of her life. The only time they'd fought was in junior high, when he'd tried to make the moves on Doris during one of the girls' many Saturday night sleepovers. They'd all been watching *The Empire Strikes Back,* snacking on Doritos and Pepsi. To be fair, Doris had been giving David the eye all night, but when David tried to put his arm around her, Cheryl shot up like a rocket, switched on the lights, and kicked David in the shins until he ran yelping to his room. Once he was gone, she told Doris their friendship was over if she ever so much as looked at her brother again. To this day, Cheryl wondered if those two sneaks had ever done anything but both of them denied it.

David and Cheryl had gotten especially close, managing life in Chicago together after college graduation. David was the first person in her family to have met Sean; in fact, he had even thrown the party where they'd met in the first place. Later, he was the only one who begged her not to marry him. If David had only said something sooner, Cheryl might have listened. Instead, he waited a few months after Cheryl had said yes to the proposal, on the day of the engagement party.

Their parents had thrown the party at the lake cottage they had once owned in northern Michigan. Sandwiches, chips, and sodas adorned the tables next to cutouts of the bride and groom. Paper plates and napkins flapped in the wind like so many wedding veils. Everyone cooed about the cute decorations and what a great couple Cheryl and Sean made but David had hung back most of the day, choosing to play with Cheryl's nieces and nephews instead of hanging out with the grown-ups. Doris had been the first to notice David's reluctance and suggested Cheryl get to the bottom of it.

Cheryl had dragged her brother away from the kids and pulled him into the woods. A path stretched out for them to follow and they walked it in silence, enjoying the sound of the loons in the distance. "So, what's up with you?" she'd finally asked, linking her arm in his. "You're acting like the grim reaper."

David hesitated. He looked over at her like a mirror, with his big brown eyes and smattering of freckles across his upturned nose. "I don't want you to marry Sean," he admitted.

Cheryl stopped short. The drink she'd been carrying sloshed over the plastic red party cup. "Oh," she said, quiet for a full minute. "I don't want to marry him either," she admitted. Cheryl started laughing, right there in the middle of the woods. "I'm making a huge mistake!" But it was too late. There was already an engagement party and a diamond ring and little dishes of pastel mints . . . At the hysterical laughter, David had looked at Cheryl like she was nuts and then finally joined in. The two leaned against the trees in the forest, clutching their sides as tears rolled down their cheeks.

"You're screwed." David finally hiccuped, wiping his eyes. "Oh, geez."

"You couldn't have said something a little sooner?" Cheryl said, punching him in the arm. "Warned me off?"

David got serious. "I thought you'd kick my ass."

"Look, it'll all work out," she said, squinting up at the sun, "I'm gonna be thirty so I just figured it was time. Maybe Mr. Right doesn't exist. Sean's not my dream man, but it will be fine."

Breaking a tiny twig off the tree, David popped it between his teeth and said, "I'm here for you. If you need anything, please come to me, okay?"

A few years later, she filed the papers for divorce and called David. He got on the first plane out of California and stayed with her for the entirety of his vacation time. He was the one who helped her find the new place and get moved in. When she was finally settled, sitting on moving boxes, talking over memories,

David apologized to her. "I should have stopped you the second you said you didn't want to do it."

"No," Cheryl said. "I should have stopped me the second I knew I didn't want to do it."

"I hope you'll be okay."

"I will be," Cheryl said. "Sean's the one I'm worried about."

Cheryl kept tabs on her ex-husband through Doris. A year or so after the divorce, Sean found someone else. She was a school-teacher and apparently, his soul mate. Cheryl couldn't have been happier for him. The fact that Cheryl was still single, in the basement moping over some guy who had broken her heart in a matter of days, was . . . well, it was just desserts.

Standing up, Cheryl shook the pins and needles out of her leg and grabbed the artificial tree. She held her breath against the dust and prayed all the spiders had vacated. Stomping up the basement stairs, tree awkward against her face, Cheryl cringed as its sharp branches poked her. Then, just like that leg lamp from *A Christmas Story,* Cheryl hoisted the tree into the center of her window.

"Ta-dum," she sang, with forced glee.

Looking down her street, Cheryl realized she was the only one with a tree already in the window. Well, good. There was nothing wrong with being first; everyone would follow soon enough. As soon as she strung the lights and plugged it in, her neighbors would most likely hang decorations by the weekend, hating her for being so prompt.

Bounding back downstairs, Cheryl rummaged for lights and ornaments. She hummed loudly, determined to enjoy the experience even though she was once again decorating for the holidays alone. As she grabbed sparkling tinsel from the boxes buried in her plastic bins, she glanced toward the stairs, sighing. The phone was ringing. She set down handfuls of gold, deciding then and there if it was Andy on the other line she would get her number changed by morning.

Chapter Thirty-eight

"DORIS WANTS TO QUIT?" CHERYL ROARED. "I KNEW IT. I KNEW this would happen. Nobody's quitting. It's too fucking late for anyone to quit."

"She doesn't want to," Jackie clarified, drumming her nails against a small statue of a horse. Jackie had sneaked into a side room at George's, knowing he wouldn't approve of her making the call. "Doug might force her. And rather than deal with that . . ."

"She'll just pull out," Cheryl railed. "I *told* you she would do this."

Jackie couldn't argue. "She might."

There was a brief silence. A buck head with an impressive ten-point rack hung on the mantel. If they hadn't been having the conversation they were, Jackie would have told Cheryl about it, then joked that Doris's rack was an eleven.

"Jackie . . ." Cheryl said. "Do you believe in this project?"

"Very much," Jackie said, absently touching a stained-glass lamp. "Why?"

"We might fail," Cheryl said glumly. "Everyone might hate our idea. We might lose everything."

"It's just butterflies, Cheryl," Jackie said. "Stay positive. We've done so much work. The staff looks great, the place looks great . . . it's going to be great."

"Well, *great*," Cheryl echoed. "Look, just find out what you can tonight. Let's have a meeting with her tomorrow. If we have to, we'll threaten her with legal action."

"We will do no such thing," Jackie insisted. "She's one of our best friends. The opening's only a few days away. She can't pull out now."

Cheryl's voice was threatening. "We won't let her."

IT TURNED OUT the girls didn't have to talk any sense into their buxom friend. Gabe did it for them. After Jackie jiggled her key in the door, she walked in to find Doris once again on the phone but, this time, she was beaming.

"I will," she crooned, smiling. "Oh, gotta go. Jackie's home. Thank you so much, Gabe. You're the best." Doris hung up and perched on a kitchen chair. Her back was straighter and she was radiant in her new makeup. "Hi, Jackie."

Jackie approached, cautious. "Which of your nineteen personalities is this?"

"Stop." Doris giggled, flushing. "I'm fine. Sorry about the other night. Do you want some dinner? There's some leftover chicken in the fridge."

"No," Jackie said, cringing. She still remembered the last time she had made the mistake of eating Doris's rubbery chicken. "I had a late dinner with George. How are you?"

"Better," Doris said. She made a move to push up her glasses and shook her head, remembering they were no longer there. Leaning forward, Doris said, "Gabe called to check in on me, to see whether or not I had put on my glasses yet. We had a bet that

I couldn't make it through forty-eight hours. If I do, I get a movie date."

"Ah," Jackie toyed with the ruby pendant on her necklace. "You do realize you have to take them out to sleep."

"I already did." Doris nodded, contemplating this for a minute. Smiling broadly, she said, "Oh, he is so bad! Should I call him back and tell him I figured it out? Ooh. I can't believe he's taking me to the movies."

"Call him later," Jackie said. "So . . . what's going on? Anything?"

Doris paused for a moment, as though having trouble remembering. She got up and started adjusting the Thanksgiving decor she'd laid out—orange and red placemats, cutouts of autumn leaves, carved napkin holders. Picking up one of the napkin holders, Doris cocked her head, squinting. "Can you tell they're supposed to be turkeys? I think they look like little shrunken heads."

"Doris . . ." Jackie sighed. She wished she had stayed at George's and gone to bed.

"Sometimes you think I'm stupid," Doris said, looking up. "You had dinner with George. So, you were there when I called. We're best friends," Doris said, setting the napkin holder in its proper place. "Just ask me what I'm going to do."

Jackie stuck out her lower lip, embarrassed. "Are you pulling out?"

Doris shook her head. "No."

In a quick gust, Jackie let out the huge breath she'd been holding. The sounds of the house came back into focus—the refrigerator running, the hallway clock ticking, distant music from Mandy's room. Her fantasy about the grand opening of the restaurant resumed. In it, she was Marilyn Monroe singing "Diamonds Are a Girl's Best Friend," being passed from gorgeous man to gorgeous man.

"Yay," Jackie whooped, hitting the table. All the decorations bounced and Doris pursed her lips. "I'm sorry, but I really thought Doug was going to . . ."

"I'm sure he'll try," Doris said firmly. "But Gabe said Doug lost his right to dictate family decisions when he left the family."

"Is Gabe in the mob?" Jackie asked, innocent.

Doris didn't even crack a smile. Instead, she clutched her hands to her chest and whispered, "No. But he's so handsome. I had such a good time yesterday. I *feel* different."

"You look amazing," Jackie said. "This is a big step, you know."

Doris nodded, pleased as a little girl. "I want to do something with my life, Jackie, just like you said. I really thought I was going to die, trapped here cleaning and cooking and knowing I'm not good at any of it anyway. I'm turning forty. I've got an entire life left to live. You know, I'll kill Doug before I let him take the restaurant away from me."

"I knew there was a killer in there somewhere," Jackie said.

"I'm really proud of us," Doris said. "We're opening a *restaurant*."

"I know," Jackie squealed, jumping around. "It's going to be huge."

"To quote my daughter," Doris added primly, "*Get it?*"

Chapter Thirty-nine

THREE DAYS LATER, THE THREE WOMEN WERE STANDING IN A cloud of perfume and hairspray, nervously posing for photos in Doris's living room like they were about to head off to the prom. But tonight, Doris would not be having sex for the first time in some hotel room. Cheryl would not be vomiting before the dance even started. Jackie would not be thanking everyone for her crown. Instead, the three friends were going to launch their first restaurant.

Doris practically hugged herself in excitement.

"You look lovely, ladies," Anthony cried. "Smile!"

The girls, the managers, and George were all at Doris's house, having a pre-party. They had enjoyed a cheese and cracker spread, toasted to the opening, and then lined up for photos.

"Doris, that dress is perfect," Gabe insisted. "You look radiant."

Doris blushed, adjusting the neck of her gown. He had helped her pick out an elegant gown with an empire waist that perfectly accentuated her cleavage. The material was soft and flowing, adorned with accent crystals.

"You look beautiful," Gabe said again, touching her arm.

Mandy glanced from him to her mother.

Coloring prettily, Doris deferred to her friends. "No, they look better," she said.

"Jacqueline is a work of art," George confirmed, "as always."

Jackie was breathtaking in a simple white satin dress that clung to her body in all the right places. Her hair was done up like a film star's, all pin curls and bejeweled combs.

"I'm in costume," she said in a breathy whisper, blowing him a kiss with her white-gloved hand.

Cheryl shifted slightly in her simple designer dress. She held up her perfectly toned arms as though to say "What about me?" and the men hooted and applauded. The dress displayed her toned and tanned body to the max.

Anthony snapped picture after picture.

"Let's get a photo with Mandy," he suggested. At Anthony's suggestion, Mandy sidled over, positioning herself between Jackie and Cheryl.

"Say cheese," Anthony sang.

Mandy showed her crookedly pretty teeth. Anthony fired away, the flash pulsing like a strobe light. Then he winked and said, "Now just with your mom, please."

Mandy looked at her mother. As Cheryl and Jackie pulled out of the shot, Mandy shifted awkwardly. "Congratulations, Mom," she finally said, putting an arm around her mother.

Doris's heart pounded until she thought it might break but the moment Anthony lowered the camera, Mandy scampered back over to the table with the food. She had been very quiet since the phone call with Doug.

"Where's your bathroom?" Anthony asked, putting away the camera.

"Use the one down the hall," Doris said.

Gabe had been walking that way and he stopped, looking back over his shoulder. Doris noticed. She added, "There's one in my bedroom. Gabe, can you show him?" After the words were out, Doris blushed, afraid she had given the false impression that Gabe had *been* in her bedroom. It didn't matter; no one was paying attention. Mandy was texting a friend, Cheryl was nibbling at a piece of cheese, and Jackie was giggling at something George had said.

Doris was just about to head to the kitchen for some seltzer water to ease her nervous stomach when the doorbell rang. Peeking out the window, Doris spotted a dark blue sedan parked in the driveway. A man dressed like a lawyer stood on the doorstep.

"What on earth?" Doris mumbled, throwing open the door.

"Doris MacLean?" the man said.

"Yes?" Coldness spread through her chest. She hadn't vandalized anyone lately—why was another formal-looking stranger standing at her door?

"I am appearing on behalf of Doug MacLean, serving you with papers for a divorce." The man's voice seemed to fade into a tunnel as Doris put her hand to her head, immediately blocking out the sound. He was holding out a clipboard and a large envelope, handing her a pen.

"I won't sign," Doris said, angrily pushing the clipboard away.

The man didn't look surprised. "It's just to say you received it."

As Doris signed her name and took the package, Cheryl walked by with the cheese platter. "I'm going to put the rest of this in the . . ." she started to say, but noticing Doris's expression, she stopped. "What's going on?"

Doris gave some sort of a strangled cry, but the words didn't come. The man was already walking back to his car, mission accomplished. Cheryl rushed to the door. The blue sedan was pulling out of the driveway.

"Who was that?" Cheryl asked.

"Papers . . ." Doris managed to say. "He sent papers."

"Papers?" Cheryl repeated. "What?" Suddenly, understanding dawned on her face. She turned to Doris, hand to her mouth. "Oh, honey. I'm so sorry."

Out of her peripheral vision, Doris could see that from across the room, no one had even noticed what was happening. Mandy was still on her phone, Jackie and George were in the middle of some animated conversation, Anthony and Gabe still off in the bathrooms.

"What do you need me to do?" Cheryl asked.

Doris stood numbly, holding the package. It was soft in her hand, like a new magazine she'd been looking forward to. "I . . . I just need five minutes," she finally mumbled.

"Five-minute warning," Cheryl shouted over her shoulder. "Then we should head out!" To Doris, she whispered, "Go to your room. Splash some cold water on your face and we will deal with this later. Fuck him. We are not going to let him ruin our big night, okay?"

Doris nodded. The weight of her heels sank into her heavy carpet as she climbed the stairs to her bedroom. Halfway up, she stopped suddenly and clutched the railing. Her gut hurt, like someone had punched it. Slitting open the envelope there on the staircase, standing underneath a painting she and Doug had once picked out for their new home, Doris pulled out the cover letter. Her eyes settled on one sentence, "Contingent upon execution of restaurant opening." So, if she still pulled out of the restaurant, the request for a divorce didn't apply?

Uncharacteristically, Doris felt rage fill her. Cheryl was right. Fuck him. *Fuck* Doug. Doris had put so much work into The Whole Package. How could he do this on her special night? How dare he?! Doris was so proud of everything she'd done. How could he try to take that away from her?

After all of Doug's years of nagging about dust and dirt, Doris knew there was something a little extra special required to get the restaurant in top form. Doris had been wholly responsible for making the place beautiful. She had taken the initiative to commission a detailing service. It had come in and given old Millstines the deep cleaning of its life.

When the detailers finished the job and Doris looked around at the sparkling setup, she put her hands to her heart, remembering the time Cheryl had told her she might be good for business after all. It seemed Cheryl had been right.

The next day, Doris had dragged Jackie and Cheryl to the restaurant to reveal her surprise. When she threw open the doors, Jackie and Cheryl stared at the sight of the cherry wood tables glistening in the low light and how the leather booths lining the walls had transformed from dark burgundy to a bright, cheerful red.

Cheryl grabbed Doris and squeezed her in a tight embrace. "I am so thankful for you. This is incredible."

Doris blushed. Gesturing at the mirrors that lined the restaurant, Doris indicated there was more. Cheryl didn't see it at first, but Jackie did. Her eyebrows lifted. The frames were copper. So were the rest of the fixtures in the restaurant. When properly cleaned, the green calcification had fallen away and they looked like works of art. If the Millstines had walked in then to pay a last visit to their place, they probably would have dropped dead on the spot, knowing they could have cashed out for a much, much better condo down in Florida. Maybe even Oceanside.

Pulling her shoulders back, Doris swept up the remainder of the stairs. She was determined to throw the whole damn packet into her top dresser drawer and leave it there. Pushing open her bedroom door, she pulled back in surprise to see . . . well, she didn't know what she was seeing.

"Gabe?" she said, horrified.

Gabe was standing with his back to her, arms around Anthony as though in an embrace. At the sound of Doris's voice, he turned suddenly. Dropping his arms, he said, "Thank goodness you're here. Where's your contact solution? I've been trying to help Anthony get something out of his eye."

Doris was instantly confused—was she out of her mind or had they been . . . *kissing?* She put her fingers to her eyes and pressed them hard. No. This night had already been too much for her to start seeing ridiculous things. Doris threw the papers into the dresser drawer and bustled forward.

"It's in the bathroom, Anthony," she said briskly. He followed behind her. Doris peered at his face, deciding his eye was indeed a little red. She smiled, relieved. "We've got to be quick about it, though. It's time for us to go."

DORIS WAS SWEATING bullets. She pulled on one of the headsets Cheryl insisted they all wear, then patted her face with a handkerchief, letting her eyes survey the room.

The waitstaff was prepped and ready, waiting for the guests in the entryway as planned. On several well-placed chairs, they sprawled out like a male version of the Garden of Eden. It was a group of perfectly coiffed Adams and Steves, dressed in next to nothing and proudly displaying their wares.

"How's it looking in there?" Cheryl said, voice crackling over the headset.

Carefully pressing the Talk button, Doris said, "Great." The earpiece gave a slight squeal and Doris fumbled to adjust the sound. She hoped she hadn't just blasted Cheryl's ear out. "Cheryl?"

"I'm here," she said. "Is everyone in their places?"

"Yes."

"Are you okay?" Cheryl's voice sounded concerned. "You holding up?"

"Fine," Doris said, instantly picturing the papers Doug had sent. "I don't want to talk about it."

Anthony walked up to the host stand, coiffed and handsome in black spandex bottoms and a bow tie. "Hi, are you excited?" Doris asked, then confirmed into her headset, "Cheryl, if you can hear me, I'm trying to talk to Anthony." When Cheryl didn't answer, Doris shook her head and tugged at the cords. "This thing's confusing."

"I can fix that," Anthony said. He reached forward and slid the set off her head and around her neck. Turning up the volume, he said, "Say something."

"Cheryl, can you hear me?" Doris practically shouted.

"Yes," a tinny voice said from somewhere around her neck.

Doris brightened. "Thanks. Much better."

"It's the least I can do," Anthony said, leaning forward and air kissing her. "I'd be blind if it wasn't for you. I'd be blind."

Back at the house, Doris had doused Anthony's contact in saline solution, then watched closely as he placed the thin piece of plastic back in his eye, Gabe hovering behind.

"You're welcome," she said. "Do you feel better?"

"My eyes do but my body is just roasting," Anthony said, indicating his sculpted form. "I made the mistake of applying body makeup to highlight my abs. *Such* a bad idea. I forgot how heavy Pancake was. I feel like I'm standing in the rain forest at high noon."

Doris patted a muscular shoulder. "Well. You look very handsome."

As Anthony adjusted his bow tie, Doris peered out the door. "Have you seen all these people?"

The line of women dressed in warm jackets, mufflers, and hats stretched down the block. An impressive group of press and photographers were also waiting patiently, eager to get a first look at what the press kits promised to be the "ride of their lives."

"I can't look," Anthony said. "I had oatmeal for lunch because I was too nervous to eat. I was too nervous." Glancing around at the restaurant, he swiveled his hips, silently mouthing the words to one of the dance numbers. After dancing for a brief moment, he slumped against the wooden stand. "Maybe I should try to eat something," he said. "Everything smells so delicious."

The smells wafting from the kitchen certainly were tantalizing: smoky meats, tangy garlic, and hints of rosemary and sage. Greg had outdone himself, even working with the limited opening-night menu Cheryl had insisted on. Even though Greg had originally protested the mini menu, the crowd at the door would probably get him to change his tune.

Regardless of how the dancing would be received, the patrons were in store for an excellent meal. The first course was either garlic-grilled prawns or sautéed scallops in a light coconut sauce, followed by a traditional Caesar or warm goat cheese salad with mixed greens. The entree options were herb-encrusted, fresh grilled salmon or a charred six-ounce filet. For dessert, Greg had prepared a to-die-for flourless chocolate cake.

"People are going to love the food," Anthony said, rubbing his palms together in anticipation. "And the men."

Doris gave him a grateful look and then said a silent prayer of thanks. The Whole Package was going to be a big success. Her heart ached that Doug wasn't here to see it but there was no point crying about it. If he wouldn't support her in the coming success, well . . . it was simply his loss.

"I love this music," Doris said to Anthony, drumming her fingers against the host stand. Sexy salsa music trilled in the background, the beat slow and sensual. "Was it your pick?"

Anthony nodded, grinning. "You'll like the music for the dance numbers, too," he promised.

Doris bit her lip, suddenly nervous. The numbers were hot, maybe too hot. That morning, she had shot up from a dead sleep, worrying about it. Doris had watched many of the rehearsals, but had been so busy staring at the way Gabe moved his hips that she hadn't spent much time wondering whether or not the dancing could be construed as offensive.

When Doris brought it up at breakfast, Jackie had laughed. "Oh, you just don't want other women to even look at Gabe," she teased, flicking a piece of muffin at Doris.

"That's not true," Doris huffed. "I am perfectly willing to share him. It's just that the dancers are so explicit. What if it's too . . ."

"Doris, it's okay," Jackie said. "Every woman has sexual fantasies."

"I know but I just hope our crowd sees it as something sexy, not something . . . sleazy."

"It's not sleazy," Jackie said, sipping her tea. "Our restaurant is high-end. The men are gorgeous. It's not like we're serving breadsticks and beer."

"I know, but . . ."

"Doris, lighten up," Jackie said. "People will love it. It's a very European idea."

"Well, Paris is a little more progressive than Schaumburg, as you've told me a million times. This could be a disaster."

Jackie hopped up and started loading their dishes into the dishwasher. "Well, let's just hope you're wrong and we are fabulous enough to prevail, because I'll tell you something. It's a little too late now."

Looking out the window at the long line of women, Doris swallowed hard. It *was* a little too late for second thoughts.

"*Bonjour*, Antonio Rico," Jackie sang out, sweeping up behind Anthony and giving him a peck on the cheek. She had taken to calling him Antonio Rico after his Latino cocktail persona, from that one night in Chicago. The two pealed with laughter every time she said it.

"*Mi chica bonita*," Anthony crooned in his best foreign accent. "You are so . . . scrumptulicious!" He giggled and pulled Jackie into his arms, making a big show of giving her a passionate kiss. She wiggled happily.

"Jackie," Doris said, shaking a finger at her. "Why aren't you wearing your headset?"

"Because I don't care to look like Britney Spears, even if we're pretending it's her good years," Jackie said. Reaching over Doris's head, she slipped off the space-age contraption and threw it into the bottom of the host stand. "There," she said, smoothing down a strand of Doris's hair. "If Cheryl needs you, she can come find you. Now, let's go ogle the crowd." Jackie grabbed her elbow and led her to the window.

Since Doris last looked, the red carpet had been laid out and the spotlight turned on. The blinding white light shot across the Schaumburg sky, over the clock tower and past the shops of the town square. A news truck was now set up; a large purple cord hung out of the back like the rings of a very large Slinky and connected to a large transmitter. Cheryl was doing an on-camera interview, gesturing toward The Whole Package and grinning at the reporter like she had discovered the cure for cancer.

At the sight, Doris's breathing quickened. She wondered if the news of The Whole Package was being broadcast to the world. Maybe it would find its way into whatever country-and-western bar Doug was in. Once he saw what a success his wife had become, he would cash in that motorcycle, get on the first plane back home, and rip up those divorce papers.

"Jackie and Doris, you two need to be out there," Anthony told them, fanning his glistening abs with a menu. "I've got it under control in here. Go get your light."

"Oh, no," Jackie said, shaking her head. "That type of attention simply is not for me."

"Like water's not for a fish," Anthony teased.

Glancing at the old-fashioned clock hanging in the entryway, Doris said, "Oh my gosh. We're going to open in ten minutes." At the thought, her heart started pounding and her palms got damp. Since that day at the mall with Gabe, Doris really hadn't been taking that much Xanax. She prayed there was one floating around somewhere in her purse.

"All right, that's all the convincing I need." Jackie grinned. "Time to make an entrance."

"In a . . . in a minute," Doris said, walking over to the host stand and opening the reservation book. "Let me check something . . ." The last thing she wanted was for Jackie to notice the start of her panic attack. If she did, there was no way Doris would ever get to the Xanax.

"Hurry," Jackie pressed, fluffing her hair. "You know what? I'm going to check my makeup in the bathroom. Back in a flash."

The moment Jackie was out of sight, Doris gave up all pretense of flipping through the reservation book and instead, slumped against the host stand. Doris was suddenly very afraid she might hit the floor. "Oh, God," she whispered, trying to fan herself with one hand.

"Doris, are you freaking out?" Anthony whispered, moving close to her. " 'Cause I am, too. Please tell me not to pass out. I'd be so embarrassed."

"You're scared?" she said, surprised.

Anthony nodded. His pupils were small and his breath was shallow. Handsome or not, he suddenly seemed very vulnerable in his bow tie and tight spandex shorts.

"Don't worry, everything will be all right," she said, touching his arm. "Let's take deep breaths."

Doris started breathing in and out, like she'd learned to do so long ago in Lamaze class. Anthony copied her breath pattern. Soon, her heart rate slowed. After another minute, listening to their heavy breathing, she realized how ridiculous she and Anthony must look. Practically at the same time, they both looked at each other and burst out laughing. Anthony glanced over at the waiters lying in their Garden of Eden poses. Happily, they were too far out of earshot to have even noticed.

"Thank you," he said. "I don't get stage fright but tonight is . . . something different. It's important."

"Maybe we'll be just fine," Doris said. "Maybe it will be fun."

"Amen," Anthony whispered. Taking one more deep breath, he shouted over to the waiters, "We've got five minutes, boys."

Jackie flew down the hallway toward them, her smile sparkling like fine champagne. "All right, Doris. Let's go!"

"Now *I* have to use the restroom," Doris said. At Jackie's frustrated look, she giggled. "Go without me. I'll be right there."

Jackie blew her a kiss and Doris dashed over to the ladies room, determined to make it a fast trip. She was not about to miss the ribbon-cutting ceremony but she always had to go to the bathroom at the most inconvenient times. Concerts, graduations, movies . . . she was even in the bathroom when everyone else found out Bruce Willis was a ghost. Doug had teased her about that one for years.

Doris rushed through the process and barely glanced at her reflection on the way out. But when she rushed out of the bathroom doors, she stopped short. Gabe was once again standing in front of Anthony. Chest puffed out, skin shiny and golden, silky shorts majestically filled.

"I have something for you," Gabe said, his face flushed. "I got you a present."

Doris stepped back into the shadows.

Anthony put his hand to his chest. "You did?"

"It's not much, but I thought you'd like it." Unfolding his fist, Gabe revealed a thin, gold necklace. It shimmered as he passed it over to Anthony. "Hold it up," Gabe said.

Eyes still on Gabe, Anthony did. A tiny star dangled from the delicate chain.

Doris watched as his Adam's apple worked up and down. She put her hand to her chest, secretly wishing that Gabe had also bought a lovely present for her. At the same time, she understood that Gabe was just extending an olive branch. He wanted to stop all the fighting and finally make friends with Anthony.

"I can't wear this. It's not uniform," Anthony said, making a move to hand it back. "Can't wear this."

In spite of the moment Doris had shared with Anthony, her loyalty was still with Gabe. At Anthony's protests, she wanted to leap out from the shadows and tell Anthony that he would wear it and he would like it. But she bit her tongue, curious to see what else would be said.

"I don't expect you to wear it," Gabe said, still flushed. "But maybe after and . . . you can just know that I . . . appreciate you. I admire you."

Anthony stared at his feet.

"It's time," a voice crackled over Doris's headset. She jumped a mile, hearing it all the way from the hostess stand.

"We're about to open," Doris said, rushing out into the hall. Both Gabe and Anthony almost jumped out of their skin for the second time that night. Gabe gave her a quick nod, then practically ran to his post by the door.

"Doris, you need to get out there," he said, gesturing toward the crowd.

Taking a deep breath, Doris gathered up her dress and stepped toward the entrance. Her heart leaped as Anthony cried, "Places, everyone, get in your places. It's show time!"

CHERYL WAS AFRAID that if she took a deep enough breath of air, her body might inflate like a helium balloon and go dancing up and over the horizon. She was thrilled to appear in front of her contacts and investors as a success once again.

Everyone in the marketing world had heard about her dismissal, and although there had been a chorus of apologies and well wishes to her face, Cheryl knew that many of them were happy to see her fall. But she was back and this time, she wasn't going anywhere. Cheryl almost wished stinking Stan and his henchman Andy were there to see it but they'd hear about The Whole Package soon enough on the local news. Cheryl had used just the right sound bites to guarantee the interview would air with all sorts of fanfare.

"The Whole Package is the utmost in male sensuality," Cheryl had purred into the camera. "It's a place where women can be women and men can be men, as men were meant to be . . ." At that, she had thrust a teaser photo of Gabe into the lens. He was blond, beautiful, and erotically posed, surrounded by the half-dressed waiters.

The cameraman had zoomed in on the shot but cleared his throat, looking uncomfortable. Cheryl winked at him. "You'll have to bring your wife in here."

"Yup," he said, lifting his baseball cap and running a hand over his head. "It seems like something she'd like."

Giggling to herself at the memory, Cheryl looked out at the fevered crowd of estrogen. The line was long and surpassed even her wildest expectations. She wondered who from the crowd would be their radio winners.

To save money on advertising, Cheryl had decided to run an on-air contest. Nine contestants won dinner on the house and a signed T-shirt from The Whole Package dancers and one grand-prize winner won a girls' trip to Las Vegas. The contest had gotten everyone excited. Practically every time Cheryl turned on the radio, she heard the rabid DJ screaming, "Grab The Whole Package—be the twentieth caller now."

Thanks to that promotion and girls like Betsy giving them great word of mouth, not to mention the spectacle they were making with the red carpet and camera crews, even more women were bound to show up than were already here. Cheryl just hoped they'd have enough food for all of them to eat.

Briefly, she closed her eyes and ran through a mental checklist. There was enough food prepped to serve three hundred guests from the prix fixe menu. Leaving room for mistakes in the kitchen, that left about two hundred and seventy actual servings. Cheryl opened her eyes and considered the line. Before blinking, she counted at least eighty people, with even more on the horizon. A smile tugged at the corner of her mouth. There were worse problems to have. If they ran out of food, Greg could always get creative with salads. They had more than enough arugula; just that morning, she had seen bins of it lining the massive walk-in refrigerator.

"Excuse me, but can we go in yet?" asked a tiny woman with wire-rim glasses. She was with her mother, an older arthritic lady. They were both giddy with anticipation.

Cheryl laughed. Putting an arm around the older woman, she angled the two of them toward one of the photographers. He snapped a picture. Perfect.

"Almost." Cheryl smiled. "The doors to The Whole Package are going to open in five minutes."

Just then, Jackie walked outside and started blowing kisses at people she knew. "Amy," she cried, bounding down the steps with her arms stretched wide. "Don't you look smashing?! Sandy! And Trish . . . How *are* you?"

Cheryl laughed out loud. To the older woman that she still had her arm around, she confided, "I have loved that girl for over twenty-five years. She's my best friend."

"That's lovely, dear," the older lady said, tapping Cheryl's face. "Now, when can we see the men?"

"Are you ready to find out what makes up The Whole Package?" Cheryl cried.

The crowd roared.

At Cheryl's cue, Jackie bopped back up to the front doors. Doris pushed her way outside, giving a shy wave to the crowd and then taking her place next to Jackie. Cheryl scampered up the steps and linked arms with her friends, heart overflowing with happiness.

"This is amazing," Doris gushed.

"Fabulous," Jackie said.

"I love you girls," Cheryl told them. "Money, work, and men may come and go, but we'll always have each other."

Doris's face crumpled. For a minute, Cheryl was afraid she might burst into tears but at that moment, loud music cued and Gabe pirouetted out and onto the foyer. There was an audible gasp from the crowd. Drums began to pound over the loudspeakers and Doris was struck dumb with adoration.

Cheryl took a good look at Gabe. She had to admit, the man was gorgeous. His body was lustrous, shining with an oil that highlighted every angle of his cut physique. Those arm muscles were perfectly designed for a woman to nestle her head against in times of passion or pain. His abs were the ultimate betrayal of modesty, with sharp lines that seemed to lead like a treasure map to his pelvis and there, his tight golden shorts revealed just enough to remind a woman of ancient battlefields and a fight for honor.

As Gabe posed for the crowd, his powerful thighs flexed and it was impossible not to imagine the force they would hold, wrapped around the female body. At the sight, every woman in that crowd was suddenly single, even if her husband had once been the man of her dreams.

Jackie, Cheryl, and Doris lifted their arms to the heavens. "The Whole Package!"

In unison, they stepped away from the front door. A red velvet ribbon was blocking the entrance and Gabe fell to his knees before it. Playfully, he teased the material with his tongue as raucous hoots and hollers sounded from the crowd. Ever so wickedly, Gabe untied the ribbon with his teeth. Leaping back to his feet, Gabe took a moment to stare out into the crowd as though appreciating the sight of each and every woman. Finally, he crossed his arms and gave a slow smile.

"Well, ladies?" he drawled. "What are you waiting for?"

After a brief moment of silent, orgasmic ecstasy, women of all shapes and sizes rushed inside. Doris bustled in behind them, plump hands already grabbing at thrown-off jackets, coats, and scarves for the coat check. When the women grabbed their coat check tickets, they would meet Christoph the German model. The women would probably linger and cause the area to get too crowded. It was Doris's job to help move them along. Jackie would be on her way over to the host stand, to greet guests and serve as Anthony's assistant. Cheryl was in charge of wrapping up loose ends outdoors, gifting thank-you vouchers to the press, and saying final good-byes. Even though camera crews were eager to get inside, Cheryl had decided to refuse entry to have better control over their media output. Only photographers and roving reporters would be allowed inside.

Just as the last guest was ushered in and Cheryl had thanked her final media contact, a new group of people approached. As they got closer, Cheryl stopped short. It was a group of men . . . led by Andy.

Before she had a chance to duck inside the restaurant and avoid him, Andy raised his hand and called, "Hey!" as though she were some train conductor who could hold the departure.

Andy was wearing his black overcoat and a pair of perfectly shined shoes. Cheryl knew this because as he strolled up to her, she made it a point to look anywhere but at him. Otherwise, she would have seen that soft hair flopping carelessly over his forehead or the guilt in those green eyes. Instead, she stared at his shoes. Once she realized the shoes next to his were even shinier, she looked up and found herself facing a group of well-dressed Japanese men.

"Well, hello," Cheryl said, surprised.

As one of the men nodded and returned the greeting, Andy said, "They can't speak English. They're my clients. I thought they'd be a perfect crowd for your grand opening."

Like a blow to the stomach, Cheryl was pulled back to that moment in her kitchen, the day after she and Andy had made love. She'd been sitting at the kitchen table, knees to her chest, insisting that she'd bring clients to The Whole Package. But Cheryl certainly hadn't meant foreign ones. To them, custom was everything. If Stan knew Andy had pulled this stunt, he'd be furious. Cheryl had half a mind to pick up a phone and tell him.

"Sounds good," Cheryl said, bowing at the men. "Go see the host, he'll seat you."

Andy said something in Japanese and they followed him in. Cheryl closed her eyes and exhaled slowly.

A moment later, Doris came rushing out the front door, Andy's coat in hand. Doris shook the coat like she wanted to strangle it. It wafted his familiar smell in Cheryl's direction.

"Did you see?" Doris cried. "That guy from TurnKey is here."

"Yup. And he speaks Japanese." Cheryl nodded. "Un-fucking-believable."

"I'm going to tell him to leave," Doris said. She started to stomp back up the steps but Cheryl reached out a hand to stop her.

"Don't." Little specks of snow began to fall, spinning through the air in front of her. "Did you see those men with him? They're clients. Unless they're gay, it'll be the quickest way for Andy to lose them."

"Oh," Doris said, folding the coat across her arm. "Good."

Thanks to Andy's arrival, Cheryl suddenly felt exhausted. All her euphoria seemed to drain to the bottom of her Louboutins, straight into the snow on the ground. "So," she asked, voice dull. "How's it going in there?"

"Well, we do have a *little* problem," Doris said.

There was a member of the news crew lingering, still packing up his stuff. The last headline Cheryl wanted to read was THE

WHOLE PACKAGE—A LITTLE PROBLEM? so Cheryl gave him a big smile, then ushered Doris toward the entrance.

"What is it?" she whispered.

Doris adjusted her cleavage, then sneaked another look around. "Some of the guests are complaining about the waiters and their . . . ah, lack of clothing."

"What are you talking about?" Cheryl said. "That's what they're *here* for."

"Yes, but . . ." Doris smoothed her hair.

Without waiting for an explanation, Cheryl rushed in through the double doors. The sudden warmth made her shiver, not to mention the feel of Andy's eyes on her, all the way from the bar. Thrusting out her chin, Cheryl waltzed into the foyer to survey the scene. After a moment, she nodded. Everything looked good.

Female voices clamored as women milled about the low-lit interior, giggling over well-placed statues of naked men and sneaking looks at live models sprawled over marble benches. Salsa music trilled in the background, its steady beat creating a sultry vibe. The waiters who were not posing walked around, greeting women and passing appetizer plates. Although some hesitated to take food from a stranger dressed in a thong, most were enjoying the apricot-brie bites and pancetta-wrapped asparagus.

"Everything looks great," Cheryl said to Doris, once again tallying the numbers in her head. "I think we'll have just enough food and . . ."

"But look," Doris said, grabbing her arm. "Look over there."

Cheryl squinted. Back in the corner, one of their hairiest waiters had successfully served a tray of appetizers but had dropped a tray full of forks on the ground. Just like a man, Bronco thought little about grace as he bent to pick them up. From the back of his hairy thighs all the way up to his buttocks, Bronco's posterior practically pressed into the faces of three shocked women at a nearby table. Plus, he was wearing a tight banana hammock and it ground up the back of his buns, revealing an unfortunate amount of shaggy black hair.

"Ah, I see," Cheryl said. She was at the table in ten seconds. "Hello, ladies," she trilled.

"Hi," Doris chimed in, right by her side.

A group of older women barely looked at them. Instead, they gaped at the way Bronco's male accessories squashed against the back of his tight silk thong, creating a misshapen alien form. He bent forward to pick up the forks one at a time, again and again. The persistent rhythm should have been saved for sex or push-ups.

"It seems like there's a problem," Cheryl said.

"There certainly is," an older lady said, turning to her.

The woman next to her nodded. "If I wanted to see a hairy ass, I would have stayed home with my husband."

Cheryl laughed, clapping a hand on the woman's shoulder. "Doris, get these ladies a round of drinks on the house."

As Doris rushed off, Cheryl pushed the hairy waiter out of the way and scooped up the remaining silverware. In a hushed voice, she told him, "Book an afternoon at the waxing salon, tomorrow."

At a nearby table, a Russian lady grabbed Cheryl's elbow. "I like 'em hairy," she said, smacking her lips together in satisfaction.

Bronco beamed.

"That's great," Cheryl said, clapping the woman on the back. "Another satisfied customer."

"Hi, Cheryl," Betsy called, waving like a flag from her table.

Cheryl excused herself and headed over to Betsy's group. The table was crammed full of young professionals, all sipping on The Whole Package's signature drink. Cheryl, Jackie, and Doris had spent hours trying to find the perfect combination to capture the mood of the restaurant. They'd finally settled on freshly squeezed pomegranate juice mixed with champagne. "Girls' Night" was born.

"This place is so cool," Betsy gushed. "It's everything I dreamed it would be."

"And the guys are hot," squealed a pretty dishwater blonde, and Betsy giggled.

Cheryl smiled and extended her hand to the blonde. "Hi. You must be Jenny."

The girl nodded, sparkling hoop earrings bobbing along with her head. She gestured at Christoph. "And that's my future husband."

"I'm glad you're having fun," Cheryl said, beckoning to him. "And it's just going to get better."

Christoph strutted over to the table. His smile practically glowed in the dim light. "I am Christoph," he said, leaning one muscular arm on the table and leaning in. "You like The Package?"

"What's not to like?" Cheryl mouthed to the girls but they were no longer looking at her. Jenny was eyeing Christoph like the first course on a menu.

With a tiny smile, Cheryl shook her head and stepped away from the table. She took a moment to appreciate the murmur of pleased voices, bright music, and the fire popping in the fireplace, then breathed in the heady aroma in the air. The scent of rosemary, garlic, and roasted meat wafted from the kitchen, cutting through the musky cologne of their waiters. The ambiance was perfect.

"We did it," she said out loud.

"You sure did," said a familiar, male voice.

Cheryl's body flushed. Slowly, she turned to face Andy. Those green eyes held hers for a second, then dropped to the ground. He shoved his hands into his pants pockets. The move pulled his cashmere sweater down tight over his stomach. The material clung to his abs in a way that put The Whole Package dancers to shame.

Cheryl gritted her teeth. "Can I help you with something?"

Andy looked up. In a brief, unwelcome flashback, Cheryl saw him as he had been in her bed. Sweat glistening off his skin, the sheet falling off his shoulder, his lips moving in to touch hers.

"I just wanted to tell you, it looks really good in here," Andy said.

Cheryl surveyed the restaurant, mainly to give herself somewhere else to look. The salads were just being delivered. Although the women seemed to like the colorful blend of frisée leaves, walnuts, goat cheese, pear, and pomegranate, they clearly liked the waiters even more. The women blushed as the men circled the tables in their tight spandex bottoms, leaning in close to offer fresh ground pepper.

"You did a great job," Andy said.

"Yup," Cheryl said lightly. "Now, what can I help you with? The bar's in the front, the entrees should be coming out in just a minute . . ."

"Cheryl," Andy said, face dark. "I just wanted to say . . ." He reached out and gently touched her arm. "I'm sorry."

His hand was warm on her skin. Cheryl's knees went weak and for a moment, her gaze softened. What was the problem? She liked this guy. For a moment, she thought she could have loved him. But he had betrayed her. Humiliated her. Picked Stan. Pushing his hand off, she stepped back, almost knocking over the tray of salads the food runner had just set down.

"I need you to leave me alone," Cheryl said.

Andy's face fell. "Cheryl . . ."

Just then, Jackie swooped in. "I hope I'm not interrupting anything," she chirped. "Are you the young man responsible for the lovely Japanese men up at the bar?"

Andy's eyes still held Cheryl's. "Yes."

"Darling," Jackie said, physically turning him to face them. "It seems that, without you to translate, our gorgeous little waiters don't know whether or not your men are gay."

Andy peered up at the bar area, confused. Sure enough, Anthony had led Marco, a spicy Italian of ambiguous sexual orientation, over to the Japanese clients. Marco was batting his eyelashes and running his hands over his washboard. The Japanese were nodding and smiling, but looked incredibly confused.

"Shit," Andy said. "Cheryl, I have to—"

Cheryl shrugged. "Have a good night."

The moment Andy was out of earshot, Jackie whispered, "Are you all right?"

Cheryl nodded. "Of course," she said, too brightly. "Another day, another guy."

Jackie frowned slightly, her pretty face concerned. "It seemed like . . ."

"And you're absolutely right," Cheryl admitted, eyes still on Andy. He was back up at the bar, arm draped across Marco like a good buddy. At Andy's command, the bartender lined up a row of shots and, in quick succession, the Japanese pounded them. They hit the table, cheering. "But sometimes, that's the way it goes."

Jackie nodded. "Well, if you want me to do anything . . ."

"The only thing I want you to do is to stand there and look pretty," Cheryl said, forcing herself back to the present. She gestured at the bustling room, determined not to let Andy ruin her good time. "I'm so excited. It's going perfectly."

"I know," Jackie squealed, fluffing her hair. "It's the most fun ever."

Just then, the lights dimmed and 2 Live Crew blasted out over the speakers. From across the room, Cheryl saw Betsy and Jenny turn to each other, eyes wide and screaming. They started bouncing up and down in their chairs. Jenny reached into her purse, pulling out a handful of dollar bills and waving them in the air.

"Oh, my God," Cheryl murmured. "Betsy's friend just pulled money out. Does she think it's a strip club?"

As the pulsating notes of "Me So Horny" pumped through the dining room, flashing lights drawing attention to the stage, Jackie giggled. "Now, why in the world would she think that?"

Everyone in the restaurant set down his or her fork in confusion, necks craning to see what all the commotion was about. With a flourish, Gabe leaped to the center of the room. At the sight of him, the women in the restaurant cheered. Gabe began a slow gyration, his eyes grazing the room. Spotting two women who were standing up, drinking cocktails, he turned and gave three quick thrusts. It took him just seconds to slide across the room and grab the hand of the blond woman. Setting down her drink, Gabe pulled her to the center of the dance floor and started a dirty dance. Instead of playing along, the poor woman froze. She put her hands up to her face and turned a slow, bright red.

"Uh-oh," Cheryl said. "Should we—"

"It's fine," Jackie said, squeezing her arm. "Gabe will figure it out."

Sure enough, Gabe had noticed the woman's discomfort. He gave her a saucy wink, then deliberately, moved toward the opposite edge of the dance floor. Everyone in the restaurant stared in admiration as Gabe's body writhed under the hot lights.

Noticing the attention was off her, the woman peeked out between her fingers. She darted backward, dangerously close to one of the fully nude male statues lining the floor. Gabe chose that moment to turn. He flashed a smile and gave one simple, suggestive pelvic thrust. This was enough to send the woman into a full panic. Scrambling toward the safety of the tables, she crashed full-on into the naked statue.

"Watch out!" Jackie cried, but it was too late.

The white plaster statue toppled to the ground, pulling the woman down with it. The flaccid plaster member broke off, rolled, and landed next to her face. As the woman made slow and intimate eye contact with the penis, her mouth gaped open, creating an even more scandalous sight.

Lawsuit, Cheryl thought, mind panicked. *On-premise injury.*

Cheryl and Jackie tried to push through the crowd but Doris got there first. She succeeded in pulling the woman up, but then lost her own footing in the process. Trapped by her long dress, Doris straddled the statue like a bull at a sawdust-floored bar. As Doris put her hands on the ground and struggled to stand, a photographer from the local paper snapped pictures. The flash on his camera pulsed like a strobe light. This heightened the sight of Doris's movements and created the utmost picture of vulgarity.

"Go for it, Mom," Mandy cheered.

Doris's daughter was the youngest person in the room. It had been a battle to get Doris to let her come but Mandy had won her over with some line about being proud. The young girl sat sandwiched between a group of Doris's friends from bridge club. It only took a quick look for Cheryl to realize that the other women at the table were not amused.

Marjorie McClemens, the president of the bridge club, was at least twenty years older than Doris. Apparently, when she first heard about The Whole Package, she suggested bringing the members of the bridge club to the grand opening. In spite of Doris's protests, Marjorie had put together a field trip. As Doris had predicted, the women were shocked. Instead of cheering on Doris's wild ride like every other woman in the restaurant, Marjorie stared glumly into a glass of Chardonnay.

Cheryl glanced around, trying to spot any camera phones documenting the incident with the statue for YouTube. Instead, her eyes fell on an old lady. Even in her hunched and fragile state, this grandma had managed to find her footing on top of a chair. She was standing there at full height, overlooking the crowd from above.

"Get down," Cheryl cried, trying to push through the crowd. "We don't have death insurance!"

The old lady gave Cheryl a beatific grin. As a line of oily backup dancers took the stage, the old woman raised her arms in the air and screamed, "Aiyee aiyee aiyee." The catcall was louder than a cab whistle. Everyone in the restaurant turned to stare.

Delighted to have an audience, the old lady ran her hands over her sagging body and eyeballed the line of handsome young men.

"Hi, honey," the old woman called. "You looking for a date?"

Guests laughed and cheered, swiveling their heads. They were clearly torn between watching Doris, the dancers, and the old lady.

Most of them just kept their eyes on Gabe, who had managed to thrust his way over to Doris and was in the process of helping Doris up. Finally on her feet, Doris gazed at Gabe with adoration.

"You all right?" he asked.

Doris nodded, tugging at her dress. With a grin, Gabe leaned forward and gave her a quick, sexy kiss on the lips. Doris's eyes widened. In spite of all the chaos, Cheryl grabbed Jackie's arm and whispered, "Did that just happen?"

Jackie squealed, "That just happened!"

Gabe leaped back into the center of the restaurant. He started snapping his fingers like Patrick Swayze in the last, triumphant dance scene of *Dirty Dancing*. The dancers crowded round. To the beat of the music, they gyrated in unison.

The old woman remained on the chair, gyrating right along with them.

Gabe looked at Cheryl, who waved her hands in a panic. "Get her down," she shouted. Gabe nodded. He rushed over to the woman, thrusting his huge package with every step.

"Aiyee aiyee aiyee," the old lady cried, wiggling her hips to the music. "Come and get it!"

Through the pulsing lights of the room, Cheryl could see that Mandy was doubled over, laughing hysterically. Jackie was clutching George's arm, and he was saying something to her in earnest. Andy's clients were speaking to each other rapidly. Andy's face was expressionless.

As everyone watched, the old woman fumbled with the top buttons of her shirt. Luckily, her arthritic fingers protested the action, so instead the woman grabbed for her heavy leather purse and began swinging it over her head.

Cheryl grabbed Gabe and practically shoved him toward the old lady. "Get her down."

Gabe nodded. He moved forward with careful, measured steps. The crowd leaned forward, hanging on every motion of the hunt. Just as he got close enough to grab her, the old woman took a flying leap off the chair. The crowd gasped as, for a moment, she hung in the air like a broken piñata. Before she could hit the ground, Anthony pushed Gabe aside and dove between him and the old woman. With strong arms and a heavy coat, Anthony caught her just before she could crash to the floor and shatter.

"I've got her," he shouted. "I've got her!"

The restaurant cheered. Gabe let out a huge breath, flashed a sexy grin at Anthony, then concentrated on working his way back across the room. He blew kisses and gyrated as though his life depended on it.

Just then, a shout went up from the other side of the room. Wearily, Cheryl twisted her neck to see. A drunken Jenny had taken up where the old lady had left off. She was on top of the table, tantalizing Christoph with a dance number of her own as her friends egged her on. Waiters were trying to place entrees on the tables but at this point, no one was paying attention to food.

Doris rushed over and pulled Jenny down from the table. "That is inappropriate!"

"I'm sorry, Doris, but this entire place is inappropriate," said a woman from the bridge club. "I think I have to leave."

"You haven't even eaten," Doris said. "Look, the entrees are coming out."

Marjorie shook her head. "I think it's best if we go." The rest of the group nodded, standing up. "We'll take Mandy home."

"No," Mandy pleaded. "Mom, let me stay."

Doris was on the verge of tears. "No, honey. Go home."

In spite of Mandy's protests, the group of women moved toward the exit. Doris leaned against the table, clearly upset. Cheryl headed in her direction but the Russian woman who liked hairy men stepped into her path.

"Excuse me," the Russian woman hissed, holding Cheryl's elbow in a talonlike grip and guiding her back to their table. "You manager?"

"Yes, I'm one of the owners," Cheryl said, proud to say it in spite of everything.

"This is too oily," the woman said.

Confused, Cheryl peered at the table. The woman had pushed the fish entree away. A slight gloss of lemon caper sauce shimmered from the plate. Although the overall presentation was perfect, Cheryl nodded. "Absolutely. I will bring you back another one, this time with the sauce on the side."

"I don't mean fish," the woman scoffed. "I mean him."

One of their younger waiters, Eric, was standing by the table and offering fresh ground pepper. The Russian lady was right. The oil on him was so thick he could have slid across the restaurant like a Ferrari in an ice spin. "Hot though, no?" Cheryl tried.

The Russian lady downed her drink and grabbed her purse. "Everyone else is leaving, we may as well, too."

"Everyone else is not leaving," Cheryl said. "*One* table left." She knew the danger of the lemming effect. If she let this happen, the entire restaurant could clear out. "Help!" she mouthed to Jackie.

Jackie raced over and started speaking French to the woman. The Russian woman cursed at her and grabbed her coat. The rest of the women at the table got up and pushed their way to the front door.

"Cheryl, she wanted me to give her a lap dance," Eric protested, rushing over to her. "I wouldn't do it. That's why she's leaving."

"You better pay for your meal," Cheryl called, but the Russian was already gone.

"Damn," Cheryl said. Closing her eyes, she tried to regain control of the night. Mentally, she ran through another checklist. First, they needed to turn down the music. The bass was giving the night a frantic air. Second, they should get some of the more offensively dressed waiters off the floor. They could rethink the outfits tomorrow. Third . . . Someone tapped her hard on the arm and Cheryl's eyes flew open. It was Doris, neck practically rubbed raw with worry. A breathless Anthony stood behind her.

"We need your help," Doris gasped.

"It's an emergency," Anthony cried.

"Calm down," Cheryl said, forcing her voice to stay level.

"Everything's okay. Doris, why don't you go turn down the music. Anthony, I need you to—"

"There's no time for that," Anthony said. "The old lady is naked in the bathroom. Gabe's guarding the door."

"And there are picketers outside," Doris added, near tears. "My church is picketing us."

"Call the cops," Cheryl ordered. "Now."

Anthony nodded and rushed for the phone. Cheryl beckoned to Jackie. Together, the three friends went to the front door and threw it open. Fifteen figures were on the lawn, waving signs and chanting. They were bullying a group of potential customers, preventing them from approaching the door. Cheryl wondered how many customers they had already scared away.

"Go ahead, let them in," Jackie called pleasantly, as though the picketers were just doormen guarding a secret club. She grinned at the potential customers like the Cheshire Cat. "Welcome."

The group pushed by the picketers and started to move up the steps, but a woman from Doris's church group rolled a tight snowball and lobbed it at the crowd.

"Carol Ann Gracie," Doris shrieked. "That is not God-like!"

Doris reached down with her bare hands and started to scoop up some snow to throw back.

Jackie grabbed her by her hair. "Doris, *no*."

Gabe rushed up. "Are we cutting the dance numbers or continuing?"

"Gabe, you were wonderful," Doris gushed, scrambling to her feet and touching her lips.

"Decency . . . Decency . . . Decency . . ." the picketers started chanting at the top of their lungs.

"Can't you people take a joke?" Cheryl shouted back.

Sirens screamed down the block. Red and blue lights flashing, cop cars peeled to a stop on the front lawn, almost crushing the picketers. "Get 'em," Jackie cheered, but the policemen jumped out of their cars and stormed the restaurant instead.

"Hee-haw," someone shouted from inside, "more strippers!"

"What the hell are they doing?" Cheryl asked, watching the entire task force of Schaumburg tear past her. "The picketers are right there."

"I thought you wanted me to call them for the old lady," Anthony wailed. He ran his hands through his hair, rushing after the cops.

Andy and his Japanese clients came up behind her. Cheryl felt his presence before she even turned.

"We're going to go," he said, putting a hand on Cheryl's shoulder. She shook it off, refusing to even look at him.

"Don't leave," Jackie entreated.

"Stay," Doris begged.

Loud shrieks and male shouts were coming from indoors. Gabe came running out, still mostly naked. "The kitchen is on fire! The kitchen is on fire!"

Panicked, Doris and Jackie rushed inside.

"Why leave now?" Cheryl said. "The show has just begun." Then, she turned and bowed graciously at his clients.

They nodded. But they certainly didn't bow back.

Chapter Forty

AFTER THE HANDSOME MEN WITH THE LONG HOSES SECURED THE smoky kitchen, The Whole Package was forced to close for the night.

Greg was devastated, hunched over in his white chef's uniform, rhythmically pounding Manhattans at the bar. Cheryl sidled up to him and put an arm around his stooped shoulders. "I need you lucid tomorrow," she said gently.

Slamming his drink onto the counter, Greg barreled for the front door as though he were going to throw himself through the plate glass. At what seemed like the last possible moment, he grabbed for the door handle and pushed his way outside.

"Thanks for burning our kitchen down," Jackie muttered.

"What if he doesn't ever come back?" Doris asked.

"If we were on top of a high rise in Chicago, I'd worry," Cheryl said, taking a seat with them at a tiny table. "But only because he'd jump. Since that's not gonna happen, we'll see him tomorrow."

Shell-shocked, the three women took in the interior of The Whole Package. The place looked like it had hosted a Greek wedding and the Italians, Russians, and entire soccer team of Brazil decided to show up, too. There were shattered plates littered across the floor, broken glasses tossed onto tables, and pieces of gold confetti on every surface imaginable. There was also a fine layer of soot covering everything.

"It looks like a cremation," Cheryl said, wiping up a bit of ash with her finger and burying her head in her hands. "How symbolic."

After the fire, everyone on staff had been sent home, as well as George, Betsy, and any other friends who were hanging around, trying to help.

Jackie was pale and drawn, tugging at a strand of hair. "Maybe it wasn't bad. Maybe it was just outrageous." A piece of gold confetti winked from her upper lip.

"It was bad," Cheryl confirmed, forcing herself to sit up straight. "Anybody want to leave the country? I'm thinking Mexico, tonight. Margaritas, fresh fish . . ."

"It's not the end of the world," Doris said, wringing her hands. "I had a really good time."

Jackie and Cheryl swiveled toward her in shock. Laughing, Cheryl said, "And how many Xanax were *you* on?"

Doris blushed. "Well, it was more excitement than I've seen in a long time. We got the police and the fire department here. That's impressive, don't you think?"

"And your gay boyfriend finally kissed you on the lips," Jackie pointed out.

Doris practically turned purple.

Cheryl shook her head. Her disappointment was so weighted that she thought she was going to fall over. "We're so screwed."

"But it was our first try," Doris practically shouted, leaping up and pacing the bar area. She started picking up pieces of broken dishes and setting them on the counter. "It can't be perfect."

"Doris, stop that," Cheryl said firmly. "You just cut yourself."

Doris looked at her hands in surprise. There was a tiny bead of blood on her finger. She grabbed a cocktail napkin, wrapping it tightly around the wound.

"They hated it." Jackie shrugged. "They hated everything about it. We'll be bankrupt within the month."

"No they did not and no we will not," Doris insisted. She grabbed another champagne bottle and threw it full force on top of the trash. It made an exceptional crash and, involuntarily, everyone ducked.

"Doris, stop," Cheryl cried. "Look, maybe you're right. It was opening night, we had high hopes and they . . ."

"Were shattered," Jackie said simply. "They were shattered."

The silence in the room was deafening. Then there was a slight sniffle. Now Doris was crying, her back leaning against the bar and her dress falling off her plump shoulder. "What are we going to do?" she wailed. "Doug's divorcing me and he should. I spent so much of our savings. I cheated on him in front of the entire restaurant. How am I going to . . ."

"Doris, after everything Doug put you through, you are insane if you think you don't deserve a tiny kiss," Cheryl said. "Those papers are a bluff. Everything's going to work out."

"What papers?" Jackie demanded.

"Divorce papers. They came before we left," Cheryl said. "But he doesn't mean it."

"You don't know that." Doris sniffled, tugging at the arm of her white dress. "How's everything going to work out?"

"Don't sign them. Get him back here, talk about it—" Cheryl tried but Doris cut her off.

"I mean about the restaurant."

Surprised, Cheryl took a moment to regroup. Then she explained that she'd been in marketing long enough to know that the first reaction didn't always have to be the final one. The media was powerful and even though the evening had been crazy, the outcome really just depended on how the newspapers decided to spin it. If they said The Whole Package was a success, it would be. In spite of everything disastrous that had happened that night.

"There's no point in sitting around talking," Cheryl finally said, standing up and grabbing her purse. "The paper will come out and . . . it's like a horoscope. We'll know our future in the morning."

"I'm a Cancer," Doris muttered.

"Great, Doris," Jackie said. She grabbed Greg's leftover Manhattan and finished it off. "And we'll be hoping for the best with that."

ON THE WAY home from The Whole Package, Jackie was in a silent panic. She sat in the passenger's seat of Doris's car, breathing in the stifling scent of the Orangesicle air freshener and hating the way the seat belt cut into her down-filled coat. Way too hot, Jackie was afraid she might throw up. The scented satchel was only the first on a long list of things that might make it happen. Living a life of poverty and confessing her pathetic state to her friends were definitely second and third.

Staring out the window as Doris drove, hands resting on the door, Jackie noticed the way the passing headlights reflected in her diamond rings. It would be one of the last times she could enjoy that image. One ring would be kept as a memento and to the rest . . . she watched the diamonds shimmer and glint . . . it was time to say good-bye.

The rational part of her brain was trying to tell her to calm down, she could get a job or something, but Jackie shuddered at the thought. As much as she enjoyed a good fantasy where she was the CEO of a jewelry importing company or some high-powered travel agent or news reporter, the only thing she'd ever been good at was painting. Look how far that had gotten her. Her organizational skills were a disaster, her competitive edge was dull, and her financial sense? Puh-lease. The only job she could get would pay minimum wage, serving burnt espressos or decorating cupcakes until she got too frustrated and ran away.

Jackie's eyes smarted. She rubbed them quickly, before Doris could see. No need to freak Doris out, as if the poor thing needed any help with that. Doris was white-knuckling the steering wheel and peering through the windshield with complete focus, mumbling something about whether or not she should have taken a Breathalyzer. Jackie had brought up the divorce papers at the beginning of the drive but Doris had clammed up, as though not talking about it kept it from being true.

"Honey, relax," Jackie pleaded, as Doris slammed on the brakes for a squirrel at least a mile away. "You had one glass of champagne six hours ago. You're fine. But if you keep driving like this you might just wrap us around a tree and I certainly have not invested in a life insurance policy, if that's what you're hoping for."

"Maybe *I* should do that," Doris moaned. "If I kill myself, Mandy and Doug might still have enough left to live on."

Jackie reached over and tried to take her hand. Doris immediately shook it off, indicating her ten and two position on the steering wheel.

"Just being around you cheers me up." Jackie chuckled. "Darling, Doug has more money than God. You'll be fine."

"No." Doris shook her head, lowering her speed by five miles. "His *family* has money and they're going to hate me if Doug has to ask for it because of something I did. Thank God they're in Florida. If they had seen this tonight . . ."

"Doug made you live like a prisoner in that house," Jackie said. "You deserve a little something—something for that."

And Doris would probably get it, Jackie thought.

Yes, Doris would be just fine. Even if Doug's family was upset about Doris's financial failure, he'd had an affair. It didn't take a divorce lawyer to see she'd be okay. And Cheryl still had a house, a car, and a professional reputation that would make it possible for her to try again and again. Nope, they were all set.

Jackie bit her lip until she tasted blood. The only person she had looking out for her was George. He had already called six times since the firefighters came. Jackie couldn't help but wonder. If push came to shove, would she take the life raft he was offering?

Running diamond-encrusted fingers over her eyes, Jackie had to admit it was fitting. After all, it had certainly been a long time ago, but George *had* met her on his yacht.

WHAT CHERYL SHOULD have been thinking of as she drove home from the disastrous opening night was the disastrous opening night. Instead, the only thing looping through her brain was the moment Andy had started spouting off Japanese like the words from a pop song. What was it about him that she always let get to her? When he'd touched her arm, she'd actually felt a twinge of physical pain. Touching the spot now, she rubbed it like a burn.

When Cheryl pulled into her driveway, worn out to her core, she braked at the sight of a bundle lying on her front door. It looked like a baby dropped from a stork. The signs were everywhere. What was she going to do?

The cravings had started two weeks ago. For the first time in twenty years, Cheryl had wanted fast food. She could not get the idea of a soft, slightly sweet hamburger bun out of her head. At the first drive-thru she came to, Cheryl put in an order for a burger and a thing of fries, and then decided to wash it all down with that drink she'd loved as a kid, a sticky orange concoction that had an aftertaste like lighter fluid.

After polishing off the meal in the parking lot, Cheryl found herself wanting a bowl of Lucky Charms cereal. Even with the orange drink burning the back of her throat, the idea of letting a purple marshmallow melt on her tongue was unbeatable. When Cheryl pulled into the grocery store, mentally asking herself, *Are you high?* another part of her brain clicked in and said, *Or are you pregnant?*

At the thought, her body was suddenly coated with panic sweat. Cheryl tried to think over the last two months but couldn't remember the last time she'd gone on a tampon run. She'd never been one to keep track because her visits were always light and easy, generally showing up in the middle of every month. Since she'd been with Andy . . . the middle of the month had come and gone, without any sort of event. And she was way too young for menopause, wasn't she?

Instead of picking up sugary cereal, Cheryl slunk into a drugstore for a pregnancy test. She felt like a teenager buying that first box of condoms, ducking the eyes of the cashier by focusing on the latest issue of *People* magazine. Back in the car, she'd stared down at the bag and finally, threw it into the glove box like an overdue parking ticket. She vowed not to even think about it until after the grand opening of The Whole Package. Then, she'd have time to deal with the news, whatever it was.

Now, Cheryl took a deep breath and pulled the bag out of its hiding spot. After slamming the car door, she breathed in the wet cement smell her garage always gave in the cold, then stomped through her house. Throwing the pregnancy test on the counter, she went straight for the Christmas tree and plugged in its white, twinkling lights.

"I'll just open the gift first, then I'll take the test," she promised.

The package on the front doorstep was most likely from her family, either an early Christmas present or a good luck on the grand opening sort of thing. Cheryl threw open her front door. Her jaw dropped. The box on her front porch was not from her family. It was hand-delivered and topped off with a familiar red rose, wrapped in red paper from Bramble's.

Cheryl's heart sank and leaped, tearing her in too many directions. She had feelings for him, that much was obvious, but he had hurt her. Worse, he had betrayed her. Allowing herself to feel anything for him would just cause more pain. But it was too cold to stand outside, fighting him inside her mind.

With a hearty sigh, she dragged the heavy box indoors. Cheryl cut her hand in her first attempt at opening the thick cardboard, but kept tearing at it until it finally peeled back. She peered inside. A red envelope rested on top of a bag of jumbo marshmallows, two roasting pokers, a Duraflame log, and a collection of Bing Crosby

CDs. Hands shaking, Cheryl yanked open the fragile paper. His penmanship was messy—and so typically male.

Dear Cheryl,

I'm coming into the restaurant tonight to support you on your Grand Opening.

   Here's a little good luck gift, in honor of the time we got to spend together before I blew any chance of a future with you. Regardless, you should know that the dinner I was paid to spend with you was one of the most interesting nights of my life. I should have made the right choice then, but it was too late and for that, all I can do is apologize. I hope one day you'll consider me a friend.

                              All the best,
                              Andy

Cheryl blinked, then read the letter again. And again. After the fourth read, she scooped up the entire box, stomped it out to her garage, and flung it into the trash bin. At the last second, she snatched out the bag of marshmallows and of course, the Bing Crosby CDs. After another moment of deliberation, she saved the roaster, too. Cheryl did love toasted marshmallows but they would have to cook over the stove, not the fire.

   Cheryl slammed the lid on the trash bin and took a deep, steadying breath. Running inside, she grabbed the pregnancy test and took the stairs two at a time. She felt a bit more confident now. There was no way she was the baby mama of some guy who didn't even know her fire was a fake.

Chapter Forty-one

THE WHOLE PACKAGE—"CAN'T YOU PEOPLE TAKE A JOKE?" THE headline of the newspaper article perfectly quoted Cheryl as she screamed at the picketers. The photo next to it was of Doris, desperately trying to climb off the naked statue.

Doris put her head in her hands. She had driven to the newsstand in her reindeer long johns, just to be the first one to get the verdict. Now she wished she hadn't.

The article had been written by a man who, according to the grainy black-and-white photo by his column, was bald and wore thick glasses. His words seemed to take great pleasure in their disastrous opening night:

> On his way down to Georgia, the devil stopped in Schaumburg to grab a bite to eat at a pornographic little restaurant focused entirely on the male package. The lewd decorations, graphic dance numbers, and relentless objectification of men are a striking antithesis to the upscale cuisine served by executive chef Greg Wilson. Had the Millstines known their former legacy would

house a production worthy of X-rated films, they may have applauded the fact that on the opening night, The Whole Disaster almost burned to the ground . . .

Doris burst into Jackie's room, sobbing and waving the pages around like they were an obituary. "There's a strip club a mile down the road," she wailed. "Why is he picking on us?"

Jackie pushed back her satin sleep mask, sat up on her elbow, and thumbed through the paper at a lightning pace.

"It's on the third page . . ." Doris sniffled, just as Jackie held up a finger and cleared her throat and read: "Cancer. Your winning smile is your golden ticket. Flash it often at a mysterious stranger."

Doris stared in confusion, hands to her heart. "Well, Doris," Jackie mused, tossing the paper to the ground, pulling her sleep mask back on and curling into a fetal position. "You better get out there and find a mysterious stranger. Or I'll tell you this much— we're fucked."

IN SPITE OF the bad review, everyone still reported to work at four o'clock. The waiters were gelled and handsome; Jackie, Cheryl, and Doris dressed in black.

"Keep your heads up, people," Cheryl instructed, nodding with approval at her comely staff. "If they would have run the pictures of you guys, women would be beating down the doors. That said, anyone who read that article and still shows up tonight is looking for a good time, so that's exactly what we'll give them!"

"If anyone complains about the food," Greg spoke from the kitchen door, holding a large kitchen knife. "Send 'em to me."

As the waiters dispersed to polish silverware, Jackie, Cheryl, and Doris linked arms and huddled. A shadow crossed Cheryl's face and she eyed her best friends, thinking over what she now knew; the secret she wasn't ready to confront. She smiled tightly and shook her head. "Here's to a great night."

Anthony was watching from the host stand. He nodded, as though to say "My sentiments exactly."

At four thirty, the staff manned their stations. By five o'clock, they began polishing wineglasses and the trays of silverware. By six o'clock, all but one of them had settled onto the stage or into the plush chairs, waiting for anyone to arrive.

Jackie, Doris, and Cheryl remained huddled at the front door, peering out like party planners waiting for the first guest. Finally, Doris screeched, "Someone's coming!" and a battalion of male bodies clambered to their feet.

A middle-aged couple, well-dressed, was walking up the steps toward The Whole Package. They stopped suddenly, noticing the sign. Confused, the man considered his options, then guided his wife away, arm wrapped around her shoulders.

"Millstines," Jackie moaned. "They were looking for Millstines."

The disappointment in the room was tangible. Cheryl cocked her head and indicated the bar. The three friends walked over and took a seat.

Anthony remained diligently at his post. At eight o'clock, he clapped his hands and shrieked, "There's a party!" and everyone once again leaped up.

A group of five women threw open the doors, hooting and hollering. They were dressed in tight jeans and low-cut, sparkling tops. The scent of cigarettes and alcohol followed them in, along with the smell of drugstore perfume. The men went on full performance. Jackie, Cheryl, and Doris immediately plastered smiles on their faces.

"They remind me of Katherine Rigney," Doris said.

"Keep smiling," Cheryl whispered. Out of the side of her mouth, she said, "They're money in the bank."

Jackie rushed forward, gushing, "Welcome, ladies."

Once the party was seated, it seemed as though the curse had been broken. Here and there, small groups of women trickled in, looking around the restaurant with titillated confusion. The dancers blasted raunchy routines every fifteen minutes, the food was complimented, and overall, the night seemed like a success . . . if twenty-four guests could keep a restaurant in business. By ten thirty, everyone had cleared out. Only the women who'd started the trend were still hanging around. One of their friends was over by the ladies' restroom, making out with one of the dancers.

"I would fire him for that," Cheryl considered, "but it's not like he's going to have his job for long anyway."

"Come on, Malinda," her friends called. The group was finally staggering to their feet, faces sour with alcohol. "We're going to the strip club." The waiters laughed, applauding the women. "Come with us," the women clamored.

Cheryl shrugged at her waiters. "Go if you want to," she said. "It's not like there's anything going on here."

Christoph, Travis, and Brian threw off their aprons with a whoop and sashayed out the front door, hanging on to the women. Maybe one of them would wake up in Vegas, married. That would be fine; and one less person to keep on the payroll.

"This is ridiculous," Cheryl said. She flopped back down at the bar and sipped at the last drops from her soda glass. "There's no point in staying open until eleven. It's a waste of resources. Anthony, will you close up?"

Anthony considered the situation, then turned the sign to Closed. He started powering down the computers. Gabe moved in to help.

"Let's just get out of here," Doris mumbled, laying her face on the bar. "I'm ready to go home."

Jackie was silent, staring into space. If she were still a smoker, she'd be puffing away.

"What are we going to do?" Doris fretted, on the way out to their cars. She was watching the ground carefully, furry boots stepping over the ice glistening in the parking lot.

"Get someone to plow or salt this," Cheryl said, deliberately avoiding the question. "It's a total liability." She stopped walking for a moment and listened. All down the street, she could hear shouts and music from the other bars and restaurants. From the back alley, there was the sound of busboys dumping bins of wine bottles into the recycling bins.

"How can anybody slip and fall if they don't come to our restaurant?" Jackie wondered.

"Don't worry, things will get better," Cheryl promised. She looked up at the sky and inhaled the crisp evening air. "Everything will be fine in the morning."

"Because . . . ?" Jackie pulled her mink tightly around her, waiting for Doris to unlock the car.

"Because I did something to help us," Cheryl said, pulling out her keys. "I wrote a letter to the editor in rebuttal of the article that came out. I sent it in today; it'll be in tomorrow's issue."

Doris paused at the door of her car, chewing her lip. She looked like an Eskimo in her big furry hat with her big rosy cheeks. "Wait. You did what? We do those types of things together."

Cheryl let out a deep sigh, dropping her purse on the hood of her BMW like she was getting ready to roll up her sleeves for a fight. "Please don't tell me this is a problem. It's just good PR."

Jackie fingered the edge of her white cashmere scarf, watching the exchange and shivering.

"Well, we're all supposed to be partners," Doris mumbled. "So, shouldn't you have asked us before doing something like that? What does it say?"

"Nothing bad," Cheryl said, stomping her feet and rubbing her hands together. "If we're going to chat about this let's go back inside."

"Just tell us what it said," Jackie requested. "I'm ready to go home."

"Are you?" Cheryl planted her hands on her hips and glared at Jackie, who looked at her in surprise. "I just said that it's a little ridiculous that we can be picketed for having half-dressed men in our restaurant when there's an actual strip club down the road. Nobody bothers them."

"True," Jackie mused. "Is that all?"

Cheryl looked down at her boots. They were a bit scuffed, even in the dark of the parking lot. She didn't want to tell her friends this next part. It was only going to cause problems.

"What else did it say?" Doris pleaded.

Cheryl's eyes flashed. "I said that it's bullshit that this town is so willing to hold a double standard. If anyone has a problem with us, they shouldn't bother showing up because they're not invited."

Doris let out a breath. "Oh no."

"Did you sign it from all of us or just you?" Jackie demanded.

"We're a team, right?" Cheryl said, grabbing her purse from the car. "It's from all of us."

"Cheryl, you need to contact the paper and get that out of there." Doris pulled the furry hat off her head, steam seeming to rise from the now messy brown hair. "That's not going to solve anything. If we write something, we write it together."

"Exactly." Jackie nodded. Her ears were starting to tingle in the icy wind. "We have an equal partnership in this. Remember? We had that conversation a long time ago and we've had to have it several times again with you, Cheryl. This isn't anything new. We're equal investors, so we work as a team. You can't speak for us."

Cheryl considered Jackie for a long moment. Once again, she thought of the secret she knew. After a moment, she said evenly, "Women will understand. They will read my letter and realize it's not fair. That review Mark Peterson wrote was bullshit. They will understand his opinion was biased and turn out to support us, I absolutely guarantee it."

Cheryl did have a history with Mark Peterson, the jerk with the dark-framed glasses. Ages ago, his paper had tried to snake one of TurnKey's clients out of ad space, after Cheryl had already paid for it. Someone had done the layout incorrectly and didn't have enough room for everything. They tried to convince TurnKey to accept a partial ad instead of the full they'd paid for. Cheryl refused. In the end, Mark's column got bumped from that issue.

Irrationally, he had blamed the slight on Cheryl. He'd had it in for her ever since.

Due to this, Mark had not been invited to the opening. He had gotten the information about it from another source, even though his column was written as though he saw it firsthand. Cheryl was clear to address that in the letter. She also addressed the issues of equality she had mentioned to the girls and there was no way she was retracting any of that now. If her critique of Mark meant a spotlight would also shine a light on sexism, Cheryl was grateful for the chance.

After all those years at TurnKey, shouting out her own sexist remarks to avoid being a target, Cheryl had never complained about what she had been subjected to. After all, women were subjected to double standards everywhere. Be sexy—but not too sexy. Use your brains—but let the man think he's smarter. Don't make fun of a beer belly—but you better order a salad. It irritated Cheryl that everyone around her claimed to be so progressive, outraged that on the other side of the world, women were treated like property, not allowed to show flesh, not allowed to drive cars, even forbidden to think. She had to wonder . . . was that attitude really so far from home?

"I stand by what I wrote," she said.

"You don't have the right to speak for us," Jackie said, slamming her hand against the car. "This could destroy us, even more than we're already destroyed."

"I'm not retracting anything," Cheryl insisted, face heated. "We need to stand up for ourselves. We're women—let's roar."

"Oh, Cheryl." Jackie laughed imperiously, leaning against the car. "Do you mean to tell me you've stopped wearing a bra or shaving your legs? That you're not going to wear makeup or play helpless when you get a flat tire?"

"I have Triple Fucking A—" Cheryl tried to say but Jackie cut her off, taking a step forward.

"When you got engaged to Sean, you wore that ring on your left finger. When you got married, you changed your last name. When you were at TurnKey, you sucked it up and dealt with all of the nonsense, just like every woman has for years. So don't you dare tell me *now's* the time to stand up for equal rights," Jackie practically shouted, "when my money and Doris's is at stake. Now is the time to figure out how to continue to play the game as we *always* have. It's time to make our financial investment pay off."

"Uh . . . *Whose* financial investment?" Cheryl asked. She did not want to talk about this but if Jackie was going to force the issue, she would.

"What?" Jackie said, taking a tiny step away from the car.

"I think you know what I'm trying to say."

The night before, Cheryl had barely gotten a wink of sleep. She was dealing with thoughts of a little pink stick, a failed business, and Andy's unwanted presents (and presence). After a few hours of tossing and turning, Cheryl found herself up at the crack of dawn. She wanted to swing by George's office to discuss their options. If George had expected her, he probably would have thought to cover the incriminating papers perched in full view on his desk.

Instead, pleased to see anyone from Jackie's world, George bustled to the kitchen to get them some coffee. When Cheryl hopped up to grab a Werther's from his desk, she stopped and stared at a financial agreement drafted between him and Jackie. It lay nestled between the desk clock and the Waterford crystal candy dish.

At first, Cheryl hadn't thought anything of it. George was Jackie's lawyer; why wouldn't he carry contracts with her? But after a moment, her brain fully processed what she had seen. "The monies transferred to Jacqueline Windsor, on behalf of George Edwards, in the amount of $250,000 for the purpose of . . ." Cheryl peered closer at the page. There it was in black and white— Princess Jackie wasn't fiscally responsible for their project at all.

"I don't understand," Doris implored, through chattering teeth. "What are you two fighting about?"

Cheryl was silent for a moment, waiting on Jackie to speak. She did look uncharacteristically vulnerable—soft curls blowing in the wind, blue eyes scared—but Cheryl refused to feel sorry for her. After sacrificing everything for their project—her life savings, a second mortgage, her professional reputation—she wasn't about to feel pity. Jackie never had to worry about a damn thing.

Putting her hands on her hips, Cheryl said, "Doris, I think it's time for you to know that—"

"Cheryl, don't!" Jackie's voice was desperate.

"I'm sorry," Cheryl said, shaking her head. "But I am the only one standing here that's actually funding *our* restaurant out of *my* money. So, why do the two of you think you have the right to call all the shots? Not to mention the fact that you two don't know shit about the corporate world."

"That's not fair," Doris argued. "Besides, it might not be my money but I had to fight Doug to be a part of this, especially when Mandy told him what was going on. What difference does it make if it's Doug's money or Jackie's husband's money . . ."

"Not Robert's money," Cheryl said, back straight as a rod. "It's George's."

Doris turned to Jackie, confused. "What?"

Fidgeting, Jackie tugged at the black beads that hung like a flapper chain around her neck. She shook her head, unable to speak.

"I have been a friend to you for over twenty-five years and I have never met anyone I've felt further away from," Cheryl told Jackie. "You are so manipulative. It's such bullshit because we're supposed to be your best friends. I would have done anything for you."

"I never meant to hurt you," Jackie said softly.

"You've always hurt me," Cheryl said. Out of the corner of her eye, she saw Doris's face fall, realizing Cheryl intended to take it all the way. "You thought we didn't know about your father. And I get it, I'm sure what was going on when we were younger wasn't easy for you to deal with. But to call us your best friends and try to keep something like that from us? Of course we knew! Everyone knew. He was stumbling in and out of every bar in town. But here was the thing that amazed me even more—no one called you on your bullshit because everyone at that school loved you enough to help you lie. And you took it all for granted. You didn't even go to the high school reunion."

Doris pulled out her keys and clicked the locks on the door. "Come on, Jackie, we're leaving." Scrambling to open the Lexus, Doris slid in and turned on the ignition, as though the force of her action could stop this fight from happening.

Jackie's breathing was controlled but shallow. Ignoring Doris, she lifted her chin. "Is there more?"

"Of course there is," Cheryl said, pale face growing blotchy. "You got everything you ever wanted. Everything's been handed to you on a silver platter. You haven't had to fight for any of it; you just had to shake your pretty blond hair around like a magic wand and—poof!—done. You want to be homecoming queen? Sure. You want to be an artist? Okay. You want to travel the world? And on and on and on. Everyone thinks you're so fabulous." Cheryl shook her head sadly. "But the truth is, you're just some girl who stole a rich man from his wife. When he was dead—and don't think people didn't joke that you killed him—you trotted off to Paris, dumping us and living out your fairy-tale life on his money. And when the money ran out, you came home to people who loved and trusted you so you could use them, too."

Doris laid on the horn. "Jackie, just get in."

"I've been working my ass off since I was eighteen," Cheryl said, as Jackie made a move for the door. "I put in eighty-hour weeks and I didn't do that because I wanted to, Jackie. I did it because I had to. I don't have a gift. But you don't even give a shit about your talent. The reason you probably haven't lifted a brush in years is because no one's willing to lift it for you."

Jackie scrambled into the car and slammed the door and Doris backed out angrily. Cheryl had to leap out of the way to keep from getting run over.

Crunching across the ice toward her car, Cheryl's vision was double as though she were drunk. She felt like she was. Somehow, she got into her car, and through her rearview mirror, watched as a baffled Doris started firing questions at Jackie. But Jackie wasn't talking. She just had that pretty blond head buried in her hands.

Chapter Forty-two

IN THE CAR, JACKIE REALIZED THAT IF SHE EVER AGAIN CAME across that Orangesicle air freshener smell in another vehicle or a car wash shop, she would be transported right back to this moment. The moment when she'd never felt so humiliated in her entire life.

"I don't understand . . ." Doris said again, still trying to take in what Jackie had just explained to her. "*All* of your money? Gone?"

Jackie nodded, squeezing the tips of her fingers with all of her might, choking back the lump in her throat.

"So, Cheryl's right," Doris realized. "You're not just staying with me because Doug's gone. You're staying . . . because you don't have anywhere else to go?"

The light debated whether or not to turn red, hovering at yellow a moment too long. Doris put her foot on the gas and shot through. Jackie wanted to applaud her but at the same time knew Doris's driving recklessly was proof of how upset she really was.

"That's not true." Jackie sighed. "I could have figured something out. I always do."

Doris shook her head, automatically checking her rearview

mirror for the police. "I really don't mind, if that's what you're thinking," Doris said softly. "I'm glad you're staying with me. I mean, you're my best friend. If you'd told me about your situation I would have been the first to help you."

Jackie fought back tears.

"Have I done something to make you not trust me?" Doris wondered. "I mean, Cheryl was totally out of line with everything she just said. I really hope you know I feel that way, but I'm trying to understand why you didn't just tell me you were in trouble."

Jackie shifted her feet on the floorboards, trying to warm her cold toes through her faux alligator-skin high heels. She wanted to explain that the things she kept from her friends had never been about a lack of trust, it was about protecting herself. Born into a family of secrets, lying was the only way to avoid talking about the truth.

"It's okay." Doris sighed, reaching out and taking her hand. "I like you because of *you*. I always have. If you lost all your money and we have to add starving artist to the list, then . . ."

"But Cheryl's right, I'm not even an artist," Jackie scoffed, tugging at her mink. "I'm this middle-aged woman who was good at something twenty years ago and to be honest with you, I don't even like to paint anymore."

When she went to Paris, Jackie had joined the artistic community with the same enthusiasm she would have had for joining a dental club. The community bored her. All these artists with their petulant ideas of what life was and how they could reflect it in their sculptures, paintings, collages—ugh!—and the modern artists were the worst. The risk takers who thought it was so avant-garde to stand up on a stage and defecate or cover themselves in blood. Ick.

Half the time, Jackie thought it would have been just as meaningful to get up and flip around her shaggy blond mane, fully clothed. When she made that remark to someone who seemed as bored as she was, he'd congratulated her with, "How brave. Where do you show?"

Just as insincere were the cocktail receptions, where everyone wore black and eyed one another, trying to determine who was important. When discussions began about various types of stylistic painting, a topic Jackie should have been fascinated by, she'd find herself nodding and smiling, wondering how many pieces of shrimp the fat man with the fedora had already inhaled.

Christian determined she was just going through an artistic downtime and that, when it was over, her inner landscape would be full again. There would be color combinations and images she had never even dreamed of. She would then speak of her intent to paint, her deep desire to paint . . . but she'd only said it to make him happy. It had been a lie.

Doris turned the car onto their street. Suddenly, Jackie stiffened and grabbed for the door handle as though she'd jump out. "Wait!" she shrieked.

Doris slammed on the brakes and the car fishtailed, weaving side to side over the yellow lines. Squealing, Doris maneuvered the Lexus with her gloved hands, finally bringing it under control. "Gosh darn it, Jackie," she panted. "Don't do that. I thought I'd hit something."

"No, I . . . I . . . just realized I forgot my . . ."

Jackie was desperately trying to think of something to prevent Doris from driving down her block. She had full-on forgotten she'd told Mandy they wouldn't be home until midnight. It was 11:05. If she let Doris walk into that house, things were going to be very bad indeed.

"My medicine," Jackie lied. "I left my medicine at the restaurant."

"You're on meds?" Doris asked. "I didn't know that. For what?"

"Um . . ." Jackie tried to think of something. "Birth control? I can't skip one or I'll get pregnant." Forget the fact that it had been months since she'd had sex.

"I'll just call Gabe," Doris soothed her. "He and Anthony will be there wrapping things up until late and he can just drop off your pills on his way home."

Doris dove into her purse, rummaging for her phone. The Lexus was still parked in the middle of the road, hazards now flashing with that annoying clicking sound. It sounded like a robotic voice repeating, "You're screwed . . . you're screwed . . . you're screwed . . ."

"Please, let's just go get them," Jackie begged. "Please, Doris. Let's just go back and get them. I'm also in the mood for some ice cream." Jackie grasped to remember her favorite brand of Ben and Jerry's. "We could get some Everything But The . . . After the day we've had, we are two women who deserve to eat some ice cream."

Doris had already eased her foot off the brake, saying, "Let's drop me off, then you take the . . ." She stopped speaking, suddenly spotting Will's beat-up Toyota. "There's a car in the driveway," Doris said. She turned to Jackie, sudden understanding dawning on her face. "This had better not be what I think it is."

Doris gunned it down the block, threw the SUV in park, and slid out, slamming the door behind her. She circled Will's Corolla like a bloodhound. Black-and-white bumper stickers from various bands and the same Dumb Bunny stickers Betsy had had hanging above her cubicle were plastered on the back bumper. A math book was nestled in the front seat against a wadded-up red hooded sweatshirt, a pair of cleats, and a dirty soccer jersey. All it needed was a busty model from the auto show standing next to it with a microphone, reciting: "Typical make in our Teenage Boy category . . ."

"Maybe it was someone just stopping by to drop off homework or something," Jackie tried, grabbing her purse and following Doris, who was already bustling up the front walk.

Doris threw open the front door, ignoring her. "Mandy," she called. "Who's here?"

As Doris stomped her way up the stairs and down the hall, Jackie felt sick. This was not going to go well. A few seconds later, from Doris's screams, Jackie determined that Will and Mandy were actually in the act of . . . well, something, when Doris burst into the room.

A red-faced Will scampered out of Mandy's bedroom, yanking up his jeans and racing for the front door like it was the jump exit of a plane. Doris was chasing after him with what appeared to be a purse, but on closer inspection was actually a Trapper Keeper with a big sticker of false teeth plastered in the middle. Like a batter forced to walk when she was ready to take it all the way, Doris threw the binder out the front door and after Will with all her might. Papers scattered over the walk.

Jackie took her place on the firm love seat and waited for the axe to drop. That took about five seconds. Mandy burst down the hallway with her face splotchy and red, especially around her mouth. Her neck looked like Will had given her a hickey.

"You," she screamed, pointing at Jackie like she'd been the one to chase Will out of the house. "You wanted this to happen. You wanted me to get caught!"

Doris turned accusing eyes to her best friend. "How could you do this?"

"No, I . . ." Jackie's blue eyes were helpless, darting from mother to daughter.

"I should have known," Doris said, hands on her hips. "You added yourself to the schedule to help Mandy sneak around. You don't even *take* birth control, you . . ."

"Yes I do. She's the one who helped me get it," Mandy screamed.

Jackie's shoulders slumped.

"You did what?" Doris's face paled. "You need to get out of our home."

"You can't kick me out, I'm your daughter!" Mandy screamed, tears streaming down her face.

"She means me," Jackie said quietly.

Standing up, Jackie took a look at her best friend. *That's what betrayal looks like*, she thought. Doris's eyes were a million shades of hurt, different colors and depths of emotion. If Jackie hadn't admitted that very night she was no longer an artist, she would have put them on a canvas.

As Jackie got to her feet, the expensive rug sank under the

pressure of her heels. With Mandy's sniffles ringing in her ears, Jackie went to her room and started folding items to place into the Louis Vuitton bag she'd stolen from Christian. It was funny. Christian had always said he didn't have money for rent yet he still had the best in designer accessories. No wonder she'd liked him.

With a studied glance around the room—just in case she was never invited back, which seemed pretty likely—Jackie memorized the lace comforter, dried flowers hanging over the reading desk, and pink Tiffany lamp just aching to start a fire with its rich antiquity.

It was kind of funny. Jackie felt greater guilt over the fact that she would not strip the sheets and leave a thank-you note and a bunch of wildflowers as she typically would after being a guest in someone's home than she did for interfering with Doris's daughter. And for that, she knew she deserved to leave—immediately.

Chapter Forty-three

THE WINDOWS OF CHERYL'S BMW WERE STEAMED WITH RAGE. As she waited at a stoplight, she caught a reflection of herself in a storefront window. She took a moment to be impressed with the general girth of the front of her car. Hit or be hit. That was its motto and Cheryl couldn't think of another vehicle that could have represented her more. She was just glad the damn thing was paid for.

"Fuck it," she shouted, gunning the engine. "Fuck Jackie, fuck Doris, and fuck *everybody*."

If there was any justice in this world, Cheryl would have stayed on the open road, speeding up entrance ramps and exit ramps until she squealed to the front door of her brothers, and fell into their arms. She had no friends, no job, and no money. What better time was there to leave?

"Sorry for the language, my baby," Cheryl apologized, patting her flat stomach.

Cheryl had gone ahead and taken the pregnancy test the night before, confident it would come up negative. She'd been busy, she'd been distracted—she'd probably gotten her period and forgotten about it. The pink stick took issue with that.

It smiled.

No matter how many times Cheryl reread the directions, determined to learn that a smile meant, "No! It's okay. You're not going to have a baby at fucking forty," she finally accepted that wasn't what it meant at all.

Cheryl had ached at the news. How embarrassing—she could just imagine the flack she was going to take from her brothers. "You're pregnant at that age? Wow. Even your ovaries are overachievers." God, she'd be cashing in senior discounts when her kid turned sixteen. Cheryl had sunk down and sat on the cool edge of the tub. It was humiliating but maybe . . . She had looked in the bathroom mirror, squinting hard at her reflection. Maybe it was good, like a second chance, so late in life . . . She put her hand on her stomach, wishing she didn't have to go through it alone. A pregnancy should be a time with pink and blue parties, Doris trying to hand-sew perfect outfits, Cheryl and Jackie laughing at the result. But she wouldn't even tell them this crazy news. They were no longer her friends.

Cheryl's heart had broken into a million pieces that morning in George's office. Jackie had been lying to her for years. It hurt so much to learn that Jackie had moved back to town not to be with them as Cheryl had thought, but because she had no other options. Then the way Doris had defended Jackie, hustling her into the car like some bodyguard, protecting her from the bad guy.

That moment drew the lines quite clearly.

If the house were burning down and Doris had to save someone, Cheryl would be on her own. It had always been that way, ever since the day Jackie had flounced over to them in the cafeteria. And this nonsense about being a team . . . her former friends had been ganging up on her from the start of this project, ignoring all her experience in the business world to do whatever they wanted. No. They didn't care about her at all. It was about time Cheryl admitted it.

Cheryl couldn't believe she had been stupid enough to trap herself into a partnership with these women. It was such an amateur move, thinking with her heart instead of her business sense. When The Whole Package went under, which it most certainly would, Doris and Jackie would live the same lives they had always been living. Cheryl would be the only one left out in the cold. If Cheryl didn't think of something and fast, her poor kid was certainly going to get the short end of that pink little stick.

Her poor kid.

Just the strangeness of that thought made her squeeze the steering wheel a little harder, dreading the thought of going to the ob-gyn. Other than spiders, there was little Cheryl hated more than a needle. At her age, there were probably thousands of tests . . . Cheryl shook her head. She would put off the appointment until after Christmas. She'd already had enough pain for one year. Was it even safe to have a kid at this age? Maybe she'd die and then Jackie and Doris would really be sorry.

Speaking of making people sorry, she almost wanted to call Andy and tell him it was his. Then they'd see just how much he wanted to be her "friend." It wasn't out of the realm of possibility that he really was the father. She couldn't be that far along or they would have caught it at the hospital when she had her concussion.

Downshifting her vehicle, Cheryl focused on the road ahead. It was an icy night and it was time to start thinking about a slower pace. Forget friends. It was time to focus on family; she might even go and be with hers in California. That certainly didn't sound so bad.

Cheryl nodded, watching the snow fall. Maybe it was time to go.

THE WHOLE PACKAGE was dark when Jackie returned, lugging her Louis Vuitton carrying case. Keying in through the front door, Jackie hoped she wasn't about to discover Anthony and Gabe had come back for some reason. Other than the owners, they were the only ones who had keys.

Bells tinkled as she pushed open the front door. Jackie smiled wryly. She had hung up those bells two weeks ago, in honor of all the shops in Paris. At that point, there had not been a doubt in her mind that this place would be a success.

Jackie's heels clicked loudly as she walked across the floor. The open room reminded her of a museum or mausoleum. The shapes of the shadows seemed to shift in front of her. If a statue was actually going to come alive like in *Mannequin*, Jackie hoped it would be the one by the fireplace. He was different from the others, not as fragile or blond. From his stone form he seemed to sport a commanding quality, with his dark hair and broad chest. He had probably been modeled after a king.

Walking over to the fridge behind the bar, Jackie pulled out a bottle of San Pellegrino. Getting kicked out of Doris's wasn't the end of the world. Staying here would be kind of . . . an adventure. She thought about a children's book she used to love, *From the Mixed-Up Files of Mrs. Basil E. Frankweiler*. Growing up, Jackie had read it probably thirty times. In it, the kids had run away from home and hidden in the Metropolitan Museum of Art, surviving on cheese and crackers, sharing dreams in antiquated beds. Camping out someplace she wasn't supposed to be—away from her father, away from her life—had always sounded like such an adventure.

Jackie could have called George, instead of staying here. That bed in his guest room had been comfortable but Jackie was too embarrassed to even speak to him now. He'd invested a quarter of a million dollars in her he would never get back. It was absolutely humiliating. Jackie had never admitted her failures to anyone and regardless of what Cheryl said, it was not time for her to start. Even though it would be painful to cut him from her life, it was a lot less painful than standing face-to-face with a man she'd admired and respected, telling him the awful truth—that just like with Robert, she had squandered his money away.

With another furtive glance around, Jackie picked up her bag and crossed over the red carpet. The red and black patterns led past the tables to the office where that thick leather couch would be waiting. Jackie could camp out there for a few days, clearing out when the restaurant opened in the morning. That routine would be fine for a while; give her a little time to clear her head and figure out her next move—if there was one.

TWO DAYS LATER, a car door slammed outside of Doris's house. In her mind, she likened the sound to the first notes swelling at the end of a romantic movie. When she'd spoken to Doug during the blow-up with Mandy, Doris had put her foot down and ordered him home.

"Doug, enough is enough," she'd said, speaking into the receiver of Mandy's cell phone. Doris had called him from that number to be certain he'd pick up. "It is time for you to come home."

"I will come home when I am good and ready," Doug had said. "Where do you—"

"Doug," she interrupted, voice like steel.

Mandy was prostrate on the kitchen floor, sobbing as though her heart would break. If the weather had not been so cold, Doris was certain the kid would have bolted for the front door and ended up on the streets of Chicago somewhere.

"You need to come home immediately," Doris said. "Or I will call your parents and tell them their granddaughter is having a nervous breakdown because she's sleeping with her teenage boyfriend and got caught, then find out what they suggest I do about a son of theirs that doesn't care."

Doug was quiet on the other end, the hotel ice machine clinking behind him.

"I'll sign your papers," she said softly, clutching the receiver. "Just come home."

"I'm in Texas," Doug said. "It would take about five days. Weather's tricky."

"Then get on a plane," she said. "Trust me when I say this"—she lowered her voice—"if I don't see you here tomorrow, I will take you for everything you've got—including your daughter."

Mandy heard the threat and screamed, rolling on the floor like a drug addict.

At that, Doris hung up, her hand shaking. She marveled at whatever strength she'd found to speak to her husband that way but she had done it. And why not? Cheryl ordered around everyone within earshot, including her friends. Jackie demanded whatever she wanted and, apparently, got it. No wonder Doris's life had so little of what she needed these days. She had stopped putting her foot down years ago. That's when Doug—and everybody—started mowing her over.

People did that, Doris suddenly realized. They take advantage of the weak. That's the way history had always read. How on earth could she have been too blind to see it?

Mandy used to be a cute little kid with cute little pigtails and admiration for her mother. But after Doris had a hard time handling the death of her mother, Mandy recognized that her mother was human. And weak. Mandy had taken advantage of the situation. Whatever Mandy wanted, Mandy got. Her husband slowly followed suit.

Even Jackie had taken advantage of her. That day Jackie had ordered breakfast from her just like Mandy always did should have been a warning. Doris vividly remembered the look of surprise when Doris actually stood up and started rummaging for eggs.

"Your father will be home tomorrow," Doris said now, holding herself up with the kitchen counter. "Go to your room and stay there. After school, skip practice and come straight home."

"No," Mandy said, getting to her feet and wiping her eyes. "If I miss practice, I can't play in the game."

"Mandy," Doris's voice was quiet. "If you don't come home tomorrow after school, I will contact the principal and revoke permission for you to participate in *any* school-sponsored extracurricular activities. I mean it."

"I have to participate in extracurriculars," Mandy spat, hands on her hips. "It's the only way I can get into a good college. You and Dad would be pissed if that didn't happen."

"Oh, you'd be just fine," Doris said calmly, picking at a piece of lint that had settled on her silk sweater. "I didn't go to college. And I turned out okay."

"That's because you weren't smart enough to get in." Mandy sneered.

Doris's eyebrows shot up. Even though it was as if this entire exchange were a movie, it was still a film whose twists and turns surprised her. Was this really how little her daughter knew about her? She thought it through. Why would Mandy know the truth? The wedding pictures she and Doug had gave no indication of the year they were married. Why would Mandy notice her mother had been married in high school?

"I had a full scholarship to Florida State," Doris said, pressing her hands to her eyes. "But your father's family and my family thought it was better for me to stay here." Mandy gawked. "I got pregnant in high school, Mandy."

"I was a mistake?!" she shrieked, eyes filling with tears. "Why would you tell me I'm a mist—"

"Oh, would you *shut up*," Doris said, hitting the table with all her might. She knew the blow would hurt and that's why she did it. She needed to do something to keep her from lunging forward and wringing her child's neck.

Mandy jumped, suddenly scared.

"I lost the first baby," Doris said. Her daughter was watching her with tense concentration. "But by that time, your father and I had already gotten married. Instead of separating and going off to college like I'd planned, I made the choice to stay with him. You were not a mistake, you were a choice. But sometimes, Mandy, choices have consequences. It's time you learned that."

Doris swept by her daughter, past the guest bedroom where her former friend had stayed, and past the photo of the three of them on the wall. Doris hesitated, looking at it for a brief moment. She,

Jackie, and Cheryl all stared from a silver frame, dressed in cheer-leading outfits. Their arms were in the air, eyes bright and optimistic. Doris had pushed her way to the front, hip cocked out like a runway model, a seductive grin on her face. Cheryl's arm was around her shoulders, the other pumped toward the sky. Jackie was in motion as always, head poked playfully between them, legs bent into a long leap.

Doris pursed her lips and continued on toward her bedroom. With all her might, she slammed the door, just like Mandy would have. With satisfaction, she listened as the picture crashed to the floor and smashed into a million little pieces.

THE GLASS FROM the frame was still on the floor when Gabe came over the next morning. "Why don't I clean that up?" he suggested.

"Nah." Doris brought him a mug of coffee. "I finally ordered maid service. I just want you to teach me how to deal with my husband."

Gabe hesitated, "You really want him back?"

Doris looked over at him with shy blue eyes. The sun was bouncing off his golden curls and in that moment, Doris was convinced he was an angel. She looked down at the floor. "I miss him, Gabe. Do you . . . do you think you can forgive me for the kiss we shared?"

Gabe coughed, covering his mouth, but Doris could see he was doing it to hide a smile. She smiled back, bravely sinking through the thick carpet on her way to a seat on the couch next to him.

"I really regret it," she said. "I'm married and I . . . I have had a crush on you since we met. It's embarrassing, because I know I remind you of your mother and that's probably why you like hanging out with me, but I wanted to confess that to you so I can let it go."

Kindness scrolled across Gabe's face, as Doris read all the things he could have said, but didn't. Instead, he adjusted the light blue scarf he was wearing around his neck and opened his arms. Doris fell into them.

"You are a wonderful woman," Gabe told her, gently kissing the top of her head. "That's why I like hanging out with you. The kiss we shared was part of my performance in the restaurant so you have no reason to feel guilty about it. But I think it was special for both of us. From now on, though, I'm perfectly happy to just be your friend."

Doris nodded, feeling the soft material of his sweater caress her face. She missed the hard material of Doug's starched shirts. Sitting up, she said, "Okay."

"Okay," Gabe said. "Now, are you ready to win your husband back?"

Doris nodded eagerly. Gabe spent hours coaching Doris on how to act. He explained she was a different person from when her husband left and in order to keep him, she was going to have to prove it.

Later that day, when Doug's key turned in the lock, Doris smoothed her hair, then ran to the phone, quickly dialing an 800 number, where she was certain to be put on hold. Gabe had told her to do this to "Show Doug you are not at his beck and call."

Two seconds into the call, Doug burst through the front door. He was wearing a soft tan leather satchel with a single strap down the middle, tossed over his shoulder like a purse. It was perfectly coordinated with his men's biker jacket, a black number with silver studs, accented with matching tan leather. His chubby cheeks were tanned from sun and wind. If Doris had not sat through her three-hour instructional with Gabe, she would have raced forward and forced her way into a hug, kissing his soft lips like a drowning woman. Instead, she turned her back on him and focused on her call.

Doug stared at her in confusion. Gabe had specifically dressed her in a sleek, long-sleeved V-necked black sweater that showed off her ample cleavage, partnered with straight-legged, slimming black pants. Doug would witness her from behind first. After a minute, Doris turned slightly to let Doug have his first glimpse of her without glasses. As her husband's jaw dropped in surprise, Doris turned back to the dining room window and gave her complete focus to the phone call.

"Yes, I'll hold," she said calmly.

Doug let out a loud sigh and stomped up the stairs. She could hear him throwing his bag onto their bed and unpacking. A few moments later, he stomped back down the stairs and into the kitchen. He opened the door and started to reach for a deliberately staged box of pastries.

"Doug, don't eat those," Doris said, putting her hand over the receiver. "Those are for my bridge club." She had bought them for Marjorie McClemens, to make up for the grand opening of The Whole Package. Just as Doug's face fell, she added, "There's a salami sandwich in there. I picked it up for you from the deli."

If Gabe were in the room, which he had begged to be, he would have applauded at the efficient way Doris turned her back on her husband for the third and final time.

Half an hour later, when Doug settled into his chair in front of the television, Doris finally went down to talk with him. By that time, her husband was absolutely befuddled. When she bent forward and kissed his cheek, he said, "Hello."

"Welcome home," Doris said kindly, pulling back and settling calmly into a chair across the room. "Your daughter will be here after school. I need you to think of an appropriate punishment for what she did. That is, unless you just came to pick up the divorce papers."

Doug was watching Doris, a tiny crinkle forming in between his warm eyes, obviously confused about what to do or say next. Gabe had said Doug would expect tears and drama. When he'd left, Doris was curled up on the ground sobbing. Now, she was standing on her own two feet.

"Where's my wife?" Doug finally demanded, trying to laugh.

"She's right in front of you," Doris said. "Doug, if you want a divorce," she continued, "I will need to know by tomorrow. If not, we're starting therapy on Saturday. I have to go to work now, so I'll expect to hear your answer in the morning."

Doris got up and started to walk toward the stairs. As though an afterthought, she added, "I kicked Jackie out. So, I guess the guest bedroom is all yours." As she climbed up the stairs, Doris noticed her legs were trembling. Once out of Doug's sight, she let out a shaky breath and slid down to the floor.

Doug hadn't said he wanted to leave her, which he could have done. Maybe, just maybe . . .

Doris gave herself a hopeful hug, marveling at the way her heart was jackhammering in her chest. Maybe her life hadn't been such a waste after all.

Chapter Forty-four

THE NEXT NIGHT, JACKIE ONCE AGAIN KEYED INTO THE WHOLE Package. She had called in to the restaurant at three o'clock to let Anthony know she wouldn't be at work. He begged to know what was going on. Cheryl had come in at noon and Doris was the only one planning to show up for the evening shift. Jackie had kindly told him to mind his business and hung up.

Now, she listened carefully once she opened the door. Nothing. The place was silent as a tomb. She sneaked back to the kitchen area and pulled open the jumbo-sized fridge. The motor hummed in tandem with the cheap fluorescent light.

Thankfully, there were batches of leftover food, including something that appeared to be pumpkin ravioli. She grabbed a few squares of that and put it on a plate. There wasn't a microwave in the place so she'd have to eat the pasta cold. She slunk over to the salad area, yanking open the stainless steel refrigerator found below the cutting boards, hunting for vegetables. She selected several ripe tomato slices and a handful of mixed greens and breathed a sigh of relief. For now, this wasn't a bad system. She just prayed Anthony was lax on this part of the inventory and wouldn't notice.

Grabbing a fork, she felt her way through the dining room, then opened the door to her new bedroom. She almost dropped her plate in surprise at the sight of Anthony, curled up and crying on what should have been her bed. Jackie wracked her brain, trying to quickly think of a good excuse to be here at such a late hour.

"This pasta looks five-star," she finally gushed, coming into the tiny room. "It was the special tonight, right? I couldn't sleep—I was just dying to know how we did." She flopped down next to him, trying to pretend like nothing was wrong.

"You're so busted." Anthony sniffled. "That was *your* suitcase hiding out in the dumbwaiter, wasn't it?" He rubbed his eyes and sat up.

Jackie stared down at her plate, face on fire. Finally, she nodded.

"I love your suitcase," Anthony said, lip trembling. "You have beautiful taste. You have such good taste."

Jackie popped a piece of ravioli into her mouth, enjoying the tender texture of the pasta against her tongue. She tried to ignore the fact that Anthony was crying. He was embarrassed, she was embarrassed . . . their best bet was to pretend as though the situation wasn't happening and get out of it as soon as possible.

"This is scrumptious," she said. "Everyone should wait until midnight to eat, shouldn't they? There must have been a crowd tonight, after Cheryl's letter to the editor. Were women just beating down the doors?" Jackie tried to keep the note of sarcasm out of her voice.

Anthony shook his head, glum.

Jackie moved her fork toward the frizzy edges of a lettuce leaf. This food really was a delight. It was unfortunate that no one had shown up to enjoy it.

"When are you going to ask what I'm doing in the office, crying?" Anthony finally demanded, turning to her with wounded eyes.

"I'm not." Jackie shook her blond curls. "You didn't ask me why Doris kicked me out. I figured we were respecting each other's privacy."

Mournfully, Anthony regarded a crumpled bunch of papers he had in his hand. He lifted them up as though he was going to throw them across the room, then his hand fell back into his lap. The motion made a whiff of something good waft in Jackie's direction. It smelled like that new cologne that was out. When she mentioned this, Anthony burst into a fresh batch of tears.

Jackie stared at him, amazed. "What did I say?"

"These *pages* smell good," Anthony moaned. "Not *me*. They're scented. The pages are scented. Why does he have to be so cruel?"

"Antonio Rico, you are ridiculous," Jackie scolded. His drama was really starting to cheer her up. "Just tell me why you're crying, for heaven's sake."

At that, her manager let out yet another heartfelt sigh. Jackie set her empty plate on the floor and patted her lap. Gratefully, Anthony hopped on the couch and laid his head in her lap. As she stroked the fine black stubble covering his head, Anthony told her everything. Gabe had written a play. Anthony was the lead. It was one of the best things he had ever read.

"Impossible." Jackie said. She leaned forward, intrigued. "Gabe can't be good-looking and talented, too."

"That's what I said," Anthony squealed, half sitting up and batting at her hand. "That's exactly what I said. I couldn't have been more surprised if he'd told me he was with the FBI and investigating Doris for smuggling babies in and out of the country."

Jackie burst out laughing. Then she stopped suddenly, remembering that Doris was never going to speak to her again.

"Sorry," Anthony said. He cracked his knuckles. "Anyway, I told Gabe he was too attractive to be a writer. Just too attractive. This was when we were unpacking all this inventory stuff. So he started taking boxes out to the Dumpster and pretending like he hadn't said anything about it at all. But I told him, I lived in New

York. I know a good play. I can see a good play. So, he gave it to me and voila." He slapped the script. "It's brilliant."

Jackie lunged for the wad of pages. Anthony had crumpled them in his hand, but held them out of reach. "Darling, please . . ." she begged.

"I'm not supposed to show anyone," he said. "Jackie, I . . . I think I love him. It's like he knows and teases me with it and I . . . I just don't want to get my heart broken again!" The poor man's body shook with sobs. His eyes were squeezed shut, unable to stop the tears that pushed through like water gushing from a crack in a ceiling.

"He doesn't love you back?" Jackie asked.

Anthony shook his head. "He tries to tell me he's straight but then he'll . . . He's not straight. We all know he's not straight," Anthony said, wiping his eyes. "I'm sorry. I'm so sorry for making you listen to me."

"It's okay, honey," Jackie said. "You're not the only one with a confused heart."

That morning, she had opened the mystery box Robert left for her. Jackie wasn't quite sure why. Maybe it was waking up in an icy room with a pinched nerve in her neck, right next to the racket of the garbage trucks clanking the Dumpsters in the alley. Not sure what had prompted the decision, Jackie got up and went straight for her suitcase. In the dim morning light, she ripped open the box before she had time to reconsider. Inside was a beautifully framed picture of her, Robert, and George.

Frustrated, Jackie stared at the picture. The three of them were at some party and the photographer captured that moment just after George made one of his dumb jokes. Jackie was hanging on his arm, gazing up at him with dancing eyes. Robert was standing to the side, hands in pockets. On the front of the silver frame, her husband had inscribed, TO MY DARLING, SO FULL OF LIFE. THIS PICTURE CAPTURES YOU MORE THAN MY WORDS EVER COULD. MAY YOUR SPARKLE GLISTEN FOR ETERNITY.

That was it. An attempt at poetry on an old picture frame, probably because she'd liked that other poem so much.

Jackie sat back in disappointment. She had wanted something that could have summed up all their years together, especially something that could take the sting out of Cheryl's words. Instead, she was left with a framed photo where, basically, she was caught flirting with George. If George was even dishonest in the least, Jackie would have thought he'd set up the whole thing.

In an uncharacteristic move, Jackie told Anthony the whole story. At the end, he shook his head, baffled. "We are two peas in a pod," he said. By now, he was seated on the floor of the office, his legs drawn up and held against his chest. Jackie was lying on the couch, her hand still absently stroking his hair.

"What are we going to do?"

DORIS SHOT UP from a dead sleep, slapping her hand to her forehead. "That's it!" she said out loud. She had been dreaming of her mother. The words from their conversation seemed to echo in her head.

Doug stirred in the sheets. "What, Doris?" He reached out his hand and ran it over her arm, eyes still closed. Doris's heart leaped. In the dim light from the clock, she gazed at Doug's familiar profile. She was so happy to have him back in her bed.

That morning, her husband had come down the stairs cautiously, as though he were a stranger in his home. In a way, he was. Doris had made him sleep in the guest bedroom and she wasn't waiting on him hand and foot like she used to. Even the breakfast she was cooking up wasn't meant for Doug, it was meant for her and Mandy.

"Good morning," he said, watching as she attempted to flip a piece of French toast.

"Hello," Doris said. "I already threw out the coffee, so if you want any the filters are above the stove."

"What are you making?"

"French toast," Doris mused, studying the piece stuck to the pan. "But it's not turning out so good."

Doug laughed. "Darlin', the only thing you can cook are eggs," he said. "And even those aren't very good. Let me take you out to breakfast."

Doris was so surprised she actually dropped the spatula on the floor. Not the part about her cooking; everyone knew that. She was surprised by Doug's invitation to brunch. They hadn't had breakfast together at a restaurant in maybe ten years.

"What about Mandy?" she said, turning off the stove and tossing the spatula in the sink.

"She's still asleep," Doug said. "Why don't we just make it the two of us?"

Cautiously, Doris nodded. Pulling on a knit cap, she wrapped herself in her mother's wool coat and followed her husband to the car. Twenty minutes later, they found themselves facing each other in, of all places, a Cracker Barrel. Doris liked the little syrups and enjoyed the option of getting a little shopping done while waiting for a table. In the back of her mind, she made a mental note that The Whole Package might want to consider selling novelty T-shirts or something and maybe having a take-home of some sort. People liked that sort of thing.

When they were seated and had placed their order, Doris didn't know what to do. For the first time in weeks, she was sitting across from her husband with nothing to do but talk to him. Since she had no idea what to say, Doris picked up the little game that sat on every table and started moving the colorful tees. Doug had stopped her, putting his large hand over hers.

"Doris," he said, voice breaking. "I have been a terrible husband and I'm begging you to let me make it right. I don't want you to sign those papers."

Doris looked up at him in shock. She had never seen her husband cry for anything other than her mother's funeral. Now, tears were streaming down his face, right there in the middle of the restaurant.

"Hush, Doug. It's okay," she said. Their waitress set down their coffee and rushed away. "What . . . what do you plan to do?" Doris said, fiddling with a creamer. "To make it right, I mean?"

"Counseling," Doug said. "I think that's a good idea you had and . . . I don't know. Whatever you want me to do. I love you, Doris. I have since we were sixteen. I just don't know what came over me."

Doris ached to leap across the table and smother him with kisses, but she remembered Gabe's advice. She would wait for Doug to make those types of overtures. Instead, she stirred the creamer into her coffee and listened as Doug started talking about the history they'd shared.

"We've had some good times," he said, as the waitress set down their meal. "Do you remember when we took Mandy to the zoo the first time and that goat tried to eat her hair?" Doug asked, taking a bite out of a piece of bacon. "The look on her face . . ."

Doris burst out laughing. Four-year-old Mandy had practically turned purple, she was so outraged by those buck teeth nibbling away at her hair. "She started screaming at him," Doris said, picturing the tiny girl Mandy had been. She was shaking her finger, scolding the animal like it was one of her many dolls. "We bought her an ice cream and you put her on your shoulders and she was the happiest girl in the world."

Doug's chubby cheeks stretched into a smile. Then he said, "Remember that night in the pontoon boat? That summer?"

Doris blushed, setting down her orange juice. She and Doug had been about twenty, and had gone on a camping trip with his family for the weekend. His mom and dad were really into the experience, getting up early for trail hikes and cooking powdered eggs over the fire. After three days of sleeping in the same tent as Doug's parents, Doris and Doug were sexually frustrated. So, when the parents had fallen asleep, Doris and Doug sneaked out of the tent. They felt their way through the dark campground, then stumbled through twigs and sand down to the lake.

On a stranger's pontoon boat, Doug had pushed up Doris's shirt and suckled her full breasts with the desperation of a starved man. Then he'd eased down her pajama bottoms and pushed her against the rough turf of the boat, hungrily pressing himself inside her. They had coupled frenetically, rolling around the floor as the sultry heat of the summer night mixed with the buzz of mosquitoes in their ears. Doug had made love to Doris for hours, the bottom of the boat slapping steadily, echoing across the still water of the lake.

"We had so many good times," Doug said, reaching out his plump hand to hold hers. "When did it all go so wrong?"

"Cheryl's divorce," Doris said. "Then Mom. Then I just got so fat. I felt unattractive."

"But I love your body." Doug smiled, eyeing her ample bosom. "I always have."

Doris's blueberry pancakes tasted like heaven but for the first time in a long time, she decided to listen when her stomach felt full. Pushing her plate aside, Doris gave a sly look at her husband and whispered, "Then Doug, it's time you take me home and . . . and make love to me."

Two people had never left a brunch so fast. In the car, they kissed with frenzy. Back at the house, Doris and Doug tore at each other's bodies with a passion that would have put The Whole Package's dance numbers to shame.

That night, Doug back in her bed and promising never to leave it, Doris's heart leaped to wake up with him beside her. "Sleep, my darling," she whispered, touching his face. "Go back to sleep." When Doug was breathing rhythmically, Doris pushed back the blankets and slipped her feet into the white slippers she kept by the bed. Bustling down to the kitchen, Doris looked up Gabe's number. Even though it was just after midnight, she called him.

"Doris?" Gabe was confused, half asleep. "Are you okay?"

Gabe was such a nice man. Doris's heart swelled with pride that he'd chosen her to be his friend. "I just had this crazy dream. I was sitting there talking to my mother and . . . I need to talk to you and Anthony about The Whole Package," she said, excitedly. "Do you have time tomorrow before we open?"

After Gabe assured her he'd set up something with Anthony, Doris hung up and she sat at her kitchen table, eyes dancing in excitement. "Thanks, Mom," she said softly. Thanks to the conversation in her dream, Doris had come up with a surefire way to save them—her investment, Cheryl's, Jackie's, the guys, The Whole damn Package. All of it.

Doris crossed her fingers and her toes. She said a little prayer. And for the first time since her mother's death, Doris felt like her old self again.

Chapter Forty-five

CHERYL TOOK A DEEP BREATH AND TUCKED IN HER SHIRT. SHE was in the restroom at the courthouse, getting ready to go in and make her case against Stan. The bathroom doors and white porcelain sinks were all lined up uniformly, just like jurors on a bench. Cheryl was glad her case wasn't at that level. Today, they were just going in to see if the judge thought they had enough evidence for trial. If that happened, Stan would certainly make the move to settle.

Adjusting her light gray Donna Karan suit, Cheryl noticed she was starting to look pale around her eyes. The spray tan was fading. For the first time in years, Cheryl would not be going in for a touch-up. Her roots were also coming in. Cheryl ran her fingers through her hair, admiring her long-hidden natural color. According to one of the million baby books she'd been reading, hair dye was not good for a baby either. Caffeine was supposedly out, too but—Cheryl clutched at her Venti Starbucks as though her life depended on it—that was something she couldn't sacrifice. Maybe her baby would come out bouncing off the walls, but Cheryl was willing to pay the price.

"Cheryl?" the bathroom door squealed. Her lawyer walked into the bathroom. "Are you all right?"

Melody was just twenty-six but was at the top of her game. A graduate of the University of Chicago's law school, Melody had snapped up Cheryl's case via the recommendation from George. Melody was convinced they would win, unless Stan showed up with one hundred clients ready to swear an oath on the fact that Cheryl's marketing efforts were worthless.

"You ready?" Melody asked, punching something into her phone.

Cheryl leaned against the cool porcelain for a minute, wanting to wash her hands, but the bathroom was out of soap. Plus, the sinks were the kind that had a single circle on the faucet to push in, dictating the length of opportunity you had for your hands to get clean. She pulled a tiny bottle of hand sanitizer out of her purse, immediately thinking of Doris and that day they had all interviewed the models.

It wasn't easy living without her best friends. Thanks to Stan, Cheryl had ditched the Racquet Club, switching over to the Tennis Club instead. There, she'd met a couple women who were eager to let her fill in on their team when they needed a sub and were happy to chat with her in the locker room about their lives. Every week, this woman Suzie had invited Cheryl to join them all for lunch. Cheryl decided she may as well give it a try—as long as they didn't go to The Whole Package—but what a mistake that had been.

The lunch had been a disaster, from start to finish. When Suzie called her with the location and time, Cheryl repeated, "Leave my house at 10:45?" Suzie said, "No, lunch is *at* 10:45 a.m." Baffled, Cheryl agreed to see her there. After she hung up, she realized these women got up at 5 a.m. with their children.

Once at the restaurant, Cheryl was startled to discover she was dressed all wrong. Suzie's friends had all shown up in their Juicy sweat suits, while Cheryl sported a designer suit. When they looked her up and down, Cheryl felt obligated to fabricate a lie about some meeting. As the host walked them to their table, Suzie eyed the location in distaste. The moment they were settled in, Suzie sniffed, saying, "These air vents are blowing out cool air instead of warm, we'll have to move."

"I've got a sweater in my car—" Cheryl started, but Suzie had already swept up from the table, and Cheryl found herself trotting after the group to another table.

When the food came, it got even weirder. When she dined with Jackie and Doris, they would always grab at each other's plates, trying whatever they felt like trying. At lunch with these women, one of them started raving about the fries so Cheryl reached out and grabbed one. They exchanged glances and the woman said, "They'll let you order fries as a side, you know."

Cheryl felt herself turning red, then stayed quiet through the conversation. Most of it was about the group's book club. Apparently, the women were mad at one of the members, Allison. Allison had hosted the most recent book club and the women couldn't stop complaining about her cooking. Seeing an opportunity to relate, Cheryl jumped in with, "I know! My friend Doris is a disaster in the kitchen," and the group fell silent, once again exchanging glances.

"It's not that Allison can't cook," Suzie finally explained, "it's just that the rest of us go to the trouble of having it catered. She's just being cheap. We're sick of it."

Cheryl almost asked why someone didn't just talk to Allison instead of ripping her apart behind her back, but she decided to keep her mouth shut.

Suzie's rules about generosity apparently didn't apply to their bill. The waiter added a standard 18 percent gratuity for the large party of women and Suzie complained until it was taken off the check. Then, she tried to justify leaving fifteen percent since he "tried to pull that."

Tight-lipped, Cheryl left an extra twenty on the table as they filed out, trying not to remember how she, Jackie, and Doris always overtipped, even before they owned a restaurant.

When the horrible lunch was over, Cheryl sat alone in her car, miserable. She missed her friends and wished she were brave enough to call them. The fight had been her fault, especially that whole situation with Jackie. In fact, Cheryl kept expecting to hear from George, threatening to sue her for snooping in his paperwork. He didn't call, probably because Jackie was being her loyal self and didn't rat her out.

Now, Cheryl put her hand to her head, feeling her eyes fill with tears. When her lawyer cleared her throat, Cheryl remembered she was in the county courthouse, not living in the past. She forced herself to stand up straight and pull it together.

"You'll be fine," Melody promised. "Don't make this harder on yourself than it is."

"I make everything hard, Melody," Cheryl said ruefully, taking one last glance in the dim courthouse mirrors. "It's my schtick."

The lawyer blinked. "You ready to win?"

Cheryl nodded. "Always."

Chapter Forty-six

JACKIE STRETCHED UP HIGH TO REACH THE HOOK OVER THE window. With a gasp of relief, she tucked in the final loop of the burgundy curtains and jumped back down from the chair.

"Voila," she proclaimed, echoing Anthony's favorite expression. "Shows you what a woman's touch can do."

"Those curtains should have been gone on the first day," Anthony apologized, blushing and sinking into his couch. "The very first day."

That night when Jackie had found Anthony crying in the office of The Whole Package, he had put his foot down as a friend and a manager. "You are coming home with me," he'd insisted. "I am not going to have you living here, stealing all the food. You're eating away any profits you ladies might actually be making."

Jackie tried to protest but Anthony put a finger to her lips. "Look, honey," he told her. "Here's the truth: I'm sad and I'm lonely and will jump off the roof if I spend another night in that apartment alone. Please come stay with me," he pleaded. "Come stay."

It wasn't like she had anywhere else to go, but the dreary

condition of Anthony's sublet shocked her. Jackie immediately got to work, adding the artistic touches it needed to glimmer. She painted the main wall magenta, adding bright purple and pink accents to the floor runners and the doors. Using wine catalogues, she tore out colorful pictures and created glittery collages to hang on the walls. She even hand-sewed the curtains, recycling Anthony's burgundy velvet blanket and adding shiny gold tassels. In just a few days, her new home was fit for a princess—or a queen and a princess, as Anthony liked to say.

"It's beautiful." He beamed, hugging her. "So beautiful. What would I do without you?"

Jackie sauntered over to her bed on the couch and flopped down. "You might have a personal life."

"You're the perfect beard," Anthony said. "Besides, I love our dates."

They had gotten into the nightly ritual of having tea. Jackie would start the water boiling on the studio's hot plate, silently thinking about George and his careful lessons on tea preparation. She hadn't spoken to him in two weeks.

After her fight with Cheryl and Doris, Jackie had disconnected her phone. Her sole relationships consisted of Anthony and an orange tabby cat that lived in their building. The cat liked to poke his large paws under the door and swipe them around. Jackie would let him in and giggle as he hopped up on the couch, stalking through the apartment like he owned the place. Some days, he would let her cuddle his big, furry form, offering the soothing vibration of a friendly purr.

Most nights, Jackie heard Anthony's heavy steps on the stairs just as the tea started to whistle. The apartment was old, so the steam radiators would switch on every half hour, clanking and hissing, keeping them up at night. But sometimes, if her timing was just right, the radiators would harmonize with the whistle of the tea.

As he walked through the door, Anthony would wave the familiar waxy white bag. Every night, he brought her leftovers.

One day they would feast on pork chops and squash; the next, beet salad with warm goat cheese. Jackie never knew what would be in the bag.

"Ooh, what is it?" she asked, racing for the food. She beamed, discovering saffron risotto over a lamb shank. "That looks amazing."

"It is," Anthony said, hanging up his coat. "I already tried it."

"Didn't you lure me to your apartment because I was eating away the company's profits?" Jackie asked, after they'd devoured the tender meat and lay satiated against the back of the futon.

"Nah. I just said that to get you to move in." Anthony grinned. "I needed the company."

He pointed at the piece of tiramisu still sitting on the coffee table. Its fluffy cream accentuated the tender form of the espresso-soaked lady fingers. Jackie kicked herself forward, grabbed a plastic fork, and dove in.

"This is decadent," she said, offering some to Anthony. He waved it away. "So . . . have you seen the girls? Doris or anybody?"

Anthony raised an eyebrow. Mysteriously, he said, "Doris or anybody might have just saved the restaurant. I don't want you to get your hopes up but you really need to come in and see for yourself."

"No," Jackie said, eating a big hunk of the tiramisu. "Not going to happen."

Anthony got up and went over to his bed. He flopped down and wrapped himself in those faded sheets that smelled like old Tide. From the bedside table, he picked up the necklace Gabe had given him, letting the gold star glimmer in the lamplight.

"How is our elusive little Gabe?" Jackie asked. Anthony snorted, the sound very brief, very New York.

"As elusive as ever," Anthony said. After a long moment, he added, "I miss home."

"New York?" Jackie said, surprised. For all the information he'd managed to drag out of her in the past week, Anthony had told her next to nothing about where he was from or why he'd left.

"New Brunswick," Anthony clarified. "It's a train ride away but I'm still a New Yorker. In every fiber of my being, I'm a New Yorker."

Anthony narrated the sour smell of the hotdog vendors, the sweet scent of cinnamon nuts, that constant hum of energy and vibration of the subway underfoot. He told her about his home; the din of his father talking back to the television, the silence of his mother reading her Harlequin novels.

"Ma's been calling me lately," Anthony admitted. "She keeps reminding me there's love for me back at home."

"What's your mother like?" Jackie asked, sipping at her tea.

Anthony explained his mother had a big heart, was the type to include all the kids in their New Brunswick neighborhood, no matter what. She provided grape Popsicles for the summers and mint cocoas in the winter and had a soft spot for kids from rough families. She had spent more than one afternoon counseling bullies, convincing them to stay for dinner instead of going back to their troubled homes. Anthony's closest friends ended up being those tough kids, thanks to his mother. By the time they were all teens and everyone could see that he was gay, Anthony already had a group that would protect him, no matter what.

"She was smart, you see," he said, running his hand over his fuzzy head. "When I told my parents my big secret, Ma just laughed and said they'd known since I was five, mesmerized by the makeup counter at the corner store."

"She sounds wonderful," Jackie said, eyes shining. She had always wondered what it would be like to have a mother.

Stretching his legs to the ceiling, Anthony let his dancer's feet move in a slow jig through the shadows on the ceiling. In the silver moonlight, Jackie watched his perfect performance, imagining an audience of twelve hundred, tapping their toes and bobbing their heads.

"Why did you leave?" Jackie asked.

"A stupid boy broke my heart," Anthony said, dropping his legs with a flop. "We started dating when we were both starting out as actors. We were starting out. When he booked Broadway, he threw me in the Dumpster like last year's playbill."

After five years together, Lance hadn't even been creative about how he'd ended it. He had breezed into their coffee shop at Broadway and Sixteenth in a tight leather coat, his hair pulled back into a slick ponytail. Ordering a chamomile tea with honey to protect his (shitty) voice, Lance had sung, "It's not you, it's me." Anthony had just nodded, stuffing a brownie into his mouth.

"I hopped the first Amtrak out of New York and headed straight for Chicago." Anthony sighed. "I sat next to an old man who smelled like Swiss cheese and chewed on sunflower seeds the whole time. The whole time."

"You know, my dear . . ." Jackie said. "If Gabe wrote a good play, all you'd have to do is get it to New York and get it on Broadway and you could tell Lance to kiss your sexy little ass."

Anthony laughed, clapping his hands. "Wouldn't that be fun?"

The two friends sat in silence for a long moment, caught up in their fantasies. Finally, Jackie set down her teacup. After washing the teacups and silverware in the tiny porcelain sink, she went and got ready for bed.

Settling into the warm blankets on the futon, the lamp clicked off and the steam heater hissing, Anthony said, "Jackie? Everything's going to be okay. I just want you to know that."

After what seemed like a lifetime of silence, Jackie said, "Anthony, you can't even begin to know how long I've waited for someone to say that."

Resting her head on her pillow, Jackie fell into a safe, deep sleep.

Chapter Forty-seven

STAN SAT LIKE A STONE IN THE COURTROOM. TRYING NOT TO LOOK over at him, Cheryl took a seat in her straight-backed wooden chair. She adjusted her skirt and positioned herself gingerly, wondering if the chairs were a form of punishment from Puritan times and trying not to jostle the cargo in her belly.

Cheryl hadn't even started to show but she was surprised to find herself consistently excited. Until now, children had bugged her. She had never planned on having any and her attitude had always been an issue between her and Sean. He wanted a soccer team; she wanted box seats at the game. Thinking of Sean, she finally got up the nerve to take a look at Stan. After all, her former boss had spent more time with her than her ex-husband.

She was surprised to see that Stan's face looked pinched and drawn. Cheryl wondered how many all-nighters he had pulled lately, playing the online poker. Was it even legal anymore? She should ask the judge, just to watch Stan's fleshy face turn to her, aghast.

Melody had left Stan's criminality out of their case. She didn't think they needed it. Now that Cheryl was face-to-face with her former boss, she was happy they'd made that decision. Stan really was a sad sack. For such a successful guy, his very presence filled the room with desperation and failure. Seeing that, Cheryl no longer felt the need to make him suffer.

Stan sneaked a peek at her from the corner of his eye. Raising her hand, Cheryl gave a friendly wave as though they were at one of their racquetball games. But this time, Cheryl wouldn't be the one who would get hurt.

When the judge called their case, Melody hit the floor running. The judge was a woman and sat listening with eyes half-closed, her chin in her hand. When Melody brought up the lunches Cheryl was forced to attend at Hooters, the woman sat up straight. "We're not suing for sexual harassment," Melody assured her. "I just want to paint an accurate portrayal of my client's work life at TurnKey." From that moment on, the judge sniffed at various statements, including how much money Cheryl had brought in for the company. Once the hard-drive report was laid out, the judge didn't even move to her chamber to deliberate. A trial date was set. Melody slammed down her folder, victorious.

Stan's skinny lawyer caught up with them in the hall. Cheryl leaned against a wall, enjoying the way the cool tiles seeped through the thin material of her suit. The two lawyers stepped away from her to chat and Cheryl eyed the passersby in the courthouse.

It was interesting—cars were driving by outside the glass windows, security was checking attendants for weapons, kids were hoping their police officer wouldn't show up to follow through on a contested ticket. Cheryl watched all these different people bustle back and forth. Suddenly, her eyes settled on a tearful, tense couple. Instinctively, Cheryl knew they were here to get a divorce.

"Nice work," a voice hissed by her ear.

Cheryl's back stiffened. She turned to face Stan. He let his eyes flicker over her body, per usual.

"Hi, Stan." Cheryl sighed. "Your breath smells like egg."

Stan pulled out his trademark cherry ChapStick and smeared it across his fleshy lips.

"Look, we might be able to come to an arrangement."

"We'll see," Cheryl said.

He rocked back on his heels, looking around in that way of his; always ready to dodge the law. "Look, what is it you want? This is your shot. Door's open."

Cheryl's eyes widened. She had heard that phrase used on clients a billion times before. It meant her former boss was willing to cut a deal. She had seen it so many times with so many people that Cheryl knew, in spite of her lawyer, this was her chance to get what she needed.

"Bob Turner," she said quickly. "Let him out of his contract and let him come to me."

Stan shifted from foot to foot. "No surprise there. What else?"

Really? He'd give her more?

"Uh . . . and the fee for our last three years with Fitzgibbon Ale."

"One."

"Two."

"Fine," Stan scoffed. "Use it to open up your own place. You should have done it years ago anyway." It was the closest thing to a compliment he'd ever given her. "I still can't believe you're a part of that restaurant," Stan snickered. "I read about it today. You could have knocked me over."

"What do you mean you just read about it?" Cheryl asked. "It's old news."

Stan gave her a funny look. "It's on the front page of the *Weekend Review*. Listen, it's not going to be easy handling that *and* opening your own firm," he said, pushing his hands into his pants pockets. "I'm just saying. You both seem to think you can do it better than anyone but I taught you everything you know."

Cheryl was totally confused. "What do you mean, you both?"

"Andy," Stan scorned. "The kid left us. Like you didn't know. He's opening his own house."

"What?" Cheryl cried but Stan was done with the conversation. He turned his back on her and then walked over to his lawyer.

Melody listened to what he said, glancing at Cheryl at every other word that came out of Stan's mouth. Eventually, he slapped his skinny lawyer on the back and walked out of the courthouse. From the way the lawyer's shoulders drooped before he turned back to Melody, Cheryl knew she'd gotten everything she'd asked for.

There was still one more thing she needed. Cheryl went up to a security guard and tapped him on the shoulder. "Do you know where I can get a copy of the *Weekend Review*?"

Chapter Forty-eight

JACKIE TOOK A DEEP BREATH, LIFTED HER HAND, AND RAPPED ON George's office door.

"Come in." George's voice was gruff. It was lunchtime, just the time of day George hated to be interrupted, but when he saw Jackie peeking in, he jumped to his feet and rushed forward.

"Jacqueline," he said, taking her hands like a blind man. "Where have you been? I've been calling and calling you. None of the girls knew where you were. I thought you had gone back to Paris."

"With whose money?" Jackie laughed. "Honestly, George. Your faith in my resources is boundless."

Jackie took a long look at him. George did indeed look like a man who had been worried for several days. He was even thinner than before, his dark eyebrows adding shadow to the circles under his dark eyes. She smiled.

"It's nice to see you," she said.

"Cut the shit, darling," he said, crossing his arms. "Where have you been?"

Jackie drew back her hands and fluttered over to the leather sofa. Patting the seat next to her, she reached into her purse and pulled out a framed picture. George didn't budge.

"I don't bite," Jackie purred, fluffing her hair. "Come here. I want to show you something."

George continued to stand there, arms crossed. His jaw was pulsing and his dark eyes were flashing. After a moment, he turned his back on her and started to walk out of the room.

"George, wait," Jackie cried, leaping to her feet. "I . . . I'm sorry." He hesitated at the door. Trembling, Jackie said, "I was scared. I didn't know what to do. My friends hate me, Doris is never going to speak to me again, and I haven't exactly been honest with you either. But then I opened that gift from Robert, saw this and . . . I just needed some time to think."

Jackie walked over to George and held out the picture. "*Very* anticlimactic, I know, but . . ."

George took a brief look and nodded. He handed it back to her. "We look good."

Without thinking, Jackie reached up and caressed his face. It was soft under her fingertips. George jumped.

"I added a little something to it," Jackie said. Walking back over to the couch, she pulled out a tiny painting she'd made of the three of them. Shyly, she handed it to George.

It mirrored the picture exactly, down to the moment in the photograph when George had just finished making one of his jokes. Jackie was still hanging on his arm, mouth open with laughter, gazing up at him with her dancing eyes. Robert was the only thing changed. She had painted him as a faded image, a friendly ghost standing off to the side. His hands were still in his pockets and he was watching over them.

George stared at the painting for a long time, visibly moved.

"I want you to have this," Jackie said softly. "You were Robert's best friend and he wanted what was best for both of us. I understand that now."

Jackie's return to art had been all Anthony's doing. One night, he'd brought home some painting supplies and left them in the corner, not saying a word. There were brushes, oil paints, and even a blank canvas. Jackie had walked to the bathroom, lathered on a face mask, and put curlers in her hair. She'd walked back out saying, "Ready to watch some TV?" Anthony had sighed and clicked on a movie.

The urge to use the paints didn't strike her until several days later. Jackie was lying in bed, staring at a wall, unable to shake that image from the photograph from her mind. Finally, she drew herself up and stomped over to the blank canvas. Hours passed. Her mind pulsed as the brushes stealthily transferred the haunting image.

That night, Anthony stopped in the doorway. He hesitated like he'd stumbled on a baby bird. Silently, he came in, took off his coat, and started boiling tea on their hot plate. He placed Jackie's at her right side, a robust Earl Grey that cooled through the night. Anthony slept peacefully in spite of—or maybe because of—the lamp burning over her easel. As the dawn was starting to break, Jackie set down her brush and reached for her tea. It was cold and went down smooth. When she climbed onto the futon, Jackie was grateful to finally close her eyes and see nothing there.

"Jacqueline, I . . ." George started to say.

"I might be a good artist after all," Jackie puzzled, eyeing the painting like it had been done by someone else. "You know?"

"Yes." George chuckled. "You just might be." He was staring at the painting with reverence. "But we've always known that."

Jackie stood up on wobbly legs and walked to the door. "I'll be picking up my phone again now," she said. "So . . . feel free to call."

Doris set down the phone, wringing her hands. According to Gabe, the restaurant was on the front cover of the *Weekend Review*. She rifled through the papers on the table until she found it. Sure enough, there was a photo of The Whole Package, gleaming in the winter light.

"Who was on the phone?" Doug asked, walking into the kitchen and kissing his wife on the forehead. "Anybody exciting?"

The first time Doug met Gabe at The Whole Package, he took in the perfect body and eight-pack of abs and muttered, "Guess I should go to the gym." To his credit, Doug never told Doris she couldn't see him but since her husband had come home, Doris found herself spending less and less time with Gabe.

"Just Gabe," she said. Taking a deep breath, she held up the *Weekend Review*. "Look."

"It's all because of my wife." Doug beamed, picking her up and spinning her.

Doris smiled. "No. It wasn't just because of me."

The night Doris had a revelation about the restaurant, her mother had visited her in a dream. Doris had fallen asleep worrying about The Whole Package. Drifting off into sleep, Doris suddenly found herself sitting with her mother at the kitchen table.

"I just don't understand it," Doris said, passing her a plate of cookies. "Why is The Package failing?"

"Why do you think?" her mother said. "You designed a restaurant for men."

"Huh?"

"Men are visual, women are emotional," her mother explained. "Right now, your restaurant is for men."

"I . . . I don't understand," Doris said, taking her mother's hand. Half aware she was no longer with her, Doris took a moment to appreciate the fine lines on her mother's face, the wisdom in her eyes.

"Women want *romance*, honey," her mother said. "Your restaurant gives them about as much romance as a one-night stand."

"You're right," Doris blurted out, leaping across the table to hug her. Then, because she knew there was so little time left to say it, Doris squeezed her mother tight and said, "Thanks for everything, Mom. I love you."

When Doris sat down with Gabe and Anthony, nervous that the

dream had just been something sentimental because she missed her mom, Doris tried to downplay her idea. But the moment she repeated what her mother had said in the dream, Anthony practically tap danced his way across the table.

"Exactly," he said, slapping his chest and pointing his finger at her like that poster of Uncle Sam. "That's what I was trying to say to Cheryl in that first interview. I knew one of you would figure it out eventually. I knew it." The flamboyant manager had already pulled out a piece of paper and started partitioning it for lists. "Boy, we have a lot of work to do."

"Carolyn was here with her boyfriend opening night," Gabe said. "She said the same thing."

Carolyn had been at the restaurant with another man? And Gabe didn't mind?

Doris looked at him in surprise. Gabe gave her a half smile and a shrug. Anthony cleared his throat.

Ah. Suddenly, everything made sense. Gabe *was* gay and Anthony was his boyfriend, just like her friends had tried to tell her. Thinking back, Doris realized Gabe and Anthony had definitely been kissing that night in her bedroom. Who knows how long that had been going on? Well . . . Doris eyed her new friend . . . Anthony was a great guy. If he made Gabe happy, then so be it. She gave Gabe a smile and a little nod. He smiled back.

"Here's what I want," Doris said, clearing her throat. "I want a place where women are romanced the moment they walk through the front door. Maybe a handsome man could greet each guest with a rose or recite a line of poetry to each guest. The food should be exquisite, yet waistline conscious. The room could smell like fresh-cut roses and the soft candlelight and decor should make women believe they've stepped into a fairy tale. I want The Whole Package to be the place where it's okay to fall in love."

"This is brilliant," Anthony said. His handsome face was flushed, dark eyes bright. "This is brilliant. What do you think made you see it?"

Doris drained her Shirley Temple and played with the stem of the cherry. "Well, I've just been thinking. I had that dream about my mother and then . . ." She hesitated and Gabe squeezed her hand. "My husband and I are planning to see a therapist," she told Anthony. "And to prepare, the therapist asked us to write up a list of things we wanted the other to do to make us feel loved. I saw Doug's list. His were guy things, but mine . . . well, mine were a little more romantic."

"Good for you," Anthony told her, nodding enthusiastically. "Good for you."

As they continued to brainstorm, it was Anthony who came up with the idea that got them into the *Weekend Review*.

"What about guest love coaches?" Anthony said suddenly. "Soap operas have a huge female audience. What if . . . for special events, we bring in one of my soap opera friends from New York?"

When Doris clapped her hands, nodding, Anthony texted one of his friends. The soap opera star texted right back with a smiley face and a promise to help. When the time came for him to visit, women came out in droves.

According to the article in the *Weekend Review*, in just a few weeks The Whole Package had gone from an embarrassing misfire to a leader in the world of concept dining.

"It's not just a place for women to dine, it's a place for them to be appreciated," Doris read aloud. She looked up at Doug and beamed.

"When my parents get back from Florida, I'm going to have my mother go there," Doug said. "I think she'd really enjoy herself. My treat."

"Dougie, you don't have to pay." Doris giggled. "We own the place."

Doug's face lit up and he reached for his wife. "We do, don't we?"

As Doug kissed her, Doris couldn't help but be amazed at how well things were going. So much had changed. She had won her husband back, started to make peace with her mother's death, and taken charge of the situation with Mandy.

After Doris and Doug forced their daughter to end her relationship with Will, the poor girl wailed for two weeks straight. It was like she'd had a tooth removed without Novocain. Doris held her ground, refusing to give in to the tantrum. With time, Mandy got tired of fighting and, instead, started coming around. She'd actually spoken to Doris at the Sunday outing to the Festival of Lights, mumbling something about how the colors were "kind of pretty."

Doug had sneaked a glance over his daughter's fuzzy white hat and given his wife a smile. Doris smiled back, feeling just like the Grinch who stole Christmas. If anyone could have seen inside her chest, they would have noticed that her once shriveled-up heart seemed to have grown at least three sizes bigger.

Chapter Forty-nine

ANDY'S MARKETING FIRM WAS IN A TINY HOUSE THAT SAT ON THE corner of a residential-style business area. To his left was a candy shop shaped like a gingerbread hut and to his right a hospital for exotic animals. His company seemed friendly and accessible, a complete antithesis to the fortress style of TurnKey.

Cheryl parked her car in the driveway. The drive was empty with the exception of Andy's Toyota 4Runner. She had timed their meeting perfectly, showing up during lunch hour. At TurnKey, Andy had never left the office for lunch unless there was a group outing or a meeting with clients. Cheryl assumed it would be the same here. Her plan was to congratulate him on his business and then ask him how involved he'd like to be as a father.

After seeing the article in the *Weekend Review,* Cheryl sat at home, devastated. Cheryl had taken a formal leave from the restaurant less than two weeks ago and it seemed that Jackie and Doris had jumped on the chance to change the concept while she was gone. It broke her heart to picture the two of them working together to create a restaurant so different from their original vision, but Cheryl wasn't surprised they had left her out. The two had always been thick as thieves.

Out of some perverse need to torture herself, Cheryl had hopped into her BMW late on Saturday night. Ducking low, she performed reconnaissance. The paper had not exaggerated about the new appeal of The Whole Package—the place was lit up like a Christmas tree. There was a line out the door. Cheryl sat there for a moment in her cotton jumpsuit (too bad those women from the tennis club couldn't see her; they'd be so proud), a sandwich from a sub shop nestled between her legs. Chewing slowly on a bite of Italian melt, Cheryl watched in confusion as the guests streamed in and out of the haven that had once been her baby. It was rather shocking to realize she'd raised her kid the wrong way.

When Cheryl first read that article, she'd scoffed and crumpled up the paper like she had when they'd gotten that terrible review. Women pampered at a restaurant; what a ridiculous, totally sexist concept. What woman wanted to be treated like she was a fragile object that needed to be held and coddled all the time?

Now, Cheryl caught her reflection in the car's rearview mirror and knew the answer—she did. It would be really nice to, for once, let down her guard and let someone else take care of her. *That* had been the problem with Sean, she realized with a start. Cheryl ran the show because no matter how hard the poor man tried, he never would have been able to make her feel like he had it under control. No wonder The Whole Package was a success. Look what it offered. One night for every woman to live out the fantasy that there she had someone watching over her, all for the price of an entree.

"Whatever," Cheryl said, wiping her hands on a napkin and taking one last look. Gunning the engine, she peeled down Main Street.

Late that night, she'd picked up the phone. She was going to tell the TurnKey actor, the one she'd been sleeping with right before Andy, that he was going to be a daddy. She would make it clear she expected nothing from him, just thought it fair to let him know.

At first, the actor thought she was calling for sex, it being Saturday night and all. It took some time for the man to actually take in what she was saying. Then, to Cheryl's complete and utter shock, he said, "I'm sorry to tell you this, Cheryl, but . . . well, there's no delicate way to say it. I shoot blanks. Why do you think my wife left me?"

Cheryl hung up the phone, stunned. Andy was the father of her child.

Smoothing her hair, she got out of the car. With careful steps, she approached the door and got ready to knock. There was a tiny plate nailed to the wood, a gold square that simply read, SCHAF-FER'S. Letting out a sudden breath, Cheryl decided not to knock. Instead, she pushed her way inside.

Andy was sitting at a desk in the center of the main room, going over some papers. When she walked in, ten different expressions ran across his face in the span of two seconds. They ranged from joy, hurt, anger, sorrow, excitement, confusion, interest, attraction, insecurity, to ultimately, hope.

Gone was the cocky man who worked for a successful marketing firm. In his place sat a serious business owner with shorter hair and a rumpled shirt. Andy made a move to stand up but Cheryl waved her hand. She was feeling emotional and wasn't sure why. Maybe coming here had been a bad idea.

Cheryl looked around the main room. Bookcases lined the walls and the furniture was dark leather. It was very masculine, like something out of a scotch advertisement. "You have a fireplace," she said lamely.

Andy nodded.

Cheryl wrung her hands. Her mouth had gone dry.

"Congratulations on The Whole Package," he said. "I heard you guys made some big changes."

Staring at her scuffed boots, Cheryl shook her head. "No. *They* made some changes. I had nothing to do with it." She paused and looked around. "Congratulations on all this. I'm sure you had everything to do with this."

Andy got to his feet.

In spite of the way Cheryl backed up toward the door, as though she was about to run out of it, he walked forward and stood in front of his desk. Leaning against it, he crossed his arms protectively across his chest. The room was tiny. He was close enough for Cheryl to feel that same electricity she always felt around him, like standing in a field during a lightning storm.

"Andy, look—" she started to say.

"Let me," he cut in. "I cannot tell you how sorry I am for what I did. It was wrong. Believe it or not, I was trying to take your advice. Do what Stan wanted me to so that I could get ahead. Rather unfortunate timing, huh?"

A log popped in the fire. They both jumped.

Andy ran his hand over his face. "Anyway. That night I came to your grand opening, I'd already made my decision to leave Turn-Key. I brought those men with me because they were going to back this place and . . . I was going to ask you to be my partner. I wanted them to meet you."

Cheryl's mind started racing, imagining what working with Andy would have been like. They would think up ideas until the wee hours of the night. Hold meetings in that little boardroom to the left, with its airy windows and dry erase boards. Head out to grab a drink or a meal when they got hungry and always, always try to ignore the hope that there might be something more between them.

"So, you changed your mind when you saw what a failure The Package was?" Cheryl asked.

Andy shook his head. "Nope. The Japanese liked it, believe it or not. They were entertained by your concept. It was me." He took a deep breath and plowed on. "That night, I realized I would never be able to work with you on a strictly professional level."

Cheryl looked up. Her eyes met that familiar, penetrating gaze.

"I don't think that would have been fair to either of us," Andy said, "because the entire time, I'd know I asked you to be my partner not just because you're good at what you do, but because I was too scared to ask you to be my partner in the fullest sense of the word."

The room seemed to be frozen in time. The only thing that assured Cheryl that no, time had not stopped, was the steady ticking from the clock on the fireplace mantel.

Andy cleared his throat. "So. Sorry to hit you with all that but I thought you should know. Thanks for stopping by."

Cheryl tried to speak. Her mouth was dry and she ached to tell him she was already bound to him for life. As she opened her mouth, she suddenly felt . . . Her eyes widened.

"Andy," Cheryl said slowly. "Do you have a restroom?" Her voice was shaking.

"Sure," he said, pointing to the door to her right. "That was the response I was hoping I'd get."

Cheryl smiled weakly, then went into the tiny room and shut the door. Pulling down her pants, she took a look. Nausea filled her heart. Numbly, she went through the motions of using the restroom and fumbling in her purse for a tampon. It was only as she flushed the toilet that she started to cry with a pain that could only be expressed with full-body, full-blown convulsions. This was the type of sadness Cheryl hadn't experienced since she'd sat in her car, head against the steering wheel; right after Stan had ripped one life away from her and forced her to invent another. The pregnancy test was wrong. Cheryl was not pregnant. All this time imagining she was . . . Her heart broke at how stupid she was. And frankly, at how *lucky* she was that Andy had started speaking before she could.

"Cheryl?" Andy rapped on the door. "Are you all right?"

It was a small office. He could probably hear her sobbing out there.

Cheryl took a shaky breath and got to her feet. She opened the bathroom door. Holding his green eyes with hers, she said, "Andy, do you think that one day you'd take me to The Whole Package?"

Andy pulled her to him and held her tight. "You own me," he said brusquely. "I'll take you anywhere you want to go."

"How do you know this is right?" she tried to protest, struggling against the safety of his arms. "You barely know me . . ."

"I do know you, Cheryl," Andy promised, searching her eyes, "and I should. I've been looking for you my entire life." Ever so slowly, the man of her dreams moved closer to her. Then, finally, rested his lips on hers.

Chapter Fifty

DORIS RACED TOWARD THE RESTAURANT, DRIVING AT A SPEED that was very un-Doris-like. Gabe had just called, panicked that all their freezers had stopped working. If they couldn't get it fixed, they could lose thousands of dollars of meat. The generator men were there now and they wouldn't do anything until she signed off on the paperwork.

"Come down here, darling," he begged over the phone. "And hurry."

JACKIE WAS ALSO en route, driving at a speed that *was* very Jackie-like.

Since money had started trickling in for The Whole Package, she and George had worked out a payment plan, at her insistence, to reimburse him. The only way he'd agree to that was if she'd take a couple hundred a week, insistent that pawning the rings Robert had given her would be a crime.

With her first four hundred, she'd bought an old used Honda

with 254,000 miles. It was beaten up and gunned like a tank, but Jackie loved it. It was nice to finally have something she'd earned all on her own. She'd decorated the interior with snow white faux fur, painted the dashboard in pearly white paint, and splurged on a soft, white leather steering wheel cover. Every time she got into her car, Jackie felt like she was sliding into a sparkly cashmere sweater.

At the moment, she was zooming toward the restaurant because Anthony had called her, panicking about the stoves. Apparently, they had stopped working and none of her former friends were around to sign off on the repairs. Jackie opted for parallel parking on the street; it was quicker than dealing with that icy lot. She patted her new car's hood like a stallion, and then dashed up the steps.

Pushing open the front doors, she glanced around, curious. She hadn't been back since the night Anthony had found her in the office. According to him, the *Weekend Review*, and their sudden profit, The Whole Package must have been transformed. Sure enough, the interior was very feminine; softer somehow and much more romantic. All the naked statues were gone and the bright reds and blacks had been replaced with pale pink and ivory.

"Antonio Rico," she sang out, looking around. "It looks like a valentine in here."

"Thanks, doll," Anthony called. "Come on back."

She followed his voice to the private dining room and stopped short. A stone-faced Cheryl and Doris sat at the table, not speaking. Anthony and Gabe were guarding them like prisoners.

"Great. Jackie's here," Anthony said, clapping like a drill sergeant. "You will all thank me for this later. Here's some wine . . ."

Gabe bustled forward, pouring a lush splash into each wineglass.

"Here's some appetizers . . ." Anthony moved plates of delicacies out from under a big silver catering tray. "Now kiss and make up."

With that, he and Gabe swished out the office door.

Avoiding the eyes of her former friends, Jackie took a seat. Doris was perched on the opposite side of the table, leaning forward with folded hands. Cheryl was to her left, eyes downcast. At least five minutes passed with no one speaking.

Letting her eyes rove over the bottles of wine lining the walls, Jackie smiled in appreciation. Anthony had thought to build the wine room and humidor as something to attract the men. The wine seemed like an impressive collection. Jackie was curious to see what brands they had stocked, for both wine and cigars. George would definitely appreciate this.

Jackie and George had been spending a lot of time together, ever since the painting. Their relationship wasn't anything dramatic or loud. But the funny part was, after all her massages, retreats, and effort at relaxation, being with him was the most calming experience she'd ever had in her life.

"Gosh darn it," Doris finally said, shifting. "If no one's going to say anything, I will. They're not going to let us out of here until we talk."

"Wanna bet?" Cheryl said. "I'll call the police and report them for kidnapping."

Doris sighed, reaching for the appetizer platter and selecting a chicken skewer. "I'm on a high-protein diet," she explained. "Don't think I'm callous because I'm eating. I'm just really hungry."

Jackie sneaked a peek at her. Yes, Doris did look like she'd lost a bit of weight. Even if she hadn't been dressed up in the clever wardrobe Gabe convinced her to buy, she was starting to look like her old self again. It was as though the hard shell of anxiety had melted away.

"No, let me start," Cheryl said. "Jackie, I'm . . . I'm sorry. I was horrible to you." With that, Cheryl dropped her head into her hands. "Really inexcusable. I mean, who the fuck did I think I was? Your life is your life and if you came back here because you had to take care of some things, it was my own fault for assuming—"

"That we were friends?" Jackie cut in, incredulous. She laid a hand on the table. "Of course we are, Cheryl. We always have been and I'm sorry if . . ." Her voice trailed off.

The sigh that slipped out came from the very bottom of her core. She and George had been having long conversations about her past. Jackie was starting to realize all the emotions she'd buried and all the manipulative little games she played. It wasn't to be malicious. It was a way to protect herself. George was helping her to let go of all that.

"I didn't think you'd like me," Jackie said softly. She looked at Cheryl and then at Doris. "I didn't think anyone would like me if they knew where I'd come from. If they knew what my family was."

"So many people have alcoholic parents . . ." Cheryl started to say and Jackie held up her hand.

"That's exactly what I didn't want," she said. "To get lumped into some category, for people to assume they knew my life. So I showed them what I wanted them to see and by the time we got older, well . . . it just didn't seem like it mattered anymore. It was in the past by then, so why bring it up? My father's doing fine, just in case you're wondering. He's out of jail and working somewhere in Ohio. I'm going to visit him in the spring."

"That's . . . good news," Cheryl said, nodding. She'd rested her chin on her hand. The dangly gold disk on the tennis bracelet she was wearing seemed to shiver. "Thank you for telling me."

"Look. I'm not going to change overnight. I'm always going to be private," Jackie said, sneaking another look at Doris, who was still nibbling at that chicken skewer. "It's who I am. But, Cheryl, if you ever doubted that I love you," her voice cracked and Jackie took a breath, trying to fight back the emotion. "I'm sorry," she whispered. "If you ever doubted I love you, that's my fault. I have to be a better friend. And I will, if you'll let me."

Cheryl pressed her lips together, bobbing her head up and down. Finally, she pushed back her chair and ran around the table to Jackie, burying her face in her arms. The two held each other for a long moment, Jackie breathing in Cheryl's familiar scent. Jackie held her tight and, finally, kissed the top of her head. "I love you."

The two friends pulled back and smiled at each other. Doris was silent, steadily eating chicken. Jackie sneaked a glance at her, then brushed her blond hair back into a ponytail, held it for a moment, and then let it drop.

"Doris, you should slap me and kick me out all over again," she finally said. "What I did to you was wrong. I'm sorry."

"Huh?" Cheryl said. She looked from one friend to the other. "What happened?"

Doris picked up another chicken skewer and took a bite. "She interfered with raising my daughter," she said. "And allowed her and her boyfriend to sneak around and have sex."

"Oh," Cheryl said.

"Not smart," Jackie said, toying with her wineglass and leaning against the table. An image of George's handsome face flicked across her mind; the picture gave her strength. "Plus, I leeched off her and I lied to her. I had no business doing any of that, much less interfering with your daughter, Doris. If I could do it all over again, I . . ."

Doris reached out and grabbed Jackie's hand, accidentally stabbing her with the thin chicken prong. "Sorry, sorry," Doris said in a rush.

"No, I deserve it," Jackie said, grabbing the chicken prong and pretending to press it against her skin. "Stab me again."

"No," Doris said, yanking it out of her hand. "I forgive you, Jackie. I love you. Besides, what you did triggered another series of events. Something good."

"What?"

"Doug came home," Doris said, blushing prettily.

Jackie and Cheryl turned to her, surprised. "He did?" they chorused.

"So, you're not leaving him?" Cheryl asked.

"No," Doris said. "What he did was wrong but it wasn't just his fault. Well, the affair was, but I wasn't the best wife, either. I needed to change some things myself. So, I did and things are really good."

The room was quiet for a minute. "Jackie, where have you been staying?" Cheryl asked. "All this time I thought you were with Doris."

"Anthony's," Doris said, in between bites of chicken. "Oh, don't look so shocked," she told Jackie, who had turned to Doris in surprise. "I've been asking about you every day."

Jackie *was* still living at Anthony's, in the small, cramped apartment. When she had started dating George, it would have been much easier to migrate into his comfortable estate and never leave, but Jackie refused. She wasn't going to risk the way she felt for him by doing what was easy.

"I missed you guys," Jackie said, looking at her friends.

Cheryl reached out, tentative. The three friends dove into each other's arms, not saying anything. They held each other for a long time, hanging on like they would never let go.

Jackie was the first to draw back, saying, "I can't believe you guys were fighting, too. I thought for sure you'd be talking when Doris kicked me out!"

"Nope," Cheryl said cheerfully. "Doris ditched me because I wasn't a team player."

Doris nodded, shrugging. "We're a team," she said. "That means we call the shots together. That is, if you guys still want to be."

Jackie and Cheryl nodded animatedly.

"But I have some requests," Cheryl said, suddenly nervous. "If we stay in business together, you guys can't gang up on me. I do have a lot of experience and I need you guys to appreciate that."

Jackie opened her mouth to speak, but Doris beat her to it. "Cheryl, we do appreciate that. If it seemed like we were ganging up, it was just because we need two people to equal one of you."

"Well, in my vast experience," Cheryl said, beaming, "I have to say. You have done an amazing job saving our business."

"Hear hear," Jackie applauded.

Suddenly, Doris slapped her hand to her forehead in a Chris

Farley "stupid" move. "But I just realized something," she said. "Jackie, I can only work with you if you'll do one thing."

Cheryl had reached out for a chicken skewer but stopped in surprise, looking at Doris. Jackie nodded, already guessing. Doris was going to ask for her to put up equal money or withdraw equal ownership.

"You're right," Jackie said. "It might take some time for me to get a loan, but I will figure out how to get my own money for . . ."

"No, silly," Doris cried, lightly slapping her wrist. "It's more important than that."

Jackie was baffled. "What . . . what do you want me to do?"

"Admit you snore," Doris said, surprising both of them.

Cheryl burst out laughing. "Like a lawn mower!"

Jackie squealed, jumping up from her seat to sock them both. The three friends hugged each other, dancing around the room in glee. Anthony and Gabe came bursting through their door.

"Are we happy again?" Anthony asked.

"*Oui oui*," Jackie cried.

Anthony lifted Gabe up and spun him around. With the three women watching, he and Gabe actually hugged, holding on for just a moment too long. Anthony caught Jackie's eye over Gabe's shoulder. She grinned.

Chapter Fifty-one

"BONNE ANNÉE! IT'S ALMOST THE NEW YEAR," JACKIE SHOUTED, holding up a piece of leftover mistletoe and waggling it over her head. George leaned forward and kissed her. "You're really supposed to wait 'til midnight," she teased, sliding toward him in her clingy aquamarine dress.

Cheryl let out a raucous wolf whistle from across the restaurant and Doris clapped her hands. To celebrate the New Year and everything it would bring, everyone was at The Whole Package. A countdown clock and champagne glasses were standing by.

Doris and Doug were cuddled at a corner table, planning their second honeymoon. As soon as the weather got warm, Doug was going to take another leave from the bank and Doris from The Whole Package. He was going to take her cross-country on the back of his bike.

The Harley had arrived that day, shipped back from where he'd left it in Amarillo, Texas. Doug promised they'd hit the West Coast and explore the back mountain roads. They'd eat burgers at the rough biker bars during the day and enjoy the comfort of local bed-and-breakfasts at night. Doris was terrified at the whole concept. She couldn't wait.

As Doug explained to her how to tilt her body as they took the tight turns, Doris squeezed his arm and said, "What if I fall off?"

Doug studied his pretty wife with adoration. "You won't."

"But what if I do?"

"I'll catch you," he promised, leaning in to kiss her.

Cheryl and Andy sat at another table with Bob Turner and his wife. Bob Turner had insisted on signing with Nolan/Schaffer that day, to ring in the New Year right. Plus, he and Rachel had been dying to see The Whole Package. Now that it had been featured in the national news, Bob liked to joke that his protégée was a big star. Watching the ink dry on the contract, Cheryl's eyes nearly misted. When Andy learned she had signed Fitzgibbon Ale, he insisted that her name would be first on the company door. They'd had that discussion in front of Cheryl's fake fire, earlier that evening.

"Nolan/Schaffer works," Andy said. "Besides, I don't want you to change your last name when we're married."

"We'll cross that bridge . . ." she started to say.

Andy sat up on one knee and snapped open a beautiful black box. "I think we're crossing it."

The most beautiful emerald-cut diamond engagement ring Cheryl had ever seen was nestled against white satin. Andy slid it on her finger as she promised to be his wife. Now, Cheryl found herself gesturing madly with her left hand as she talked throughout her conversation with Bob and Rachel. The light of her love reflected across the table.

"Look at her," Anthony said to Gabe. "Remember how I used to call her The Tan One?"

The two men were perched against the host stand, enjoying the show.

"No," Gabe said, touching his hand gently. "We weren't speaking then. Because I was stupid."

Anthony's face got serious. "When are we going to tell them we're leaving?"

"Soon."

Convincing Gabe his play was worth being seen had been no small task. Anthony enlisted the help of Jackie, who sat Gabe down and gave it to him straight. The part he'd written for Anthony could take them both to the top. They needed to put it onstage.

"New York?" Gabe said, surprised.

Jackie nodded.

Gabe had never been to the Big Apple. As Anthony described the pulse and lights of the city, he became more entranced with the idea. They would get an apartment together, something overlooking the park. It would be like heaven. As though Jackie were lip-reading their conversation from across the room, she nodded at them and smiled. George leaned forward and whispered something in her ear, sneaking a glance at Anthony.

"I think he's ready," Anthony said to Gabe. "It's almost midnight."

Gabe grinned. "Let's do it."

The lights of the restaurant dimmed and the patrons looked around in surprise. A single spotlight shone toward the stage.

"Darling," George began, brushing back Jackie's blond hair.

She gazed up into his dark eyes and purred, "Yes?"

"Well," George mused, touching her lips. "I hope you'll forgive me for this, but I wanted to start the New Year off right. This one's for you, my dear Jacqueline."

George leaped up and rushed to the stage, with Doug, Andy, Bob Turner, Anthony, and Gabe right behind him.

Jackie's jaw dropped.

"What is happening?!" Cheryl and Doris cried, racing over and sliding into Jackie's booth.

In perfect unison, their men pointed at the digital clock Anthony had mounted on the wall. It read 11:59 and fifty seconds. They started the countdown to midnight, slowly swiveling their hips. "Seven . . . six . . . five . . ." The stage lights burst on, disco ball flashing crazily. The pulsating notes of 2 Live Crew pounded through the restaurant.

"Oh my God, they're going to drop the ball," Cheryl realized.

"The ball?" Doris asked, confused. Then she leaped to her feet crying, "Omigod, the *ball!*"

In perfect formation, the men ripped off their shirts and pants to reveal black bowties and sexy little bottoms made out of spandex. "The Whole Package!" George cried.

In perfect harmony, George, Doug, and Andy danced for their women as though their love depended on it.